The Love Object

Since her debut novel, *The Country Girls*, Edna O'Brien has written more than twenty works of fiction. She is the recipient of many awards, including the Irish PEN Lifetime Achievement Award, the American National Arts Gold Medal and the Frank O'Connor Prize. Born and raised in the west of Ireland, she has lived in London for many years.

Further praise for *The Love Object*:

'Edna O'Brien is one of those writers who are masters of the art of the short story as well as of the novel . . . Perfectly pitched passages, beautiful, layered with meaning and powerfully evocative, abound in these stories. O'Brien has the finely turned sensibility of the greatest artists – there is often a Mozartian flow to her work. . . . There is something miraculous about it all.' Éilís Ní Dhuibhne, *Irish Times*

'A stubbornly resilient and defiantly individual talent.' Joyce Carol Oates, *Times Literary Supplement*

'The most striking thing in this collection of the best of her stories is how well the earlier pieces have stood the test of time. The oldest were first collected in 1968, the most recent in 2011. . . For a writer whose fame sprang partly from her first novel being burned, who has been somewhat defined by that oppressive reaction to her work, her longevity is important.' Lucy Daniel, *Daily Telegraph*

'A treat indeed. O'Brien has an ability to conjure up a whole way of life within a few pages.' Leyla Sanai, *Independent on Sunday*

'O'Brien captivates us in this collection . . . few writers explore the female psyche so astutely or with such vigour.' *The Lady*

EDNA O'BRIEN

The Love Object

Selected Stories

ff

FABER & FABER

First published in 2013
by Faber and Faber Ltd
Bloomsbury House
74–77 Great Russell Street
London WC1B 3DA
This paperback edition first published in 2014

Typeset by RefineCatch Limited, Bungay, Suffolk
Printed and bound by CPI Group (UK) Ltd, Croydon, CR0 4YY

A CIP record for this book
is available from the British Library

ISBN 978-0-571-28295-1

2 4 6 8 10 9 7 5 3 1

For Philip Roth in long friendship

Contents

Introduction

The most striking aspect of Edna O'Brien's short stories, aside from the consistent mastery with which they are executed, is their diversity. This writer knows many worlds, and delineates them for us with deep insight, uncanny accuracy, wry fondness and, always, compassion. Although she left it early, she is never far from the world into which she was born and where she was brought up. She is one of the most sophisticated writers now at work, yet her sensibility is suffused with the light of the far west of Ireland, and again and again in these tales she returns to the lovely fields and melancholy towns of her youth.

In her 'international' stories – and Henry James surely would acknowledge her as a fellow traveller – she looks with an exile's measuring eye upon the racy thrills and false blandishments of life in society. The title story of this volume, 'The Love Object', one of the most celebrated of her mature short fictions, not only traces with an unflinching, almost forensic clarity the flowering and fading of a love affair, but also, and as if casually, portrays the flashy, complacent world of middle-class London in the 1960s. Only a girl from County Clare would note of her pompous lawyer lover on their first going to bed together: 'Another thing he did that endeared him was to fold back the green silk bedspread, a thing I never do myself.'

Edna O'Brien began her career as a writer – and began it early – in a golden age of the Irish short story. She and near-contemporaries such as John McGahern and William Trevor had as exemplars the likes of Sean O'Faolain, Frank O'Connor, Mary Lavin and Benedict Kiely – and, of course, the James Joyce of *Dubliners* – yet on the evidence of the work gathered in this volume her true teacher was Chekhov, for she displays a positively Chekhovian empathy with the characters and milieus that she portrays.

The mark of genius in a writer is an ability to burrow deep into the consciousness of a disparate cast of personalities. We are familiar with Edna O'Brien as an Irish cosmopolitan, the russet-haired beauty who knows her way around not only London and New York but also the pleasure gardens and yachting harbours of Europe; the friend and confidante of the great figures of contemporary art and culture; the trail-blazer who flew the nets of Catholic Ireland and made a life for herself abroad that young women – such as those so lovingly brought to life in her early *Country Girls* trilogy – used to, and no doubt still do, dream of. Yet this is the same Edna O'Brien who in 'The Shovel Kings' can portray with accuracy and aching sympathy the grindingly harsh lives of Irish navvies who dug the foundations for the rebuilding of postwar Britain.

Nor has she let slip from her artistic memory even the tiniest detail of the Ireland of those first three literally marvellous novels, *The Country Girl*, *The Lonely Girl* and *Girls in Their Married Bliss*. One of the loveliest, funniest, most evocative and hair-raisingly accurate stories in this collection, 'Irish Revel', with its faint echoes of Joyce's 'The Dead', conjures a world that is Ireland in the 1950s but that could also be Russia in the closing years of the nineteenth century, the Russia of Tolstoy, Turgenev and Chekhov. In Mary, the central character, Edna O'Brien catches all the innocence, longing and delicacy of a tender bloom set down unrescuably in a patch of weeds.

For as long as she could remember, she had been pumping bicycles, carting turf, cleaning out houses, doing a man's work. Her father and her two brothers worked for the forestry, so that she and her mother had to do all the odd jobs – there were three children to care for, and fowl and pigs and churning. Theirs was a mountainy farm in Ireland, and life was hard.

The delicacy and fond humour on display in this story are magical, but so too, in its way, is the unforgiving portrait of the grossness and cruelty of country life. It is hard to think of any contemporary writer who could match the combination of immediacy and sympathetic recall out of which this luminous story is woven.

Younger writers today, particularly younger women writers, acknowledge the revolution that Edna O'Brien wrought in Irish writing. No one before her, not even Kate O'Brien or Mary Lavin, had managed to portray in fiction an utterly convincing female sensibility. It is not so much the figuring of the female characters themselves that is so striking in these stories, but the way in which their author catches in the web of her artistry something of the essence of womanhood itself. Some of her women, such as Maisie in 'Brother', who has murder on her mind, or Ita McNamara in 'Oft in the Stilly Night', who believes herself to have been ravished by the stalk of a lily, are plainly mad – one of Edna O'Brien's story collections is titled *A Fanatic Heart* – but all are in some way damaged by the world, and specifically by the world of men. And all are spiritually vulnerable; indeed, we might say of Edna O'Brien that she is the poet of vulnerability.

Two of the most moving stories, 'Mrs Reinhardt' and 'Paradise', portray a pair of women who have been, in their different ways, betrayed by men and by men's impossible expectations of what and how they should be. Mrs Reinhardt, whose husband has left her for a spoilt young woman half her age, is almost unbearably touching in her determination to reach out and grasp anything and everything that life might still offer her, and, inevitably, ends up badly scarred. The unnamed young woman in 'Paradise' is also eager to sample life's riches, and so has given herself to an elderly millionaire playboy who does not bother to try to understand her, and who at the close rejects her, ostensibly because of her failure to learn how to swim.

Here, as so often elsewhere, Edna O'Brien mourns for the plight of her wounded women and at the same celebrates their exuberance, their generosity and, ultimately, their indomitable spirit. She is, simply, one of the finest writers of our time.

John Banville, 2013

Irish Revel

Mary hoped that the rotted front tire would not burst. As it was, the tube had a slow puncture, and twice she had to stop and use the pump, maddening, because the pump had no connection and had to be jammed on over the corner of a handkerchief. For as long as she could remember, she had been pumping bicycles, carting turf, cleaning out houses, doing a man's work. Her father and her two brothers worked for the forestry, so that she and her mother had to do all the odd jobs – there were three children to care for, and fowl and pigs and churning. Theirs was a mountainy farm in Ireland, and life was hard.

But this cold evening in early November she was free. She rode along the mountain road, between the bare thorn hedges, thinking pleasantly about the party. Although she was seventeen, this was her first party. The invitation had come only that morning from Mrs. Rodgers of the Commercial Hotel. The postman brought word that Mrs. Rodgers wanted her down that evening, without fail. At first, her mother did not wish Mary to go, there was too much to be done, gruel to be made, and one of the twins had earache and was likely to cry in the night. Mary slept with the year-old twins, and sometimes she was afraid that she might lie on them or smother them, the bed was so small. She begged to be let go.

'What use would it be?' her mother said. To her mother all outings were unsettling – they gave you a taste of something you couldn't have. But finally she weakened, mainly because Mrs. Rodgers, as owner of the Commercial Hotel, was an important woman and not to be insulted.

'You can go, so long as you're back in time for the milking in the morning; and mind you don't lose your head,' her mother warned. Mary was to stay overnight in the village with Mrs. Rodgers. She plaited her hair, and later when she combed it, it fell in dark crinkled waves over her shoulders. She was allowed to wear the black lace dress that had come from America years ago and belonged to no one in particular. Her mother had sprinkled her with Holy Water, conveyed her to the top of the lane, and warned her never to touch alcohol.

Mary felt happy as she rode along slowly, avoiding the potholes that were thinly iced over. The frost had never lifted that day. The ground was hard. If it went on like that, the cattle would have to be brought into the shed and given hay.

The road turned and looped and rose; she turned and looped with it, climbing little hills and descending again toward the next hill. At the descent of the Big Hill she got off the bicycle – the brakes were unreliable – and looked back, out of habit, at her own house. It was the only house back there on the mountain, small, whitewashed, with a few trees around it and a patch at the back which they called a kitchen garden. There was a rhubarb bed, and shrubs over which they emptied tea leaves, and a stretch of grass where in the summer they had a chicken run, moving it from one patch to the next every other day. She looked away. She was now free to think of John Roland. He had come to their district two years before, riding a motorcycle at a ferocious speed; raising dust on the milk cloths spread on the hedge to dry. He stopped to ask the way. He was staying with Mrs. Rodgers in the Commercial Hotel and had come up to see the lake, which was noted for its colors. It changed color rapidly – it was blue and green and black, all within an hour. At sunset it was often a strange burgundy, not like a lake at all, but like wine.

'Down there,' she said to the stranger, pointing to the lake below, with the small island in the middle of it. He had taken a wrong turning.

Hills and tiny cornfields descended steeply toward the water. The misery of the hills was clear, from all the boulders. The cornfields were turning, it was midsummer; the ditches throbbing with the blood-red of fuchsia; the milk sour five hours after it had been put in the tanker. He said how exotic it was. She had no interest in views herself. She just looked up at the high sky and saw that a hawk had halted in the air above them. It was like a pause in her life, the hawk above them, perfectly still; and just then her mother came out to see who the stranger was. He took off his helmet and said, 'Hello,' very courteously. He introduced himself as John Roland, an English painter, who lived in Italy.

She did not remember exactly how it happened, but after a while he walked into their kitchen with them and sat down to tea.

Two long years since; but she had never given up hoping – perhaps this evening. The mail-car man said that someone special in the Commercial Hotel expected her. She felt such happiness. She spoke to her bicycle, and it seemed to her that her happiness somehow glowed in the pearliness of the cold sky, in the frosted fields going blue in the dusk, in the cottage windows she passed. Her father and mother were rich and cheerful; the twin had no earache, the kitchen fire did not smoke. Now and then she smiled at the thought of how she would appear to him – taller and with breasts now, and a dress that could be worn anywhere. She forgot about the rotted tire, got up, and cycled.

The five streetlights were on when she pedaled into the village. There had been a cattle fair that day and the main street was covered with dung. The townspeople had their windows protected with wooden half-shutters and makeshift arrangements of planks and barrels. Some were out scrubbing their own piece of footpath with bucket and brush. There were cattle wandering around, mooing, the way cattle do when they are in a strange street, and drunken farmers with sticks were trying to identify their own cattle in dark corners.

Beyond the shop window of the Commercial Hotel, Mary heard loud conversation and men singing. It was opaque glass, so that she could not identify any of them, she could just see their heads moving about inside. It was a shabby hotel, the yellow-washed walls needed a coat of paint, as they hadn't been done since the time De Valera came to that village during the election campaign five years before. De Valera went upstairs that time and sat in the parlor and wrote his name with a penny pen in an autograph book, and sympathized with Mrs. Rodgers on the recent death of her husband.

Mary thought of resting her bicycle against the porter barrels under the shop window, and then of climbing the three stone steps that led to the hall door, but suddenly the latch of the shop door clicked and she ran in terror up the alley by the side of the shop, afraid it might be someone who knew her father and would say he saw her going in through the public bar. She wheeled her bicycle into a shed and approached the back door. It was open, but she did not enter without knocking.

Two town girls rushed to answer it. One was Doris O'Beirne, the daughter of the harness maker. She was the only Doris in the whole village, and she was famous for that, as well as for the fact that one of her eyes was blue and the other a dark brown. She was learning shorthand and typing at the local technical school, and later she meant to be a secretary to some famous man or other in the government, in Dublin.

'God, I thought it was someone important,' she said when she saw Mary standing there, blushing, beholden, and with a bottle of cream in her hand. Another girl! Girls were two a penny in that neighborhood. People said that it had something to do with the limewater that so many girls were born. Girls with pink skins and matching eyes, and girls like Mary, with long, wavy hair and gorgeous figures.

'Come in or stay out,' said Eithne Duggan, the second girl, to Mary. It was supposed to be a joke, but neither of them liked her. They hated shy mountainy people.

Mary came in, carrying cream which her mother had sent to Mrs. Rodgers as a present. She put it on the dresser and took off her coat. The girls nudged each other when they saw her dress. In the kitchen was a smell of cow dung from the street, and fried onions from a pan that simmered on the stove.

'Where's Mrs. Rodgers?' Mary asked.

'Serving,' Doris said in a saucy voice, as if any fool ought to know. Two old men sat at the table eating.

'I can't chew, I have no teeth,' said one of the men to Doris. ''Tis like leather,' he said, holding the plate of burned steak toward her. He had watery eyes and he blinked childishly. Was it so, Mary wondered, that eyes got paler with age, like bluebells in a jar?

'You're not going to charge me for that,' the old man was saying to Doris. Tea and steak cost five shillings at the Commercial.

''Tis good for you, chewing is,' Eithne Duggan said, teasing him.

'I can't chew with my gums,' he said again, and the two girls began to giggle. The old man looked pleased that he had made them laugh, and he closed his mouth and munched once or twice on a piece of fresh shop bread. Eithne Duggan laughed so much that she had to put a dishcloth between her teeth. Mary hung up her coat and went through to the shop.

Mrs. Rodgers came from the counter for a moment to speak to her.

'Mary, I'm glad you came, that pair in there are no use at all, always giggling. Now, first thing we have to do is to get the parlor upstairs straightened out. Everything has to come out of it except the piano. We're going to have dancing and everything.'

Quickly Mary realized that she was being given work to do, and she blushed with shock and disappointment.

'Pitch everything into the back bedroom, the whole shootin' lot,' Mrs. Rodgers was saying, as Mary thought of her good lace dress and of how her mother wouldn't even let her wear it to Mass on Sundays.

'And we have to stuff a goose, too, and get it on,' Mrs. Rodgers said, and went on to explain that the party was in honor of the local Customs and Excise Officer, who was retiring because his wife won some money in the sweep. Two thousand pounds. His wife lived thirty miles away at the far side of Limerick, and he lodged in the Commercial Hotel from Monday to Friday, going home for the weekends.

'There's someone here expecting me,' Mary said, trembling with the pleasure of being about to hear his name pronounced by someone else. She wondered which room was his, and if he was likely to be in at that moment. Already in imagination she had climbed the rickety stairs and knocked on the door and heard him move around inside.

'Expecting you!' Mrs. Rodgers said, and looked puzzled for a minute. 'Oh, that lad from the slate quarry was inquiring about you, he said he saw you at a dance once. He's as odd as two left shoes.'

'What lad?' Mary said, as she felt the joy leaking out of her heart.

'Oh, what's his name,' Mrs. Rodgers said, and then to the men with empty glasses who were shouting for her, 'Oh, all right, I'm coming.'

Upstairs Doris and Eithne helped Mary move the heavy pieces of furniture. They dragged the sideboard across the landing, and one of the casters tore the linoleum. She was expiring, because she had the heaviest end, the other two being at the same side. She felt that it was on purpose: they ate sweets without offering her one, and she caught them making faces at her dress. The dress worried her, too, in case anything should happen to it. If one of the lace threads caught in a splinter of wood, or on a porter barrel, she would have no business going home in the morning. They carried out a varnished bamboo whatnot, a small table, knickknacks, and a chamber pot with no handle which held some withered hydrangeas. They smelled awful.

'How much is the doggie in the window, the one with the waggledy tail?' Doris O'Beirne sang to a white china dog and swore that there wasn't ten pounds' worth of furniture in the whole shebeen.

'Are you leaving your curlers in, Dot, till it starts?' Eithne Duggan asked her friend.

'Oh, def,' Doris O'Beirne said. She wore an assortment of curlers – white pipe cleaners, metal clips, and pink plastic rollers. Eithne had just taken hers out, and her hair, dyed blond, stood out, all frizzed and alarming. She reminded Mary of a molting hen about to attempt flight. She was, God bless her, an unfortunate girl, with a squint, jumbled teeth, and almost no lips; like something put together hurriedly. That was the luck of the draw.

'Take these,' Doris O'Beirne said, handing Mary bunches of yellowed bills crammed on skewers.

Do this! Do that! They ordered her around like a maid. She dusted the piano, top and sides, and the yellow and black keys; then the surround and the wainscoting. The dust, thick on everything, had settled into a hard film because of the damp in that room. A party! She'd have been as well off at home, at least it was clean dirt attending to calves and pigs and the like.

Doris and Eithne amused themselves, hitting notes on the piano at random and wandering from one mirror to the next. There were two mirrors in the parlor and one side of the folding fire screen was a blotchy mirror, too. The other two sides were water lilies painted on black cloth, but like everything else in the room it was decrepit.

'What's that?' Doris and Eithne asked each other as they heard a hullabaloo downstairs. They rushed out to see what it was, and

Mary followed. Over the banisters they saw that a young bullock had got in the hall door and was slithering over the tiled floor, trying to find his way out again.

'Don't excite her, don't excite her, I tell ye,' said the old toothless man to the young boy who tried to drive the black bullock out. Two more boys were having a bet as to whether or not the bullock would do something on the floor, when Mrs. Rodgers came out and dropped a glass of porter. The beast backed out the way he'd come, shaking his head from side to side.

Eithne and Doris clasped each other in laughter, and then Doris drew back so that none of the boys would see her in her curling pins and call her names. Mary had gone back to the room, downcast. Wearily she pushed the chairs back against the wall and swept the linoleumed floor where they were later to dance.

'She's bawling in there,' Eithne Duggan told her friend Doris. They had locked themselves into the bathroom with a bottle of cider.

'God, she's a right-looking eejit in the dress,' Doris said. 'And the length of it!'

'It's her mother's,' Eithne said. She had admired the dress before that, when Doris was out of the room, and had asked Mary where she bought it.

'What's she crying about?' Doris wondered aloud.

'She thought some lad would be here. Do you remember that lad stayed here the summer before last and had a motorcycle?'

'He was a Jew,' Doris said. 'You could tell by his nose. God, she'd shake him in that dress, he'd think she was a scarecrow.' She squeezed a blackhead on her chin, tightened a curling pin which had come loose, and said, 'Her hair isn't natural either, you can see it's curled.'

'I hate that kind of black hair, it's like a gypsy's,' Eithne said, drinking the last of the cider. They hid the bottle under the scoured bath.

'Have a cachou, take the smell off your breath,' Doris said as she hawed on the bathroom mirror and wondered if she would get off with that fellow O'Toole from the slate quarry, who was coming to the party.

In the front room Mary polished glasses. Tears ran down her cheeks, so she did not put on the light. She foresaw how the party would be; they would all stand around and consume the goose, which was now simmering in the turf range. The men would be drunk, the girls giggling. Having eaten, they would dance and sing and tell ghost stories, and in the morning she would have to get up early and be home in time to milk. She moved toward the dark pane of window with a glass in her hand and looked out at the dirtied streets, remembering how once she had danced with John on the upper road to no music at all, just their hearts beating and the sound of happiness.

He came into their house for tea that summer's day, and on her father's suggestion he lodged with them for four days, helping with the hay and oiling all the farm machinery for her father. He understood machinery. He put back doorknobs that had fallen off. Mary made his bed in the daytime and carried up a ewer of water from the rain barrel every evening, so that he could wash. She washed the checked shirt he wore, and that day his bare back peeled in the sun. She put milk on it. It was his last day with them. After supper he proposed giving each of the grown-up children a ride on the motorbike. Her turn came last; she felt that he had planned it that way, but it may have been that her brothers were more persistent about being first. She would never forget that ride. She warmed from head to foot in wonder and joy. He praised her as a good balancer, and at odd moments he took one hand off the handlebar and gave her clasped hands a comforting pat. The sun went down, and the gorse flowers blazed yellow. They did not talk for miles; she had his stomach encased in the delicate and frantic grasp of a girl in love, and no matter how far they rode, they seemed always to be riding into a golden haze. He saw the lake at its most glorious. They got off at the bridge five miles away and sat on the limestone wall, which was cushioned by moss and lichen. She took a tick out of his neck and touched the spot where the tick had drawn one pinprick of blood; it was then they danced. A sound of larks and running water. The hay in the fields was lying green and ungathered, and the air was sweet with the smell of it. They danced.

'Sweet Mary,' he said, looking earnestly into her eyes. Her eyes were a greenish-brown. He confessed that he could not love her, because he already loved his wife and children, and anyhow, he said, 'You are too young and too innocent.'

Next day, as he was leaving, he asked if he might send her something in the post; it came eleven days later: a black-and-white drawing of her, very like her, except that the girl in the drawing was uglier.

'A fat lot of good, that is,' said her mother, who had been expecting a gold bracelet or a brooch. 'That wouldn't take you far.'

They hung it on a nail in the kitchen for a while, and then one day it fell down and someone (probably her mother) used it to sweep dust onto; ever since it was used for that purpose. Mary had wanted to keep it, to put it away in a trunk, but she was ashamed to. They were hard people, and it was only when someone died that they could give in to sentiment or crying.

'Sweet Mary,' he had said. He never wrote. Two summers passed, devil's pokers flowered for two seasons, and thistle seed blew in the wind; the trees in the forest were a foot higher. She had a feeling that he would come back, and a gnawing fear that he might not.

'Oh, it ain't gonna rain no more, no more, it ain't gonna rain no more. How in the hell can the old folks say it ain't gonna rain no more?'

So sang Brogan, whose party it was, in the upstairs room of the Commercial Hotel. Unbuttoning his brown waistcoat, he sat back and said what a fine spread it was. They had carried the goose up on a platter and it lay in the center of the mahogany table, with potato stuffing spilling out of it. There were sausages also and polished glasses rim downward, and plates and forks for everyone.

'A fork supper' was how Mrs. Rodgers described it. She had read about it in the paper; it was all the rage now in posh houses in Dublin, this fork supper where you stood up for your food and ate with a fork only. Mary had brought knives in case anyone got into difficulties.

''Tis America at home,' Hickey said, putting turf on the smoking fire.

The pub door was bolted downstairs, the shutters across, as the eight guests upstairs watched Mrs. Rodgers carve the goose and then tear the loose pieces away with her fingers. Every so often she wiped her fingers on a tea towel.

'Here you are, Mary, give this to Mr. Brogan, as he's the guest of honor.' Mr. Brogan got a lot of breast and some crispy skin as well.

'Don't forget the sausages, Mary,' Mrs. Rodgers said. Mary had to do everything: pass the food around, serve the stuffing, ask people whether they wanted paper plates or china ones. Mrs. Rodgers had bought paper plates, thinking they were sophisticated.

'I could eat a young child,' Hickey said.

Mary was surprised that people in towns were so coarse and outspoken. When he squeezed her finger, she did not smile at all. She wished that she were at home – she knew what they were doing at home: the boys at their lessons; her mother baking a cake of whole meal bread, because there was never enough time during the day to bake; her father rolling cigarettes and talking to himself. John had taught him how to roll cigarettes, and every night since, he rolled four and smoked four. He was a good man, her father, but dour. In another hour they'd be saying the Rosary in her house and going to bed; the rhythm of their lives never changed, the fresh bread was always cool by morning.

'Ten o'clock,' Doris said, listening to the chimes of the landing clock.

The party began late; the men were late getting back from the dogs in Limerick. They killed a pig on the way in their anxiety to get back quickly. The pig had been wandering in the road, and the car came around the corner; it got run over instantly.

'Never heard such a roarin' in all me born days,' Hickey said, reaching for a wing of goose, the choicest bit.

'We should have brought it with us,' O'Toole said. O'Toole worked in the slate quarry and knew nothing about pigs or farming; he was tall and thin and jagged. He had bright-green eyes and a face like a greyhound's; his hair was so gold that it looked dyed, but in fact it was bleached by the weather. No one had offered him any food.

'A nice way to treat a man,' he said.

'God bless us, Mary, didn't you give Mr. O'Toole anything to eat yet?' Mrs. Rodgers said as she thumped Mary on the back to hurry her up. Mary brought him a large helping on a paper plate, and he thanked her and said that they would dance later. To him she looked far prettier than those good-for-nothing town girls – she was tall and thin like himself; she had long black hair that some people might think streelish, but not him; he liked long hair and simple-minded girls; maybe later on he'd get her to go into one of the other rooms where they could do it. She had funny eyes when you looked into them, brown and deep, like a bloody bog hole.

'Have a wish,' he said to her as he held the wishbone up. She wished that she were going to America on an airplane, and on second thought she wished that she would win a lot of money and could buy her mother and father a house down near the main road.

'Is that your brother, the bishop?' Eithne Duggan, who knew well that it was, asked Mrs. Rodgers, concerning the flaccid-faced cleric over the fireplace. Unknown to herself, Mary had traced the letter J on the dust of the picture mirror earlier on, and now they all seemed to be looking at it, knowing how it came to be there.

'That's him, poor Charlie,' Mrs. Rodgers said proudly, and was about to elaborate, but Brogan began to sing unexpectedly.

'Let the man sing, can't you,' O'Toole said, hushing two of the girls who were having a joke about the armchair they shared; the springs were hanging down underneath and the girls said that any minute the whole thing would collapse.

Mary shivered in her lace dress. The air was cold and damp, even though Hickey had got up a good fire. There hadn't been a fire in that room since the day De Valera signed the autograph book. Steam issued from everything.

O'Toole asked if any of the ladies would care to sing. There were five ladies in all – Mrs. Rodgers, Mary, Doris, Eithne, and Crystal, the local hairdresser, who had a new red rinse in her hair and who insisted that the food was a little heavy for her. The goose was greasy and undercooked, she did not like its raw, pink color. She liked dainty things, little bits of cold chicken breast with sweet pickles. Her real name was Carmel, but when she started up as a hairdresser, she changed it to Crystal and dyed her brown hair red.

'I bet you can sing,' O'Toole said to Mary.

'Where she comes from, they can hardly talk,' Doris said.

Mary felt the blood rushing to her sallow cheeks. She would not tell them, but her father's name had been in the paper once, because he had seen a pine marten in the forestry plantation; and they ate with a knife and fork at home and had oilcloth on the kitchen table, and kept a tin of coffee in case strangers called. She would not tell them anything. She just hung her head, making it clear that she was not about to sing.

In honor of the bishop, O'Toole put 'Far Away in Australia' on the horn gramophone. Mrs. Rodgers had asked for it. The sound issued forth with rasps and scratchings, and Brogan said he could do better than that himself.

'Christ, lads, we forgot the soup!' Mrs. Rodgers said suddenly, as she threw down the fork and went toward the door. There had been soup scheduled to begin with.

'I'll help you,' Doris O'Beirne said, stirring herself for the first time that night, and they both went down to get the pot of dark giblet soup which had been simmering all that day.

'Now we need two pounds from each of the gents,' said O'Toole, taking the opportunity while Mrs. Rodgers was away to mention the delicate matter of money. The men had agreed to pay two pounds each, to cover the cost of the drink; the ladies did not have to pay anything, but were invited so as to lend a pleasant and decorative atmosphere to the party, and, of course, to help.

O'Toole went around with his cap held out, and Brogan said that as it was *his* party, he ought to give a fiver.

'I ought to give a fiver, but I suppose ye wouldn't hear of that,' Brogan said, and handed up two pound notes. Hickey paid up, too, and O'Toole himself and Long John Salmon – who had been silent up to then. O'Toole gave it to Mrs. Rodgers when she returned and told her to clock it up against the damages.

'Sure that's too kind altogether,' she said, as she put it behind the stuffed owl on the mantelpiece, under the bishop's watchful eye.

She served the soup in cups, and Mary was asked to pass the cups around. The grease floated like drops of molten gold on the surface of each cup.

'See you later, alligator,' Hickey said, as she gave him his; then he asked her for a piece of bread, because he wasn't used to soup without bread.

'Tell us, Brogan,' said Hickey to his rich friend, 'what'll you do, now that you're a rich man?'

'Oh, go on, tell us,' said Doris O'Beirne.

'Well,' said Brogan, thinking for a minute, 'we're going to make some changes at home.' None of them had ever visited Brogan's home because it was situated in Adare, thirty miles away, at the far side of Limerick. None of them had ever seen his wife either, who, it seems, lived there and kept bees.

'What sort of changes?' someone said.

'We're going to do up the drawing room, and we're going to have flower beds,' Brogan told them.

'And what else?' Crystal asked, thinking of all the lovely clothes she could buy with that money, clothes and jewelry.

'Well,' said Brogan, thinking again, 'we might even go to Lourdes. I'm not sure yet, it all depends.'

'I'd give my two eyes to go to Lourdes,' Mrs. Rodgers said.

'And you'd get 'em back when you arrived there,' Hickey said, but no one paid any attention to him.

O'Toole poured out four half tumblers of whiskey and then stood back to examine the glasses to see that each one had the same amount. There was always great anxiety among the men about being fair with drink. Then O'Toole stood bottles of stout in little groups of six and told each man which group was his. The ladies had gin-and-orange.

'Orange for me,' Mary said, but O'Toole told her not to be such a goody, and when her back was turned, he put gin in her orange.

They drank a toast to Brogan.

'To Lourdes,' Mrs. Rodgers said.

'To Brogan,' O'Toole said.

'To myself,' Hickey said.

'Mud in your eye,' said Doris O'Beirne, who was already unsteady from tippling cider.

'Well, we're not sure about Lourdes,' Brogan said. 'But we'll get the drawing room done up anyhow, and the flower beds put in.'

'We've a drawing room here,' Mrs. Rodgers said, 'and no one ever sets foot in it.'

'Come into the drawing room, Doris,' said O'Toole to Mary, who was serving the jelly from the big enamel basin. They'd had no china bowl to put it in. It was red jelly with whipped egg white in it, but something had gone wrong, because it hadn't set properly. She served it in saucers, and thought to herself what a rough-and-ready party it was. There wasn't a proper cloth on the table either, just a plastic one, and no napkins, and that big basin with the jelly in it. Maybe people washed in that basin downstairs.

'Well, someone tell us a bloomin' joke,' said Hickey, who was getting fed up with talk about drawing rooms and flower beds.

'I'll tell you a joke,' said Long John Salmon, erupting out of his silence.

'Good,' said Brogan, as he sipped from his whiskey glass and his stout glass alternately. It was the only way to drink enjoyably.

That was why, in pubs, he'd be much happier if he could buy his own drink and not rely on anyone else's meanness.

'Is it a funny joke?' Hickey asked of Long John Salmon.

'It's about my brother,' said Long John Salmon, 'my brother Patrick.'

'Oh no, don't tell us that old rambling thing again,' said Hickey and O'Toole together.

'Oh, let him tell it,' said Mrs. Rodgers, who'd never heard the story anyhow.

Long John Salmon began, 'I had this brother Patrick and he died; the heart wasn't too good.'

'Holy Christ, not this again,' said Brogan, recollecting which story it was.

But Long John Salmon went on, undeterred by the abuse from the three men.

'One day I was standing in the shed, about a month after he was buried, and I saw him coming out of the wall, walking across the yard.'

'Oh, what would you do if you saw a thing like that?' Doris said to Eithne.

'Let him tell it,' Mrs. Rodgers said. 'Go on, Long John.'

'Well, it was walking toward me, and I said to myself, "What do I do now?"; 'twas raining heavy, so I said to my brother Patrick, "Stand in out of the wet or you'll get drenched."'

'And then?' said one of the girls anxiously.

'He vanished,' said Long John Salmon.

'Ah, God, let us have a bit of music,' said Hickey, who had heard that story nine or ten times. It had neither a beginning, a middle, nor an end. They put a record on, and O'Toole asked Mary to dance. He did a lot of fancy steps and capering; and now and then he let out a mad 'Yippee.' Brogan and Mrs. Rodgers were dancing, too, and Crystal said that she'd dance if anyone asked her.

'Come on, knees up, Mother Brown,' O'Toole said to Mary, as he jumped around the room, kicking the legs of chairs as he moved. She felt funny: her head was swaying around and around, and in the pit of her stomach there was a nice ticklish feeling that made her want to lie back and stretch her legs. A new feeling that frightened her.

'Come into the drawing room, Doris,' he said, dancing her right out of the room and into the cold passage, where he kissed her clumsily.

Inside, Crystal O'Meara had begun to cry. That was how drink affected her; either she cried or talked in a foreign accent and said, 'Why am I talking in a foreign accent?'

This time she cried.

'Hickey, there is no joy in life,' she said as she sat at the table with her head laid in her arms and her blouse slipping up out of her skirtband.

'What joy?' said Hickey, who had all the drink he needed, and a pound note which he slipped from behind the owl when no one was looking.

Doris and Eithne sat on either side of Long John Salmon, asking if they could go out next year when the sugar plums were ripe. Long John Salmon lived by himself, way up the country, and he had a big orchard. He was odd and silent in himself; he took a swim every day, winter and summer, in the river at the back of his house.

'Two old married people,' Brogan said, as he put his arm around Mrs. Rodgers and urged her to sit down because he was out of breath from dancing. He said he'd go away with happy memories of them all, and sitting down, he drew her onto his lap. She was a heavy woman, with straggly brown hair that had once been a nut color.

'There is no joy in life,' Crystal sobbed, as the gramophone made crackling noises and Mary ran in from the landing, away from O'Toole.

'I mean business,' O'Toole said, and winked.

O'Toole was the first to get quarrelsome.

'Now, ladies, now, gentlemen, a little laughing sketch, are we ready?' he asked.

'Fire ahead,' Hickey told him.

'Well, there was these three lads, Paddy th'Irishman, Paddy th'Englishman, and Paddy the Scotsman, and they were badly in need of a . . .'

'Now, no smut,' Mrs. Rodgers snapped, before he had uttered a wrong word at all.

'What smut?' asked O'Toole, getting offended. 'Smut!' And he asked her to explain an accusation like that.

'Think of the girls,' Mrs. Rodgers said.

'Girls,' O'Toole sneered, as he picked up the bottle of cream – which they'd forgotten to use with the jelly – and poured it into the carcass of the ravaged goose.

'Christ's sake, man,' Hickey said, taking the bottle of cream out of O'Toole's hand.

Mrs. Rodgers said that it was high time everyone went to bed, as the party seemed to be over.

The guests would spend the night in the Commercial. It was too late for them to go home anyhow, and also, Mrs. Rodgers did not want them to be observed staggering out of the house at that hour. The police watched her like hawks, and she didn't want any trouble, until Christmas was over at least. The sleeping arrangements had been decided earlier on – there were three bedrooms vacant. One was Brogan's, the room he always slept in. The other three men were to pitch in together in the second big bedroom, and the girls were to share the back room with Mrs. Rodgers herself.

'Come on, everyone, blanket street,' Mrs. Rodgers said, as she put a guard in front of the dying fire and took the money from behind the owl.

'Sugar you,' O'Toole said, pouring stout now into the carcass of the goose, and Long John Salmon wished that he had never come. He thought of daylight and of his swim in the mountain river at the back of his gray, stone house.

'Ablution,' he said aloud, taking pleasure in the word and in the thought of the cold water touching him. He could do without people, people were waste. He remembered catkins on a tree outside his window, catkins in February as white as snow; who needed people?

'Crystal, stir yourself,' Hickey said, as he put on her shoes and patted the calves of her legs.

Brogan kissed the four girls and saw them across the landing to the bedroom. Mary was glad to escape without O'Toole noticing; he was very obstreperous and Hickey was trying to control him.

In the bedroom she sighed; she had forgotten all about the furniture being pitched in there. Wearily they began to unload the things. The room was so crammed that they could hardly move in it. Mary suddenly felt alert and frightened, because O'Toole could be heard yelling and singing out on the landing. There had been gin in her orangeade, she knew now, because she breathed closely onto the palm of her hand and smelled her own breath. She had broken her Confirmation pledge, broken her promise; it would bring her bad luck.

Mrs. Rodgers came in and said that five of them would be too crushed in the bed, so that she herself would sleep on the sofa for one night.

'Two of you at the top and two at the bottom,' she said, as she warned them not to break any of the ornaments, and not to stay talking all night.

'Night and God bless,' she said, as she shut the door behind her.

'Nice thing,' said Doris O'Beirne, 'bunging us all in here; I wonder where she's off to.'

'Will you loan me curlers?' Crystal asked. To Crystal, hair was the most important thing on earth. She would never get married because you couldn't wear curlers in bed then. Eithne Duggan said she wouldn't put curlers in now if she got five million for doing it, she was that jaded. She threw herself down on the quilt and spread her arms out. She was a noisy, sweaty girl, but Mary liked her better than the other two.

'Ah, me old segotums,' O'Toole said, pushing their door in. The girls exclaimed and asked him to go out at once, as they were preparing for bed.

'Come into the drawing room, Doris,' he said to Mary, and curled his forefinger at her. He was drunk and couldn't focus on her properly, but he knew that she was standing there somewhere.

'Go to bed, you're drunk,' Doris O'Beirne said, and he stood very upright for an instant and asked her to speak for herself.

'Go to bed, Michael, you're tired,' Mary said to him. She tried to sound calm because he looked so wild.

'Come into the drawing room, I tell you,' he said as he caught her wrist and dragged her toward the door. She let out a cry, and Eithne Duggan said she'd brain him if he didn't leave the girl alone.

'Give me that flowerpot, Doris,' Eithne Duggan called, and then Mary began to cry in case there might be a scene. She hated scenes. Once, she heard her father and a neighbor having a row about boundary rights and she'd never forgotten it; they had both been a bit drunk, after a fair.

'Are you cracked or are you mad?' O'Toole said, when he perceived that she was crying.

'I'll give you two seconds,' Eithne warned, as she held the flowerpot high, ready to throw it at O'Toole's stupefied face.

'You're a nice bunch of hard-faced aul crows, crows,' he said. 'Wouldn't give a man a squeeze,' and he went out, cursing each one of them. They shut the door very quickly and dragged the sideboard in front of the door, so that he could not break in when they were asleep.

They got into bed in their underwear; Mary and Eithne at one end, with Crystal's feet between their faces.

'You have lovely hair,' Eithne whispered to Mary. It was the nicest thing she could think of to say. They each said their prayers and shook hands under the covers and settled down to sleep.

'Hey,' Doris O'Beirne said a few seconds later, 'I never went to the lav.'

'You can't go now,' Eithne said, 'the sideboard's in front of the door.'

'I'll die if I don't go,' Doris O'Beirne said.

'And me, too, after all that orange we drank,' Crystal said. Mary was shocked that they could talk like that. At home you never spoke of such a thing, you just went out behind the hedge and that was that. Once a workman saw her squatting down, and from that day she never talked to him, or acknowledged that she knew him.

'Maybe we could use that old pot,' Doris O'Beirne said, and Eithne Duggan sat up and said that if anyone used a pot in that room she wasn't going to sleep there,

'We have to use something,' Doris said. By now she had got up and had switched on the light. She held the pot up to the naked bulb and saw what looked to be a crack in it.

'Try it,' Crystal said, giggling.

They heard feet on the landing, and then the sound of choking and coughing, and later O'Toole cursing and swearing and hitting the wall with his fist. Mary curled down under the bedclothes, thankful for the company of the girls. They stopped talking.

'I was at a party. Now I know what parties are like,' Mary said to herself, as she tried to force herself asleep. She heard a sound as of water running, but it did not seem to be raining outside. Later she dozed, but at daybreak she heard the hall door bang and she sat up in bed abruptly. She had to be home early to milk, so she got up, took her shoes and her lace dress, let herself out by dragging the sideboard forward, and opening the door slightly.

There were newspapers spread on the landing floor and in the lavatory, and a heavy smell pervaded. Downstairs, porter had flowed out of the bar into the hall. It was probably O'Toole who had turned on the taps of the five porter barrels; the stone-floored bar and sunken passage outside were swimming with black porter. Mrs. Rodgers would kill somebody. Mary put on her high-heeled shoes and picked her steps carefully across the room to the door. She left without even making a cup of tea.

She wheeled her bicycle down the alley and into the street. The front tire was dead flat. She pumped for half an hour, but it remained flat.

The frost lay like a spell upon the street, upon the sleeping windows and the slate roofs of the narrow houses. It had magically made the dunged street white and clean. She did not feel tired but relieved to be out, and stunned by lack of sleep, she inhaled the beauty of the morning. She walked briskly, sometimes looking back to see the track which her bicycle and her feet made on the white road.

Mrs. Rodgers wakened at eight and stumbled out in her big nightgown from Brogan's warm bed. She smelled disaster instantly and hurried downstairs to find the porter in the bar and the hall; then she ran to call the others.

'Porter all over the place; every drop of drink in the house is on the floor – Mary Mother of God, help me in my tribulation! Get up, get up.' She rapped on their door and called the girls by name.

The girls rubbed their sleepy eyes, yawned, and sat up.

'She's gone,' Eithne said, looking at the place on the pillow where Mary's head had been.

'Oh, a sneaky country one,' Doris said, as she got into her taffeta dress and went down to see the flood. 'If I have to clean that in my good clothes, I'll die,' she said. But Mrs. Rodgers had already brought brushes and pails and got to work. They opened the bar door and began to bail the porter into the street. Dogs came to lap it up, and Hickey, who had by then come down, stood and said what a crying shame it was, to waste all that drink. Outside, it washed away an area of frost and revealed the dung of yesterday's fair day. O'Toole, the culprit, had fled since the night; Long John Salmon was gone for his swim, and upstairs in bed Brogan snuggled down for a last-minute warm and deliberated on the joys that he would miss when he left the Commercial for good.

'And where's my lady with the lace dress?' Hickey asked, recalling very little of Mary's face, but distinctly remembering the sleeves of her black dress, which dipped into the plates.

'Sneaked off, before we were up,' Doris said. They all agreed that Mary was no bloody use and should never have been asked.

'And 'twas she set O'Toole mad, egging him on and then disappointing him,' Doris said, and Mrs. Rodgers swore that O'Toole, or Mary's father, or someone, would pay dear for the wasted drink.

'I suppose she's home by now,' Hickey said, as he rooted in his pocket for a butt. He had a new packet, but if he produced that, they'd all be puffing away at his expense.

Mary was half a mile from home, sitting on a bank.

If only I had a sweetheart, something to hold on to, she thought, as she cracked some ice with her high heel and watched the crazy splintered pattern it made. The poor birds could get no food, as the ground was frozen hard. Frost was everywhere; it coated the bare branches and made them like etchings, it starched the grass and blurred the shape of a plow that stood in a field, above all it gave the world an appearance of sanctity.

Walking again, she wondered if and what she would tell her mother and her brothers about it, and if all parties were as bad. She was at the top of the hill now, and could see her own house, like a little white box at the end of the world, waiting to receive her.

The Connor Girls

To know them would be to enter an exalted world. To open the stiff green iron gate, to go up their shaded avenue and to knock on their white hall door was a journey I yearned to make. No one went there except the gardener, the postman, and a cleaning woman who told none of their secrets, merely boasted that the oil paintings on the walls were priceless and the furniture was all antique. They had a flower garden with fountains, a water-lily pond, kitchen garden and ornamental trees that they called monkey-puzzle trees. Mr Connor, the Major, and his two daughters lived there. His only son had been killed in a car accident. It was said that the accident was due to his father's bullying of him, always urging him to drive faster since he had the most expensive car in the neighbourhood. Not even their tragedy brought them closer to the people in the town, partly because they were aloof, but being Protestants, the Catholics could not attend the service in the church or go to the Protestant graveyard where they had a vault with steps leading down to it, just like a house. It was smothered in creeper. They never went into mourning and had a party about a month later to which their friends came.

The Major had friends who owned a stud farm and these were invited two or three times a year along with a surgeon and his wife, from Dublin. The Connor girls were not beauties but they were distinguished and they talked in an accent that made everyone else's seem flat and sprawling, like some familiar estuary or a puddle in a field. They were dark haired with dark eyes and leathery skin. Miss Amy wore her hair in plaits which she folded over the crown of her head and Miss Lucy's hair, being more bushy, was kept flattened with brown slides. If they as much as nodded to a local or stopped to admire a new baby in its pram the news spread throughout the parish and those who had never had a salute felt such a pang of envy, felt left out. We ourselves had been saluted and it was certain that we would become on better terms since they were under a sort of compliment to us. My father had given them permission to walk their dogs over our fields so that most afternoons we saw the two girls in their white mackintoshes and biscuit-coloured walking sticks drawing these fawn unwieldy beasts, on leashes. Once they had passed our house they used to let their dogs go, whereupon our own sheep-dogs barked fiercely but kept inside our own paling being as I think terrified of the thorough-breds, who were beagles. Though they had been passing by for almost a year, they never stopped to talk to my mother if they met her returning from the hen-house with an empty pail, or going there with the foodstuff. They had merely saluted and passed on. They talked to my father of course and called him Mick, although his real name was Joseph, and they joked with him about his hunters which had never won cup or medal. They ignored my mother and she resented this. She longed to bring them in so that they could admire our house with all its knicknacks, and admire the thick wool rugs which she made in the winter nights and which she folded up when no visitors were expected.

'I'll ask them to tea this coming Friday,' she said to me. We planned to ask them impromptu, thinking that if we asked them ahead of time they were more likely to refuse. So we made cakes and sausage rolls and sandwiches of egg mayonnaise, some with onion, some without. The milk jelly we had made was whisked and seemed like a bowl of froth with a sweet confectionery smell. I was put on watch by the kitchen window and as soon as I saw them coming in at the gate I called to Mamma.

'They're coming, they're coming.'

She swept her hair back, pinned it with her brown tortoiseshell comb and went out and leaned on the top rung of the gate as if she was posing for a photograph, or looking at a view. I heard her say 'Excuse me Miss Connor, or rather Miss Connors,' in that exaggerated accent which she had picked up in America, and which she used when strangers came, or when she went to the city. It was like putting on new clothes or new shoes which did not fit her. I saw them shake their heads a couple of times and long before she had come back into the house I knew that the Connor girls had refused our invitation and that the table which we had laid with such ceremony was a taunt and a downright mockery.

Mamma came back humming to herself as if to pretend that it hadn't mattered a jot. The Connor girls had walked on and their dogs which were off the leashes were chasing our young turkeys into the woods.

'What will we do with this spread?' I asked Mamma as she put on her overall.

'Give it to the men, I expect,' she said wearily.

You may know how downcast she was when she was prepared to give iced cake and dainty sandwiches to workmen who were ploughing and whose appetites were ferocious.

'They didn't come,' I said stupidly, being curious to know how the Connor girls had worded their refusal.

'They never eat between meals,' Mamma said, quoting their exact phrase in an injured sarcastic voice.

'Maybe they'll come later on,' I said.

'They're as odd as two left shoes,' she said, tearing a frayed tea towel in half. When in a temper, she resorted to doing something about the house. Either she took the curtains down, or got on her knees to scrub the floor and the legs and rungs of the wooden chairs.

'They see no one except that Mad Man,' she said mainly to herself.

The Connor girls kept very much to themselves and did most of their shopping in the city. They attended church on Sundays, four Protestant souls comprising the congregation in a stone church that was the oldest in our parish. Moss covered the stones and various plants grew between the cracks so that in the distance the side wall of the church was green both from verdure and centuries of rain. Their father did not attend each Sunday but once a month the girls wheeled him down to the family vault where his wife and son were interred. Local people who longed to be friends with them would rush out and offer their sympathy as if the Major was the only one to have suffered bereavement. Always he remained brusque and asked his daughters the name of the man or woman who happened to be talking to him. He was known to be crotchety but this was because of his rheumatism which he had contracted years before. He could not be persuaded to go to any of the holy wells where other people went, to pray, and seek a cure for their ailments. He was a large man with a very red face and he always wore grey mittens. The Rector visited him twice a month and in the dapping season sent up two fresh trout on the mail car. Soon after the Connor girls invited the Rector for dinner and some of the toffs who had come for the dapping.

Otherwise they entertained rarely, except for the Mad Man who visited them every Sunday. He was a retired captain from the next town and he had a brown moustache with a red tint in it and very large bloodshot eyes. People said that he slept with the Connor girls and hence he had been given the nickname of Stallion. It was him my mother referred to as the Mad Man. On Sundays he drove over in his sports car, in time for afternoon tea, which in summer time they had out of doors on an iron table. Us children used to go over there to look at them through the trees and though we could not clearly see them we could hear their voices, hear the girls' laughter and then the tap of a croquet mallet when they played a game. Their house was approached from the road by a winding avenue that was dense with evergreen trees. Those trees were hundreds of years old but also there were younger trees that the Major had planted for the important occasions in his life – the Coronation, the birth of his children, England's victory in the last war. For his daughters he had planted quinces. What were quinces we wondered and never found out. Nailed to the blue cedar, near the gate was a sign which said 'Beware of dogs' and the white pebble-dashed walls that surrounded their acres of garden were topped with broken glass so that children could not climb over and steal from the orchard.

Everyone vetted them when they came out of their stronghold on Sunday evening. Their escort, the Stallion, walked the girls to the Greyhound Hotel. Miss Amy, who was younger, wore brighter clothes but they both wore tweed costumes, and flat shoes with ornamental tongues that came over the insteps and hid the laces. Miss Amy favoured red or maroon while Miss Lucy wore dark brown with a matching dark-brown beret. In the hotel they had the exclusive use of the sitting room and sometimes when they were a little intoxicated Miss Lucy played the piano while her sister and the Stallion sang. It was a saucy song, a duet in which the man asked the pretty maid where she was going to, and eventually asked for her hand in marriage. Refusing him she said, 'I will not marry, marry, marry you', and then stamped her feet to emphasise it, whereupon the men in the bar would start laughing and saying Miss Amy was 'bucking'. There was much suggestiveness about their lives because the Stallion always spent Sunday night in their house. Hickey our hired help said they were all so drunk that they probably tumbled into bed together. Walking home on the frosty nights Hickey said it was a question of the blind leading the blind, as they slithered all over the road, and according to Hickey used language that was not ladylike. He would report these things in the morning to my mother and since they had rebuffed her she was pleased, and emphasised the fact that they had no breeding. Naturally she thought the very worst of the Stallion and could never bring herself to pronounce his christian name. To her he was 'that Mad Man'.

The Stallion was their sole escort until fate sent another man in the form of a temporary bank clerk. We reckoned that he was a Protestant because he didn't go to Mass on the first Sunday. He was most dashing. He had brown hair, he too had a moustache but it was fuller than the Stallion's and was a soft dark brown. Mostly he wore a tweed jacket and matching plus-fours. Also he had a motor cycle and when he rode it, he wore goggles. Within two weeks he was walking Miss Amy out and escorting her to the Greyhound Hotel. She began to pay more attention to her clothes, she got two new accordion-pleated skirts and some tight-fitting jumpers that made her bust more pronounced. They were called Sloppy Joe's but although they were long and sloppy they were also sleek, and they flattered the figure. Formerly her hair was wound in a staid plait around her head but now it was allowed to tumble down in thick coils over her shoulders and she toned down the colour in her cheeks with pale powder. No one ever said she was pretty but certainly she looked handsome when she cycled to the village to collect the morning paper, and hummed to herself as she went free-wheel down the hill that led to the town.

The bank clerk and herself were in love. Hickey saw them embrace in the porch of the Greyhound Hotel when Miss Lucy had gone back in to get a packet of cigarettes. Later they kissed shamelessly when walking along the towpath and people said that Miss Amy used to nibble the hairs of his luxurious moustache. One night she took off her sandal in the Greyhound Hotel and put her bare foot into the pocket of his sports jacket and the two of them giggled at her proceedings. Her sister and the Stallion often tagged along but Miss Amy and the bank clerk would set off on his motor cycle, down the

Shannon Road, for fun. It was said that they swam naked but no one could verify that and it was possible that they just paddled their feet.

As it happened, someone brought mischievous news about the bank clerk. A commercial traveller who was familiar with other parts, told it on good authority that the bank clerk was a lapsed Catholic and had previously disgraced himself in a seaside town. People were left to guess the nature of the mistake and most concluded that it concerned a girl or a woman. Instantly the parish turned against him. The next evening when he came out from the bank he found that both wheels of his pedal bicycle had been ripped and punctured and on the saddle there was an anonymous letter which read 'Go to Mass or we'll kill you.' His persecutors won. He attended the last Mass the following Sunday, knelt in the back pew with no beads and no prayer book, with only his fingers to pray on.

However it did not blight the romance. Those who had predicted that Miss Amy would ditch him because he was a Catholic were proven wrong. Most evenings they went down the Shannon Road, a couple full of glee, her hair and her headscarf flying, and chuckles of laughter from both of them as they frightened a dog or hens that strayed on to the roadside. Much later he saw her home, and the lights were on in their front parlour until all hours. A local person (the undertaker actually) thought of fitting up a telescope to try and see into the parlour but as soon as he went inside their front gate to reconnoitre, the dogs came rearing down the avenue and he ran for his life.

'Can it be serious I wonder.' So at last my mother admitted to knowing about the romance. She could not abide it, she said that Catholics and Protestants just could not mix. She recalled a grievance held for many years of a time in her girlhood when she and all the others from the national school were invited to the big house to a garden party, and were made to make fools of themselves by doing running jumps and sack races and were then given watery lemonade

with flies in it. Her mind was firmly made up about the incompati-
bility of Catholics and Protestants. That very night Miss Amy
sported an engagement ring in the Greyhound Hotel and the
following morning the engagement was announced in the paper.
The ring was star-shaped and comprised of tiny blue stones that
sparkled and trembled under the beam of the hanging lamp. People
gasped when told that it was insured for a hundred pounds.

'Do we have to give Miss Amy some sort of present,' my mother
said grudgingly that evening. She had not forgotten how they
snubbed her and how they barely thanked her for the fillets of
pork that she gave them every time that we killed a pig.

'Indeed we do, and a good present,' my father said, so they
went to Limerick some time after, and got a carving knife and
fork that was packed in a velvet-lined box. We presented it to
Miss Amy the next time she was walking her dogs past our house.

'It *is* kind of you, thanks awfully,' she said as she smiled at each
one of us, and told my father coyly that as she was soon to be
hitched up they ought to have that night out. She was not serious
of course but yet we all laughed and my mother did a 'tch tch' in
mock disapproval. Miss Amy looked ravishing that day. Her skin
was soft and her brown eyes had caught the reflection of her
orange neck scarf and gave her a warm theatrical glow. Also she
was amiable. It was a damp day, with shreds of mist on the mountains and the trees dripped quietly as we spoke. Miss Amy held
out the palms of her hands to take the drips from the walnut
tree and announced to the heavens what a 'lucky gal' she was.
My mother enquired about her trousseau and was told that she
had four pairs of court shoes, two camel-hair coats, a saxe-blue
going-away suit and a bridal dress in voile that was a cross between
peach and champagne colour. I loved her then, and wanted to
know her and wished with all my heart that I could have gone
across the fields with her and become her confidante but I was ten
and she was thirty or thirty-five.

There was much speculation about the wedding. No one from the village had been invited but then that was to be expected. Some said that it was to be in a Register Office in Dublin but others said that the bank clerk had assured the Parish Priest that he would be married in a Catholic church, and had guaranteed a huge sum of money in order to get his letter of freedom. It was even said that Miss Amy was going to take instruction so as to be converted but that was only wishful thinking. People were stunned the day the bank clerk suddenly left. He left the bank at lunchtime, after a private talk with the Manager. Miss Amy drove him to the little railway station ten miles away, and they kissed several times before he jumped on to the moving train. The story was that he had gone ahead to make the plans and that the Connor girls and their father would travel shortly after. But the postman who was a Protestant said that the Major would not travel one inch to see his daughter marry a Papist.

We watched the house and gate carefully but we did not see Miss Amy emerge throughout the week. No one knows when she left, or what she wore or in what frame of mind. All we knew was that suddenly Miss Lucy was out walking with the Stallion and Miss Amy was not to be seen.

'And where's the bride-to-be tonight?' enquired Mrs O'Shea, the hotel proprietor. Miss Lucy's reply was clipped and haughty.

'My sister's gone away, for a change,' she said.

The frozen voice made everyone pause and Mrs O'Shea gave some sort of untoward gasp that seemed to detect catastrophe.

'Is there anything else you would care to know, Mrs O'Shea,' Miss Lucy asked and then turned on her heel and with the Stallion left. Never again did they drink in the Greyhound Hotel but moved to a public house up the street, where several of the locals soon followed them.

The mystery of Miss Amy was sending people into frenzies of conjecture and curiosity. Everyone thought that everyone else knew something. The postman was asked but he would just nod his head and say 'Time will tell', although it was plain to see that he was pleased with the outcome. The priest when asked in confidence by my mother said that the most Christian thing to do would be to go down on one's knees and say a prayer for Miss Amy. The phrase 'star-crossed lovers' was used by many of the women and for a while it even was suggested that Miss Amy had gone berserk and was shut up in an asylum. At last the suspense was ended as each wedding present was returned, with an obscure but polite note from Miss Lucy. My mother took ours back to the shop and got some dinner plates in exchange. The reason given was that there had been a clash of family interests. Miss Lucy came to the village scarcely at all. The Major had got more ill and she was busy nursing him. A night nurse cycled up their avenue every evening at five to nine, and the house itself, without so much coming and going, began to look forlorn. In the summer evenings I used to walk up the road and gaze in at it, admiring the green jalousies, the bird-table nailed to the tree, the tall important flowers and shrubs, that for want of tending had grown apace. I used to wish that I could unlock the gate and go up and be admitted there and find the clue to Miss Amy's whereabouts and her secret.

We did in fact visit the house the following winter when the Major died. It was much more simply furnished than I had imagined and the loose linen covers on the armchairs were a bit frayed. I was studying the portraits of glum puffy dark-looking ancestors when suddenly there was a hush and into the parlour came Miss Amy wearing a fur coat looking quite different. She looked older and her face was coarse.

'Miss Amy, Miss Amy,' several people said aloud, and flinching she turned to tell the driver to please leave her trunk on the landing upstairs. She had got much fatter and was wearing no engagement ring. When the people sympathised with her, her eyes became cloudy with tears and then she ran out of the room, and up the stairs to sit with the remains.

It did not take long for everyone to realise that Miss Amy had become a drinker. As the coffin was laid in the vault she tried to talk to her father which everyone knew was irrational. She did not just drink at night in the bar, but drank in the daytime and would take a miniature bottle out of her bag when she queued in the butcher's shop to get chops and a sheep's head for the dogs. She drank with my father when he was on a drinking bout. In fact she drank with anyone that would sit with her, and had lost all her snootiness. She sometimes referred to her engagement as 'My flutter'. Soon after, she was arrested in Limerick for drunken driving but was not charged because the Superintendent had been a close friend of her father's. Her driving became calamitous. People were afraid to let their children play in the street in case Miss Amy might run them over in her Peugeot car. No one had forgotten that her brother had killed himself driving and even her sister began to confide to my mother, telling her worries in tense whispers, spelling the words that were the most incriminating.

'It must be a broken heart,' my mother said.

'Of course with Dad gone there is no one to raise any objections now, to the wedding.'

'So why don't they marry,' my mother asked and in one fell swoop surrendered all her prejudices.

'Too late, too late,' Miss Lucy said and then added that Miss Amy could not get the bank clerk out of her system, that she sat in the breakfast room staring at photographs they had taken the day of her engagement and was always looking for an excuse to use his name.

One night the new Curate found Miss Amy drunk in a hedge under her bicycle. By then her driving licence had been taken away for a year. He picked her up, brought her home in his car and the next day called on her because he had found a brooch stuck to the fuchsia hedge where she became entangled. Furthermore he had put her bicycle in to be repaired. This gesture worked wonders. He was asked to stay to tea, and invited again the following Sunday. Due to his influence or perhaps secretly due to his prayers, Miss Amy began to drink less. To everyone's amazement the Curate went there most Sunday nights and played bridge with the two girls and the Stallion. In no time Miss Amy was overcome with resolve and industry. The garden which had been neglected began to look bright and trim again and she bought bulbs in the hardware shop, whereas formerly she used to send away to a nursery for them. Everyone remarked on how civil she had become. Herself and my mother exchanged recipes for apple jelly and lemon curd, and just before I went away to boarding school she gave me a present of a bound volume of Aesop's Fables. The print was so small that I could not read it, but it was the present that mattered. She handed it to me in the field and then asked if I would like to accompany her to gather some flowers. We went to the swamp to get the yellow irises. It was a close day, the air was thick with midges and they lay in hosts over the murky water. Holding a small bunch to her chest she said that she was going to post them to somebody, somebody special.

'Won't they wither,' I said, though what I really wanted to know was who they were meant for.

'Not if I pack them in damp moss,' she said and it seemed that the thought of despatching this little gift was bringing joy to her, though there was no telling who the recipient would be. She asked me if I'd fallen in love yet or had a 'beau'. I said that I had liked an actor who had come with the travelling players and had in fact got his autograph.

'Dreams', she said, 'dreams', and then using the flowers as a bat swatted some midges away. In September I went to boarding school and got involved with nuns and various girl friends, and in time the people in our parish, even the Connor girls, almost disappeared from my memory. I never dreamt of them any more and I had no ambitions to go cycling with them or to visit their house. Later when I went to university in Dublin I learnt quite by chance that Miss Amy had worked in a beauty parlour in Stephens Green, had drank heavily, and had joined a golf club., By then the stories of how she teetered on high heels, or wore unmatching stockings or smiled idiotically and took ages to say what she intended to say, had no interest for me.

Somewhat precipitately and unknown to my parents I had become engaged to a man who was not of our religion. Defying threats of severing bonds, I married him and incurred the wrath of family and relatives just as Miss Amy had done, except that I was not there to bear the brunt of it. Horrible letters, some signed and some anonymous, used to reach me and my mother had penned an oath that we would never meet again, this side of the grave. I did not see my family for a few years, until long after my son was born, and having some change of heart they proposed by letter that my husband, my son and I, pay them a visit. We drove down one blowy autumn afternoon and I read stories aloud as much to distract myself as to pacify my son. I was quaking. The sky was watery and there were pale green patches like holes or voids in it. I shall never forget the sense of awkwardness, sadness and dismay when I stepped out of my husband's car and saw the large gaunt cut-stone house with thistles in the front garden. The thistle seed was blowing wildly, as were the leaves and even those that had already fallen were rising and scattering about. I introduced my husband to my parents and very proudly I asked my little son to shake hands with his grandfather, and his grandmother. They admired his gold hair but he ignored them and ran to cuddle the two sheepdogs. He was going to be the one that would make our visit bearable.

In the best room my mother had laid the table for tea and we sat and spoke to one another in thin, strained, unforgiving voices. The tea was too strong for my husband, who usually drank China tea anyhow, and instantly my mother jumped up to get some hot water. I followed her out to apologise for the inconvenience.

'The house looks lovely and clean,' I said.

She had polished everywhere and she had even dusted the artificial flowers which I remembered as being clogged with dust.

'You'll stay a month,' she said in a warm commandeering voice, and she put her arms around me in an embrace.

'We'll see,' I said prudently, knowing my husband's restlessness.

'You have a lot of friends to see,' she said.

'Not really,' I said with a coldness that I could not conceal.

'Do you know who is going to ask you to tea – the Connor girls.' Her voice was urgent and grateful. It meant a victory for her, for me, and an acknowledgement of my husband's non-religion. In her eyes Protestants and atheists were one and the same thing.

'How are they?' I asked.

'They've got very sensible, and aren't half as stuck up,' she said and then ran as my father was calling for her to cut the iced cake. Next afternoon there was a gymkhana over in the village and my parents insisted that we go.

'I don't want to go to this thing,' my husband said to me. He had intended to do some trout fishing in one of the many mountain rivers, and to pass his few days, as he said, without being assailed by barbarians.

'Just for this once,' I begged and I knew that he had consented because he put on his tie, but there was no affability in it. After lunch my father, my husband, my little son and I set out. My mother did not come as she had to guard her small chickens. She had told us in the most graphic details of her immense sorrow one morning upon finding sixty week-old chicks laid out on the flag dead, with their necks wrung, by weasels.

In the field where the gymkhana was held there were a few caravans, strains of accordion music, a gaudy sign announcing a Welsh clairvoyant, wild restless horses, and groups of self-conscious people in drab clothes, shivering as they waited for the events to begin. It was still windy and the horses looked unmanageable. They were being held in some sort of order by youngsters who had little power over them. I saw people stare in my direction and a few of them gave reluctant half-smiles. I felt uneasy and awkward and superior all at once.

'There's the Connor girls,' my father said. They were perched on their walking sticks which opened up to serve as little seats.

'Come on, come on,' he said excitedly and as we approached them they hailed me and said my name. They were older but still healthy and handsome, and Miss Amy showed no signs of her past despair. They shook my hand, shook my husband's hand and were quick to flirt with him, to show him what spirited girls they were.

'And what do you think of this young man,' my father said proudly as he presented his grandson.

'What a sweet little chap,' they said together, and I saw my husband wince. Then from the pocket of her fawn coat Miss Amy took two unwrapped jelly sweets and handed them to the little boy. He was on the point of eating them when my husband bent down until their faces were level and said very calmly, 'But you don't eat sweets, now give them back.' The little boy pouted, then blushed, and held out the palm of his hand on which rested these absurd two jellies that were dusted over with granular sugar. My father protested, the Connor girls let out exclamations of horror, and I said to my husband, 'Let him have them, it's a day out.' He gave me a menacing look and very firmly he repeated to the little boy what he had already said. The sweets were handed back and with scorn in her eyes Miss Amy looked at my husband and said, 'Hasn't the mummy got any say over her own child.'

There was a moment's strain, a moment's silence and then my father produced a packet of cigarettes and gave them one each. Since we didn't smoke we were totally out of things.

'No vices,' Miss Lucy said and my husband ignored her.

He suggested to me that we take the child across to where a man had a performing monkey clinging to a stick. He raised his cap slightly to say his farewell and I smiled as best I could. My father stayed behind with the Connor girls.

'They were going to ask us to tea,' I said to my husband as we walked downhill. I could hear the suction of his galoshes in the soggy ground.

'Don't think we missed much,' he said and at that moment I realised that by choosing his world I had said goodbye to my own and to those in it. By such choices we gradually become exiles, until at last we are quite alone.

Tough Men

'Throw more paraffin in it,' Morgan said as he went out to the shop to serve Mrs. Gleeson for the sixth time that morning. Hickey threw paraffin and a fist of matches onto the gray cinders, then put the top back on the stove quickly in case the flames leaped into his face. The skewers of curled-up bills on the shelf overhead were scorched, having almost caught fire many a time before. It was a small office, partitioned off from the shop, where Morgan did his accounts and kept himself warm in the winter. A cozy place with two chairs, a sloping wooden desk, and ledgers going back so far that most of the names entered in the early ones were the names of dead people. There was a safe as well, and everything had the air of being undisturbed, because the ashes and dust had congealed evenly on things. It was called The Snug.

'Bloody nuisance, that Gleeson woman,' Morgan said as he came in from the counter and touched the top of the iron stove to see if it was warming up.

'She doesn't do a tap of work; hubby over in England earning money, all the young ones out stealing firewood and milk, and anything else they can lay hands on,' Hickey said.

Mrs. Gleeson was an inquisitive woman, always dressed in black, with a black kerchief over her head and a white, miserable, nosy face.

'We'll need to get a good fire up,' Morgan said. 'That's one thing we'll need,' and he popped a new candle into the stove to get it going. He swore by candle grease and paraffin for lighting fires, and neither cost him anything, because he sold them, along with every other commodity that country people needed – tea, flour, hen food, hardware, Wellington boots, and gaberdine coats. In the summer he hung the coats outside the door on a window ledge, and once a coat had fallen into a puddle. He offered it to Hickey cheap, but was rejected.

'Will they miss you?' Morgan said.

'Miss, my eye! Isn't poor man in bed with hot-water bottles and Sloan's liniment all over Christmas, and she's so murdered minding him, she doesn't know what time of day it is.'

'Poor man' was Hickey's name for his boss, Mr. James Brady, a gentleman farmer who was given to drink, rheumatic aches, and a scalding temper.

'Say the separating machine got banjaxed up at the creamery,' Morgan said.

'Of course,' said Hickey, as if any fool would know enough to say that. It was simple; Hickey had been to the creamery with Brady's milk, and when he got home he could say he had been held up because a machine broke down.

'Of course I'll tell them that,' he said again, and winked at Morgan. They were having an important caller that morning and a lot of strategy was required. Morgan opened the lower flap door of the stove and a clutter of ashes fell onto his boots. The grating was choked with ashes too, and Hickey began to clean it out with a stick, so that they could at least make the place presentable. Then he rooted in the turf basket, and finding two logs, he popped them in and emptied whatever shavings and turf dust were in the basket over them.

'That stove must be thirty years old,' Morgan said, remembering how he used to light it with balls of paper and dry sticks when he first came to work in the shop as an apprentice. He lit it all the years he served his time and he still lit it when he began to get wise to fiddling money and giving short weight. That was when he was saving to buy the shop from the mean blackguard who owned it. He even lit it when he hired the new shopgirl, because she was useless at it. She had chilblains and hence wore a dress down to her ankles, and he pitied her for her foolishness. Finally he married her. Now he had a shopboy who usually lit the stove for him.

'His nibs is off again today,' he said to Hickey, remembering the squint-eyed shopboy whom he hired but did not trust.

'He'd stay at home with a gumboil, he would,' Hickey said, though neither of them objected very much, as they needed the privacy. Also, business was slack just after Christmas.

'If this thing comes off we'll go to the dogs, Fridays and Saturdays,' Morgan said.

'Shanks' mare?' Hickey asked with a grin.

'We'll hire a car,' Morgan said, and the dreams of these pleasant outings began to buoy him up and make him smile in anticipation. He liked the dogs and already envisaged the crowds, the excitement, the tote board, the tracks artificially lit up, and the six or seven sleek hounds following the hare with such grace as if it were wind and not their own legs that propelled them.

'Let's do our sums,' he said, and together Hickey and himself counted *the* number of big farmers who had hay sheds. Not having been up the country for many a day, Morgan was, as he admitted, hazy about who lived beyond the chapel road, or up the commons, or down the Coolnahilla way and in the byroads and over the hills. In this Hickey was fluent because he did a bit of shooting on Sundays and had walked those godforsaken spots. They counted the farmers and hence the number of hay sheds, and their eyes shone with cupidity and glee. The stranger who was coming to see them had patented a marvelous stuff that, when sprayed on hay sheds, prevented rusting. Morgan was hoping to be given the franchise for the whole damn parish.

'Jaysus, there must be a hundred hay sheds,' Hickey said, and marveled at Morgan's good luck at meeting a man who put him on to such a windfall.

''Twas pure fluke,' Morgan said, and recalled the holiday he took at the spa town and how one day when he was trying to down this horrible sulphur water a man sat next to him and asked him where he was from, and eventually he heard about this substance that was a godsend to farmers.

'Pure fluke,' he said again, and lifted the whiskey bottle from its hiding place, behind a holy picture which was laid against the wall. He took a quick slug.

'I think that's him,' Hickey said, buttoning his waistcoat so as not to seem like a barbarian. In fact, it was John Ryan, a medical student, who had been asked not for reasons of his education but because he had a bit of pull. He tiptoed toward the entrance and from the outside played on the frosted glass as if it were a piano.

'Come in,' said Morgan.

He knew it was John Ryan by the shape of the long eejitty fingers. Ryan was briefed to tell them if any other shopkeepers up the street had been approached by the bloke. Being home on holidays, Ryan did nothing but hatch in houses, drink tea, and click girls in the evening.

'All set,' said Ryan as he looked at the two men and the saucepan waiting on the stove. Morgan had decided that they would do a bit of cooking, having reasoned that if a man came all that way, a bit of grub would not go amiss. Hickey, who couldn't even go to the creamery without bringing a large agricultural sandwich in his pocket, declared that no man does good business on an empty stomach. The man was from the North of Ireland.

'Is the bird on yet?' said John Ryan, splaying his hands fanwise to get a bit of heat from the stove.

'We haven't got her yet,' said Hickey, and Morgan cursed aloud the farmer that had promised him a cockerel.

'Get us a few logs while you're standing,' Morgan said, and John Ryan reluctantly went out. At the back of the shop by a mossy wall he gathered a bundle of damp, roughly sawn logs. He was in dread that he would stain the new fawn Crombie coat that his mother had given him at Christmas.

'Any sign of anyone?' Morgan said. It was important that the man with the chicken got to them before the stranger.

'Not a soul,' John Ryan said.

'Bloody clown,' Morgan said, and he went to the door to see if there was a sound of a horse and cart. Hickey lifted the lid of the saucepan to show Ryan the little onions that were in it simmering. He had peeled them earlier at the outside tap and had cried buckets. It was a new saucepan that afterward would be cleaned and put back in stock.

'How's the ladies, John?' he asked. Ryan had a great name with ladies and wasn't a bad-looking fellow. He had a long face and a longish nose and a great crop of brown, thick, curly, oily hair. His eyes were a shade of green that Hickey had never seen on any other human being, only in a shade of darning wool.

'I bet you're clicking like mad,' said Morgan, coming back to the snug. He wished that he was John Ryan's age and not a middle-aged married man with a flushed face and a rank liver.

'I get places,' Ryan boasted, and gave a nervous laugh, because he remembered his date of the night before. He had arranged to meet a girl behind the shop, on the back road which led to the creamery, the same road where Hickey had the mare and cart tethered to a gate and where Morgan kept the logs in a stack against a wall under a tarpaulin. She'd cycled four miles to meet him because he was damned if he was going to put himself out for any girl. No sooner had she arrived than she asked him the time and said that she'd have to be thinking of getting back soon.

'Take off your scarf,' he said. She was so muffled with scarf and gloves and things that he couldn't get near her.

'I'm fine this way,' she said, standing with her bicycle between them. Half a dozen words were exchanged and she rode off again, making a date for the following Sunday night.

'So 'twas worthwhile,' Morgan said, although he had no interest in women anymore. He knew well enough that nothing much went on between men and women. His own wife nearly drove him mad, sitting in front of the kitchen fire saying she could see faces in the flames and then getting up suddenly and running upstairs to see if there was a man under her bed. He had sent her to Lourdes the summer before to see if that would straighten her out, but she came back worse.

'Love, it's all bull . . .' he said. His wife had developed a craze for putting sugar and peaches into every bit of meat she cooked. Then she had a fegary to buy an egg timer. She played with the egg timer at night, turning it upside down and watching the passage of the sand as it flowed down into the underneath tube. Childish she was.

'I wish he'd come,' Hickey said.

'Which of them?' said John Ryan.

'Long John with the chicken,' said Hickey.

'He sent word yesterday that he'd be here this morning with my Christmas box,' Morgan said.

''Twill be plucked and all?' John Ryan asked.

'Oh, ready for the oven,' Morgan said. 'Other years I brought it up home, but I don't want it dolled up with peaches and sugar and that nonsense.'

'No man wants food ruined,' said Hickey. He pitied Morgan with the wife he had. Everyone could see she was getting more peculiar, talking to herself as she rode on her bicycle to Mass and hiding behind walls if she saw a man coming.

They heard footsteps in the shop, and Ryan opened the door a crack to see who it was.

'Is it him?'

'No, it's a young Gleeson one.'

'She can wait,' Morgan said, making no effort to get up. He was damned if he'd weigh three pennies' worth of sugar on a cold day like this. The child tapped the counter with a coin, then began to cough to let them know she was there, and finally she hummed a song. In the end she had to go away unserved.

'In a month from now you'll be well away,' Hickey said.

'It's not a dead cert,' Morgan said. He had to keep some curb on his dreams, because more than once he or his wife had had a promise of a legacy and were diddled out of it. Yet inwardly his spirits were soaring and made better each minute by the great draughts of whiskey which he took from the bottle. The other two men drank from mugs. In that way he was able to ration them a bit.

He had to go out to the shop for the next customer because it was the schoolteacher's maid, and they gave him quite a bit of trade. She wanted particular toilet rolls for her mistress, but he had none.

'Will you order them?' the maid said, and Morgan made a great to-do about entering the request in the day book. Afterward the three men had a great laugh and Morgan said it wasn't so long ago since the teacher had to use grass, but now that she was taking a correspondence course in Latin, there was no stopping of her and her airs.

'And do you know,' said Hickey, although he'd probably told them before a hundred times, 'she cancels the paper if she's going away for a day, what do you think of that for meanness, a twopenny paper?'

'There he is!' said Hickey suddenly. They heard a cart being drawn up outside and a mare whinny. Hickey knew that mare belonged to Long John Salmon, because like her owner, she went berserk when she got into civilized surroundings.

'Now,' said Morgan, raising his short, fat finger in warning. 'Sit tight and don't let neither of you stir or he'll be in here boring us about that dead brother of his.'

Morgan went out to the shop, shook hands with Long John Salmon, and wished him a Happy New Year. He was relieved to see that Long John had a rush basket under his arm, which no doubt contained the cockerel. They talked about the weather, both uttering the usual rigmarole about how bad it had been. Patches of snow still lodged in the hollows of the field across the road from the shop. The shop was situated between two villages and looked out on a big empty field with a low stone wall surrounding it. Long John said that the black frost was appalling, which was why he had to come at a snail's pace in case the mare slipped. Long John said that Christmas had been quieter than usual and Morgan agreed, though as far as he could remember, Christmas Day was always the most boring day in his married life; the pubs were closed and he was alone with his missus from Mass time until bedtime. This year, of course, she had added peaches and sugar to the turkey, so there wasn't even that to enjoy.

'I had a swim Christmas Day,' Long John said. He believed in a daily swim, and flowers of sulphur on Saturdays to purify the blood.

'We had a goose but no plum pudding,' Long John added, giving Morgan the cue to hand him a small plum pudding wrapped in red glassette paper.

'Your Christmas box,' Morgan said, hoping to God Long John would hand him the chicken and get it over with. He could hear the men murmuring inside.

'Do you eat honey?' Long John asked.

'No,' said Morgan in a testy voice. He knew that Long John kept bees and had a crooked inked sign on his gate which said HONEY FOR SALE.

'No wonder you have no children,' said Long John with a grin.

Morgan was tempted to turn on him for a remark like that. He had no children, not because he didn't eat honey, but because Mrs. Morgan screamed the night of their honeymoon and screamed ever after when he went near her. Finally they got separate rooms.

'Well, here's a jar,' said Long John, handing over a jar of honey that looked like white wax.

'That's too good altogether,' said Morgan, livid with rage in case Long John was trying to do it cheap this Christmas.

'Christ Almighty,' Hickey muttered inside. 'If he doesn't hand over a chicken, I'll go out the country to his place and flog a goose.'

As if prompted, Long John then did it. He handed over the chicken wrapped in newspaper, ordered some meal stuffs, and said he was on his way to the forge to get the mare's shoes off.

'I'll have it all ready for you,' said Morgan, almost running from the counter.

'You'd think it was a boar he was giving away,' said Hickey as Morgan came in and unwrapped the chicken.

'Don't talk to me,' said Morgan, 'get it on.'

The water had boiled away, so John Ryan had to run in his patent-leather shoes to the pump, which was about a hundred yards up the road. He thought to himself that when he was a qualified doctor he'd run errands for no one, and Hickey and Morgan would be tipping their hats to him.

'It's a nice bird,' said Hickey, feeling the breast, 'but you'd think he'd wrap it in butter paper.'

'Oh, a mountainy man,' said Morgan. 'What can you expect from a mountainy man.'

They put the chicken in and added lashings of salt. In twenty minutes or so it began to simmer and Morgan timed it on his pocket watch. Later Hickey put a few cubes of Oxo in the water to flavor the soup. Morgan was demented from explaining to customers that all he was cooking was a sheep's head for a dog. Hickey and John Ryan sat tight in the snug and smoked ten cigarettes apiece. Hickey got it out of John Ryan that the girl of the night before was a waste of time. He liked knowing these things, because although he did not have many dates with girls, he liked to be sure that a girl was amenable.

'I didn't get within a mile of her,' John Ryan said, and regretted telling it two seconds later. He had his name to keep up and most of the local men thought that, because of being a medical student, he did extraordinary things with girls and took terrible risks.

'I didn't fancy her anyhow,' John Ryan said, 'I've had too many women lately, women have no shame in them nowadays.'

'Ah, stop,' said Hickey, hoping that John Ryan would tell him some juicy incidents about orgies in Dublin and streetwalkers who wore nothing under their dresses. At that moment Morgan came in from the shop and said they ought to have a drop of the soup. He was getting irritable because he had been so busy at the counter, and the whiskey was going to his head and fuddling him.

'If I could begin my life again I'd be in the demolition business,' Morgan said for no reason. He imagined that there must be great satisfaction in destroying houses and breaking up ornamental mantelpieces and smashing windows. He sometimes had a dream in which Mrs. Morgan lay under a load of mortar and white rubble, with her clothes well above her knees. Hickey got three new cups from the shop and lifted out the soup with one of them. By now the stove was so hot that dribbles of spilled soup sizzled on the black iron top. It was the finest soup any of them had ever tasted.

'Whoever comes in now can wait, 'cos I'm not budging,' Morgan said as he sat on the principal chair and drank the soup noisily. It was at that very moment Hickey said, 'Wisht,' and a car was heard to pull up. The three of them were at the door instantly, and saw the rather battered V8 come to a halt close to the wall. The driver was a small butty fellow with red hair and a red beard.

'Oh, Red Hugh of the North,' said Hickey, casting aspersions on the car and the rust on the radiator.

'I don't like his attire,' said John Ryan.

The man wore no jacket but a grayish jersey that looked like a dishcloth, as it was full of holes.

'Shag his attire,' said Morgan, and went forward to greet the stranger and apologize for the state of the weather. It had begun to

rain, or rather to hail, and the snow in the field was being turned
to slime. The stranger winked at the three of them and gave a little
toss of the head to denote how sporting he was. He was by far the
smallest of them. He spoke in the clipped accent of the North, and
they could see at once that he was briary. He seemed to be looking
at them severely, as if he was mentally assessing their characters.

'Matt O'Meara's the name,' he said, shaking hands with Morgan
but merely nodding to the others. In the snug he was handed a
large whiskey without being asked whether he was teetotal or not.
He made them uneasy with his silence and his staring blue eyes.

'Knock that back,' Morgan said, 'and then we'll talk turkey.'

He winked at John Ryan. Ryan was briefed to open the proceedings by telling the fellow how rain played havoc with every
damned thing, even gates, and how one didn't know whether it
was the oxygen or the hydrogen or some trace minerals that did
such damage.

'You'd ask yourself what they add to the rain,' Ryan said, and
secretly congratulated himself for his erudition.

'Like what the priest said about the French cheese,' said Hickey,
but Morgan did not want Hickey to elaborate on that bloody story
before they got things sorted out. It would have been better if
Hickey had been given porter, because he had no head
for spirits.

'Well, we have plenty of hay sheds,' Morgan said, and the man
smiled coldly as if that was a foregone conclusion.

'How many have you contracted?' the man asked. He showed
no courtesy but, Morgan thought, business is business, and toler-
ated it.

'If we get the gentlemen farmers, the others will follow suit,'
Morgan said.

'How many gentlemen farmers are there?' the fellow asked,
and by doing a quick count and with much interruption and
counter-interruption from Ryan and Hickey, it was concluded

that there were at least twenty gentlemen farmers. The man did his sums on the back of his hand with the stub of a pencil and said that that would yield a thousand pounds and stared icily at his future partners. Five hundred each. Morgan could not repress a smile, already in his mind he had reserved the hackney car for Friday and Saturday evenings. He asked if by any chance the man had brought a sample and was told no. There were dozens of hay sheds in the North where it had been used, and if Morgan wanted to go up there and vet them, he was quite welcome. This man had a very abrasive manner.

'If you want, I can go elsewhere,' he said.

Hickey saw that the fellow could become obstreperous, and sensing a rift, he said that if they were going to be partners they must all shake on it, and they did.

'Comrades,' said the fellow, much to their astonishment. They abhorred that word. Stalin used that word and a woman in South America called Eva Perón. It was the moment for Morgan to remind Hickey to produce the eats, as their visitor must be starving. Hickey sharpened his knife, drew up his sleeves, and began to carve like an expert. He resolved to give Ryan and the visitor a leg each and keep the breast for himself and Morgan. Up at Brady's, where he had worked for seventeen years, he had never tasted a bit of the breast. She always gave it to her husband, even though he drank acres of arable land away, threatened to kill her more than once, and indeed might have, only that he, Hickey, had intervened and swiped the revolver or pitchfork or whatever weapon Brady had to hand. The stranger, deferring food, began to ask a few practical questions, such as where they would get lodging, whose hay shed they ought to do first, and where he could store the ladders and various equipment if they came on Sunday. The plan was that he and his two men would arrive at the weekend and start on Monday. Morgan said he would get them fixed up in digs, and it was agreed that, pest though she was, Mrs. Gleeson wasn't such a bad landlady, being liberal with tea and cake at any hour. The stranger then inquired about the fishing and set Hickey off on a rigmarole about eels.

'We'll take you on the lake when the May fly is up,' Morgan said, and boasted about his boat, which was moored down at the pier.

'There is one thing,' said the stranger. 'It's the deposit.' He smiled as he said this and pursed his lips.

Morgan, who had been extremely cordial up to then, looked sour and stared at the newcomer with disbelief. 'Do you think I came up the river on a bicycle?'

'I don't,' said the stranger, 'but do *you* think I came up the river on a bicycle?' and then very matter-of-factly he explained that three men, the lorry, the gallons of the expensive stuff and equipment had to be carted from the North. He then reminded them that farmers all over Ireland were crying out for his services. A brazen fellow he was. 'I want a hundred pounds,' he said.

'That's a fortune,' said Hickey.

'I'll give you fifty,' said Morgan flatly, only to be told that it wasn't worth a tinker's curse, that if Morgan & Co. preferred, he would gladly take his business elsewhere. Morgan saw that he had no alternative, so he slowly moved to the safe and undid the creaky brass catch.

'That needs oiling,' said Hickey pointlessly. The place seethed with tension and bad feeling.

The money was in small brown envelopes, and the notes were kept together with rubber bands, some of them shredding. Morgan did not go to the bank often, as it only gave people the wrong idea. He did not even like this villain watching him as he parted them and counted.

The man did not seem either embarrassed or exhilarated at receiving the money; he simply made a poor joke about its being dirty. He confirmed the arrangements and said to make only two appointments for the first week in case the weather was bad or there was any other hitch. He put the money into an old mottled wallet and said he'd be off. Despite the fact that Morgan had provided eats, he did not press the fellow to stay. He did not like him. They'd have a better time of it themselves, so he was quite pleased to mouth formalities and shake hands coldly with the blackguard.

Once he had gone, they fled to the snug to devour their dinner and discuss him. John Ryan took an optimistic view, pointing out that he did not want to slinge and was therefore a solid worker. Hickey said that for a small butty he wasn't afraid to stand up to people, but that wasn't it significant that he hadn't cracked a joke. Hickey could see that Morgan was a bit on edge, so he thought to bolster him.

'Anyhow, he'll bring in the spondulicks,' and he reminded Morgan to make a note of the fact that he had paid him a hundred pounds, as if Morgan could forget. Morgan dipped the plain pen in the bottle of ink and asked aloud what date it was, though he knew it already.

No sooner had they sat down to eat than John Ryan started sniffing. Every forkful was put to his nose before being consigned to his mouth. Hickey commented on this and on the fact that John Ryan wouldn't eat a shop egg if you paid him.

'It doesn't smell right,' John Ryan said.

'God's sake, it's the tastiest chicken I ever ate,' Hickey said.

'First class, first class,' Morgan said, though he didn't fancy it that much. That blackguard had depressed him and hadn't given him any sense of comradeship, but hoofed it soon as he got the hundred pounds. Had the others not been there, Morgan would have haggled, and he resolved in future to do business alone.

'Are you in, Morgan?' They heard Long John Salmon call from the shop, and sullenly Morgan got up and put his plate of dinner on top of the stove.

'Coming,' he said as he wiped his mouth.

Out in the shop he asked Long John if he had any other calls to do, because business had been so brisk he hadn't got around to weighing the meal stuff.

'Nicest chicken I ever had,' he then said, humoring Long John.

'They're a good table fowl, the Rhode Islands,' said Long John.

'They are,' said Morgan, 'they're the best.'

'If I'd known you were eating it so soon, I'd have got it all ready for you,' said Long John.

'It *was* ready, hadn't a thing to do only put it in the pot with some onions and salt, and Bob's your uncle.'

' ''Twasn't cleaned,' said Long John Salmon.

'What?' said Morgan, not fully understanding.

'Christ, that's what it is,' said John Ryan, dropping his plate and making one leap out of the snug and through the shop, around to the back where he could be sick.

'He's in a hurry,' said Long John as he saw Ryan go out with his hand clapped across his mouth.

'You mean it wasn't drawn,' said Morgan, and he felt queasy. Then he remembered being in Long John's farmyard and he writhed as he contemplated the muck of the place. Sorrows never come in single file. At that moment Guard Tighe came into the shop in uniform, looking agitated.

'Was there a bloke here about spraying hay sheds?' he asked.

'What business is it of yours,' Morgan said.

Morgan was thinking that Tighe was nosy and probably wanted the franchise for his wife's people, who had a hardware shop up the street.

'Was he or wasn't he?'

'He was here,' said Morgan, and he was on the point of boasting of his new enterprise when the guard forestalled him.

'He's a bounder,' he said. 'He's going all over the country bamboozling people.'

'How do you know that?' Morgan said.

Hickey had come from inside the snug, wild with curiosity.

'I know it because the man who invented the damn stuff got in touch with us, warning us about this bounder, this pretender.'

'Jaysus,' said Morgan. 'Why didn't you tell me sooner.'

'We're a guard short,' said Tighe, and at that instant Morgan hit the counter with his fist and kept hitting it so that billheads and paper bags flew about.

'You're supposed to protect citizens,' he said.

'You didn't give him any money?' said the guard.

'Only *one hundred pounds*,' said Morgan with vehemence, as if the guard were the cause of it all, instead of his own importunity. The guard then asked particulars of the car, the license plate, the man's appearance, dismissing the man's name as fictitious. When the guard asked if the man's beard looked to be dyed, Morgan lost his temper completely and called upon his Maker to wreak vengeance on embezzlers, chancers, bounders, thieves, layabouts, liars, and the Garda Siotchana.

'Christ, I didn't even give myself a Christmas box,' Morgan said, and Hickey, sensing that worse was to follow, picked up his cap and said it was heinous, heinous altogether. Outside, he found Ryan, white as a sheet, over near the wall where the mare and cart were tethered.

'Red Hugh of the North was a bounder,' he said.

'I don't care what he was,' said Ryan, predicting his own demise.

'You're very chicken,' said Hickey, thrilled at making such an apt joke.

'If you had stayed inside I was all right,' said Ryan, as he commenced to retch again. Hickey looked up and saw that Mrs. Gleeson was crouched behind the other side of the wall observing. In her black garb she looked like a witch. She'd tell the whole country.

'She'll tell my mother,' said Ryan, and drew his coat collar up around him to try and disguise his appearance.

'Good, good Bess,' Hickey said to the mare as he unknotted the reins. Morgan had come out and like a lunatic was waving his arms in all directions and calling for action. Hickey was damned if he was going to stay for any postmortem. It was obvious that the whole thing was a swindle and the fellow was now in some smart hotel eating his fill or more likely heading for the boat to Holyhead. Exit the gangsters.

'Get rid of this bloody chicken,' Morgan called.

'Add peaches to it,' said Hickey.

'Come back,' said Morgan. 'Come back, you hooligan.'

But Hickey had already set out and the mare was trotting at a merry pace, having been unaccountably idle for a couple of hours.

A Scandalous Woman

Everyone in our village was unique and one or two of the girls were beautiful. There were others before and after but it was with Eily I was connected. Sometimes one finds oneself in the swim, one is wanted, one is favoured, one is privy, and then it happens, the destiny, and then it is over and one sits back and knows alas that it is someone else's turn.

Hers was the face of a madonna. She had brown hair, a great crop of it, fair skin and eyes that were as big and as soft and as transparent as ripe gooseberries. She was always a little out of breath and gasped when one approached, then embraced, and said 'darling'. That was when we met in secret. In front of her parents and others she was somewhat stubborn and withdrawn, and there was a story that when young she always lived under the table to escape her father's thrashings. For one Advent she thought of being a nun but that fizzled out and her chief interests became clothes and needlework. She helped on the farm and used not to be let out much, in the summer, because of all the extra work. She loved the main road with the cars and the bicycles and the buses, and had no interest at all in the sidecar that her parents used for conveyance. She would work like a horse to get to the main road before dark to see the passers-by. She was swift as a colt. My father never stopped praising this quality in her and put it down to muscle. It was well known that Eily and her family hid their shoes in a hedge near the road, so that they would have clean footwear when they went to Mass, or to market, or later on, in Eily's case, to the dress dance.

The dress dance in aid of the new mosaic altar marked her debut. She wore a georgette dress and court shoes threaded with silver and gold. The dress had come from America long before but had been re-styled by Eily, and during the week before the dance she was never to be seen without a bunch of pins in her mouth as she tried out some different fitting. Peter the Master, one of the local tyrants, stood inside the door with two or three of his cronies both to count the money and to survey the couples and comment on their clumsiness or on their dancing 'technique'. When Eily arrived in her tweed coat and said 'Evening gentlemen' no one passed any remark, but the moment she slipped off the coat and the transparency of the georgette plus her naked shoulders were revealed, Peter the Master spat into the palm of his hand and said didn't she strip a fine woman.

The locals were mesmerized. She was not off the floor once, and the more she danced the more fetching she became, and was saying 'ooh' and 'aah' as her partners spinned her round and round. Eventually one of the ladies in charge of the supper had to take her into the supper room and fan her with a bit of cardboard. I was let to look in the window, admiring the couples and the hanging streamers and the very handsome men in the orchestra with their sideburns and the striped suits. Then in the supper room where I had stolen to, Eily confided to me that something out of this world had taken place. Almost immediately after she was brought home by her sister Nuala.

Eily and Nuala always quarrelled – issues such as who would milk, or who would separate the milk, or who would draw water from the well, or who would churn, or who would bake bread. Usually Eily got the lighter tasks because of her breathlessness and her accomplishments with the needle. She was wonderful at knitting and could copy any stitch just from seeing it in a magazine or in a knitting pattern. I used to go over there to play and though they were older than me they used to beg me to come and bribe me with empty spools or scraps of cloth for my dolls. Sometimes we played hide and seek, sometimes we played families and gave ourselves posh names and posh jobs, and we used to paint each other with the dye from plants or blue bags and treat each other's faces as if they were palettes, and then laugh and marvel at the blues and indigos and pretend to be natives and do hula hula and eat dock leaves. Once Nuala made me cry by saying I was adopted and that my mother was not my real mother at all. Eily had to pacify me by spitting on dock leaves and putting them all over my face as a mask.

Nuala was happiest when someone was upset and almost always she trumped for playing hospital. She was doctor and Eily was nurse. Nuala liked to operate with a big black carving knife, and long before she commenced, she gloated over the method and over what tumours she was going to remove. She used to say that there would be nothing but a shell by the time she had finished, and that one wouldn't be able to have babies, or women's complaints ever. She had names for the female parts of one, Susies for the breasts, Florries for the stomach, and Matilda for lower down. She would sharpen and re-sharpen the knife on the steps, order Eily to get the hot water, the soap, to sterilize the utensils and to have to hand a big winding sheet.

Eily also had to don an apron, a white apron, that formerly she had worn at cookery classes. The kettle always took an age to boil on the open hearth, and very often Nuala threw sugar on it to encourage the flame. The two doors would be wide open, a bucket to one, and a stone to the other. Nuala would be sharpening the knife and humming 'Waltzing Matilda', the birds would almost always be singing or chirruping, the dogs would be outside on their hind quarters, snapping at flies and I would be lying on the kitchen table terrified and in a state of undress. Now and then, when I caught Eily's eye she would raise hers to heaven as much as to say 'you poor little mite' but she never contradicted Nuala or disobeyed orders. Nuala would don her mask. It was a bright red papier mâché mask that had been in the house from the time when some mummers came on the day of the Wren, got bitten by the dog, and lost some of their regalia including the mask and a legging. Before she commenced she let out a few dry, knowing coughs, exactly imitating the doctor's dry, knowing coughs. I shall never stop remembering those last few seconds as she snapped the elastic band around the back of her head, and said to Eily 'All set Nurse?'

For some reason I always looked upwards and backwards and therefore could see the dresser upside down, and the contents of it. There was a whole row of jugs, mostly white jugs with sepia designs of corn, or cattle, or a couple toiling in the fields. The jugs hung on hooks at the edge of the dresser and behind them were the plates with ripe pears painted in the centre of each one. But most beautiful of all were the little dessert dishes of carnival glass, with their orange tints and their scalloped edges. I used to say good-bye to them, and then it would be time to close eyes before the ordeal.

She never called it an operation, just an 'op', the same as the doctor did. I would feel the point of the knife like the point of a compass going around my scarcely formed breasts. My bodice would not be removed just lifted up. She would comment on what she saw and say 'interesting', or 'quite' or 'oh dearie me' as the case may be, and then when she got at the stomach she would always say 'tut tut tut' and 'what nasty business have we got here.' She would list the unwholesome things I had been eating, such as sherbet or rainbow toffees, hit the stomach with the flat of the knife and order two spoons of turpentine and three spoons of castor oil before commencing. These potions had then to be downed. Meanwhile Eily, as the considerate nurse, would be mopping the doctor's brow, handing extra implements such as sugar tongs, spoon or fork. The spoon was to flatten the tongue and make the patient say 'Aah'. Scabs or cuts would be regarded as nasty devils, and elastic marks a sign of iniquity. I would also have to make a general confession. I used to lie there praying that their mother would come home unexpectedly. It was always a Tuesday, the day their mother went to the market to sell things, to buy commodities and to draw her husband's pension. I used to wait for a sound from the dogs. They were vicious dogs and bit everyone except their owners, and on my arrival there I used to have to yell for Eily to come out and escort me past them.

All in all it was a woeful event but still I went each Tuesday, on the way home from school, and by the time their mother returned all would be over, and I would be sitting demurely by the fire, waiting to be offered a shop biscuit, which of course at first I made a great pretence of refusing.

Eily always conveyed me down the first field as far as the white gate, and though the dogs snarled and showed their teeth, they never tried biting once I was leaving. One evening, though it was nearly milking time, she came further and I thought it was to gather a few hazelnuts because there was a little tree between our boundary and theirs that was laden with them. You had only to shake the tree for the nuts to come tumbling down, and you had only to sit on the nearby wall, take one of the loose stones and crack away to your heart's content. They were just ripe, and they tasted young and clean, and helped as well to get all fur off the backs of the teeth. So we sat on the wall but Eily did not reach up and draw a branch and therefore a shower of nuts down. Instead she asked me what I thought of Romeo. He was a new bank clerk, a Protestant, and to me a right toff in his plus-fours with his white sports bicycle. The bicycle had a dynamo attached so that he was never without lights. He rode the bicycle with his body hunched forwards so that as she mentioned him I could see his snout and his lock of falling hair coming towards me on the road. He also distinguished himself by riding the bicycle into shops or hallways. In fact he was scarcely ever off it. It seems he had danced with her the night she wore the green georgette, and next day left a note in the hedge where she and her family kept their shoes. She said it was the grace of God that she had gone there first thing that morning otherwise the note might have come into someone else's hand. He had made an assignation for the following Sunday, and she did not know how she was going to get out of her house and under what excuse. At least Nuala was gone, back to Technical School where she was learning to be a domestic economy instructress, and my sisters had returned to the convent so that we were able to hatch it without the bother of them eavesdropping on us. I said yes that I would be her accomplice, without knowing what I was letting myself in for. On the Sunday I told my parents that I was going with Eily to visit a cousin of theirs, in the hospital, and she in turn told her parents that we were visiting a cousin of mine. We met at the white gate and both of us were peppering. She had an old black dirndl skirt which she slipped out of, and underneath was her cerise dress with the slits at the side. It was a most compromising garment. She wore a brooch at the bosom. Her mother's brooch, a plain flat gold pin with a little star in the centre, that shone feverishly. She took out her little gold flapjack and proceeded to dab powder on. The puff was dry so she removed the little muslin cover, made me hold it delicately while she dipped into the powder proper. It was ochre stuff and completely wrecked her complexion. Then she applied lipstick, wet her kiss curl and made me kneel down in the field and promise never ever to split.

We went towards the hospital, but instead of going up that dark cedar-lined avenue, we crossed over a field, nearly drowning ourselves in the swamp, and permanently stooping so as not to be sighted. I said we were like soldiers in a war and she said we should have worn green or brown as camouflage. Her bright bottom, bobbing up and down, could easily have been spotted by anyone going along the road. When we got to the thick of the woods Romeo was there. He looked very indifferent, his face forward, his head almost as low as the handlebars of the bicycle, and he surveyed us carefully as we approached. Then he let out a couple of whistles to let her know how welcome she was. She stood beside him, and I faced them and we all remarked what a fine evening it was. I could hardly believe my eyes when I saw his hand go round her waist, and then her dress crumpled as it was being raised up from the back, and though the two of them stood perfectly still, they were both looking at each other intently and making signs with their lips. Her dress was above the back of her knees. Eily began to get very flushed and he studied her face most carefully, asking if it was nice, nice. I was told by him to run along: 'Run along Junior,' was what he said. I went and adhered to the bark of a tree, eyes closed, fists closed, and every bit of me in a clinch. Not long after, Eily hollered and on the way home and walking very smartly she and I discussed growing pains and she said there were no such things but that it was all rheumatism.

So it continued Sunday after Sunday, with one holy day, Ascension Thursday, thrown in. We got wizard in our excuses – once it was to practise with the school choir, another time it was to teach the younger children how to receive Holy Communion, and once – this was our riskiest ploy – it was to get gooseberries from an old crank called Miss MacNamara. That proved to be dangerous because both our mothers were hoping for some, either for eating or stewing, and we had to say that Miss MacNamara was not home, whereupon they said weren't the bushes there anyhow with the gooseberries hanging off. For a moment I imagined that I had actually been there, in the little choked garden, with the bantam hens and the small mouldy bushes, weighed down with the big hairy gooseberries that were soft to the touch and that burst when you bit into them. We used to pray on the way home, say prayers and ejaculations, and very often when we leant against the grass bank while Eily donned her old skirt and her old canvas shoes, we said one or other of the mysteries of the Rosary. She had new shoes that were clogs really and that her mother had not seen. They were olive green and she bought them from a gypsy woman in return for a table cloth of her mother's, that she had stolen. It was a special cloth that had been sent all the way from Australia by a nun. She was a thief as well. One day all these sins would have to be reckoned with. I used to shudder at night when I went over the number of commandments we were both breaking, but I grieved more on her behalf, because she was breaking the worst one of all in those embraces and transactions with him. She never discussed him except to say that his middle name was Jack.

During those weeks my mother used to say I was pale and why wasn't I eating and why did I gargle so often with salt and water. These were forms of atonement to God. Even seeing her on Tuesdays was no longer the source of delight that it used to be. I was wracked. I used to say 'Is this a dagger which I see before me,' and recalled all the queer people around who had visions and suffered from delusions. The same would be our cruel cup. She flared up. 'Marry, did I or did I not love her?' Of course I loved her and would hang for her but she was asking me to do the two hardest things on earth – to disobey God, and my own mother. Often she took huff, swore that she would get someone else – usually Una my greatest rival – to play gooseberry for her, and be her dogsbody in her whole secret life. But then she would make up, and be waiting for me on the road as I came from school, and we would climb in over the wall that led to their fields, and we would link and discuss the possible excuse for the following Sunday. Once she suggested wearing the green georgette, and even I, who also lacked restraint in matters of dress, thought it would draw untoward attention to her, since it was a dance dress and since as Peter the Master said 'She looked stripped in it.' I said Mrs Bolan would smell a rat. Mrs Bolan was one of the many women who were always prowling and turning up at graveyards, or in the slate quarry to see if there were courting couples. She always said she was looking for stray turkeys or turkey eggs but in fact she had no fowl, and was known to tell tales to be calumnious and as a result, one temporary school teacher had to leave the neighbourhood, do a flit in the night, and did not even have time to get her shoes back from the cobblers. But Eily said that we would never be found out, that the god Cupid was on our side, and while I was with her I believed it.

I had a surprise a few evenings later. Eily was lying in wait for me on the way home from school. She peeped up over the wall, said 'yoo hoo' and then darted down again. I climbed over. She was wearing nothing under her dress since it was such a scorching day. We walked for a bit, then we flopped down against a cock of hay, the last one in the field, as the twenty-three other cocks had been brought in the day before. It looked a bit silly and was there only because of an accident, the mare had bolted, broke away from the hay cart and nearly strangled the driver, who was himself an idiot and whose chin was permanently smeared with spittle. She said to close my eyes, open my hand and see what God would give me. There are moments in life when the pleasure is more than one can bear, and one descends willy nilly into a wild tunnel of flounder and vertigo. It happens on swing boats and chairoplanes, it happens maybe at waterfalls, it is said to happen to some when they fall in love, but it happened to me that day, propped against the cock of hay, the sun shining, a breeze commencing, the clouds like cruisers in the heavens on their way to some distant port. I had closed my eyes, and then the cold thing hit the palm of my hand, fitting it exactly, and my fingers came over it to further the hold on it, and to guess what it was. I did not dare say in case I should be wrong. It was of course a little bottle, with a screw-on cap, and a label adhering to one side, but it was too much to hope that it would be my favourite perfume, the one called 'Mischief'. She was urging me to guess. I feared that it might be an empty bottle, though such a gift would not be wholly unwelcome, since the remains of the smell always lingered; or that it might be a cheaper perfume, a less mysterious one named after a carnation or a poppy, a perfume that did not send shivers of joy down my throat and through my swallow to my very heart. At last I opened my eyes, and there it was, my most prized thing, in a little dark blue bottle, with a silverish label and a little rubber stopper, and inside, the precious stuff itself. I unscrewed the cap, lifted off the little rubber top and a drop of the precious stuff was assigned to the flat of my finger and then conveyed to a particular spot in the hollow behind the left ear. She did exactly the same and we kissed each other and breathed in the rapturous smell. The smell of hay intervened so we ran to where there was no hay and kissed again. That moment had an air of mystery and sanctity about it, what with the surprise and our speechlessness, and a realization somewhere in the back of my mind that we were engaged in rotten business indeed, and that our larking days were over.

If things went well my mother had a saying that it was all too good to be true. It proved prophetic the following Saturday because as my hair was being washed at the kitchen table, Eily arrived and sat at the end of the table and kept snapping her fingers in my direction. When I looked up from my expanse of suds I saw that she was on the verge of tears and was blotchy all over. My mother almost scalded me, because in welcoming Eily she had forgotten to add the cold water to the pot of boiling water and I screamed and leapt about the kitchen shouting hellfire and purgatory. Afterwards Eily and I went around to the front of the house, sat on the step where she told me that all was U.P. She had gone to him as was her wont, under the bridge, where he did a spot of fishing each Friday and he told her to make herself scarce. She refused, whereupon he moved downstream and the moment she followed he waded into the water. He kept telling her to beat it, beat it. She sat on the little milk stool, where he in fact had been sitting, then he did a terrible thing which was to cast his rod in her direction and almost remove one of her eyes with the nasty hook. She burst into tears and I began to plait her hair for comfort's sake. She swore that she would throw herself in the self-same river before the night was out, then said it was only a lovers' quarrel, then said that he would have to see her, and finally announced that her heart was utterly broken, in smithereens. I had the little bottle of perfume in my pocket, and I held it up to the light to show how sparing I had been with it, but she was interested in nothing only the ways and means of recovering him, or then again of taking her own life. Apart from drowning she considered hanging, the intake of a bottle of Jeyes Fluid, or a few of the grains of strychnine that her father had for foxes.

Her father was a very gruff man who never spoke to the family except to order his meals and to tell the girls to mind their books. He himself had never gone to school but had great acumen in the buying and selling of cattle and sheep, and put that down to the fact that he had met the scholars. He was an old man with an atrocious temper, and once on a fair day had ripped the clothing off an auctioneer who tried to diddle him over the price of an Aladdin lamp.

My mother came to sit with us, and this alarmed me since my mother never took the time to sit, either indoors or outdoors. She began to talk to Eily about knitting, about a new tweedex wool, asking if she secured some would Eily help her knit a three-quarter length jacket. Eily had knitted lots of things for us including the dress I was wearing – a salmon pink, with scalloped edges and a border of white angora decorating those edges. At that very second as I had the angora to my face tickling it, my mother said to Eily that once she had gone to a fortune teller, had removed her wedding ring as a decoy, and when the fortune teller asked was she married, she had replied no, whereupon the fortune teller said 'How come you have four children?' My mother said they were uncanny, those ladies, with their gypsy blood and their clairvoyant powers. I guessed exactly what Eily was thinking. Could we find a fortune teller or a witch who could predict her future?

There was a witch twenty miles away who ran a public house and who was notorious, but who only took people on a whim. When my mother ran off to see if it was a fox because of the racket in the henhouse I said to Eily that instead of consulting a witch we ought first to resort to other things, such as novenas, putting wedding cake under our pillows or gathering bottles of dew in the early morning and putting them in a certain fort to make a wish. Anyhow how could we get to a village twenty miles away, unless it was on foot or by bicycle, and neither of us had a machine. Nevertheless, the following Sunday, we were to be found setting off with a bottle of tea, a little puncture kit, and eight shillings, which was all the money we managed to scrape together.

We were not long started when Eily complained of feeling weak, and suddenly the bicycle was wobbling all over the road and she came a cropper as she tried to slow it down, by heading for a grass bank. Her brakes were non-existent as indeed were mine. They were borrowed bicycles. I had to use the same method to dismount, and the two of us with our front wheels wedged into the bank, and our handlebars askew, caused a passing motorist to call out that we were a right pair of Mohawks and a danger to the county council.

I gave her a sup of tea, and forced on her one of the eggs which we had stolen from various nests, and which were intended as a bribe for our witch. Along with the eggs we had a little flitch of home-cured bacon. She cracked it on the handlebars, and with much persuasion from me swallowed it whole, saying it was worse than castor oil. It being Sunday, she recalled other Sundays and where she would be at that exact moment and she prayed to St Anthony to please bring him back. We had heard that he went to Limerick most weekends now, and there was rumour that he was going out with a bacon curer's daughter, and that they were getting engaged.

The woman who opened the side door of the pub, said that the witch did not live there any longer. She was very cross, had eyebrows that met, and these as well as the hairs in her head were a yellowish grey. She told us to leave her threshold at once, and how dare we intrude upon her Sunday leisure. She closed the door in our faces. I said to Eily 'That's her.' And just as we were screwing up our courage to knock again, she reopened the door and said who in the name of Jacob had sent us. I said we'd come a long way, miles and miles, I showed the eggs and the bacon in its dusting of saltpetre, and she said she was extremely busy, seeing as it was her birthday and that sons and daughters and cousins were coming for a high tea. She opened and closed the door numerous times, and through it all we stood our ground, until finally we were brought in, but it was my fortune she wanted to tell. The kitchen was tiny and stuffy, and the same linoleum was on the floor as on the little wobbling table. There was a little wooden armchair for her, a form for visitors and a stove that was smoking. Two rhubarb tarts were cooling on top, and that plus a card were the only indications of a birthday celebration. A small man, her husband, excused himself and wedged sideways through another door. I pleaded with her to take Eily rather than me, and after much dithering, and even going out to the garden to empty tea leaves, she said that maybe she would, but that we were pests the pair of us. I was sent to join her husband, in the little pantry, and was nearly smothered from the puffing of his pipe. There was also a strong smell of flour, and no furniture except a sewing machine with a half-finished garment, a shift, wedged in under the needle. He talked in a whisper, said that Mau Mau would come to Ireland, and that St Columbus would rise from his grave, to make it once again the island of saints and scholars. I was certain that I would suffocate. But it was worth it. Eily was jubilant. Things could not have been better. The witch had not only seen his initial, J, but seen it twice in a concoction that she had done with the whites of one of the eggs and some gruel. Yes things had been bad, very bad, there had been grievous misunderstandings, but all was to be changed, and leaning across the table she said to Eily 'Ah sure, you'll end your days with him.'

Cycling home was a joy, we spinned downhill, saying to hell with safety, to hell with brakes, saluted strangers, admired all the little cottages and the outhouses and the milk tanks and the whining mongrels, and had no nerves passing the haunted house. In fact we would have liked to see an apparition on that most buoyant of days. When we got to the cross roads, that led to our own village, Eily had a strong presentiment, as indeed had I, that he would be there waiting for us, contrite, in a hair shirt, on bended knees. But he was not. There was the usual crowd of lads playing pitch and toss. A couple of the younger ones tried to impede us by standing in front of the bikes and Eily blushed red. She was a favourite with everyone that summer, and she had a different dress for every day of the week. She was called a fashion plate. We said good night and knew that it did not matter, that though he had not been waiting for us, before long he and Eily would be united. She resolved to be patient and be a little haughty and not seek him out.

Three weeks later, on a Saturday night, my mother was soaking her feet in a mixture of warm water and washing soda, when a rap came on the scullery window. We both trembled. There was a madman who had taken up residence in a bog-hole and we were certain that it must be him. 'Call your father,' she said. My father had gone to bed in a huff, because she had given him a boiled egg instead of a fry for his tea. I didn't want to leave her alone and unattended so I yelled up to my father, and at the same time a second assault was delivered on the window pane. I heard the words 'Sir, Sir'.

It was Eily's father, since he was the only person who called my father Sir. When we opened the door to him the first thing I saw was the slash hook in his hand, and then the condition of his hair which was upstanding and wild. He said 'I'll hang, draw, and quarter him,' and my mother said 'Come in Mr Hogan,' not knowing who this graphic fate was intended for. He said he had found his daughter in the lime kiln, with the bank clerk, in the most satanic position, with her belly showing.

My first thought was one of delight at their reunion, and then I felt piqued that Eily hadn't told me but had chosen instead to meet him at night in that disused kiln that reeked of damp. Better the woods I thought and the call of the cuckoo, and myself keeping some kind of watch, though invariably glued to the bark of a tree.

He said he had come to fetch a lantern, to follow them as they had scattered in different directions, and he did not know which of them to kill first. My father, whose good humour was restored by this sudden and unexpected intrusion, said to hold on for a moment, to step inside and that they would consider a plan of campaign. Mr Hogan left his cap on the step, a thing he always did, and my mother begged of him to bring it in, since the new pup ate every article of clothing that it could find. Only that very morning my mother looked out on the field and thought it was flakes of snow, but in fact it was her line of washing, chewed to pieces. He refused to bring in his cap which to me was a perfect example of how stubborn he was, and how awkward things were going to be. At once, my father ordered my mother to make tea, and though still gruff, there was between them now an understanding, because of the worse tragedy that loomed. My mother seemed the most perturbed, made a hopeless cup of tea, cut the bread in agricultural hunks, and did everything wrong as if she herself had just been found out in some base transaction. After the men had gone out on their search party, she got me to go down on my knees to pray with her, and I found it hard to pray because I was already thinking of the flogging I would get for being implicated. She cross-examined me. Did I know anything about it? Had Eily ever met him? Why had she made herself so much style, especially that slit skirt.

I said no to everything. These noes were much too hastily delivered, and only that my mother was so busy cogitating and surmising, she would have suspected something for sure. Kneeling there I saw them trace every movement of ours, get bits of information from this one and that one, the so-called cousins, the woman who had promised us the gooseberries, and Mrs Bolan. I knew we had no hope. Eily! Her most precious thing was gone, her jewel. The inside of one was like a little watch and once the jewel or jewels were gone the outside was nothing but a sham. I saw her die in the cold lime kiln and then again in a sick room, and then stretched out on an operating table the very way that I used to be. She had joined that small sodality of scandalous women who had conceived children without securing fathers and who were damned in body and soul. Had they convened they would have been a band of seven or eight, and might have sent up an unholy wail to their maker and their covert seducers. The one thing I could not endure was the thought of her stomach protuberant, and a baby coming out saying 'ba ba'. Had I had the chance to see her I should have suggested that we run away with gypsies.

Poor Eily, from then on she was kept under lock and key, and allowed out only to Mass, and then so concealed was she, with a mantilla over her face that she was not even able to make a lip sign to me. Never did she look so beautiful as those subsequent Sundays in chapel, her hair and her face veiled, her eyes like smoking tragedies peering through. I once sat directly in front of her, and when we stood up for the first gospel, I stared up into her face, and got such a dig in the ribs from my mother that I toppled over.

A mission commenced the following week, and a strange priest with a beautiful accent, and a strong sense of rhetoric, delivered the sermons each evening. It was better than a theatre – the chapel in a state of hush, scores of candles like running stairways, all lit, extra flowers on the altar, a medley of smells, the white linen, and the place so packed that we youngsters had to sit on the altar steps and saw everything clearer, including the priest's adam's apple as it bobbed up and down. Always I could sight Eily, hemmed in by her mother, and some other old woman, pale and impassive, and I was certain that she was about to die. On the evening that the sermon centred on the sixth commandment, we youngsters were kept outside until Benediction time. We spent the time wandering through the stalls, looking at the tiers of rosary beads that were as dazzling as necklaces, all hanging side by side and quivering in the breeze, all colours, and of different stones, then of course the bright scapulars, and all kinds of little medals and beautiful crucifixes that were bigger than the girth of one's hand, and even some that had a little cavity within, where a relic was contained, and also beautiful prayer books and missals, some with gold edging and little holdalls made of filigree.

When we trooped in for the Benediction Eily slipped me a holy picture. It said 'Remembrance is all I ask, but if Remembrance should prove a task Forget me.' I was musing on it and swallowing back my tears at the very moment that Eily began to retch, and was hefted out by four of the men. They bore her aloft as if she was a corpse on a litter. I said to my mother that most likely Eily would die and my mother said if only such a solution could occur. My mother already knew. The next evening Eily was in our house, in the front room, and though I was not admitted, I listened at the door, and ran off only when there was a scream or a blow or a thud. She was being questioned about each and every event, and about the bank clerk and what exactly were her associations with him. She said no, over and over again, and at moments was quite defiant, and as they said an 'upstart'. One minute they were asking her kindly, another minute they were heckling, another minute her father swore that it was to the lunatic asylum that she would be sent, and then at once her mother was condemning her for not having milked for two weeks.

They were contrariness itself. How could she have milked since she was locked in the room off the kitchen, where they stowed the oats and which was teeming with mice. I knew for a fact that her meals – a hunk of bread and a mug of weak tea – were handed into her, twice a day, and that she had nothing else to do only cry, and think, and sit herself upon the oats and run her fingers through it, and probably have to keep making noises to frighten off the mice. When they were examining her my mother was the most reasonable but also the most exacting. My mother would ask such things as 'Where did you meet? How long were you together, were others present?' Eily denied ever having met him and was spry enough to say 'What do you take me for, Mrs Brady, a hussy?' But that incurred some sort of a belt from her father, because I heard my mother say that there was no need to resort to savagery. I almost swooned when on the glass panel of our hall door I saw a shadow, then knuckles, and through the glass the appearance of a brown habit, such as the missioner wore.

He saw Eily alone, and we all waited in the kitchen, the men supping tea, my mother segmenting a grapefruit to offer to the priest. It seemed odd fare to give him in the evening, but she was used to entertaining priests only at breakfast time, when one came every five or ten years to say Mass in the house to re-bless it, and put paid to the handiwork of the devil. When he was leaving, the missioner shook hands with each of us, then patted my hair, and watching his sallow face and his rimless spectacles, and drinking in his beautiful speaking voice, thought that if I were Eily I would prefer him to the bank clerk, and would do anything to get to be in his company.

I had one second with Eily, while they all trooped out to open the gate for the priest, and to wave him off. She said for God's sake not to split on her. Then she was taken upstairs by my mother, and when they re-emerged Eily was wearing one of my mother's mackintoshes, a Mrs Miniver hat, and a pair of old sunglasses. It was a form of disguise since they were setting out on a journey. Eily's father wanted to put a halter round her but my mother said it wasn't the Middle Ages. I was enjoined to wash cups and saucers, to empty the ashtray, and plump the cushions again, but once they were gone I was unable to move because of a dreadful pain that gripped the lower part of my back and stomach, and I was convinced that I too was having a baby and that if I were to move or part my legs some terrible thing would come ushering out.

The following morning Eily's father went to the bank, where he broke two glass panels, sent coins flying about the place, assaulted the bank manager, and tried to saw off part of the bank clerk's anatomy. The two customers – the butcher and the undertaker – had to intervene, and the lady clerk who was in the cloakroom managed to get to the telephone to call the barracks. When the Sergeant came on the scene, Eily's father was being held down, his hands tied with a skipping rope, but he was still trying to aim a kick at the blackguard who had ruined his daughter. Very quickly the Sergeant got the gist of things. It was agreed that Jack, that was the culprit's name, would come to their house that evening. Though the whole occasion was to be fraught with misfortune, my mother upon hearing of it, said some sort of buffet would have to be considered.

It proved to be an arduous day. The oats had to be shovelled out of the room and the women were left to do it, since my father was busy seeing the solicitor and the priest, and Eily's father remained in the town and boasting about what he wouldn't have done to the bugger only for the Sergeant coming on the scene.

Eily was silence itself. She didn't even smile at me when I brought the basket of groceries that her mother had sent me to fetch. Her mother kept referring to the fact that they would never provide bricks and mortar for the new house now. For years she and her husband had been skimping and saving, intending to build a house, two fields nearer the road. It was to be identical to their own house, that is to say a cement two-storey house, but with the addition of a lavatory, and a tiny hall inside the front door, so that, as she said, if company came, they could be vetted there instead of plunging straight into the kitchen. She was a backward woman and probably because of living in the fields she had no friends, and had never stepped inside anyone else's door. She always washed out of doors at the rain barrel, and never called her husband anything but Mister. Unpacking the groceries she said that it was a pity to waste them on him, and the only indulgence she permitted herself was to smell these things, especially the packet of raspberry and custard biscuits. There was blackcurrant jam, a Scribona swiss roll, a tin of herrings in tomato sauce, a loaf, and a large tin of fruit cocktail.

Eily kept whitening and re-whitening her buckskin shoes. No sooner were they out on the window than she would bring them in and whiten again. The women were in the room putting the oats into sacks. They didn't have much to say. My mother used always to laugh because when they met Mrs Hogan used to say 'any newses' and look up at her, with that wild stare, opening her mouth to show the big gaps between her front teeth, but the 'newses' had at last come to her own door, and though she must have minded dreadfully she seemed vexed more than ashamed, as if it was inconvenience rather than disgrace that had hit her. But from that day on she almost stopped calling Eily by her pet name which was Babbie.

I said to Eily that if she liked we could make toffee, because making toffee always humoured her. She pretended not to hear. Even to her mother she refused to speak, and when asked a question she bared her teeth like one of the dogs. She even wanted one of the dogs, Spot, to bite me, and led him to me by the ear, but he was more interested in a sheep's head that I had brought from the town. It was an arduous day, what with carting out the oats in cans and buckets, and refilling it into sacks, moving a table in there and tea chests, finding suitable covers for them, laying the table properly, getting rid of all the cobwebs in the corners, sweeping up the soot that had fallen down the chimney, and even running up a little curtain. Eily had to hem it and as she sat outside the back door I could see her face and her expression and she looked very stubborn and not nearly so amenable as before. My mother provided a roast chicken, some pickles and freshly boiled beets. She skinned the hot beets with her hands and said 'Ah you've made your bed now' but Eily gave no evidence of having heard. She simply washed her face in the aluminium basin, combed her hair severely back, put on her whitened shoes, and then turned around to make sure that the seams of her stockings were straight. Her father came home drunk, and he looked like a younger man trotting up the fields in his oatmeal-coloured socks – he'd lost his shoes. When he saw the sitting-room that had up to then been the oats room, he exclaimed, took off his hat to it and said 'Am I in my own house at all mister?' My father arrived full of important news which as he kept saying he would discuss later. We waited in a ring, seated around the fire, and the odd words said were said only by the men and then without any point. They discussed a beast that had had fluke.

The dogs were the first to let us know. We all jumped up and looked through the window. The bank clerk was coming on foot, and my mother said to look at that swagger, and wasn't it the swagger of a hobo. Eily ran to look in the mirror that was fixed to the window ledge. For some extraordinary reason my father went out to meet him and straight away produced a packet of cigarettes. The two of them came in smoking, and he was shown to the sitting-room which was directly inside the door to the left. There were no drinks on offer since the women decided that the men might only get obstreperous. Eily's father kept pointing to the glories of the room, and lifted up a bit of cretonne, to make sure that it was a tea chest underneath, and not a piece of pricey mahogany. My father said 'Well Mr Jacksie, you'll have to do your duty by her and make an honest woman of her.' Eily was standing by the window looking out at the oncoming dark. The bank clerk said 'Why so' and whistled in a way that I had heard him whistle in the past. He did not seem put out. I was afraid that on impulse he might rush over and put his hands somewhere on Eily's person. Eily's father mortified us all by saying she had a porker in her, and the bank clerk said so had many a lass, whereupon he got a slap across the face, and was told to sit down and behave himself.

From that moment on he must have realized he was lost. On all other occasions I had seen him wear a khaki jacket and plus-fours, but that evening he wore a brown suit that gave him a certain air of reliability and dullness. He didn't say a word to Eily, or even look in her direction, as she sat on a little stool staring out the window and biting on the little lavalier that she wore around her neck. My father said he had been pup enough and the only thing to do was to own up to it, and marry her. The bank clerk put forward three objections – one that he had no house, two that he had no money, and three that he was not considering marrying. During the supper Eily's mother refused to sit down, and stayed in the kitchen nursing the big tin of fruit cocktail, and having feeble jabs at it with the old iron tin opener. She talked aloud to herself about the folks 'hither' in the room and what a sorry pass things had come to. As usual my mother ate only the pope's nose, and served the men the breasts of chicken. Matters changed every other second, they were polite to him remembering his status as a bank clerk, then they were asking him what kind of crops grew in his part of the country, and then again they would refer to him as if he was not there saying 'The pup likes his bit of meat.' He was told that he would marry her on the Wednesday week, that he was being transferred from the bank, that he would go with his new wife and take rooms in a midland town. He just shrugged and I was thinking that he would probably vanish on the morrow but I didn't know that they had alerted everyone, and that when he did in fact try to leave at dawn the following morning, three strong men impeded him and brought him up the mountain for a drive in their lorry. For a week after he was indisposed, and it is said that his black eyes were as big as bubble gum. It left a perma-nent hole in his lower cheek as if a little pebble of flesh had been tweezed out of him.

Anyhow they discussed the practicalities of the wedding while they ate their fruit cocktail. It was served in the little carnival dishes and I thought of the numerous operations that Nuala had done, and how if it was left to Eily and me that things would not be nearly so crucial. I did not want her to have to marry him and I almost blurted that out. But the plans were going ahead, he was being told that it would cost him ten pounds, that it would be in the sacristy of the Catholic church, since he was a Protestant and there were to be no guests except those present, and Eily's former teacher a Miss Melody. Even her sister Nuala was not going to be told until after the event. They kept asking him was that clear, and he kept saying 'Oh yeh,' as if it were a simple matter of whether he would have more fruit cocktail or not. The number of cherries were few and far between, and for some reason had a faint mauve hue to them. I got one and my mother passed me hers. Eily ate well but listlessly, as if she weren't there at all. Towards the end my father sang 'Master Mc-Grath', a song about a greyhound, and Mr Hogan told the ghost story about seeing the headless liveried man at a cross roads, when he was a boy.

Going down the field Eily was told to walk on ahead with her intended, probably so that she could discuss her trousseau or any last-minute things. The stars were never so bright or so numerous, and the moonlight cast as white a glow as if it were morning and the world was veiled with frost. Eily and he walked in utter silence. At last, she looked up at him, and said something, and all he did was to draw away from her, and there was such a distance between them as a cart or a car could pass through. She edged a little to the right to get nearer, and as she did he moved further away so that eventually she was on the edge of a path and he was right in by the hedge hitting the bushes with a bit of a stick he had picked up. We followed behind, the grown-ups discussing whether or not it would rain the next day, but no doubt wondering what Eily had tried to say to him.

They met twice more before the wedding, once in the sitting-room of the hotel, when the travelling solicitor drew up the papers guaranteeing her a dowry of two hundred pounds, and once in the city when he was sent with her to the jewellers to buy a wedding ring. It was the same city as where he had been seeing the bacon curer's daughter and Eily said that in the jewellers he expressed the wish that she would drop dead. At the wedding breakfast itself there were only sighs and tears, and the teacher as was her wont stood in front of the fire, and mindless of the mixed company hitched up her dress behind, the better to warm the cheeks of her bottom. In his giving away speech my father said they had only to make the best of it. Eily snivelled, her mother wept and wept and said 'Oh Babbie, Babbie', and the groom said 'Once bitten twice shy.' The reception was in their new lodgings, and my mother said that she thought it was bad form the way the landlady included herself in the proceedings. My mother also said that their household utensils were pathetic, two forks, two knives, two spoons, an old kettle, an egg saucepan, a primus, and as she said not even a nice enamel bin for the bread but a rusted biscuit tin. When they came to leave Eily tried to dart into the back of the car, tried it more than once, just like an animal trying to get back to its lair.

On returning home my mother let me put on her lipstick, and praised me untowardly for being such a good, such a pure little girl and never did I feel so guilty because of the leading part I had played in Eily's romance. The only thing that my mother had eaten at the wedding was a jelly made with milk. We tried it the following Sunday, a raspberry flavoured jelly made with equal quantities of milk and water – and then whisked. It was like a beautiful pink tongue, dotted with spittle, and it tasted slippery. I had not been found out, had received no punishment, and life was getting back to normal again. I gargled with salt and water, on Sundays longed for visitors that never came, and on Monday mornings had all my books newly covered so that the teacher would praise me. Ever since the scandal she was enjoining us to go home in pairs, to speak Irish and not to walk with any sense of provocation.

Yet she herself stood by the fire grate, and after having hitched up her dress petted herself. When she lost her temper she threw chalk or implements at us, and used very bad language.

It was a wonderful year for lilac and the window sills used to be full of it, first the big moist bunches, with the lovely cool green leaves, and then a wilting display, and following that, the seeds in pools all over the sill and the purple itself much sadder and more dolorous than when first plucked off the trees.

When I daydreamed, which was often, it hinged on Eily. Did she have a friend, did her husband love her, was she homesick and above all was her body swelling up? She wrote to her mother every second week. Her mother used to come with her apron on, and the letter in one of those pockets, and sit on the back step and hesitate before reading it. She never came in, being too shy, but she would sit there while my mother fetched her a cup of raspberry cordial. We all had sweet tooths. The letters told next to nothing, only such things as that their chimney had caught fire, or a boy herding goats found an old coin in a field, or could her mother root out some old clothes from a trunk and send them to her as she hadn't got a stitch. 'Tis style enough she has' her mother would say bitterly, and then advise that it was better to cut my hair and not have me go around in ringlets, because as she said 'Fine feathers make fine birds.' Now and then she would cry and then feed the birds the crumbs of the biscuit or shortbread that my mother had given her.

She liked the birds and in secret in her own yard made little perches for them, and if you please hung bits of coloured rags, and the shaving mirror for them, to amuse themselves by. My mother had made a quilt for Eily and I believe that was the only wedding present she received. They parcelled it together. It was a red flannel quilt, lined with white and had a herringbone stitch around the edge. It was not like the big soft quilt that once occupied the entire window of the draper's, a pink satin onto which one's body could sink, then levitate. One day her mother looked right at me and said 'Has she passed any more worms?' I had passed a big tapeworm and that was a talking point for a week or so after the furore of the wedding had died down. Then she gave me half a crown. It was some way of thanking me for being a friend of Eily's. When her son was born the family received a wire. He was given the name of Jack, the same as his father and I thought how the witch had been right when she had seen the initial twice, but how we had misconstrued it and took it to be glad tidings.

Eily began to grow odd, began talking to herself, and then her lovely hair began to fall out in clumps. I would hear her mother tell my mother these things. The news came in snatches, first from a family who had gone up there to rent grazing, and then from a private nurse who had to give Eily pills and potions. Eily's own letters were disconnected and she asked about dead people or people she'd hardly known. Her mother meant to go by bus one day and stay overnight, but she postponed it until her arthritis got too bad and she was not able to travel at all.

Four year later, at Christmas time Eily, her husband and their three children paid a visit home and she kept eyeing everything and asking people to please stop staring at her, and then she went round the house and looked under the beds, for some male spy whom she believed to be there. She was dressed in brown and had brown fur-backed gloves. Her husband was very suave, had let his hair grow long, and during the tea kept pressing his knee against mine, and asking me which did I like best, sweet or savoury. The only moment of levity was when the three children, got in, clothes and all, to a pig trough and began to bask in it. Eily laughed her head off as they were being hosed down by her mother. Then they had to be put into the settle bed, alongside the sacks of flour, and the brooms, and the bric-à-brac, while their clothes were first washed and then put on a little wooden horse to dry before the fire. They were laughing but their teeth chattered. Eily didn't remember me very clearly and kept asking me if I was the eldest or the middle girl in the family. We heard later that her husband got promoted, and was running a little shop and had young girls working as his assistants.

I was pregnant, and walking up a street in a city, with my own mother, under not very happy circumstances, when we saw this wild creature coming towards us talking and debating to herself. Her hair was grey and frizzed, her costume was streelish, and she looked at us, and then peered, as if she were going to pounce on us, and then she started to laugh at us, or rather to sneer, and she stalked away and pounced on some other persons. My mother said 'I think that was Eily,' and warned me not to look back. We both walked on, in terror, and then ducked into the porch-way of a shop, so that we could follow her with our eyes, without ourselves being seen. She was being avoided by all sorts of people, and by now she was shouting something and brandishing her fist and struggling to get heard. I shook, as indeed the child within me was induced to shake, and for one moment I wanted to go down that street to her, but my mother held me back and said that she was dangerous, and that in my condition I must not go. I did not need much in the way of persuading. She moved on and by now several people were laughing, and looking after her and I was unable to move, and all the gladness of our summer day, and a little bottle of 'Mischief', pressed itself into the palm of my hand again, and I saw her lithe and beautiful as she once was, and in the street a great flood of light wrapped itself around a cock of hay that was dancing about, on its own.

I did go in search of her years later. My husband waited up at the cross, and I went down the narrow steep road with my son, who was thrilled to be approaching a shop. Eily was inside the counter, her head bent over a pile of bills that she was attaching to a skewer. She looked up and smiled. The same face but much coarser. Her hair was permed and a newly-pared pencil protruded from it. She was pleased to see me and at once reached out and handed my son a fistful of rainbow toffees.

It was the very same as if we'd parted only a little while ago. She didn't shake hands, or make any special fuss, she simply said 'Talk of an angel', because she had been thinking of me that very morning. Her children were helping, one was weighing sugar, the little girl was funnelling castor oil into four-ounce bottles, and her eldest son was up on a ladder fixing a flex to a ceiling light. He said my name, said it with a sauciness as soon as she introduced me, but she told him to whist. For her own children she had no time, because they were already grown but for my son she was full of welcome and kept saying he was a cute little fellow. She weighed him on the big meal scales, and then let him scoop the grain with a trowel, and let it slide down the length of his arm and made him gurgle.

People kept coming in and out and she went on talking to me while still serving them. She was complete mistress of her surroundings and said what a pity that her husband was away, off on the lorry, doing the door-to-door orders. He had given up banking, found the business more profitable. She winked each time she hit the cash register, letting me see what an expert she was. Whenever there was a lull, I thought of saying something but my son's pranks commandeered the occasion. She was very keen to offer me something and ripped the glass paper off a two-pound box of chocolates and lay them before me, slantwise, propped against a can or something. They were eminently inviting, and when I refused she made some reference to the figure.

'You were always too generous,' I said sounding like my mother or some stiff relation.

'Go on,' she said and biffed me.

It seemed the right moment to broach it, but how?

'How are you,' I said. She said that as I could see she was topping, getting on a bit, and the children were great sorts and the next time I came I'd have to give her notice so that we could have a singsong. I didn't say that my husband was up at the road, and by now would be looking at his watch and saying 'Damn' and maybe would have got out to polish or do some cosseting to the vintage motor car, that he loved so. I said and again it was lamentable, 'Remember the old days Eily.'

'Not much,' she said.

'The good old days,' I said.

'They're all much of a muchness,' she said.

'Bad,' I said.

'No, busy,' she said. My first thought was that they must have drugged the feelings out of her, they must have given her strange brews and along with quelling her madness they had taken her spark away.

She kissed me and put holy water on my forehead, delving it in deeply, as if I were dough. They waved to us and my son could not return those waves encumbered as he was with the various presents that both the children and Eily had showered on him. It was beginning to spot with rain, and what with that and the holy water and the red rowan tree bright and instinct with life, I thought that ours indeed was a land of shame, a land of murder and a land of strange sacrificial women.

The Rug

I went down on my knees upon the brand-new linoleum and smelled the strange smell. It was rich and oily. It first entered and attached itself to something in my memory when I was nine years old. I've since learned that it is the smell of linseed oil, but coming on it unexpectedly can make me both a little disturbed and sad.

I grew up in the west of Ireland, in a gray cut-stone farmhouse which my father inherited from his father. My father came from lowland, better-off farming people, my mother from the windswept hungry hills above a great lake. As children, we played in a small forest of rhododendrons – thickened and tangled and broken under scratching cows – around the house and down the drive. The avenue up from the front gates had such great potholes that cars had to lurch off into the field and out again.

But though all outside was neglect, overgrown with ragwort and thistle, strangers were surprised when they entered the house; my father might fritter his life away watching the slates slip from the outhouse roof – but within, that same, square, lowland house of stone was my mother's pride and joy. It was always spotless. It was stuffed with things – furniture, china dogs, Toby mugs, tall jugs, trays, tapestries, and whatnots. Each of the four bedrooms had holy pictures on the walls and a gold mantelpiece surmounting each fireplace. In the fireplaces there were paper fans or lids of chocolate boxes. Mantelpieces carried their own close-packed array of wax flowers, holy statues, broken alarm clocks, shells, photographs, soft rounded cushions for sticking pins in.

My father was generous, foolish, and so idle that it could only have been some sort of malcontent. That year in which I was nine and first experienced the wonderful smell, he sold another of the meadows to pay off some debt, and for the first time in many years my mother got a lump of money.

She went out early one morning and caught the bus to the city, and through a summer morning and afternoon she trudged around looking at linoleum. When she came home in the evening, her feet hurting from high heels, she said she had bought some beautiful light-brown linoleum, with orange squares on it.

The day came when the four rolls were delivered to the front gates, and Hickey, our farm help, got the horse and cart ready to bring it up. We all went; we were that excited. The calves followed the cart, thinking that maybe they were to be fed down by the roadside. At times they galloped away but came back again, each calf nudging the other out of the way. It was a warm, still day, the sounds of cars and neighbors' dogs carried very distinctly; and the cow pats on the drive were brown and dry like flake tobacco.

My mother did most of the heaving and shoving to get the rolls onto the cart. She had early accepted that she had been born to do the work.

She may have bribed Hickey with the promise of hens to sell for himself, because that evening he stayed in to help with the floor – he usually went over to the village and drank a pint or two of stout. Mama, of course, always saved newspapers, and she said that the more we laid down under the lino the longer it would wear. On her hands and knees, she looked up once – flushed, delighted, tired – and said, 'Mark my words, we'll see a carpet in here yet.'

There was calculation and argument before cutting the difficult bits around the door frames, the bay window, and the fireplace. Hickey said that without him my mother would have botched the whole thing. In the quick flow of argument and talk, they did not notice that it was past my bedtime. My father sat outside in the kitchen by the stove all evening while we worked. Later, he came in and said what a grand job we were doing. A grand job, he said. He'd had a headache.

The Rug

The next day must have been Saturday, for I sat in the sitting room all morning admiring the linoleum, smelling its smell, counting the orange squares. I was supposed to be dusting. Now and then I rearranged the blinds, as the sun moved. We had to keep the sun from fading the bright colors.

The dogs barked and the postman cycled up. I ran out and met him carrying a huge parcel. Mama was away up in the yard with the hens. When the postman had gone, I went up to tell her.

'A parcel?' she said. She was cleaning the hens' trough before putting their food in it. The hens were moiling around, falling in and out of the buckets, pecking at her hands. 'It's just binding twine for the baling machine,' she said. 'Who'd be sending parcels?' She was never one to lose her head.

I said that the parcel had a Dublin postmark – the postman told me that – and that there was some black woolly thing in it. The paper was torn at the corner, and I'd pushed a finger in, fearfully.

Coming down to the house, she wiped her hands with a wad of long grass. 'Perhaps somebody in America has remembered us at last.' One of her few dreams was to be remembered by relatives who had gone to America. The farm buildings were some way from the house; we ran the last bit. But even in her excitement, her careful nature forced her to unknot every length of string from the parcel and roll it up, for future use. She was the world's most generous woman, but was thrifty about saving twine and paper, and candle stumps, and turkey wings, and empty pill boxes.

'My God,' she said reverently, folding back the last piece of paper and revealing a black sheepskin hearthrug. We opened it out. It was a half-moon shape and covered the kitchen table. She could not speak. It was real sheepskin, thick and soft and luxurious. She examined the lining, studied the maker's label in the back, searched through the folds of brown paper for a possible letter, but there was nothing at all to indicate where it had come from.

'Get me my glasses,' she said. We read the address again, and the postmark. The parcel had been sent from Dublin two days before. 'Call your father,' she said. He was in bed with rheumatic pains. Rug or no rug, he demanded a fourth cup of tea before he could get up.

We carried the big black rug into the sitting room and laid it down upon the new linoleum, before the fireplace.

'Isn't it perfect, a perfect color scheme?' she said. The room had suddenly become cozy. She stood back and looked at it with surprise, and a touch of suspicion. Though she was always hoping, she never really expected things to turn out well. At nine years old, I knew enough about my mother's life to say a prayer of thanks that at last she had got something she wanted, and without having to work for it. She had a round, sallow face and a peculiarly uncertain, timid smile. The suspicion soon left her, and the smile came out. That was one of her happiest days; I remember it as I remember her unhappiest day to my knowledge – the day the bailiff came, a year later. I hoped she would sit in the newly appointed room on Sundays for tea, without her apron, with her brown hair combed out, looking calm and beautiful. Outside, the rhododendrons, though wild and broken, would bloom red and purple, and inside, the new rug would lie upon the richly smelling linoleum. She hugged me suddenly, as if I were the one to thank for it all; the hen mash had dried on her hands and they had the mealy smell I knew so well.

For spells during the next few days, my mother racked her brain, and she racked our brains, for a clue. It had to be someone who knew something of her needs and wants – how else could he have decided upon just the thing she needed? She wrote letters here and there, to distant relations, to friends, to people she had not seen for years.

'Must be one of *your* friends,' she would say to my father.

'Oh, probably, probably. I've known a lot of decent people in my time.'

She was referring – ironically, of course – to the many strangers to whom he had offered tea. He liked nothing better than to stand down at the gates on a fair day or a race day, engaging passersby in conversation and finally bringing someone up to the house for tea and boiled eggs. He had a gift for making friends.

'I'd say that's it,' my father said, delighted to take credit for the rug.

In the warm evenings we sat around the fireplace – we'd never had a fire in that room throughout the whole of my childhood – and around the rug, listening to the radio. And now and then, Marna or Dada would remember someone else from whom the rug might have come. Before a week had passed, she had written to a dozen people – an acquaintance who had moved up to Dublin with a greyhound pup Dada had given him, which greyhound had turned out a winner; an unfrocked priest who had stayed in our house for a week, gathering strength from Mama to travel on home and meet his family; a magician who had stolen Dada's gold watch and never been seen since; a farmer who once sold us a tubercular cow and would not take it back.

Weeks passed. The rug was taken out on Saturdays and shaken well, the new lino polished. Once, coming home early from school, I looked in the window and saw Mama kneeling on the rug saying a prayer. I'd never seen her pray like that, in the middle of the day, before. My father was going into the next county the following day to look at a horse he thought he might get cheap; she was, of course, praying that he would keep his promise and not touch a drink. If he did, he might be off on a wild batter and would not be seen for a week.

He went the next day; he was to stay overnight with relations. While he was away, I slept with Mama, for company, in the big brass bed. I wakened to see a candle flame and Mama hurriedly putting on her cardigan. Dada had come home? No, she said, but she had been lying awake thinking, and there was something she had to tell Hickey or she would not get a wink of sleep. It was not yet twelve; he might be awake. I didn't want to be left in the dark, I said, but she was already hurrying along the landing. I nipped out of bed and followed. The luminous clock said a quarter to twelve. From the first landing, I looked over and saw her turning the knob of Hickey's door.

Why should he open his door to her then, I thought; he never let anyone in at any time, keeping the door locked when he was out on the farm. Once, we climbed in through the window and found things in such a muddle – his good suit laid out flat on the floor, a shirt soaking in a bucket of dirty green water, a milk can in which there was curdled buttermilk, a bicycle chain, a broken Sacred Heart, and several pairs of worn, distorted, cast-off boots – that she resolved never to set foot in it again.

'What the hell is it?' Hickey said. Then there was a thud. He must have knocked something over while he searched for his flashlamp.

'If it's fine tomorrow, we'll cut the turf,' Mama said.

Hickey asked if she'd wakened him at that hour to tell him something he already knew – they discussed it at teatime.

'Open the door,' she said. 'I have a bit of news for you, about the rug.'

He opened the door just a fraction. 'Who sent it?' he asked.

'That party from Ballinsloe,' she said.

'That party' was her phrase for her two visitors who had come to our house years before – a young girl and an older man who wore brown gauntlet gloves. Almost as soon as they'd arrived, my father went out with them in their motorcar. When they returned to our house an hour later, I gathered from the conversation that they had been to see our local doctor, a friend of Dada's. The girl was the sister of a nun who was headmistress at the convent where my sisters were. She had been crying. I guessed then, or maybe later, that her tears had to do with her having a baby and that

Dada had taken her to the doctor so that she could find out for certain if she was pregnant and make preparations to get married. It would have been impossible for her to go to a doctor in her own neighborhood, and I had no doubt but that Dada was glad to do a favor for the nun, as he could not always pay the fees for my sisters' education. Mama gave them tea on a tray – not a spread with hand-embroidered cloth and bone-china cups – and shook hands with them coolly when they were leaving. She could not abide sinful people.

'Nice of them to remember,' Hickey said, sucking air between his teeth and making bird noises. 'How did you find out?'

'I just guessed,' Mama told him.

'Oh, Christ!' Hickey said, closing his door with a fearful bang and getting back into bed with such vehemence that I could hear the springs revolt.

Mama carried me up the stairs, because my feet were cold, and said that Hickey had not one ounce of manners.

Next day, when Dada came home sober, she told him the story, and that night she wrote to the nun. In due course, a letter came to us – with holy medals and scapulars enclosed for me – saying that neither the nun nor her married sister had sent a gift. I expect the girl had married the man with the gauntlet gloves.

' 'Twill be one of life's mysteries,' Mama said, as she beat the rug against the pier, closed her eyes to escape the dust, and reconciled herself to never knowing.

But a knock came on our back door four weeks later, when we were upstairs changing the sheets on the beds. 'Run down and see who it is,' she said.

It was a namesake of Dada's from the village, a man who always came to borrow something – a donkey, or a mowing machine, or even a spade.

'Is your mother in?' he asked, and I went halfway up the stairs and called her down.

'I've come for the rug,' he said.

'What rug?' Mama said. It was the nearest she ever got to lying.
Her breath caught short and she blushed a little.

'I hear you have a new rug here. Well, 'tis our rug, because my
wife's sister sent it to us months ago and we never got it.'

'What are you talking about?' she said in a very sarcastic voice.
He was a cowardly man, and it was said that he was so ineffectual
he would call his wife in from the garden to pour him a cup of tea.
I suppose my mother hoped that she would frighten him off.

'The rug the postman brought here one morning and handed it
to your youngster there.' He nodded at me.

'Oh, that,' Mama said, a little stunned by the news that the
postman had given information about it. Then a ray of hope, or a
ray of lunacy, must have struck her, because she asked what color
rug he was inquiring about.

'A black sheepskin,' he said.

There could be no more doubt about it. Her whole being
drooped – shoulders, stomach, voice, everything.

'It's here,' she said absently, and she went through the hall into
the sitting room.

'Being namesakes and that, the postman got us mixed up,' he
said stupidly to me.

She had winked at me to stay there and see he did not follow her,
because she did not want him to know that we had been using it.

It was rolled and had a piece of cord around the middle when
she handed it to him. As she watched him go down the avenue she
wept, not so much for the loss – though the loss was enormous – as
for her own foolishness in thinking that someone had wanted to
do her a kindness at last.

'We live and learn,' she said, as she undid her apron strings, out
of habit, and then retied them slowly and methodically, making a
tighter knot.

The Creature

She was always referred to as The Creature by the townspeople, the dressmaker for whom she did buttonholing, the sacristan, who used to search for her in the pews on the dark winter evenings before locking up, and even the little girl Sally, for whom she wrote out the words of a famine song. Life had treated her rottenly, yet she never complained but always had a ready smile, so that her face with its round rosy cheeks, was more like something you could eat or lick; she reminded me of nothing so much as an apple fritter.

I used to encounter her on her way from devotions or from Mass, or having a stroll, and when we passed she smiled, but she never spoke, probably for fear of intruding. I was doing a temporary teaching job in a little town in the west of Ireland and soon came to know that she lived in a tiny house facing a garage that was also the town's undertaker. The first time I visited her, we sat in the parlour and looked out on the crooked lettering on the door. There seemed to be no one in attendance at the station. A man helped himself to petrol. Nor was there any little muslin curtain to obscure the world, because, as she kept repeating, she had washed it that very day and what a shame. She gave me a glass of rhubarb wine, and we shared the same chair, which was really a wooden seat with a latticed wooden back, that she had got from a rubbish heap and had varnished herself. After varnishing, she had dragged a nail over the wood to give a sort of mottled effect, and you could see where her hand had shaken, because the lines were wavery.

I had come from another part of the country; in fact, I had come to get over a love affair, and since I must have emanated some sort of sadness she was very much at home, with me and called me 'dearest' when we met and when we were taking leave of one another. After correcting the exercises from school, filling in my diary, and going for a walk, I would knock on her door and then sit with her in the little room almost devoid of furniture – devoid even of a plant or a picture – and oftener than not I would be given a glass of rhubarb wine and sometimes a slice of porter cake. She lived alone and had done so for seventeen years. She was a widow and had two children. Her daughter was in Canada; the son lived about four miles away. She had not set eyes on him for the seventeen years – not since his wife had slung her out – and the children that she had seen as babies were big now, and, as she heard, marvellously handsome. She had a pension and once a year made a journey to the southern end of the country, where her relatives lived in a cottage looking out over the Atlantic.

Her husband had been killed two years after their marriage, shot in the back of a lorry, in an incident that was later described by the British Forces as regrettable. She had had to conceal the fact of his death and the manner of his death from her own mother, since her mother had lost a son about the same time, also in combat, and on the very day of her husband's funeral, when the chapel bells were ringing and re-ringing, she had to pretend it was for a travelling man, a tinker, who had died suddenly. She got to the funeral at the very last minute on the pretext that she was going to see the priest.

She and her husband had lived with her mother. She reared her children in the old farmhouse, eventually told her mother that she, too, was a widow, and as women together they worked and toiled and looked after the stock and milked and churned and kept a sow to whom she gave the name of Bessie. Each year the bonhams would become pets of hers, and follow her along the road to Mass or whenever and to them, too, she gave pretty names. A migrant workman helped in the summer months, and in the autumn he would kill the pig for their winter meat. The killing of the pig always made her sad, and she reckoned she could hear those roars – each successive roar – over the years, and she would dwell on that, and then tell how a particular naughty pig stole into the house one time and lapped up the bowls of cream and then lay down on the floor, snoring and belching like a drunken man. The workman slept downstairs on the settle bed, got drunk on Saturdays, and was the cause of an accident; when he was teaching her son to shoot at targets, the boy shot off three of his own fingers. Otherwise, her life had passed without incident.

When her children came home from school, she cleared half the table for them to do their exercises – she was an untidy woman – then every night she made blancmange for them, before sending them to bed. She used to colour it red or brown or green as the case may be, and she marvelled at these colouring essences almost as much as the children themselves did. She knitted two sweaters each year for them – two identical sweaters of bowneen wool – and she was indeed the proud mother when her son was allowed to serve at Mass.

Her finances suffered a dreadful setback when her entire stock contracted foot-and-mouth disease, and to add to her grief she had to see the animals that she so loved die and be buried around the farm, wherever they happened to stagger down. Her lands were disinfected and empty for over a year, and yet she scraped enough to send her son to boarding school and felt lucky in that she got a reduction of the fees because of her reduced circumstances. The parish priest had intervened on her behalf. He admired her and used to joke her on account of the novelettes she so cravenly read. Her children left, her mother died, and she went through a phase of not wanting to see anyone – not even a neighbour – and she reckoned that was her Garden of Gethsemane. She contracted shingles, and one night, dipping into the well for a bucket of water, she looked first at the stars then down at the water and thought how much simpler it would be if she were to drown. Then she remembered being put into the well for sport one time by her brother, and another time having a bucket of water douched over her by a jealous sister, and the memory of the shock of these two experiences and a plea to God made her draw back from the well and hurry up through the nettle garden to the kitchen, where the dog and the fire, at least, awaited her. She went down on her knees and prayed for the strength to press on.

Imagine her joy when, after years of wandering, her son returned from the city, announced that he would become a farmer, and that he was getting engaged to a local girl who worked in the city as a chiropodist. Her gift to them was a patchwork quilt and a special border of cornflowers she planted outside the window, because the bride-to-be was more than proud of her violet-blue eyes and referred to them in one way or another whenever she got the chance. The Creature thought how nice it would be to have a border of complementary flowers outside the window, and how fitting, even though *she* preferred wallflowers, both for their smell and their softness. When the young couple came home from the honeymoon, she was down on her knees weeding the bed of flowers, and, looking up at the young bride in her veiled hat, she thought, an oil painting was no lovelier or no more sumptuous. In secret, she hoped that her daughter-in-law might pare her corns after they had become intimate friends

Soon, she took to going out to the cowshed to let the young couple be alone, because even by going upstairs she could over-hear. It was a small house, and the bedrooms were directly above the kitchen. They quarrelled constantly. The first time she heard angry words she prayed that it be just a lovers' quarrel, but such spiteful things were said that she shuddered and remembered her own dead partner and how they had never exchanged a cross word between them. That night she dreamed she was looking for him, and though others knew of his whereabouts they would not guide her. It was not long before she realized that her daughter-in-law was cursed with a sour and grudging nature. A woman who automatically bickered over everything – the price of eggs, the best potato plants to put down, even the fields that should be pasture and those that should be reserved for tillage. The women got on well enough during the day, but rows were inevitable at night when the son came in and, as always, The Creature went out to the cowshed or down the road while things transpired. Up in her bedroom, she put little swabs of cotton wool in her ears to hide whatever sounds might be forthcoming. The birth of their first child did everything to exacerbate the young woman's nerves, and after three days the milk went dry in her breasts. The son called his mother out to the shed, lit a cigarette for himself, and told her that unless she signed the farm and the house over to him he would have no peace from his young barging wife.

This The Creature did soon after, and within three months she was packing her few belongings and walking away from the house where she had lived for fifty-eight of her sixty years. All she took was her clothing, her Aladdin lamp, and a tapestry denoting ships on a hemp-coloured sea. It was an heirloom. She found lodgings in the town and was the subject of much curiosity, then ridicule, because of having given her farm over to her son and daughter-in-law. Her son defected on the weekly payments he was supposed to make, but though she took the matter to her solicitor, on the appointed day she did not appear in court and as it happened spent the entire night in the chapel, hiding in the confessional.

Hearing the tale over the months, and how The Creature had settled down and made a soup most days, was saving for an electric blanket, and much preferred winter to summer, I decided to make the acquaintance of her son, unbeknownst to his wife. One evening I followed him to the field where he was driving a tractor. I found a sullen, middle-aged man, who did not condescend to look at me but proceeded to roll his own cigarette.

I recognized him chiefly by the three missing fingers and wondered pointlessly what they had done with them on that dreadful day. He was in the long field where she used to go twice daily with buckets of separated milk, to feed the suckling calves. The house was to be seen behind some trees, and either because of secrecy or nervousness he got off the tractor, crossed over and stood beneath a tree, his back balanced against the knobbled trunk. It was a little hawthorn and, somewhat superstitious, I hesitated to stand under it. Its flowers gave a certain dreaminess to that otherwise forlorn place. There is something gruesome about ploughed earth, maybe because it suggests the grave.

He seemed to know me and he looked, I thought distastefully at my patent boots and my tweed cape. He said there was nothing he could do, that the past was the past, and that his mother had made her own life in the town. You would think she had prospered or remarried, his tone was so caustic when he spoke of 'her own life'. Perhaps he had relied on her to die. I said how dearly she still held him in her thoughts, and he said that she always had a soft heart and if there was one thing in life he hated it was the sodden handkerchief.

With much hedging, he agreed to visit her, and we arranged an afternoon at the end of that week. He called after me to keep it to myself, and I realized that he did not want his wife to know. All I knew about his wife was that she had grown withdrawn, that she had had improvements made on the place – larger windows and a bathroom installed – and that they were never seen together, not even on Christmas morning at chapel.

By the time I called on The Creature that eventful day, it was long after school, and, as usual, she had left the key in the front door for me. I found her dozing in the armchair, very near the stove, her book still in one hand and the fingers of the other hand fidgeting as if she were engaged in some work. Her beautiful embroidered shawl was in a heap on the floor, and the first thing she did when she wakened was to retrieve it and dust it down. I could see that she had come out in some sort of heat rash, and her face resembled nothing so much as a frog's, with her little raisin eyes submerged between pink swollen lids.

At first she was speechless; she just kept shaking her head. But eventually she said that life was a crucible, life was a crucible. I tried consoling her, not knowing what exactly I had to console her about. She pointed to the back door and said things were kiboshed from the very moment he stepped over that threshold. It seems he came up the back garden and found her putting the finishing touches to her hair. Taken by surprise, she reverted to her long-lost state of excitement and could say nothing that made sense. 'I thought it was a thief,' she said to me, still staring at the back door, with her cane hanging from a nail there.

When she realized who he was, without giving him time to catch breath, she plied both food and the drink on him, and I could see that he had eaten nothing, because the ox tongue in its mould of jelly was still on the table, untouched. A little whisky bottle lay on its side, empty. She told me how he'd aged and that when she put her hand up to his grey hairs he backed away from her as if she'd given him an electric shock. He who hated the soft heart and the sodden handkerchief must have hated that touch. She asked for photos of his family, but he had brought none. All he told her was that his daughter was learning to be a mannequin, and she put her foot in it further by saying there was no need to gild the lily. He had newspapers in the soles of his shoes to keep out the damp, and she took off those damp shoes and tried polishing them. I could see how it all had been, with her jumping up and down trying to please him but in fact just making him edgy. 'They were drying on the range,' she said, 'when he picked them up and put them on.' He was gone before she could put a shine on them, and the worst thing was that he had made no promise concerning the future. When she asked 'Will I see you?'

he had said 'Perhaps,' and she told me that if there was one word in the English vocabulary that scalded her, it was the word 'perhaps'.

'I did the wrong thing,' I said, and, though she didn't nod, I knew that she also was thinking it – that secretly she would consider me from then on a meddler. All at once I remembered the little hawthorn tree, the bare ploughed field, his heart as black and unawakened as the man I had come away to forget, and there was released in me, too, a gigantic and useless sorrow. Whereas for twenty years she had lived on that last high tightrope of hope, it had been taken away from her, leaving her without anyone, without anything, and I wished that I had never punished myself by applying to be a sub in that stagnant, godforsaken little place.

The Doll

Every Christmas there came a present of a doll from a lady I scarcely knew. She was a friend of my mother's and though they only met rarely, or accidentally at a funeral, she kept up the miraculous habit of sending to me a doll. It would come on the evening bus shortly before Christmas and it added to the hectic glow of those days when everything was charged with bustle and excitement. We made potato stuffing, we made mince pies, we made bowls of trifle, we decorated the window sills with holly and with tinsel, and it was as if untoward happiness was about to befall us.

Each year's doll seemed to be more beautiful, more bewitching and more sumptuously clad than the previous year's. They were of both sexes. There was a jockey in bright red and saffron, there was a Dutch drummer boy in maroon velvet, there was a sleeping doll in a crinoline, a creature of such fragile beauty that I used to fear for her when my sisters picked her up clumsily or tried to make her flutter her eyelashes. Her eyes were suggestive of china and small blue flowers, having the haunting colour of one and the smooth glaze of the other. She was named Rosalind.

My sisters, of course, were jealous and riled against the unfairness of my getting a doll whereas they only got the usual dull flannel sock with tiny things in it, necessary things such as pencils, copybooks, plus some toffees and a liquorice pipe. Each of my dolls was given a name, and a place of rest, in a corner or on a whatnot, or in an empty biscuit tin, and each had special conversations allotted to them, special endearments, and if necessary special chastisements. They had special times for fresh air – a doll would be brought out and splayed on a window sill, or sunk down in the high grass and apparently abandoned. I had no favourites until the seventh doll came and she was to me the living representation of a princess. She too was a sleeping doll but a sizeable one and she was dressed in a pale-blue dress, with a gauze overdress, a pale-blue bonnet and white kid button shoes. My sisters – who were older – were as smitten with her as I. She was uncanny. We all agreed that she was almost lifelike and that with coaxing she might speak. Her flaxen hair was like a feather to finger, her little wrists moved on a swivel, her eyelashes were black and sleek and the gaze in her eyes so fetching that we often thought she was not an inanimate creature, that she had a soul, and a sense of us. Conversations with her were the most intense and the most incriminating of all.

It so happened that the teacher at school harboured a dislike for me and this for unfathomable reasons. I loved lessons, was first with my homework, always early for class, then always lit the school fire, raked the ashes, and had a basket full of turf and wood when she arrived. In fact my very diligence was what annoyed her and she would taunt me about it and proclaim what a 'goody-goody' I was. She made jokes about my cardigan or my shoe laces or the slide in my hair and to make the other girls laugh she referred to me as 'It'. She would say 'It has a hole in its sock', or 'It hasn't got a proper blazer', or 'It has a daub on its copybook.' I believe she hated me. If in an examination I came first – and I usually did – she would read out everyone's marks, leave mine until last and say, 'We know who swotted the most', as if I were in disgrace. If at cookery classes I made pancakes and offered her one she would make a face as if I had offered her tripe or strychnine. She once got a big girl to give me fruit laxatives pretending that they were sweets and made great fun when I had to go in and out to the closets all day. It was a cruel cross to bear. When the Inspector came and praised me she said that I was brainy but that I lacked versatility. In direct contrast she was lovely to my sisters and would ask them occasionally how was my mother, and when was she going to send over a nice pot of homemade jam or a slab cake. I used to pray and make novenas that one day she would examine her conscience and think on how she wronged me and repent.

One day my prayers seemed on the point of being answered. It was November and already the girls were saving up for Christmas and we knew that soon there would be the turkey market and soon after hams and little seedless oranges in the grocery shop window. She said that since we'd all done so well in the Catechism exam she was going to get the infants to act in the school play and that we would build a crib and stack it with fresh hay and statues. Somebody said that my doll would make a most beautiful Virgin. Several girls had come home with me to see the doll and had been allowed to peep in at her in her box that was lined with silver chaff. I brought her next day and every head in the classroom craned as the teacher lifted the lid of the black lacquered box and looked in.

'She's passable,' she said, and told one of the girls to put the doll in the cookery press until such time as she was needed. I grieved at being parted from her but I was proud of the fact that she would be in the school play and be the cynosure of all. I had made her a cloak, a flowing blue cloak with a sheath of net over it and a little diamante clasp. She was like a creature of moonlight, shimmering, even on dark wet days. The cookery press was not a fit abode for her but what could I do?

The play did not pass off without incident. The teacher's cousin, Milo, was drunk, belligerent and offensive. He called girls up to the fire to pretend to talk to them and then touched the calves of their legs and tickled the backs of their knees. He called me up and asked would I click. He was an auctioneer from the city and unmarried. The teacher's two sons also came to look at the performance but one of them left in the middle. He was strange and would laugh for no reason and although over twenty he called the teacher 'Mammy'. He had very bright red hair and a peculiar stare in his eyes. For the most part the infants forgot their lines, lost their heads and the prompter was always late so that the wrong girls picked up her cues. She was behind a curtain but could be heard out on the street. The whole thing was a fiasco. My doll was the star of the occasion and everyone raved about her.

Afterwards there was tea and scones and the teacher talked to those few mothers who had come. My mother had not come because at that time she was unable to confront crowds and even dreaded going to Mass on Sundays, but believed that God would preserve her from the dizziness and suffocations that she was suffering from. After they had all left and a few of us had done the washing up, I went to the teacher and to my delight she gave me a wide genial smile. She thanked me for the doll, said that there was no denying but that the doll saved the play and then as I reached out she staved my hand with a ruler and laughed heartily.

'You don't think I'm going to let you have her now, I've got quite fond of her . . . the little mite,' she said and gave the china cheek a tap. At home I was berserk. My mother said the teacher was probably teasing and that she would return the doll in a day or two. My father said that if she didn't she would have to answer to him, or else get a hammering. The days passed and the holidays came and not only did she not give me my doll but she took it to her own home and put it in the china cabinet along with cups and ornaments. Passing by their window I would look in. I could not see her because the china cabinet was in a corner, but I knew where she was as the maid Lizzie told me. I would press my forehead to the window and call to the doll and say that I was thinking of her, and that rescue was being hatched.

Everyone agreed that it was monstrous but no one talked to the teacher, no one tackled her. The truth is they were afraid of her. She had a bitter tongue and also, being superstitious, they felt that she could give us children brains or take them away as a witch might. It was as if she could lift the brains out of us with a forceps and pickle them in brine. No one did anything and in time I became reconciled to it. I asked once in a fit of bravura and the teacher said wasn't I becoming impudent. No longer did I halt to look in the window of her house but rather crossed the road and I did not talk to Lizzie in case she should tell me something upsetting.

Once I was sent to the teacher's house with a loin of pork and found her by the fire with her queer son, both of them with their stockings down, warming themselves. There were zigzags of heat on their shins. She asked if I wanted to go in and see the doll, but I declined. By then I was preparing to go away to boarding school and I knew that I would be free of her for ever, that I would forget her, that I would forget the doll, forget most of what happened, or at least remember it without a quiver.

The years go by and everything and everyone gets replaced. Those we knew, though absent, are yet merged inextricably into new folk so that each person is to us a sum of many others and the effect is of opening box after box in which the original is forever hidden.

The teacher dies a slow death, wastes to a thread through cancer, yet strives against it and says she is not ready. I hear the amount of money she left and her pitiable last words but I feel nothing. I feel none of the rage and none of the despair. She does not matter to me any more. I am on the run from them. I have fled. I live in a city. I am cosmopolitan. People come to my house, all sorts of people, and they do feats like dancing, or jesting, or singing, inventing a sort of private theatre where we all play a part. I too play a part. My part is to receive them and disarm them, ply them with food and drink and secretly be wary of them, be distanced from them. Like them I smile, and drift, like them I smoke or drink to induce a feverishness or a pleasant wandering hallucination. It is not something I culti-vated. It developed of its own accord, like a spore that breathes in the darkness. So I am far from those I am with, and far from those

I have left. At night I enjoy the farness. In the morning I touch a table or a teacup to make sure that it is a table or a teacup and I talk to it, and I water the flowers and I talk to them, and I think how tender flowers are, and woods and woodsmoke and possibly how tender are my new friends but that like me they are intent on concealment. None of us ever says where we come from or what haunts us. Perhaps we are bewildered or ashamed.

I go back. Duty hauls me back to see the remaining relatives and I play the expected part. I had to call on the teacher's son. He was the undertaker and was in charge of my aunt's burial. I went to pay him, to 'fix up' as it is called, and his wife whom I knew to be a bit scattered admitted me amidst peals of laughter. She said she always thought I had jet-black hair, as she ran down the hall calling his name. His name is Denis. He shakes hands with me very formally, asks what kind of wreath I want and if it should be heart-shaped, circular, or in the form of a cross. I leave it all to him. There in the over-stuffed china cabinet is my confiscated doll and if dolls can age, it certainly had done. Grey and mouldy, the dress and cloak are as a shroud and I thought if I were to pick her up she would disintegrate.

'God, my mother was fond of her,' he said, as if he were trying to tell me that she had been fond of me too. Had he said so I might have hissed. I was older now and it was clear to me that she had kept the doll out of perversity, out of pique and jealousy. In some way she had divined that I would have a life far away from them and adventures such as she herself would never taste. Sensing my chill, he boasted that he had not let his own children play with the doll, thereby implying that she was a sacred object, a treasured souvenir. He hauled out a brandy bottle and winked expecting me to say yes. I declined.

A sickness had come over me, a sort of nausea for having cared so much about the doll, for having let them maltreat me and now for no longer caring at all. My abrupt departure puzzled him. He did something untoward. He tried to kiss me. He thought perhaps that in my world it was the expected thing. Except that the kiss was proffered as a sympathy kiss, a kiss of condolence over my aunt's death. His face had the sour smell of a towel that he must have dried himself on, just before he came to welcome me. The kiss was clumsiness personified. I pitied him but I could not stay, and I could not reminisce, and I could not pretend to be the fast kiss-easy woman he imagined me to be.

Walking down the street, where I walk in memory, morning noon and night, I could not tell what it was, precisely, that reduced me to such wretchedness. Indeed it was not death but rather the gnawing conviction of not having yet lived. All I could tell was that the stars were as singular and as wondrous as I remembered them and that they still seemed like a link, an enticement to the great heavens, and that one day I would reach them and be absorbed into their glory, and pass from a world that, at that moment, I found to be rife with cruelty and stupidity, a world that had forgotten how to give.

'Tomorrow . . .' I thought. 'Tomorrow I shall be gone', and realised that I had not lost the desire to escape or the strenuous habit of hoping.

Sister Imelda

Sister Imelda did not take classes on her first day back in the convent but we spotted her in the grounds after the evening Rosary. Excitement and curiosity impelled us to follow her and try and see what she looked like, but she thwarted us by walking with head bent and eyelids down. All we could be certain of, was that she was tall and limber and that she prayed while she walked. No looking at nature for her, or no curiosity about seventy boarders in gaberdine coats and black shoes and stockings. We might just as well have been crows, so impervious was she to our stares and to abortive attempts at trying to say 'Hello Sister'.

We had returned from our long summer holiday and we were all wretched. The convent with its high stone wall and green iron gates enfolding us again, seeming more of a prison than ever – for after our spell in the outside world we all felt very much older and more sophisticated, and my friend Baba and I were dreaming of our final escape, which would be in a year. And so, on that damp autumn evening when I saw the chrysanthemums and saw the new nun intent on prayer I pitied her and thought how alone she must be, cut off from her friends and conversation with only God as her intangible spouse.

The next day she came into our classroom to take Geometry. Her pale, slightly long face I saw as formidable but her eyes were different, being blue-black and full of verve. Her lips were very purple as if she had put puce pencil on them. They were the lips of a woman who might sing in cabaret and unconsciously she had formed the habit of turning them inwards as if she too was aware of their provocativeness. She had spent the last four years – the same span that Baba and I had spent in the convent – at the university in

Dublin where she studied languages. We couldn't understand how she had resisted the temptations of the hectic world and willingly come back to this. Her spell in the outside world made her different from the other nuns, there was more bounce in her walk, more excitement in the way she tackled teaching, reminding us that it was the most important thing in the world as she uttered the phrase 'Praise be the Incarnate World'. She began each day's class by reading from Cardinal Newman who was a favourite of hers. She read how God dwelt in light unapproachable, and how with Him there was neither change nor shadow of alteration. It was amazing how her looks changed. Some days when her eyes were flashing she looked almost profane and made me wonder what events inside the precincts of the convent caused her to be suddenly so excited. She might have been a girl going to a dance except for her habit.

'Hasn't she wonderful eyes,' I said to Baba. That particular day they were like blackberries, large and soft and shiny.

'Something wrong in her upstairs department,' Baba said and added that with make-up Imelda would be a cinch.

'Still she has a vocation!' I said and even aired the idiotic view that I might have one. At certain moments it did seem enticing to become a nun, to lead a life unspotted by sin, never to have to have babies and to wear a ring that singled one out as the Bride of Christ. But there was the other side to it, the silence, the gravity of it, having to get up two or three times a night to pray and above all never having the opportunity of leaving the confines of the place except for the funeral of one's parents. For us boarders it was torture but for the nuns it was nothing short of doom. Also we could complain to each other and we did, food being the source of the greatest grumbles. Lunch was either bacon and cabbage or a peculiar stringy meat followed by tapioca pudding; tea consisted of bread dolloped with lard and occasionally, as a treat, fairly green rhubarb jam, which did not have enough sugar. Through the long curtainless windows we saw the conifer trees and a sky that was scarcely ever without the promise of rain or a downpour.

She was a right lunatic then, Baba said, having gone to university for four years and willingly come back to incarceration, to poverty, chastity and obedience. We concocted scenes of agony in some Dublin hostel, while a boy, or even a young man, stood beneath her bedroom window throwing up chunks of clay or whistles or a supplication. In our version of it he was slightly older than her, and possibly a medical student since medical students had a knack with women, because of studying diagrams and skeletons. His advances, like those of a sudden storm would intermittently rise and over-whelm her and the memory of these sudden flaying advances of his, would haunt her until she died, and if ever she contracted fever these secrets would out. It was also rumoured that she possessed a fierce temper and that while a postulant she had hit a girl so badly with her leather strap that the girl had to be put to bed because of wounds. Yet another black mark against Sister Imelda was that her brother Ambrose had been sued by a nurse for breach of promise.

That first morning when she came into our classroom and modestly introduced herself I had no idea how terribly she would infiltrate my life, how in time she would be not just one of those teachers or nuns, but rather a special one almost like a ghost who passed the boundaries of common exchange and who crept inside one, devouring so much of one's thoughts, so much of one's passion, invading the place that was called one's heart. She talked in a low voice as if she did not want her words to go beyond the bounds of the wall and constantly she stressed the value of work both to enlarge the mind and discipline the thought. One of her eyelids was red and swollen as if she was getting a sty. I reckoned that she over-mortified herself by not eating at all. I saw in her some terrible premonition of sacrifice which I would have to emulate. Then in direct contrast she absently held the stick of chalk between her first and second fingers the very same as if it were a cigarette and Baba whispered to me that she might have been a smoker when in Dublin. Sister Imelda looked down sharply at me and said what was the secret and would I like to share it since it seemed so comical. I said 'Nothing Sister, nothing', and her dark eyes yielded such vehemence that I prayed she would never have occasion to punish me.

November came and the tiled walls of the recreation hall oozed moisture and gloom. Most girls had sore throats and were told to suffer this inconvenience to mortify themselves in order to lend a glorious hand in that communion of spirit that linked the living with the dead. It was the month of the Suffering Souls in Purgatory, and as we heard of their twofold agony, the yearning for Christ and the ferocity of the leaping flames that burnt and charred their poor limbs, we were asked to make acts of mortification. Some girls gave up jam or sweets and some gave up talking and so in recreation time they were like dummies making signs with thumb and finger to merely say 'How are you?' Baba said that saner people were locked in the lunatic asylum which was only a mile away. We saw them in the grounds, pacing back and forth, with their mouths agape and dribble coming out of them, like icicles. Among our many fears was that one of those lunatics would break out and head straight for the convent and assault some of the girls.

Yet in the thick of all these dreads I found myself becoming dreadfully happy. I had met Sister Imelda outside of class a few times and I felt that there was an attachment between us. Once it was in the grounds when she did a reckless thing. She broke off a chrysanthemum and offered it to me to smell. It had no smell or at least only something faint that suggested autumn and feeling this to be the case herself she said it was not a gardenia was it. Another time we met in the chapel porch and as she drew her shawl more tightly around her body I felt how human she was, and prey to the cold.

In the classroom things were not so congenial between us. Geometry was my worst subject and indeed a total mystery to me.

She had not taken more than four classes when she realised this and threw a duster at me in a rage. A few girls gasped as she asked me to stand up and make a spectacle of myself. Her face had reddened and presently she took out her handkerchief and patted the eye which was red and swollen. I not only felt a fool but I felt in imminent danger of sneezing as I inhaled the smell of chalk that had fallen onto my gym-frock. Suddenly she fled from the room leaving us ten minutes free until the next class. Some girls said it was a disgrace, said I should write home and say I had been assaulted. Others welcomed the few minutes in which to gabble. All I wanted was to run after her and say that I was sorry to have caused her such distemper because I knew dimly that it was as much to do with liking as it was with dislike. In me then there came a sort of speechless tenderness for her and I might have known that I was stirred.

'We could get her de-frocked,' Baba said and elbowed me in God's name to sit down.

That evening at Benediction I had the most overwhelming surprise. It was a particularly happy evening with the choir nuns in full soaring form and the rows of candles like so many little ladders to the golden chalice that glittered all the more because of the beams of fitful flame. I was full of tears when I discovered a new holy picture had been put in my prayer book and before I dared look on the back to see who had given it to me I felt and guessed that this was no ordinary picture from an ordinary girl friend, that this was a talisman and a peace offering from Sister Imelda. It was a pale-blue picture so pale that it was almost grey like the down of a pigeon and it showed a mother looking down on the infant child. On the back, in her beautiful ornate handwriting, she had written a verse:

> *Trust Him when dark doubts assail thee,*
> *Trust Him when thy faith is small,*
> *Trust Him when to simply trust Him*
> *Seems the hardest thing of all.*

This was her atonement. To think that she had located the compartment in the chapel where I kept my prayer book and to think that she had been so naked as to write in it and give me a chance to boast about it and to show it to other girls. When I thanked her next day she bowed but did not speak. Mostly the nuns were on silence and only permitted to talk during class.

In no time I had received another present, a little miniature prayer book with a leather cover and gold edging. The prayers were in French and the lettering so minute it was as if a tiny insect had fashioned them. Soon I was publicly known as her pet. I opened doors for her, raised the blackboard two pegs higher (she was taller than other nuns) and handed out the exercise books which she had corrected. Now, in the margins of my geometry propositions I would find 'Good' or 'Excellent', when in the past she used to splash 'Disgraceful'. Baba said it was foul to be a nun's pet and that any girl who sucked up to a nun could not be trusted.

About a month later Sister Imelda asked me to carry her books up four flights of stairs to the cookery kitchen. She taught cookery to a junior class. As she walked ahead of me I thought how supple she was and how thoroughbred and when she paused on the landing to look out through the long curtainless window, I too paused. Down below two women in suede boots were chatting and smoking as they moved down the street with shopping baskets. Nearby a lay nun was down on her knees scrubbing the granite steps and the cold air was full of the smell of raw Jeyes Fluid. There was a potted plant on the landing and Sister Imelda put her fingers in the earth and went 'tch tch tch', saying it needed water. I said I would water it later on. I was happy in my prison then, happy to be near her, happy to walk behind her as she twirled her beads and bowed to the servile nun. I no longer cried for my mother, no longer counted the days on a pocket calendar, until the Christmas holidays.

'Come back at five,' she said as she stood on the threshold of the cookery kitchen door. The girls all in white overalls were arraigned around the long wooden table waiting for her. It was as if every girl was in love with her. Because, as she entered, their faces broke into smiles and in different tones of audacity they said her name. She must have liked cookery class because she beamed and called to someone, anyone, to get up a blazing fire. Then she went across to the cast-iron stove and spat on it to test its temperature. It was hot because her spit rose up and sizzled.

When I got back later she was sitting on the edge of the table swaying her legs. There was something reckless about her pose, something defiant. It seemed as if any minute she would take out a cigarette case, snap it open and then archly offer me one. The wonderful smell of baking made me realise how hungry I was, but far more so, it brought back to me my own home, my mother testing orange cakes with a knitting needle and letting me lick the line of half-baked dough down the length of the needle. I wondered if she had supplanted my mother and I hoped not, because I had aimed to outstep my original world and take my place in a new and hallowed one.

'I bet you have a sweet tooth,' she said and then she got up, crossed the kitchen and from under a wonderful shining silver cloche she produced two jam tarts with a criss-cross design on them, where the pastry was latticed over the dark jam. They were still warm.

'What will I do with them?' I asked.

'Eat them, you goose,' she said and she watched me eat as if she herself derived some peculiar pleasure from it whereas I was embarrassed about the pastry crumbling and the bits of blackberry jam staining the lips. She was amused. It was one of the most awkward yet thrilling moments I had lived, and inherent in the pleasure was the terrible sense of danger. Had we been caught she, no doubt, would have to make massive sacrifice. I looked at her and thought how peerless and how brave and I wondered if she felt hungry. She had a white overall over her black habit and this made her warmer, freer, and caused me to think of the happiness that would be ours, the laissez-faire if we were away from the convent in an ordinary kitchen doing something easy and customary. But we weren't. It was clear to me then that my version of pleasure was inextricable from pain and they existed side by side and were interdependent like the two forces of an electric current.

'Had you a friend when you were in Dublin at university?' I asked daringly.

'I shared a desk with a sister from Howth and stayed in the same hostel,' she said.

'But what about boys?' I thought, 'and what of your life now and do you long to go out into the world?' But could not say it.

We knew something about the nuns' routine. It was rumoured that they wore itchy, wool underwear, ate dry bread for breakfast, rarely had meat, cakes or dainties, kept certain hours of strict silence with each other, as well as constant vigil on their thoughts; so that if their minds wandered to the subject of food or pleasure they would quickly revert to thoughts of God and their eternal souls. They slept on hard beds with no sheets and hairy blankets. At four o'clock in the morning while we slept, each nun got out of bed, in her habit – which was also her death habit – and, chanting, they all flocked down the wooden stairs like ravens, to fling themselves on the tiled floor of the chapel. Each nun – even the Mother Superior – flung herself in total submission, saying prayers in Latin and offering up the moment to God. Then silently back to their cells for one more hour of rest. It was not difficult to imagine Sister Imelda face downwards, arms outstretched, prostrate on the tiled floor. I often heard their chanting when I wakened suddenly from a nightmare, because, although we slept in a different building, both adjoined, and if one wakened one often heard that monotonous Latin chanting, long before the birds began, long before our own bell summoned us to rise at six.

'Do you eat nice food?' I asked.

'Of course,' she said and smiled. She sometimes broke into an eager smile which she did much to conceal.

'Have you ever thought of what you will be?' she asked.

I shook my head. My design changed from day to day.

She looked at her man's silver pocket watch, closed the damper of the range and prepared to leave. She checked that all the wall presses were locked by running her hand over them.

'Sister,' I called, gathering enough courage at last. We must have some secret, something to join us together, 'What colour hair have you?'

We never saw the nuns' hair, or their eyebrows, or ears, as all that part was covered by a stiff, white guimp.

'You shouldn't ask such a thing,' she said, getting pink in the face, and then she turned back and whispered, 'I'll tell you on your last day here, provided your geometry has improved.'

She had scarcely gone when Baba, who had been lurking behind some pillar, stuck her head in the door and said 'Christ sake save me a bit.' She finished the second pastry, then went around looking in kitchen drawers. Because of everything being locked she found only some castor sugar in a china shaker. She ate a little and threw the remainder into the dying fire so that it flared up for a minute with a yellow spluttering flame. Baba showed her jealousy by putting it around the school that I was in the cookery kitchen every evening, gorging cakes with Sister Imelda and telling tales.

I did not speak to Sister Imelda again in private until the evening of our Christmas theatricals. She came to help us put on make-up and get into our stage clothes and fancy headgears. These clothes were kept in a trunk from one year to the next and though sumptuous and though strewn with braiding and gold they smelt of camphor. Yet as we donned them we felt different and as we sponged pancake make-up onto our faces we became saucy and emphasised these new guises by adding dark pencil to the eyes and making the lips bright orange. There was only one tube of lipstick and each girl clamoured for it. The evening's entertainment was to comprise scenes from Shakespeare and laughing sketches. I had been chosen to recite Mark Antony's lament over Caesar's body and for this I was to wear a purple toga, white knee-length socks and patent buckle shoes. The shoes were too big and I moved in them as if in clogs. She said to take them off, to go barefoot. I realised that I was getting nervous and that in an effort to memorise my speech the words were getting all askew and flying about in my head, like the separate pieces of a jigsaw puzzle. She sensed my panic and very slowly put her hand on my face and enjoined me to look at her. I looked into her eyes which seemed fathomless and saw that she was willing me to be calm and obliging me to be master of my fears and I little knew that one day she would have to do the same as regards the swoop of my feelings for her. As we continued to stare I felt myself becoming calm and the words were restored to me in their right and fluent order. The lights were being lowered out in the recreation hall and we knew now that all the nuns had arrived, had settled themselves down and were eagerly awaiting this annual hotchpotch of amateur entertainment. There was that fearsome hush as the hall went dark and the few spotlights turned on. She kissed her crucifix and I realised that she was saying a prayer for me. Then she raised her arm as if depicting the stance of a Greek goddess and walking onto the stage I was fired by her ardour.

Baba could say that I bawled like a bloody bull but Sister Imelda who stood in the wings said that temporarily she had felt the streets of Rome had seen the corpse of Caesar as I delivered those poignant, distempered lines. When I came off stage she put her arms around me and I was encased in a shower of silent kisses. After we had taken down the decorations and put the fancy clothes back in the trunk, I gave her two half-pound boxes of chocolates – bought for me illicitly by one of the day-girls – and she gave me a casket made from the insides of match boxes and covered over with gilt paint and gold dust. It was like holding moths and finding their powder adhering to the fingers.

'What will you do on Christmas Day, Sister?' I said.

'I'll pray for you,' she said.

It was useless to say 'Will you have turkey?' or 'Will you have plum pudding?' or 'Will you loll in bed?', because I believed that Christmas Day would be as bleak and deprived as any other day in her life. Yet she was radiant as if such austerity was joyful. Maybe she was basking in some secret realisation involving her and me.

On the cold snowy afternoon three weeks later when we returned from our holidays Sister Imelda came up to the dormitory to welcome me back. All the other girls had gone down to the recreation hall to do barn dances and I could hear someone banging on the piano. I did not want to go down and clump around with sixty other girls, having nothing to look forward to, only tea and the Rosary and early bed. The beds were damp after our stay at home and when I put my hand between the sheets it was like feeling dew but did not have the freshness of outdoors. What depressed me further was that I had seen a mouse in one of the cupboards, seen its tail curl with terror as it slipped away into a crevice. If there was one mouse, there was God knows how many, and the cakes we hid in secret would not be safe. I was still unpacking as she came down the narrow passage between the rows of iron beds and I saw in her walk such agitation.

'Tut, tut, tut, you've curled your hair,' she said, offended.

Yes, the world outside was somehow declared in this perm and for a second I remembered the scalding pain as the trickles of ammonia dribbled down my forehead and then the joy as the hair-dresser said that she would make me look like Movita, a Mexican star. Now suddenly that world and those aspirations seemed trite and I wanted to take a brush and straighten my hair and revert to the dark gawky sombre girl that I had been. I offered her iced queen cakes that my mother had made but she refused them and said she could only stay a second. She lent me a notebook of hers, which she had had as a pupil, and into which she had copied favourite quotations, some religious, some not. I read at random:

> *Twice or thrice had I loved thee*
> *Before I knew thy face or name*
> *So in a voice, so in a shapeless flame*
> *Angels affect us oft.*

'Are you well?' I asked.

She looked pale. It may have been the day, which was wretched and grey with sleet or it may have been the white bedspreads but she appeared to be ailing.

'I missed you,' she said.

'Me too,' I said.

At home, gorging, eating trifle at all hours, even for breakfast, having little ratafias to dip in cups of tea, fitting on new shoes and silk stockings, I wished that she could be with us, enjoying the fire and the freedom.

'You know it is not proper for us to be so friendly.'

'It's not wrong,' I said.

I dreaded that she might decide to turn away from me, that she might stamp on our love and might suddenly draw a curtain over it, a black crêpe curtain that would denote its death. I dreaded it and knew it was going to happen.

'We must not become attached,' she said and I could not say we already were, no more than I could remind her of the day of the revels and the intimacy between us. Convents were dungeons and no doubt about it.

From then on she treated me as less of a favourite. She said my name sharply in class and once she said if I must cough could I wait until class had finished. Baba was delighted as were the other girls because they were glad to see me receding in her eyes. Yet I knew that that crispness was part of her love because no matter how callously she looked at me, she would occasionally soften. Reading her notebook helped me and I copied out her quotations into my own book, trying as accurately as possible to imitate her handwriting.

But some little time later when she came to supervise our study one evening I got a smile from her as she sat on the rostrum looking down at us all. I continued to look up at her and by slight frowning indicated that I had a problem with my geometry. She beckoned to me lightly and I went up bringing my copybook and the pen. Standing close to her, and also because her guimp was crooked, I saw one of her eyebrows for the first time. She saw that I noticed it and said did that satisfy my curiosity. I said not really. She said what else did I want to see, her swan's neck perhaps, and I went scarlet. I was amazed that she would say such a thing in the hearing of other girls and then she said a worse thing, she said that G. K. Chesterton was very forgetful and had once put on his trousers backwards. She expected me to laugh. I was so close to her that a rumble in her stomach seemed to be taking place in my own and about this she also laughed. It occurred to me for one terrible moment that maybe she had decided to leave the convent to jump over the wall. Having done the theorem for me she marked it 'one hundred out of one hundred' and then asked if I had any other problems. My eyes filled with tears as I wanted her to realise that her recent coolness had wrought havoc with my nerves and my peace of mind.

'What is it?' she said.

I could cry or I could tremble to try and convey the emotion but I could not tell her. As if on cue, the Mother Superior came in, and saw this glaring intimacy and frowned as she approached the rostrum.

'Would you please go back to your desk,' she said, 'and in future kindly allow Sister Imelda to get on with her duties.'

I tiptoed back and sat with head down, bursting with fear and shame. Then she looked at a tray on which the milk cups were laid and finding one cup of milk untouched she asked which girl had not drunk her milk.

'Me, Sister,' I said, and I was called up to drink it and stand under the clock as a punishment. The milk was tepid and dusty and I thought of cows on the fairs days at home and the farmers hitting them as they slid and slithered over the muddy streets.

For weeks I tried to see my nun in private and I even lurked outside doors where I knew she was due, only to be rebuffed again and again. I suspected the Mother Superior had warned her against making a favourite of me. But I still clung to a belief that a bond existed between us and that her coldness and even some glares which I had received were a charade, a mask. I would wonder how she felt alone in bed and what way she slept and if she thought of me, or refusing to think of me if she dreamt of me as I did of her. She certainly got thinner because her nun's silver ring slipped easily and sometimes unavoidably off her marriage finger. It occurred to me that she was having a nervous breakdown.

One day in March the sun came out, the radiators were turned off, and though there was a lashing wind we were told that officially Spring had arrived, and that we could play games. We all trooped up to the games field and to our surprise, saw that Sister Imelda was officiating that day. The daffodils in the field tossed and turned and they were a very bright shocking yellow but they were not as fetching as the little timid snowdrops that trembled in the wind. We played rounders and when my turn came to hit the ball with the long wooden pound I crumbled and missed, fearing that the ball would hit me.

'Champ . . .' said Baba jeering.

After three such failures Sister Imelda said that if I liked I could sit and watch, and when I was sitting in the greenhouse swallowing my shame she came in and said that I must not give way to tears because humiliation was the greatest test of Christ's love or indeed *any* love.

'When you are a nun you will know that,' she said and instantly I made up my mind that I would be a nun and that though we might never be free to express our feelings we would be under the same roof, in the same cloister, in mental and spiritual conjunction all our lives.

'Is it very hard at first?' I said.

'It's awful,' she said and she slipped a little medal into my gym frock pocket. It was warm from being in her pocket and as I held it, I knew that once again we were near and that in fact we had never severed. Walking down from the playing field to our Sunday lunch of mutton and cabbage everyone chattered to Sister Imelda. The girls milled around her, linking her, trying to hold her hand, counting the various keys on her bunch of keys and asking impudent questions.

'Sister, did you ever ride a motor bicycle?'

'Sister, did you ever wear seamless stockings?'

'Sister, who's your favourite film star – male!'

'Sister, what's your favourite food?'

'Sister, if you had a wish what would it be?'

'Sister, what do you do when you want to scratch your head?'

Yes, she had ridden a motor bicycle, and she had worn silk stockings but they were seamed. She liked bananas best and if she had a wish it would be to go home for a few hours to see her parents, and her brother.

That afternoon as we walked through the town the sight of closed shops with porter barrels outside, and mongrel dogs did not dispel my re-found ecstasy. The medal was in my pocket and every other second I would touch it for confirmation. Baba saw a Swiss roll in a confectioner's window laid on a doily and dusted with caster sugar

and its appeal made her cry out with hunger, and rail against being
in a bloody reformatory, surrounded by drips and mopes. On impulse
she took her nail file out of her pocket and dashed across to the
window to see if she could cut the glass. The prefect rushed up from
the back of the line and asked Baba if she wanted to be locked up.

'I am anyhow,' Baba said and sawed at one of her nails, to main-
tain her independence and vent her spleen. Baba was the only girl
who could stand up to a prefect. When she felt like it she dropped
out of a walk, sat on a stone wall and waited until we all came
back. She said that if there was one thing more boring than
studying it was walking. She used to roll down her stockings and
examine her calves and say that she could see varicose veins coming
from this bloody daily walk. Her legs like all our legs were black
from the dye of the stockings and we were forbidden to bathe
because baths were immoral. We washed each night in an enamel
basin beside our beds. When girls splashed cold water onto their
chests they let out cries, though this was forbidden.

After the walk we wrote home. We were allowed to write home
once a week; our letters were always censored. I told my mother
that I had made up my mind to be a nun, and asked if she could
send me bananas, when a batch arrived at our local grocery shop.
That evening, perhaps as I wrote to my mother on the ruled white
paper, a telegram arrived which said that Sister Imelda's brother
had been killed in a van, while on his way home from a hurling
match. The Mother Superior announced it, and asked us to pray
for his soul and write letters of sympathy to Sister Imelda's parents.
We all wrote identical letters, because in our first year at school we
had been given specimen letters for various occasions, and we all
referred back to our specimen letter of sympathy.

Next day the town hire-car drove up to the convent and Sister
Imelda, accompanied by another nun, went home for the funeral.
She looked as white as a sheet with eyes swollen and she wore a
heavy knitted shawl over her shoulders. Although she came back

that night (I stayed awake to hear the car) we did not see her for a whole week, except to catch a glimpse of her back, in the chapel. When she resumed class she was peaky and distant, making no reference at all to her recent tragedy.

The day the bananas came I waited outside the door and gave her a bunch wrapped in tissue paper. Some were still a little green, and she said that Mother Superior would put them in the glass-house to ripen. I felt that Sister Imelda would never taste them; they would be kept for a visiting priest or bishop.

'Oh Sister, I'm sorry about your brother,' I said, in a burst.

'It will come to us all, sooner or later,' Sister Imelda said dolefully.

I dared to touch her wrist to communicate my sadness. She went quickly, probably for fear of breaking down. At times she grew irritable and had a boil on her cheek. She missed some classes and was replaced in the cookery kitchen by a younger nun. She asked me to pray for her brother's soul and to avoid seeing her alone. Each time as she came down a corridor towards me I was obliged to turn the other way. Now, Baba or some other girl moved the blackboard two pegs higher and spread her shawl, when wet, over the radiator to dry.

I got 'flu and was put to bed. Sickness took the same bleak course, a cup of hot senna delivered in person by the head-nun who stood there while I drank it, tea at lunch-time with thin slices of brown bread (because it was just after the war food was still rationed, so the butter was mixed with lard and had white streaks running through it and a faintly rancid smell), hours of just lying there surveying the empty dormitory, the empty iron beds with white counterpanes on each one, and metal crucifixes laid on each white, frilled, pillow-slip. I knew that she would miss me and hoped that Baba would tell her where I was. I counted the number of tiles from the ceiling to the head of my bed, thought of my mother at home on the farm mixing hen food, thought of my father, losing his temper perhaps and stamping on the kitchen floor with nailed boots and I recalled the money owing for my school fees and hoped that Sister Imelda would never get to hear of it. During the Christmas holiday I had seen a bill sent by the head-nun to my father which said, 'Please remit this week without fail.' I hated being in bed causing extra trouble and therefore reminding the head-nun of the unpaid liability. We had no clock in the dormitory, so there was no way of guessing the time, but the hours dragged.

Marigold, one of the maids, came to take off the counterpanes at five and brought with her two gifts from Sister Imelda – an orange and a pencil sharpener. I kept the orange peel in my hand, smelling it, and planning how I would thank her. Thinking of her I fell into a feverish sleep and was wakened when the girls came to bed at ten and switched on the various ceiling lights.

At Easter Sister Imelda warned me not to give her chocolates so I got her a flashlamp instead and spare batteries. Pleased with such a useful gift (perhaps she read her letters in bed), she put her arms round me and allowed one cheek to adhere but not to make the sound of a kiss. It made up for the seven weeks of withdrawal, and as I drove down the convent drive with Baba she waved to me, as she had promised, from the window of her cell.

In the last term at school studying was intensive because of the examinations which loomed at the end of June. Like all the other nuns Sister Imelda thought only of these examinations. She crammed us with knowledge, lost her temper every other day and gritted her teeth whenever the blackboard was too greasy to take the imprint of the chalk. If ever I met her in the corridor she asked if I knew such and such a thing, and coming down from Sunday games she went over various questions with us. The fateful examination day arrived and we sat at single desks supervised by some strange woman from Dublin. Opening a locked trunk she took out the pink examination papers and distributed them around.

Geometry was on the fourth day. When we came out from it, Sister Imelda was in the hall with all the answers, so that we could compare our answers with hers. Then she called me aside and we went up towards the cookery kitchen and sat on the stairs while she went over the paper with me, question for question. I knew that I had three right and two wrong, but did not tell her so.

'It is black,' she said then, rather suddenly. I thought she meant the dark light where we were sitting.

'It's cool though,' I said.

Summer had come, our white skins baked under the heavy uniform and dark violet pansies bloomed in the convent grounds. She looked well again and her pale skin was once more unblemished.

'My hair,' she whispered, 'is black.' And she told me how she had spent her last night before entering the convent. She had gone cycling with a boy and ridden for miles, and they'd lost their way up a mountain and she became afraid she would be so late home that she would sleep it out next morning. It was understood between us that I was going to enter the convent in September and that I could have a last fling too.

Two days later we prepared to go home. There were farewells and outlandish promises, and autograph books signed, and girls trudging up the recreation hall, their cases bursting open with clothes and books. Baba scattered biscuit crumbs in the dormitory for the mice, and stuffed all her prayer books under a mattress. Her father promised to collect us at four. I had arranged with Sister Imelda secretly that I would meet her in one of the summer houses around the walks, where we would spend our last half-hour together. I expected that she would tell me something of what my life as a postulant would be like. But Baba's father came an hour early. He had something urgent to do later and came at three instead. All I could do was ask Marigold to take a note to Sister Imelda.

Remembrance is all I ask,
But if remembrance should prove a task,
Forget me.

I hated Baba, hated her busy father, hated the thought of my mother standing in the doorway in her good dress, welcoming me home at last. I would have become a nun that minute if I could.

I wrote to my nun that night and again next day and then every week for a month. Her letters were censored so I tried to convey my feelings indirectly. In one of her letters to me (they were allowed one letter a month) she said that she looked forward to seeing me in September. But by September Baba and I had left for the university in Dublin. I stopped writing to Sister Imelda then, reluctant to tell her that I no longer wished to be a nun.

In Dublin we enrolled at the college where she had surpassed herself. I saw her maiden name on a list, for having graduated with special honours, and for days was again sad and remorseful. I rushed out and bought batteries for the flashlamp I'd given her, and posted them without any note enclosed. No mention of my missing vocation, no mention of why I had stopped writing.

One Sunday about two years later Baba and I were going out to Howth on a bus. Baba had met some businessmen who played golf there and she had done a lot of scheming to get us invited out. The bus was packed, mostly mothers with babies and children on their way to Dollymount Strand. We drove along the coast road and saw the sea, bright green and glinting in the sun and because of the way the water was carved up into millions of little wavelets its surface seemed like an endless heap of dark green broken bottles. Near the shore the sand looked warm and was biscuit-coloured. We never swam or sunbathed, we never did anything that was good for us. Life was geared to work and to meeting men and yet one knew that mating could only but lead to one's being a mother and hawking obstreperous children out to the seaside on Sunday. 'They know not what they do' could surely be said of us.

We were very made up and even the conductor seemed to disapprove and snapped at having to give the change of ten shillings. For no reason at all I thought of our make-up rituals before the school play and how innocent it was in comparison because now our skins were smothered beneath layers of it and we never took it off at night. Thinking of the convent I suddenly thought of Sister Imelda and then as if prey to a dream, I heard the rustle of serge, smelt the Jeyes Fluid and the boiled cabbage and saw her pale shocked face in the months after her brother died. Then I looked around and saw her in earnest and at first thought that I was imagining things. But no, she had got on accompanied by another nun and they were settling themselves in the back seat nearest the door. She looked older but she had the same aloof quality and the same eyes and my heart began to race with a mixture of excitement and dread. At first it raced with a prodigal strength and then it began to falter and I thought it was going to give out. My fear of her and my love came back in one fell realisation. I would have gone through the window except that it was not wide enough. The thing was how to escape her. Baba gurgled with delight, stood up and in the most flagrant way looked around to make sure that it was Imelda. She recognised the other nun as one with the nickname of Johnny who taught piano lessons. Baba's first thought was revenge, as she enumerated the punishments they had meted out to us and said how nice it would be to go back and shock them and say 'Mud in your eye, Sisters', or 'Get lost', or something worse. Baba could not understand why I was quaking no more than she could understand why I began to wipe off the lipstick. Above all I knew that I could not confront them.

'You're going to have to,' Baba said.

'I can't,' I said.

It was not just my attire, it was the fact of never having written and of my broken promise. Baba kept looking back and said they weren't saying a word and that children were gawking at them. It wasn't often that nuns travelled in buses and we speculated as to where they might be going.

'They might be off to meet two fellows,' Baba said, and visualised them in the golf club getting blotto and hoisting up their skirts. For me it was no laughing matter. She came up with a strategy and it was that as we approached our stop and the bus was still moving I was to jump up and go down the aisle and pass them without even looking. She said most likely they would not notice us as their eyes were lowered and they seemed to be praying.

'I can't run down the bus,' I said. There was a matter of shaking limbs and already a terrible vertigo.

'You're going to,' Baba said, and though insisting that I couldn't I had already begun to rehearse an apology. While doing this I kept blessing myself over and over again and Baba kept reminding me that there was only one more stop before ours. When the dreadful moment came I jumped up and put on my face what can only be called an apology of a smile. I followed Baba to the rear of the bus. But already they had gone. I saw the back of their two sable, identical figures with their veils being blown wildly about in the wind. They looked so cold and lost as they hurried along the pavement and I wanted to run after them. In some way I felt worse than if I had confronted them. I cannot be certain what I would have said. I knew that there is something sad and faintly distasteful about love's ending, particularly love that has never been fully realised. I might have hinted at that but I doubt it. In our deepest moments we say the most inadequate things.

A Rose in the Heart of New York

December night. Jack Frost in scales along the outside of the windows giving to the various rooms a white filtered light. The ice like bits of mirror beveling the puddles of the potholes. The rooms were cold inside, and for the most part identically furnished. The room with no furniture at all – save for the apples gathered in the autumn – was called the Vacant Room. The apples were all over the place. Their smell was heady, many of them having begun to rot. Rooms into which no one had stepped for days, and yet these rooms and their belongings would become part of the remembered story. A solemn house, set in its own grounds, away from the lazy bustle of the village. A lonesome house, it would prove to be, and with a strange lifelikeness, as if it were not a house at all but a person observing and breathing, a presence amid a cluster of trees and sturdy wind-shorn hedges.

The overweight midwife hurried up the drive, her serge cape blowing behind her. She was puffing. She carried her barrel-shaped leather bag in which were disinfectant, gauze, forceps, instruments, and a small bottle of holy water lest the new child should prove to be in danger of death. More infants died around Christmastime than in any other month of the year. When she passed the little syca-more tree that was halfway up, she began to hear the roaring and beseeching to God. Poor mother, she thought, poor poor mother. She was not too early, had come more or less at the correct time, even though she was summoned hours before by Donai, the serving boy who worked on the farm. She had brought most of the children of that parish into the world, yet had neither kith nor kin of her own. Coming in the back door, she took off her bonnet and then attached it to the knob by means of its elastic string.

*

It was a blue room – walls of dark wet morose blue, furniture made of walnut, including the bed on which the event was taking place. Fronting the fireplace was a huge lid of a chocolate box with the representation of a saucy-looking lady. The tassel of the blind kept bobbing against the frosted windowpane. There was a washstand, a basin and ewer of off-white, with big roses splashed throughout the china itself, and a huge lumbering beast of a wardrobe. The midwife recalled once going to a house up the mountain, and finding that the child had been smothered by the time she arrived, the fatherless child had been stuffed in a drawer. The moans filled that room and went beyond the distempered walls out into the cold hall outside, where the black felt doggie with the amber eyes stood sentinel on a tall varnished whatnot. At intervals the woman apologized to the midwife for the untoward commotion, said sorry in a gasping whisper, and then was seized again by a pain that at different times she described as being a knife, a dagger, a hell on earth. It was her fourth labor. The previous child had died two days after being born. An earlier child, also a daughter, had died of whooping cough. Her womb was sick unto death. Why be a woman. Oh, cruel life; oh, merciless fate; oh, heartless man, she sobbed. Gripping the coverlet and remembering that between those selfsame, much-patched sheets, she had been prized apart, again and again, with not a word to her, not a little endearment, only rammed through and told to open up. When she married she had escaped the life of a serving girl, the possible experience of living in some grim institution, but as time went on and the bottom drawer was emptied of its gifts, she saw that she was made to serve in an altogether other way. When she wasn't screaming she was grinding her head into the pillow and praying for it to be all over. She dreaded the eventual bloodshed long before they saw any. The midwife made her ease up as she put an old sheet under her and over that a bit of oilcloth. The midwife said it was no joke and repeated the hypothesis that if men had to give birth there would not be a child born in the whole wide world. The husband was downstairs getting paralytic. Earlier when his wife had announced that she would have to go upstairs because of her labor, he said, looking for the slightest pretext for a celebration, that if there was any homemade wine or altar wine stacked away, to get it out, to produce it, and also the cut glasses. She said there was none and well he knew it, since they could hardly afford tea and sugar. He started to root and to rummage, to empty cupboards of their contents of rags, garments, and provisions, even to put his hand inside the bolster case, to delve into pillows; on he went, rampaging until he found a bottle in the wardrobe, in the very room into which she delivered her moans and exhortations. She begged of him not to, but all he did was to wield the amber-colored bottle in her direction, and then put it to his head so that the spirit started to go glug-glug. It was intoxicating stuff. By a wicked coincidence a crony of his had come to sell them another stove, most likely another crock, a thing that would have to be coaxed alight with constant attention and puffing to create a draft. The other child was with a neighbor, the dead ones in a graveyard six or seven miles away, among strangers and distant relatives, without their names being carved on the crooked rain-soaked tomb.

'O Jesus,' she cried out as he came back to ask for a knitting needle to skewer out the bit of broken cork.

'Blazes,' he said to her as she coiled into a knot and felt the big urgent ball – that would be the head – as it pressed on the base of her bowels and battered at her insides.

Curses and prayers combined to issue out of her mouth, and as time went on, they became most pitiful and were interrupted with screams. The midwife put a facecloth on her forehead and told her to push, in the name of the Lord to push. She said she had no strength left, but the midwife went on enjoining her and simulating a hefty breath. It took over an hour. The little head showing its tonsure would recoil, would reshow itself, each time a fraction more, although, in between, it was seeming to shrink from the world that it was hurtling toward. She said to the nurse that she was being burst apart, and that she no longer cared if she died, or if they drank themselves to death. In the kitchen they were sparring over who had the best greyhound, who had the successor to Mick the Miller. The crucifix that had been in her hand had fallen out, and her hands themselves felt bony and skinned because of the way they wrenched one another.

'In the name of God, push, missus.'

She would have pushed everything out of herself, her guts, her womb, her craw, her lights, and her liver, but the center of her body was holding on and this center seemed to be the governor of her. She wished to be nothing, a shell, devoid of everything and everyone, and she was announcing that, and roaring and raving, when the child came hurtling out, slowly at first, as if its neck could not wring its way through, then the shoulder – that was the worst bit – carving a straight course, then the hideous turnabout, and a scream other than her own, and an urgent presage of things, as the great gouts of blood and lymph followed upon the mewling creature itself. Her last bit of easiness was then torn from her, and she was without hope. It had come into the world lopsided, and the first announcement from the midwife was a fatality, was that it had clubbed feet. Its little feet, she ventured to say, were like two stumps adhering to one another, and the blasted cord was bound around its neck. The result was a mewling piece of screwed-up, inert, dark-purple misery. The men subsided a little when the announcement was shouted down and they came to say congrats. The father waved a strip of pink flesh on a fork that he was carrying and remarked on its being unappetizing. They were cooking a goose downstairs and he said in future he would insist on turkey, as goose was only for gobs and goms. The mother felt green and disgusted, asked them to leave her alone. The salesman said was it a boy or a child, although he had just been told that it was a daughter. The mother could feel the blood gushing out of her, like water at a weir. The midwife told them to go down and behave like gentlemen.

Then she got three back numbers of the weekly paper, and a shoe box with a lid, and into it she stuffed the mess and the unnecessaries. She hummed as she prepared to do the stitching down the line of torn flesh that was gaping and coated with blood. The mother roared again and said this indeed was her vinegar and gall. She bit into the crucifix and dented it further. She could feel her mouth and her eyelids being stitched, too; she was no longer a lovely body, she was a vehicle for pain and for insult. The child was so quiet it scarcely breathed. The afterbirth was placed on the stove, where the dog, Shep, sniffed at it through its layers of paper and for his curiosity got a kick in the tail. The stove had been quenched, and the midwife said to the men that it was a crying shame to leave a good goose like that, neither cooked nor uncooked. The men had torn off bits of the breast so that the goose looked wounded, like the woman upstairs, who was then tightening her heart and soul, tightening inside the array of catgut stitches, and regarding her whole life as a vast disappointment. The midwife carried the big bundle up to the cellar, put an oil rag to it, set a match to it, and knew that she would have to be off soon to do the same task elsewhere. She would have liked to stay and swaddle the infant, and comfort the woman, and drink hot sweet tea, but there was not enough time. There was never enough time, and she hadn't even cleaned out the ashes or the cinders in her grate that morning.

The child was in a corner of the room in a brown cot with slats that rattled because of the racket they had received from the previous children. The mother was not proud, far from it. She fed the child its first bottle, looked down at its wizened face, and thought, Where have you come from and why? She had no choice of a name. In fact, she said to her first visitor, a lieutenant from the army, not to tell her a pack of lies, because this child had the ugliest face that had ever seen the light of day. That Christmas the drinking and sparring went on, the odd neighbor called, the mother got up on the third day and staggered down to do something about the unruly kitchen. Each evening at nightfall she got a bit of a candle to have handy and re-oiled the Sacred Heart lamp for when the child cried. They both contracted bronchitis and the child was impounded in masses of flannel and flannelette.

Things changed. The mother came to idolize the child, because it was so quiet, never bawling, never asking for anything, just weirdly still in its pram, the dog watching over it, its eyes staring out at whatever happened to loom in. Its very ugliness disappeared. It seemed to drink them in with its huge, contemplating, slightly hazed-over, navy eyes. They shone at whatever they saw. The mother would look in the direction of the pram and say a little prayer for it, or smile, and often at night she held the candle shielded by her hand to see the face, to say pet or tush, to say nonsense to it. It ate whatever it was given, but as time went on, it knew what it liked and had a sweet tooth. The food was what united them, eating off the same plate, using the same spoon, watching one another's chews, feeling the food as it went down the other's neck. The child was slow to crawl and slower still to walk, but it knew everything, it perceived everything. When it ate blancmange or junket, it was eating part of the lovely substance of its mother.

They were together, always together. If its mother went to the post office, the child stood in the middle of the drive praying until its mother returned safely. The child cut the ridges of four fingers along the edge of a razor blade that had been wedged upright in the wood of the dresser, and seeing these four deep, horizontal identical slits the mother took the poor fingers into her own mouth and sucked them, to lessen the pain, and licked them to abolish the blood, and kept saying soft things until the child was stilled again.

Her mother's knuckles were her knuckles, her mother's veins were her veins, her mother's lap was a second heaven, her mother's forehead a copybook onto which she traced A B C D, her mother's body was a recess that she would wander inside forever and ever, a sepulcher growing deeper and deeper. When she saw other people, especially her pretty sister, she would simply wave from that safe place, she would not budge, would not be lured out. Her father took a hatchet to her mother and threatened that he would split open the head of her. The child watched through the kitchen window, because this debacle took place outdoors on a hillock under the three beech trees where the clothesline stretched, then sagged. The mother had been hanging out the four sheets washed that morning, two off each bed. The child was engaged in twisting her hair, looping it around bits of white rag, to form ringlets, decking herself in the kitchen mirror, and then every other minute running across to the window to reconnoiter, wondering what she ought to do, jumping up and down as if she had a pain, not knowing what to do, running back to the mirror, hoping that the terrible scene would pass, that the ground would open up and swallow her father, that the hatchet would turn into a magic wand, that her mother would come through the kitchen door and say 'Fear not,' that travail would all be over. Later she heard a verbatim account of what had happened. Her father demanded money, her mother refused same on the grounds that she had none, but added that if she had it she would hang sooner than give it to him. That did it. It was then he really got bucking, gritted his teeth and his muscles, said that he would split the head of her, and the mother said that if he did so there was a place for him. That place was the lunatic asylum. It was twenty or thirty miles away, a big gray edifice, men and women lumped in together, some in strait-jackets, some in padded cells, some blindfolded because of having sacks thrown over their heads, some strapped across the chest to quell and impede them. Those who did not want to go there were dragged by relatives, or by means of rope, some being tied on to the end of a plow or a harrow and brought in on all fours, like beasts of the earth. Then when they were not so mad, not so rampaging, they were let home again, where they were very peculiar and given to smiling and to chattering to themselves, and in no time they were ripe to go off again or to be dragged off. March was the worst month, when everything went askew, even the wind, even the March hares. Her father did not go there. He went off on a batter and then went to a monastery, and then was brought home and shook in the bed chair for five days, eating bread and milk and asking who would convey him over the fields, until he saw his yearlings, and when no one volunteered to, it fell to her because she was the youngest. Over in the fields he patted the yearlings and said soppy things that he'd never say indoors, or to a human, and he cried and said he'd never touch a drop again, and there was a dribble on his pewter-brown mustache that was the remains of the mush he had been eating, and the yearling herself became fidgety and fretful as if she might bolt or stamp the ground to smithereens.

The girl and her mother took walks on Sundays – strolls, picked blackberries, consulted them for worms, made preserve, and slept side by side, entwined like twigs of trees or the ends of the sugar tongs. When she wakened and found that her mother had got up and was already mixing meals for the hens or stirabout for the young pigs, she hurried down, carrying her clothes under her arm, and dressed in whatever spot she could feast on the sight of her mother most. Always an egg for breakfast. An egg a day and she would grow strong. Her mother never ate an egg but topped the girl's egg and fed her it off the tarnished eggy spoon and gave her little sups of tea with which to wash it down. She had her own mug, red enamel and with not a chip. The girl kept looking back as she went down the drive for school, and as time went on, she mastered the knack of walking backward to be able to look all the longer, look at the aproned figure waving or holding up a potato pounder or a colander, or whatever happened to be in her hand.

The girl came home once and the mother was missing. Her mother had actually fulfilled her promise of going away one day and going to a spot where she would not be found. That threatened spot was the bottom of the lake. But in fact her mother had gone back to her own family, because the father had taken a shotgun to her and had shot her but was not a good aim like William Tell, had missed, had instead made a hole in the Blue Room wall. What were they doing upstairs in the middle of the day, an ascent they never made except the mother alone to dress the two beds. She could guess. She slept in a neighbor's house, slept in a bed with two old people who reeked of eucalyptus. She kept most of her clothes on and shriveled into herself, not wanting to touch or be touched by these two old people buried in their various layers of skin and hair and winceyette. Outside the window was a climbing rose with three or four red flowers along the bow of it, and looking at the flowers and thinking of the wormy clay, she would try to shut out what these two old people were saying, in order that she could remember the mother whom she despaired of ever seeing again. Not far away was their own house, with the back door wide open so that any stranger or tinker could come in or out. The dog was probably lonely and bloodied from hunting rabbits, the hens were forgotten about and were probably in their coops, hysterical, picking at one another's feathers because of their nerves. Eggs would rot. If she stood on the low whitewashed wall that fronted the cottage, she could see over the high limestone wall that boundaried their fields and then look to the driveway that led to the abandoned house itself.

To her it was like a kind of castle where strange things had happened and would go on happening. She loved it and she feared it. The sky behind and above gave it mystery, sometimes made it broody, and gave it a kind of splendor when the red streaks in the heavens were like torches that betokened the performance of a gory play. All of a sudden, standing there, with a bit of grass between her front teeth, looking at her home and imagining this future drama, she heard the nearby lych-gate open and then shut with a clang, and saw her father appear, and jumped so clumsily she thought she had broken everything, particularly her ribs. She felt she was in pieces. She would be like Humpty-Dumpty, and all the king's horses and all the king's men would not be able to put her together again. Dismemberment did happen, a long time before, the time when her neck swelled out into a big fleshed balloon. She could only move her neck on one side, because the other side was like a ball and full of fluid and made gluggles when she touched it with her fingers. They were going to lance it. They placed her on a kitchen chair. Her mother boiled a saucepan of water. Her mother stood on another chair and reached far into the rear of a cupboard and hauled out a new towel. Everything was in that cupboard, sugar and tea and round biscuits and white flour and linen and must and mice. First one man, then another, then another man, then a last man who was mending the chimney, and then last of all her father each took hold of her – an arm, another arm, a shoulder, a waist, and her two flying legs that were doing everything possible not to be there. The lady doctor said nice things and cut into the big football of her neck, and it was like a pig's bladder bursting all over, the waters flowing out, and then it was not like that at all; it was like a sword on the bone of her neck sawing, cutting into the flesh, deeper and deeper, the men pressing upon her with all their might, saying that she was a demon, and the knife went into her swallow or where she thought of forever more as her swallow, and the lady doctor said, 'Drat it,' because she had done the wrong thing – had cut too deep and had to start scraping now, and her older sister danced a jig out on the flagstones so that neighbors going down the road would not get the impression that someone was being murdered. Long afterward she came back to the world of voices, muffled voices, and their reassurances, and a little something sweet to help her get over it all, and the lady doctor putting on her brown fur coat and hurrying to her next important work of mercy.

When she slept with the neighbors the old man asked the old woman were they ever going to be rid of her, were they going to have this dunce off their hands, were they saddled with her for the rest of their blooming lives. She declined the milk they gave her because it was goat's milk and too yellow and there was dust in it. She would answer them in single syllables, just yes or no, mostly no. She was learning to frown, so that she, too, would have A B C's. Her mother's forehead and hers would meet in heaven, salute, and all their lines would coincide. She refused food. She pined. In all, it was about a week.

The day her mother returned home – it was still January – the water pipes had burst, and when she got to the neighbors' and was told she could go on up home, she ran with all her might and resolution, so that her windpipe ached and then stopped aching when she found her mother down on her knees dealing with pools of water that had gushed from the red pipes. The brown rag was wet every other second and had to be wrung out and squeezed in the big chipped basin, the one she was first bathed in. The lodges of water were everywhere, lapping back and forth, threatening to expand, to discolor the tiles, and it was of this hazard they talked and fretted over rather than the mother's disappearance, or the dire cause of it, or the reason for her return. They went indoors and got the ingredients and the utensils and the sieve so as to make an orange cake with orange filling and orange icing. She never tasted anything so wonderful in all her life. She ate three big hunks, and her mother put her hand around her and said if she ate any more she would have a little corporation.

The father came home from the hospital, cried again, said that sure he wouldn't hurt a fly, and predicted that he would never break his pledge or go outside the gate again, only to Mass, never leave his own sweet acres. As before, the girl slept with her mother, recited the Rosary with her, and shared the small cubes of dark raisin-filled chocolate, then trembled while her mother went along to her father's bedroom for a tick, to stop him bucking. The consequences of those visits were deterred by the bits of tissue paper, a protection between herself and any emission. No other child got conceived, and there was no further use for the baggy napkins, the bottle, and the dark-brown mottled teat. The cot itself was sawn up and used to back two chairs, and they constituted something of the furniture in the big upstairs landing, where the felt dog still lorded over it but now had an eye missing because a visiting child had poked wire at it. The chairs were painted oxblood red and had the sharp end of a nail dragged along the varnish to give a wavering effect. Also on the landing was a bowl with a bit of wire inside to hold a profusion of artificial tea roses. These tea roses were a two-toned color, were red and yellow plastic, and the point of each petal was seared like the point of a thorn. Cloth flowers were softer. She had seen some once, very pale pink and purple, made of voile, in another house, in a big jug, tumbling over a lady's bureau. In the landing at home, too, was the speared head of Christ, which looked down on all the proceedings with endless patience, endless commiseration. Underneath Christ was a pussy cat of black papier-mâché which originally had sweets stuffed into its middle, sweets the exact image of strawberries and even with a little leaf at the base, a leaf made of green-glazed angelica. They liked the same things – applesauce and beetroot and tomato sausages and angelica. They cleaned the windows, one the inside, the other the outside, they sang duets, they put newspapers over the newly washed dark-red tiles so as to keep them safe from the muck and trampalations of the men. About everything they agreed, or almost everything.

In the dark nights the wind used to sweep through the window and out on the landing and into the other rooms, and into the Blue Room, by now uninhabited. The wardrobe door would open of its own accord, or the ewer would rattle, or the lovely buxom Our Lady of Limerick picture would fall onto the marble wash-stand and there was a rumpus followed by prognostications of bad luck for seven years. When the other child came back from boarding school, the girl was at first excited, prepared lovingly for her, made cakes, and, soon after, was plunged into a state of wretchedness. Her mother was being taken away from her, or, worse, was gladly giving her speech, her attention, her hands, and all of her gaze to this intruder. Her mother and her older sister would go upstairs, where her mother would have some little treat for her, a hanky or a hanky sachet, and once a remnant that had been got at the mill at reduced price, due to a fire there. Beautiful, a flecked salmon pink.

Downstairs *she* had to stack dishes onto the tray. She banged the cups, she put a butter knife into the two-pound pot of blackcurrant jam and hauled out a big helping, then stuck the greasy plates one on top of the other, whereas normally she would have put a fork in between to protect the undersides. She dreamed that her mother and her rival sister were going for a walk and she asked to go too, but they sneaked off. She followed on a bicycle, but once outside the main gate could not decide whether to go to the left or the right, and then, having decided, made the wrong choice and stumbled on a herd of bullocks, all butting one another and endeavoring to get up into one another's backside. She turned back, and there they were strolling up the drive, like two sedate ladies linking and laughing, and the salmon-flecked remnant was already a garment, a beautiful swagger coat which her sister wore with a dash.

'I wanted to be with you,' she said, and one said to the other, 'She wanted to be with us,' and then no matter what she said, no matter what the appeal, they repeated it as if she weren't there. In the end she knew that she would have to turn away from them, because she was not wanted, she was in their way. As a result of that dream, or rather the commotion that she made in her sleep, it was decided that she had worms, and the following morning they gave her a dose of turpentine and castor oil, the same as they gave the horses.

When her sister went back to the city, happiness was restored again. Her mother consulted her about the design on a leather bag which she was making. Her mother wanted a very old design, something concerning the history of their country. She said there would have to be battles and then peace and wonderful scenes from nature. Her mother said that there must be a lot of back history to a land and that education was a very fine thing. Preferable to the bog, her mother said. The girl said when she grew up that she would get a very good job and bring her mother to America. Her mother mentioned the street in Brooklyn where she had lodged and said that it had adjoined a park. They would go there one day. Her mother said maybe.

The growing girl began to say the word 'backside' to herself and knew that her mother would be appalled. The girl laughed at bullocks and the sport they had. Then she went one further and jumped up and down and said 'Jumping Jack,' as if some devil were inside her, touching and tickling the lining of her. It was creepy. It was done outdoors, far from the house, out in the fields, in a grove, or under a canopy of rhododendrons. The buds of the rhododendrons were sticky and oozed with life, and everything along with herself was soaking wet, and she was given to wandering flushes and then fits of untoward laughter, so that she had to scold herself into some state of normality and this she did by slapping both cheeks vehemently. As a dire punishment she took cups of Glauber's salts three times a day, choosing to drink it when it was lukewarm and at its most nauseating. She would be told by her father to get out, to stop hatching, to get out from under her mother's apron strings, and he would send her for a spin on the woeful brakeless bicycle. She would go to the chapel, finding it empty of all but herself and the lady sacristan, who spent her life in there polishing and rearranging the artificial flowers; or she would go down into a bog and make certain unattainable wishes, but always at the end of every day, and at the end of every thought, and at the beginning of sleep and the precise moment of wakening, it was of her mother and for her mother she existed, and her prayers and her good deeds and her ringlets and the ire on her legs – created by the serge of her gym frock – were for her mother's intention, and on and on. Only death could part them, and not even that, because she resolved that she would take her own life if some disease or some calamity snatched her mother away. Her mother's three-quarter-length jacket she would don, sink her hands into the deep pockets, and say the name 'Delia,' her mother's, say it in different tones of voice, over and over again, always in a whisper and with a note of conspiracy.

A lovely thing happened. Her mother and father went on a journey by hire car to do a transaction whereby they could get some credit on his lands, and her father did not get drunk but ordered a nice pot of tea, and then sat back gripping his braces and gave her mother a few bob, with which her mother procured a most beautiful lipstick in a ridged gold case. It was like fresh fruit, so moist was it, and coral red. Her mother and she tried it on over and over again, were comical with it, trying it on, then wiping it off, trying it on again, making cupids so that her mother expostulated and said what scatterbrains they were, and even the father joined in the hilarity and daubed down the mother's cheek and said Fanny Anny, and the mother said that was enough, as the lipstick was liable to get broken. With her thumbnail she pressed on the little catch, pushing the lipstick down into its case, into its bed. As the years went on, it dried out and developed a peculiar shape, and they read somewhere that a lady's character could be told by that particular shape, and they wished that they could discover whether the mother was the extrovert or the shy violet.

The girl had no friends, she didn't need any. Her cup was full. Her mother was the cup, the cupboard, the sideboard with all the things in it, the tabernacle with God in it, the lake with the legends in it, the bog with the wishing well in it, the sea with the oysters and the corpses in it, her mother a gigantic sponge, a habitation in which she longed to sink and disappear forever and ever. Yet she was afraid to sink, caught in that hideous trap between fear of sinking and fear of swimming, she moved like a flounderer through this and that; through school, through inoculation, through a man who put his white handkerchief between naked her and naked him, and against a galvanized outhouse door came, gruntling and disgruntling like a tethered beast upon her; through a best friend, a girl friend who tried to clip the hairs of her vagina with a shears. The hairs of her vagina were mahogany-colored, and her best friend said that that denoted mortal sin. She agonized over it. Then came a dreadful blow. Two nuns called and her mother and her father said that she was to stay outside in the kitchen and see that the kettle boiled and then lift it off so that water would not boil over. She went on tiptoe through the hall and listened at the door of the room. She got it in snatches. She was being discussed. She was being sent away to school. A fee was being discussed and her mother was asking if they could make a reduction. She ran out of the house in a dreadful state. She ran to the chicken run and went inside to cry and to go berserk. The floor was full of damp and gray-green mottled droppings. The nests were full of sour sops of hay. She thought she was going out of her mind. When they found her later, her father said to cut out the 'bull,' but her mother tried to comfort her by saying they had a prospectus and that she would have to get a whole lot of new clothes in navy blue. But where would the money come from?

In the convent to which they sent her she eventually found solace. A nun became her new idol. A nun with a dreadfully pale face and a master's degree in science. This nun and she worked out codes with the eyelids, and the flutter of the lashes, so they always knew each other's moods and feelings, so that the slightest hurt imposed by one was spotted by the other and responded to with a glance. The nun gave another girl more marks at the mid-term examination, and did it solely to hurt her, to wound her pride; the nun addressed her briskly in front of the whole class, said her full name and asked her a theological conundrum that was impossible to answer. In turn, she let one of the nun's holy pictures fall on the chapel floor, where of course it was found by the cleaning nun, who gave it back to the nun, who gave it to her with a 'This seems to have got mislaid.' They exchanged Christmas presents and notes that contained blissful innuendos. She had given chocolates with a kingfisher on the cover, and she had received a prayer book with gilt edging and it was as tiny as her little finger. She could not read the print but she held it to herself like a talisman, like a secret scroll in which love was mentioned.

Home on holiday it was a different story. Now *she* did the avoiding, the shunning. All the little treats and the carrageen soufflé that her mother had prepared were not gloated over. Then the pink crepe-de-Chine apron that her mother had made from an old dance dress did not receive the acclamation that the mother expected. It was fitted on and at once taken off and flung over the back of a chair with no praise except to remark on the braiding, which was cleverly done.

'These things are not to be sniffed at,' her mother said, passing the plate of scones for the third or fourth time. The love of the nun dominated all her thoughts, and the nun's pale face got between her and the visible world that she was supposed to be seeing. At times she could taste it. It interfered with her studies, her other friendships, it got known about. She was called to see the Reverend Mother. The nun and she never had a tête-à-tête again and never swapped holy pictures. The day she was leaving forever they made an illicit date to meet in the summerhouse, out in the grounds, but neither of them turned up. They each sent a message with an apology, and it was, in fact, the messengers who met, a junior girl and a postulant carrying the same sentence on separate lips – 'So-and-so is sorry – she wishes to say she can't . . .' They might have broken down or done anything, they might have kissed.

Out of school, away from the spell of nuns and gods and flower gardens and acts of contrition, away from the chapel with its incense and its brimstone sermons, away from surveillance, she met a bakery man who was also a notable hurley player and they started up that kind of courtship common to their sort – a date at Nelson's pillar two evenings a week, then to a café to have coffee and cream cakes, to hold hands under the table, to take a bus to her digs, to kiss against a railing and devour each other's face, as earlier they had devoured the mock cream and the sugar-dusted sponge cakes. But these orgies only increased her hunger, made it into something that could not be appeased. She would recall her mother from the very long ago, in the three-quarter-length jacket of salmon tweed, the brooch on the lapel, the smell of face powder, the lipstick hurriedly put on so that a little of it always smudged on the upper or the lower lip and appeared like some kind of birthmark. Recall that they even had the same mole on the back of the left hand, a mole that did not alter winter or summer and was made to seem paler when the fist was clenched. But she was recalling someone whom she wanted to banish. The bakery man got fed up, wanted more than a cuddle, hopped it. Then there was no one, just a long stretch, doing novenas, working in the library, and her mother's letters arriving, saying the usual things, how life was hard, how inclement the weather, how she'd send a cake that day or the next day, as soon as there were enough eggs to make it with. The parcels arrived once a fortnight, bound in layers of newspaper, and then a strong outer layer of brown paper, all held with hideous assortments of twines — binding twine, very white twine, and colored plastic string from the stools that she had taken to making; then great spatters of sealing wax adorning it. Always a registered parcel, always a cake, a pound of butter, and a chicken that had to be cooked at once, because of its being nearly putrid from the four-day journey. It was not difficult to imagine the kitchen table, the bucket full of feathers, the moled hand picking away at the pin feathers, the other hand plunging in and drawing out all the undesirables, tremulous, making sure not to break a certain little pouch, since its tobacco-colored fluid could ruin the taste of the bird. Phew. Always the same implications in each letter, the same cry —

'Who knows what life brings. Your father is not hard-boiled despite his failings. It makes me sad to think of the little things that I used to be able to do for you.' She hated those parcels, despite the fact that they were most welcome.

She married. Married in haste. Her mother said from the outset that he was as odd as two left shoes. He worked on an encyclopedia and was a mine of information on certain subjects. His specialty was vegetation in pond life. They lived to themselves. She learned to do chores, to bottle and preserve, to comply, to be a wife, to undress neatly at night, to fold her clothes, to put them on a cane chair, making sure to put her corset and her underthings respectfully under her dress or her skirt. It was like being at school again. The mother did not visit, being at odds with the censuring husband. Mother and daughter would meet in a market town midway between each of their rural homes, and when they met they sat in some hotel lounge, ordered tea, and discussed things that can easily be discussed – recipes, patterns for knitting, her sister, items of furniture that they envisaged buying. Her mother was getting older, had developed a slight stoop, and held up her hands to show the rheumatism in her joints. Then all of a sudden, as if she had just remembered it, she spoke about the cataracts, and her journey to the specialist, and how the specialist had asked her if she remembered anything about her eyes and how she had to tell him that she had lost her sight for five or six minutes one morning and that then it came back. He had told her how lucky it was, because in some instances it does not come back at all. She said yes, the shades of life were closing in on her. The daughter knew that her marriage would not last, but she dared not say so. Things were happening such as that they had separate meals, that he did not speak for weeks on end, and yet she defended him, talked of the open pine dresser he had made, and her mother rued the fact that she never had a handyman to do odd things for her. She said the window had broken in a storm and that there was still a bit of cardboard in it. She said she had her heart on two armchairs, armchairs with damask covers. The daughter longed to give them to her and thought that she might steal from her husband when he was asleep, steal the deposit, that is, and pay for them on hire purchase. But they said none of the things that they should have said.

'You didn't get any new style,' the mother said, restating her particular dislike for a sheepskin coat.

'I don't want it,' the girl said tersely.

'You were always a softie,' the mother said, and inherent in this was disapproval for a man who allowed his wife to be dowdy. Perhaps she thought that her daughter's marriage might have amended for her own.

When her marriage did end, the girl wrote and said that it was all over, and the mother wrote posthaste, exacting two dire promises – the girl must write back on her oath and promise her that she would never touch an alcoholic drink as long as she lived and she would never again have to do with any man in body or soul. High commands. At the time the girl was walking the streets in a daze and stopping strangers to tell of her plight. One day in a park she met a man who was very sympathetic, a sort of tramp. She told him her story, and then all of a sudden he told her this terrible dream. He had wakened up and he was swimming in water and the water kept changing color, it was blue and red and green, and these changing colors terrified him. She saw that he was not all there and invented an excuse to go somewhere. In time she sold her bicycle and pawned a gold bracelet and a gold watch and chain. She fled to England. She wanted to go somewhere where she knew no one. She was trying to start afresh, to wipe out the previous life. She was staggered by the assaults of memory – a bowl with her mother's menstrual cloth soaking in it and her sacrilegious idea that if lit it could resemble the heart of Christ, the conical wick of the Aladdin lamp being lit too high and disappearing into a jet of black; the roses, the five freakish winter roses that were in bloom when the pipes burst; the mice that came out of the shoes, then out of the shoe closet itself, onto the floor where the newspapers had been laid to prevent the muck and manure of the trampling men; the little box of rouge that almost asked to be licked, so dry and rosy was it; the black range whose temperature could be tested by just spitting on it and watching the immediate jig and trepidation of the spit; the pancakes on Shrove Tuesday (if there wasn't a row); the flitches of bacon hanging to smoke; the forgotten jam jars with inevitably the bit of moldy jam in the bottom; and always, like an overseeing spirit, the figure of the mother, who was responsible for each and every one of these facets, and always the pending doom in which the mother would perhaps be struck with the rim of a bucket, or a sledgehammer, or some improvised weapon; struck by the near-crazed father. It would be something as slight as that the mother had a splinter under her nail and the girl felt her own nail being lifted up, felt hurt to the quick, or felt her mother's sputum, could taste it like a dish. She was possessed by these thoughts in the library where she worked day in and day out, filing and cataloguing and handing over books. They were more than thoughts, they were the presence of this woman whom she resolved to kill. Yes, she would have to kill. She would have to take up arms and commit a murder. She thought of choking or drowning. Certainly the method had to do with suffocation, and she foresaw herself holding big suffocating pillows or a bolster, in the secrecy of the Blue Room, where it had all begun. Her mother turned into the bursting red pipes, into the brown dishcloths, into swamps of black-brown blooded water. Her mother turned into a streetwalker and paraded. Her mother was taking down her knickers in public, squatting to do awful things, left little piddles, small as puppies' piddles, her mother was drifting down a well in a big bucket, crying for help, but no help was forthcoming. The oddest dream came along. Her mother was on her deathbed, having just given birth to her – the little tonsured head jutted above the sheet – and had a neck rash, and was busy trying to catch a little insect, trying to cup it in the palms of her hands, and was saying that in the end 'all there is, is yourself and this little insect that you're trying to kill.' The word 'kill' was everywhere, on the hoardings, in the evening air, on the tip of her thoughts. But life goes on. She bought a yellow two-piece worsted, and wrote home and said, 'I must be getting cheerful, I wear less black.' Her mother wrote, 'I have only one wish now and it is that we will be buried together.' The more she tried to kill, the more clinging the advances became. Her mother was taking out all the old souvenirs, the brown scapulars salvaged from the hurtful night in December, a mug, with their similar initial on it, a tablecloth that the girl had sent from her first earnings when she qualified as a librarian. The mother's letters began to show signs of wandering. They broke off in midsentence; one was written on blotting paper and almost indecipherable;

they contained snatches of information such as 'So-and-so died, there was a big turnout at the funeral,' 'I could do with a copper bracelet for rheumatism,' 'You know life gets lonelier.'

She dreaded the summer holidays, but still she went. The geese and the gander would be trailing by the riverbank, the cows would gape at her as if an alien had entered their terrain. It was only the horses she avoided – always on the nervy side, as if ready to bolt. The fields themselves as beguiling as ever, fields full of herbage and meadowsweet, fields adorned with spangles of gold as the buttercups caught the shafts of intermittent sunshine. If only she could pick them up and carry them away. They sat indoors. A dog had a deep cut in his paw and it was thought that a fox did it, that the dog and the fox had tussled one night. As a result of this, he was admitted to the house. The mother and the dog spoke, although not a word passed between them. The father asked pointed questions, such as would it rain or was it teatime. For a pastime they then discussed all the dogs that they had had. The mother especially remembered Monkey and said that he was a queer one, that he'd know what you were thinking of. The father and daughter remembered further back to Shep, the big collie, who guarded the child's pram and drove thoroughbred horses off the drive, causing risk to his own person. Then there were the several pairs of dogs, all of whom sparred and quarreled throughout their lives, yet all of whom died within a week of one another, the surviving dog dying of grief for his pal. No matter how they avoided it, death crept into the conversation. The mother said unconvincingly how lucky they were never to have been crippled, to have enjoyed good health and enough to eat. The curtains behind her chair were a warm red velveteen and gave a glow to her face. A glow that was reminiscent of her lost beauty.

She decided on a celebration. She owed it to her mother. They would meet somewhere else, away from that house, and its skeletons and its old cunning tug at the heartstrings. She planned it a year in advance, a holiday in a hotel, set in beautiful woodland surroundings on the verge of the Atlantic Ocean. Their first hours were happily and most joyfully passed as they looked at the rooms, the view, the various tapestries, found where things were located, looked at the games room and then at the display cabinets, where there were cut-glass and marble souvenirs on sale. The mother said that everything was 'poison, dear.' They took a walk by the seashore and remarked one to the other on the different stripes of color on the water, how definite they were, each color claiming its surface of sea, just like oats or grass or a plowed land. The brown plaits of seaweed slapped and slathered over rocks, long-legged birds let out their lonesome shrieks, and the mountains that loomed beyond seemed to hold the specter of continents inside them so vast were they, so old. They dined early. Afterward there was a singsong and the mother whispered that money wasn't everything; to look at the hard-boiled faces. Something snapped inside her, and forgetting that this was her errand of mercy, she thought instead how this mother had a whole series of grudges, bitter grudges concerning love, happiness, and her hard impecunious fate. The angora jumpers, the court shoes, the brown and the fawn garments, the milk complexion, the auburn tresses, the little breathlessnesses, the hands worn by toil, the sore feet, these were but the trimmings, behind them lay the real person, who demanded her pound of flesh from life. They sat on a sofa. The mother sipped tea and she her whiskey. They said, 'Cheers.' The girl tried to get the conversation back to before she was born, or before other children were born, to the dances and the annual race day and the courtship that preempted the marriage. The mother refused to speak, balked, had no story to tell, said that even if she had a story she would not tell it. Said she hated raking up the past. The girl tweezed it out of her in scraps. The mother said yes, that as a young girl she was bold and obstinate and she did have fancy dreams but soon learned to toe the line. Then she burst out laughing and said she climbed up a ladder once into the chapel, and into the confessional, so as to be the first person there to have her confession heard by the missioner. The missioner nearly lost his life because he didn't know how anyone could possibly have got in, since the door was bolted and he had simply come to sit in the confessional to compose himself, when there she was, spouting sins. What sins?

The mother said, 'Oh, I forget, love. I forget everything now.'

The girl said, 'No, you don't.'

They said night-night and arranged to meet in the dining room the following morning.

The mother didn't sleep a wink, complained that her eyes and her nose were itchy, and she feared she was catching a cold. She drank tea noisily, slugged it down. They walked by the sea, which was now the color of gunmetal, and the mountains were no longer a talking point. They visited a ruined monastery where the nettles, the sorrel, the clover, and the seedy dock grew high in a rectangle. Powder shed from walls that were built of solid stone. The mother said that probably it was a chapel, or a chancery, a seat of sanctity down through the centuries, and she genuflected. To the girl it was just a ruin, unhallowed, full of weeds and buzzing with wasps and insects. Outside, there was a flock of noisy starlings. She could feel the trouble brewing. She said that there was a lovely smell, that it was most likely some wild herb, and she got down on her knees to locate it. Peering with eyes and fingers among the low grass, she came upon a nest of ants that were crawling over a tiny bit of ground with an amazing amount of energy and will. She felt barely in control.

They trailed back in time for coffee. The mother said hotel life was demoralizing as she bit into an iced biscuit. The porter fetched the paper. Two strange little puppies lapped at the mother's feet, and the porter said they would have to be drowned if they were not claimed before dusk. The mother said what a shame and recalled her own little pups, who didn't eat clothes on the line during the day but when night came got down to work on them.

'You'd be fit to kill them, but of course you couldn't,' she said lamely. She was speaking of puppies from ten or fifteen years back.

He asked if she was enjoying it, and the mother said, 'I quote the saying "See Naples and die," the same applies to this.'

The daughter knew that the mother wanted to go home there and then, but they had booked for four days and it would be an admission of failure to cut it short. She asked the porter to arrange a boat trip to the island inhabited by seabirds, then a car drive to the Lakes of Killarney and another to see the home of the liberator Daniel O'Connell, the man who had asked to have his dead heart sent to Rome, to the Holy See. The porter said certainly and made a great to-do about accepting the tip she gave him. It was he who told them where Daniel O'Connell's heart lay, and the mother said it was the most rending thing she had ever heard, and the most devout. Then she said yes, that a holiday was an uplift, but that it came too late, as she wasn't used to the spoiling. The girl did not like that. To change the conversation the girl produced a postcard that she used as a bookmark. It was a photograph of a gouged torso and she told the porter that was how she felt, that was the state of her mind. The mother said later she didn't think the girl should have said such a thing and wasn't it a bit extreme. Then the mother wrote a six-page letter to her friend Molly and the girl conspired to be the one to post it so that she could read it and find some clue to the chasm that stretched between them. As it happened, she could not bring herself to read it, because the mother gave it to her unsealed, as if she had guessed those thoughts, and the girl bit her lower lip and said, 'How's Molly doing?'

The mother became very sentimental and said, 'Poor creature, blind as a bat,' but added that people were kind and how when they saw her with the white cane, they knew. The letter would be read to her by a daughter who was married and overweight and who suffered with her nerves. The girl recalled an autograph book, the mother's, with its confectionery-colored pages and its likewise rhymes and ditties. The mother recalled ice creams that she had eaten in Brooklyn long before. The mother remembered the embroidery she had done, making the statement in stitches that there was a rose in the heart of New York. The girl said stitches played such an important role in life and said, 'A stitch in time saves nine.' They tittered. They were getting nearer. The girl delicately inquired into the name and occupation of the mother's previous lover, in short, the father's rival. The mother would not divulge, except to say that he loved his mother, loved his sister, was most thoughtful, and that was that. Another long silence. Then the mother stirred in her chair, coughed, confided, said that in fact she and this thoughtful man, fearing, somehow sensing, that they would not be man and wife, had made each other a solemn pact one Sunday afternoon in Coney Island over an ice. They swore that they would get in touch with each other toward the end of their days. Lo and behold, after fifty-five years the mother wrote that letter! The girl's heart quickened, and her blood danced to the news of this tryst, this long-sustained clandestine passion. She felt that something momentous was about to get uttered. They could be true at last, they need not hide from one another's gaze. Her mother would own up. Her own life would not be one of curtained shame. She thought of the married man who was waiting for her in London, the one who took her for delicious weekends, and she shivered. The mother said that her letter had been returned; probably his sister had returned it, always being jealous. The girl begged to know the contents of the letter. The mother said it was harmless. The girl said go on. She tried to revive the spark, but the mother's mind was made up. The mother said that there was no such thing as love between the sexes and that it was all bull. She reaffirmed that there was only one kind of love and that was a mother's love for her child. There passed between them then such a moment, not a moment of sweetness, not a moment of reaffirmation, but a moment dense with hate – one hating and the other receiving it like rays, and then it was glossed over by the mother's remark about the grandeur of the ceiling. The girl gritted her teeth and resolved that they would not be buried in the same grave, and vehemently lit a cigarette, although they had hardly tasted the first course.

'I think you're very unsettled,' her mother said.

'I didn't get that from the ground,' the daughter said.

The mother bridled, stood up to leave, but was impeded by a waiter who was carrying a big chafing dish, over which a bright blue flame riotously spread. She sat down as if pushed down and said that that remark was the essence of cruelty. The girl said sorry. The mother said she had done all she could and that without maid or car or checkbook or any of life's luxuries. Life's dainties had not dropped on her path, she had to knit her own sweaters, cut and sew her own skirts, be her own hairdresser. The girl said for God's sake to let them enjoy it. The mother said that at seventy-eight one had time to think.

'And at thirty-eight,' the girl said.

She wished then that her mother's life had been happier and had not exacted so much from her, and she felt she was being milked emotionally. With all her heart she pitied this woman, pitied her for having her dreams pulped and for betrothing herself to a life of suffering. But also she blamed her. They were both wild with emotion. They were speaking out of turn and eating carelessly; the very food seemed to taunt them. The mother wished that one of those white-coated waiters would tactfully take her plate of dinner away and replace it with a nice warm pot of tea, or better still, that she could be home in her own house by her own fireside, and furthermore she wished that her daughter had never grown into the cruel feelingless hussy that she was.

'What else could I have done?' the mother said.

'A lot,' the girl said, and gulped at once.

The mother excused herself.

'When I pass on, I won't be sorry,' she said.

Up in the room she locked and bolted the door, and lay curled up on the bed, knotted as a foetus, with a clump of paper handkerchiefs in front of her mouth. Downstairs she left behind her a grown girl, remembering a woman she most bottomlessly loved, then unloved, and cut off from herself in the middle of a large dining room while confronting a plate of undercooked lamb strewn with mint.

Death in its way comes just as much of a surprise as birth. We know we will die, just as the mother knows that she is primed to deliver around such and such a time, yet there is a fierce inner exclamation from her at the first onset of labor, and when the water breaks she is already a shocked woman. So it was. The reconciliation that she had hoped for, and indeed intended to instigate, never came. She was abroad at a conference when her mother died, and when she arrived through her own front door, the phone was ringing with the news of her mother's death. The message though clear to her ears was incredible to her. How had her mother died and why? In a hospital in Dublin as a result of a heart attack. Her mother had gone there to do shopping and was taken ill in the street. How fearful that must have been. Straightaway she set back for the airport, hoping to get a seat on a late-night flight.

Her sister would not be going, as she lived now in Australia, lived on a big farm miles from anywhere. Her letters were always pleas for news, for gossip, for books, for magazines. She had mellowed with the years, had grown fat, and was no longer the daffodil beauty. To her it was like seeing pages of life slip away, and she did not bend down to pick them up. They were carried away in the stream of life itself. And yet something tugged. The last plane had gone, but she decided to sit there until dawn and thought to herself that she might be sitting up at her mother's wake. The tube lighting drained the color from all the other waiting faces, and though she could not cry, she longed to tell someone that something incalculable had happened to her. They seemed as tired and as inert as she did. Coffee, bread, whiskey, all tasted the same, tasted of nothing, or at best of blotting paper. There was no man in her life at the moment, no one to ring up and tell the news to. Even if there was, she thought that lovers never know the full story of one another, only know the bit they meet, never know the iceberg of hurts that have gone before, and therefore are always strangers, or semi-strangers, even in the folds of love. She could not cry. She asked herself if perhaps her heart had turned to lead. Yet she dreaded that on impulse she might break down and that an attendant might have to lead her away.

When she arrived at the hospital next day, the remains had been removed and were now on their way through the center of Ireland. Through Joyce's Ireland, as she always called it, and thought of the great central plain open to the elements, the teeming rain, the drifting snow, the winds that gave chapped faces to farmers and cattle dealers and croup to the young calves. She passed the big towns and the lesser towns, recited snatches of recitation that she remembered, and hoped that no one could consider her disrespectful because the hire car was a bright ketchup red. When she got to her own part of the world, the sight of the mountains moved her, as they had always done – solemn, beautiful, unchanging except for different ranges of color. Solid and timeless. She tried to speak to her mother, but found the words artificial. She had bought a sandwich at the airport and now removed the glacé paper with her teeth and bit into it. The two days ahead would be awful. There would be her father's wild grief, there would be her aunt's grief, there would be cousins and friends, and strays and workmen; there would be a grave wide open and as they walked to it they would walk over other graves, under hawthorn, stamping the nettles as they went. She knew the graveyard very well, since childhood. She knew the tombs, the headstones, and the hidden vaults. She used to play there alone and both challenge and cower from ghosts. The inside of the grave was always a rich broody brown, and the gravedigger would probably lace it with a trellis of ivy or convolvulus leaf.

At that very moment she found that she had just caught up with the funeral cortege, but she could hardly believe that it would be her mother's. Too much of a coincidence. They drove at a great pace and without too much respect for the dead. She kept up with them. The light was fading, the bushes were like blurs, the air bat-black; the birds had ceased, and the mountains were dark bulks. If the file of cars took a right from the main road toward the lake town, then it must certainly be her mother's. It did. The thought of catching up with it was what made her cry. She cried with such delight, cried like a child who has done something good and is being praised for it and yet cannot bear the weight of emotion. She cried the whole way through the lakeside town and sobbed as they crossed the old bridge toward the lovely dark leafy country road that led toward home. She cried like a homing bird. She was therefore seen as a daughter deeply distressed when she walked past the file of mourners outside the chapel gate, and when she shook the hands or touched the sleeves of those who had come forward to meet her. Earlier a friend had left flowers at the car-hire desk and she carried them as if she had specially chosen them. She thought, They think it is grief, but it is not the grief they think it is. It is emptiness more than grief. It is a grief at not being able to be wholehearted again. It is not a false grief, but it is unyielding, it is blood from a stone.

Inside the chapel she found her father howling, and in the first rows closest to the altar and to the coffin the chief mourners, both men and women, were sobbing, or, having just sobbed, were drying their eyes. As she shook hands with each one of them, she heard the same condolence – 'Sorry for your trouble, sorry for your trouble, sorry for your trouble.'

That night in her father's house people supped and ate and reminisced. As if in mourning a huge bough of a nearby tree had fallen down. Its roots were like a hand stuck up in the air. The house already reeked of neglect. She kept seeing her mother's figure coming through the door with a large tray, laden down with things. The undertaker called her out. He said since she had not seen the remains he would bring her to the chapel and unscrew the lid. She shrank from it, but she went, because to say no would have brought her disgrace. The chapel was cold, the wood creaked, and even the flowers at night seemed to have departed from themselves, like ghost flowers. Just as he lifted the lid he asked her to please step away, and she thought, Something fateful has happened, the skin has turned black or a finger moves or, the worst, she is not dead, she has merely visited the other world. Then he called her and she walked solemnly over and she almost screamed. The mouth was trying to speak. She was sure of it. One eyelid was not fully shut. It was unfinished. She kissed the face and felt a terrible pity. 'O soul,' she said, 'where are you, on your voyaging, and O soul, are you immortal.'

Suddenly she was afraid of her mother's fate and afraid for the fact that one day she, too, would have to make it. She longed to hold the face and utter consolations to it, but she was unable. She thought of the holiday that had been such a fiasco and the love that she had first so cravenly and so rampantly given and the love that she had so callously and so pointedly taken back. She thought why did she have to withdraw, why do people have to withdraw, why?

After the funeral she went around the house tidying and searching, as if for some secret. In the Blue Room damp had seeped through the walls, and there were little burrs of fungus that clung like bobbins on a hat veiling. In drawers she found bits of her mother's life. Emblems. Wishes. Dreams contained in such things as an exotic gauze rose of the darkest drenchingest red. Perfume bottles, dance shoes, boxes of handkerchiefs, and the returned letter. It was to the man called Vincent, the man her mother had intended to marry but whom she had forsaken when she left New York and came back to Ireland, back to her destiny. For the most part it was a practical letter outlining the size of her farm, the crops they grew, asking about mutual friends, his circumstances, and so forth. It seems he worked in a meat factory. There was only one little leak – 'I think of you, you would not believe how often.' In an instinctive gesture she crumpled the letter up as if it had been her own. The envelope had marked on the outside – *Return to sender.* The words seemed brazen, as if he himself had written them. There were so many hats, with flowers and veiling, all of light color, hats for summer outings, for rainless climes. Ah, the garden parties she must have conceived. Never having had the money for real style, her mother had invested in imitation things – an imitation crocodile handbag and an imitation fur bolero. It felt light, as if made of hair.

There were, too, pink embroidered corsets, long bloomers, and three unworn cardigans.

For some reason she put her hand above the mantelpiece to the place where they hid shillings when she was young. There wrapped in cobweb was an envelope addressed to her in her mother's handwriting. It sent shivers through her, and she prayed that it did not bristle with accusations. Inside, there were some trinkets, a gold sovereign, and some money. The notes were dirty, crumpled, and folded many times. How long had the envelope lain there? How had her mother managed to save? There was no letter, yet in her mind she concocted little tendernesses that her mother might have written – words such as 'Buy yourself a jacket,' or 'Have a night out,' or 'Don't spend this on Masses.' She wanted something, some communiqué. But there was no such thing.

A new wall had arisen, stronger and sturdier than before. Their life together and all those exchanges were like so many spilt feelings, and she looked to see some sign or hear some murmur. Instead, a silence filled the room, and there was a vaster silence beyond, as if the house itself had died or had been carefully put down to sleep.

The Love Object

He simply said my name. He said 'Martha,' and once again I could feel it happening. My legs trembled under the big white cloth and my head became fuzzy, though I was not drunk. It's how I fall in love. He sat opposite. The love object. Elderly. Blue eyes. Khaki hair. The hair was graying on the outside and he had spread the outer gray ribs across the width of his head as if to disguise the khaki, the way some men disguise a patch of baldness. He had what I call a very religious smile. An inner smile that came on and off, governed as it were by his private joy in what he heard or saw: a remark I made, the waiter removing the cold dinner plates that served as ornament and bringing warmed ones of a different design, the nylon curtain blowing inward and brushing my bare, summer-ripened arm. It was the end of a warm London summer.

'I'm not mad about them, either,' he said. We were engaged in a bit of backbiting. Discussing a famous couple we both knew. He kept his hands joined all the time as if they were being put to prayer. There were no barriers between us. We were strangers. I am a television announcer; we had met to do a job, and out of courtesy he asked me to dinner. He told me about his wife – who was thirty like me – and how he knew he would marry her the very first moment he set eyes on her. (She was his third wife.) I made no inquiries as to what she looked like. I still don't know. The only memory I have of her is of her arms sheathed in big, mauve, crocheted sleeves; the image runs away with me and I see his pink, praying hands vanishing into those sleeves and the two of them waltzing in some large, grim room, smiling rapturously at their good fortune in being together. But that came much later.

We had a pleasant supper and figs for afters. The first figs I'd ever tasted. He tested them gently with his fingers, then put three on my side plate. I kept staring down at their purple-black skins, because with the shaking I could not trust myself to peel them. He took my mind off my nervousness by telling me a little story about a girl who was being interviewed on the radio and admitted to owning thirty-seven pairs of shoes and buying a new dress every Saturday, which she later endeavored to sell to friends or family. Somehow I knew that it was a story he had specially selected for me and also that he would not risk telling it to many people. He was in his way a serious man, and famous, though that is hardly of interest when one is telling about a love affair. Or is it? Anyhow, without peeling it, I bit into one of the figs.

How do you describe a taste? They were a new food and he was a new man and that night in my bed he was both stranger and lover, which I used to think was the ideal bed partner.

In the morning he was quite formal but unashamed; he even asked for a clothes brush because there was a smudge of powder on his jacket where we had embraced in the taxi coming home. At the time I had no idea whether or not we would sleep together, but on the whole I felt that we would not. I have never owned a clothes brush. I own books and records and various bottles of scent and beautiful clothes, but I never buy cleaning stuffs or aids for prolonging property. I expect it is improvident, but I just throw things away. Anyhow, he dabbed the powder smear with his handkerchief and it came off quite easily. The other thing he needed was a piece of sticking plaster because a new shoe had cut his heel. I looked but there was none left in the tin. My children had cleared it out during the long summer holidays. In fact, for a moment I saw my two sons throughout those summer days, slouched on chairs, reading comics, riding bicycles, wrestling, incurring cuts which they promptly covered with Elastoplast, and afterward, when the plasters fell, flaunting the brown-rimmed marks as proof of their valor. I missed them badly and longed to hold them in my arms – another reason why I welcomed his company. 'There's no plaster left,' I said, not without shame. I thought how he would think me neglectful. I wondered if I ought to explain why my sons were at boarding school when they were still so young. They were eight and ten. But I didn't. I had ceased to want to tell people the tale of how my marriage had ended and my husband, unable to care for two young boys, insisted on boarding school in order to give them, as he put it, a stabilizing influence. I believed it was done in order to deprive me of the pleasure of their company. I couldn't.

We had breakfast outdoors. The start of another warm day. The dull haze that precedes heat hung from the sky, and in the garden next door the sprinklers were already on. My neighbors are fanatic gardeners. He ate three pieces of toast and some bacon. I ate also, just to put him at his ease, though normally I skip breakfast. 'I'll stock up with plaster, clothes brush, and cleaning fluids,' I said. My way of saying, 'You'll come again?' He saw through it straightaway. Hurrying down the mouthful of toast, he put one of his prayer hands over mine and told me solemnly and nicely that he would not have a mean and squalid little affair with me, but that we would meet in a month or so and he hoped we would become friends. I hadn't thought of us as friends, but it was an interesting possibility. I remembered the earlier part of our evening's conversation and his referring to his earlier wives and his older grown-up children, and I thought how honest and unnostalgic he was. I was really sick of sorrows and people multiplying them even to themselves. Another thing he did that endeared him was to fold back the green silk bedspread, a thing I never do myself.

When he left I felt quite buoyant and in a way relieved. It had been nice and there were no nasty aftereffects. My face was pink from kissing and my hair tossed from our exertions. I looked a little wanton. Feeling tired from such a broken night's sleep, I drew the curtains and got back into bed. I had a nightmare. The usual one, where I am being put to death by a man. People tell me that a nightmare is healthy and from that experience I believe it. I wakened calmer than I had been for months and passed the remainder of the day happily.

Two mornings later he rang and asked was there a chance of our meeting that night. I said yes, because I was not doing anything and it seemed appropriate to have supper and seal our secret decently. But we started recharging.

'We did have a very good time,' he said. I could feel myself making little petrified moves denoting love, shyness; opening my eyes wide to look at him, exuding trust. This time he peeled the figs for both of us. We positioned our legs so that they touched and withdrew them shortly afterward, confident that our desires were flowing. He brought me home. I noticed when we were in bed that he had put cologne on his shoulder and that he must have set out to dinner with the hope if not the intention of sleeping with me. I liked the taste of his skin better than the foul chemical and I had to tell him so. He just laughed. Never had I been so at ease with a man. For the record, I had slept with four other men, but there always seemed to be a distance between us, conversation-wise. I mused for a moment on their various smells as I inhaled his, which reminded me of some herb. It was not parsley, not thyme, not mint, but some nonexistent herb compounded of these three smells. On this second occasion our lovemaking was more relaxed.

'What will you do if you make an avaricious woman out of me?' I asked.

'I will pass you on to someone very dear and suitable,' he said. We coiled together, and with my head on his shoulder I thought of pigeons under the railway bridge nearby, who passed their nights nestled together, heads folded into mauve breasts. In his sleep we kissed and murmured. I did not sleep. I never do when I am overhappy, overunhappy, or in bed with a strange man.

Neither of us said, 'Well, here we are, having a mean and squalid little affair.' We just started to meet. Regularly. We stopped going to restaurants because of his being famous. He would come to my house for dinner. I'll never forget the flurry of those preparations – putting flowers in vases, changing the sheets, thumping knots out of pillows, trying to cook, putting on makeup, and keeping a hairbrush nearby in case he arrived early. The agony of it! It was with difficulty that I answered the doorbell when it finally rang.

'You don't know what an oasis this is,' he would say. And then in the hallway he would put his hands on my shoulders and squeeze them through my thin dress and say, 'Let me look at you,' and I would hang my head, both because I was overwhelmed and because I wanted to be. We would kiss, often for a full five minutes. He kissed the inside of my nostrils. Then we would move to the sitting room and sit on the chaise longue still speechless. He would touch the bone of my knee and say what beautiful knees I had. He saw and admired parts of me that no other man had ever bothered with. Soon after supper we went to bed.

Once, he came unexpectedly in the late afternoon when I was dressed to go out. I was going to the theater with another man.

'How I wish I were taking you,' he said.

'We'll go to the theater one night?' He bowed his head. We would. It was the first time his eyes looked sad. We did not make love because I was made up and had my false eyelashes on and it seemed impractical. He said, 'Has any man ever told you that to see a woman you desire when you cannot do a thing about it leaves you with an ache?'

The ache conveyed itself to me and stayed all through the theater. I felt angry for not having gone to bed with him, and later I regretted it even more, because from that evening onward our meetings were fewer. His wife, who had been in France with their children, returned. I knew this when he arrived one evening in a motorcar and in the course of conversation mentioned that his small daughter had that day peed over an important document. I can tell you now that he was a lawyer.

From then on it was seldom possible to meet at night. He made afternoon dates and at very short notice. Any night he did stay, he arrived with a travel bag containing toothbrush, clothes brush, and a few things a man might need for an overnight, loveless stay in a provincial hotel. I expect she packed it. I thought, How ridiculous. I felt no pity for her. In fact, the mention of her name – it was Helen – made me angry. He said it very harmlessly. He said they'd been burgled in the middle of the night and he'd gone down in his pajamas while his wife telephoned the police from the extension upstairs.

'They only burgle the rich,' I said hurriedly, to change the conversation. It was reassuring to find that he wore pajamas with her, when he didn't with me. My jealousy of her was extreme, and of course grossly unfair. Still, I would be giving the wrong impression if I said her existence blighted our relationship at that point. Because it didn't. He took great care to speak like a single man, and he allowed time after our lovemaking to stay for an hour or so and depart at his leisure. In fact, it is one of those after-love sessions that I consider the cream of our affair. We were sitting on the bed, naked, eating smoked-salmon sandwiches. I had lighted the gas fire because it was well into autumn and the afternoons got chilly. The fire made a steady, purring noise. It was the only light in the room. It was the first time he noticed the shape of my face, because he said that up to then my coloring had drawn all of his admiration. His face and the mahogany chest and the pictures also looked better. Not rosy, because the gas fire did not have that kind of glow, but resplendent with a whitish light. The goatskin rug underneath the window had a special luxurious softness. I remarked on it. He happened to say that he had a slight trace of masochism, and that often, unable to sleep at night in a bed, he would go to some other room and lie on the floor with a coat over him and fall fast asleep. A thing he'd done as a boy. The image of the little boy sleeping on the floor moved me to enormous compassion, and without a word from him, I led him across to the goatskin and laid him down. It was the only time our roles were reversed. He was not my father. I became his mother. Soft and totally fearless. Even my nipples, about which I am squeamish, did not shrink from his rabid demands. I wanted to do everything and anything for him. As often happens with lovers, my ardor and inventiveness stimulated his. We stopped at nothing. Afterward, remarking on our achievement – a thing he always did – he reckoned it was the most intimate of all our intimate moments. I was inclined to agree. As we stood up to get dressed, he wiped his armpits with the white blouse I had been wearing and asked which of my lovely dresses I would wear to dinner that night. He chose my black one for me. He said it gave him great pleasure to know that although I was to dine with others my mind would ruminate on what he and I had done. A wife, work, the world, might separate us, but in our thoughts we were betrothed.

'I'll think of you,' I said.

'And I, of you.'

We were not even sad at parting.

It was after that I had what I can only describe as a dream within a dream. I was coming out of sleep, forcing myself awake, wiping my saliva on the pillow slip, when something pulled me, an enormous weight dragged me down into the bed, and I thought: I have become infirm. I have lost the use of my limbs and this accounts for my listlessness for several months when I've wanted to do nothing except drink tea and stare out the window. I am a cripple. All over. Even my mouth won't move. Only my brain is ticking away. My brain tells me that a woman downstairs doing the ironing is the only one who could locate me, but she might not come upstairs for days, she might think I'm in bed with a man, committing a sin. From time to time I sleep with a man, but normally I sleep alone. She'll leave the ironed clothes on the kitchen table, and the iron itself upright on the floor so that it won't set fire to anything. Blouses will be on hangers, their frilled collars white and fluid like foam. She's the sort of woman who even irons the toes and heels of nylon stockings. She'll slip away, until Thursday, her next day in. I feel something at my back or, strictly speaking, tugging at my bedcovers, which I have mounted right up the length of my back to cover my head. For shelter. And I know now that it's not infirmity that's dragging me down, but a man. How did he get in there? He's on the inside, near the wall. I know what he's going to do to me, and the woman downstairs won't ever come to rescue me, she'd be too ashamed or she might not think I want to be rescued. I don't know which of the men it is, whether it's the big tall bruiser that's at the door every time I open it innocently, expecting it's the laundry boy and find it's Him, with an old black carving knife, its edge glittering because he's just sharpened it on a step. Before I can scream, my tongue isn't mine anymore. Or it might be the Other One. Tall too, he gets me by my bracelet as I slip between the banisters of the stairs. I've forgotten that I am not a little girl anymore and that I don't slip easily between banisters. If the bracelet snapped in two I would have made my escape, leaving him with one half of a gold bracelet in his hand, but my goddamn provident mother had a safety chain put on it because it was nine-carat. Anyhow, he's in the bed. It will go on forever, the thing he wants. I daren't turn around to look at him. Then something gentle about the way the sheet is pulled down suggests that he might be the New One. The man I met a few weeks ago. Not my type at all, tiny broken veins on his cheeks, and red, actually red, hair. We were on a goatskin. But it was raised off the ground, high as a bed. I had been doing most of the

loving; breasts, hands, mouth, all yearned to minister to him. I felt
so sure, never have I felt so sure of the rightness of what I was
doing. Then he started kissing me down there and I came to his
lapping tongue and his head was under my buttocks and it was
like I was bearing him, only there was pleasure instead of pain. He
trusted me. We were two people, I mean, he wasn't someone on
me, smothering me, doing something I couldn't see. I could see. I
could have shat on his red hair if I wanted. He trusted me. He
stretched the come to the very last. And all the things that I loved
up to then, like glass or lies, mirrors and feathers, and pearl
buttons, and silk, and willow trees, became secondary compared
with what he'd done. He was lying so that I could see it: so
delicate, so thin, with a bunch of worried blue veins along its sides.
Talking to it was like talking to a little child. The light in the
room was a white glow. He'd made me very soft and wet, so I put
it in. It was quick and hard and forceful, and he said, 'I'm not
considering you now, I think we've considered you,' and I said
that was perfectly true and that I liked him roughing away. I said
it. I was no longer a hypocrite, no longer a liar. Before that he
had often remonstrated with me, he had said, 'There are words
we are not going to use to each other, words such as "Sorry" and
"Are you angry?"' I had used these words a lot. So I think from
the gentle shuffle of the bedcovers – like a request really – that it
might be him, and if it is I want to sink down and down into the
warm, dark, sleepy pit of the bed and stay in it forever, coming
with him. But I am afraid to look in case it is not Him but One of
the Others.

When I finally woke up I was in a panic and I had a dreadful
urge to telephone him, but though he never actually forbade it, I
knew he would have been most displeased.

When something has been perfect, as our last encounter in the
gaslight had been, there is a tendency to try hard to repeat it.
Unfortunately, the next occasion was clouded. He came in the

afternoon and brought a suitcase containing all the paraphernalia for a dress dinner which he was attending that night. When he arrived he asked if he could hang up his tails, as otherwise they would be very creased. He hooked the hanger on the outer rim of the wardrobe, and I remember being impressed by the row of war medals along the top pocket. Our time in bed was pleasant but hasty. He worried about getting dressed. I just sat and watched him. I wanted to ask about his medals and how he had merited them, and if he remembered the war, and if he'd missed his then wife, and if he'd killed people, and if he still dreamed about it. But I asked nothing. I sat there as if I were paralyzed.

'No braces,' he said as he held the wide black trousers around his middle. His other trousers must have been supported by a belt.

'I'll go to Woolworth's for some,' I said. But that was impractical because he was already in danger of being late. I got a safety pin and fastened the trousers from the back. It was a difficult operation because the pin was not really sturdy enough.

'You'll bring it back?' I said. I am superstitious about giving people pins. He took some time to reply because he was muttering 'Damn' under his breath. Not to me. But to the stiff, inhuman, starched collar, which would not yield to the little gold studs he had wanted to pierce through. I tried. He tried. Each time when one of us failed the other became impatient. He said if we went on, the collar would be grubby from our hands. And that seemed a worse alternative. I thought he must be dining with very critical people, but of course I did not give my thoughts on the matter. In the end we each managed to get a stud through and he had a small sip of whiskey as a celebration. The bow tie was another ordeal. He couldn't do it. I daren't try.

'Haven't you done it before?' I said. I expect his wives – in succession – had done it for him. I felt such a fool. Then a lump of hatred. I thought how ugly and pink his legs were, how repellent the shape of his body, which did not have anything in the way of a waist, how deceitful his eyes, which congratulated himself in the mirror when he succeeded in making a clumsy bow. As he put on the coat the sound of the medals tinkling enabled me to remark on their music. There was so little I could say. Lastly he donned a white silk scarf that came below his middle. He looked like someone I did not know. He left hurriedly. I ran with him down the road to help get a taxi, and trying to keep up with him and chatter was not easy. All I can remember is the ghostly sight of the very white scarf swinging back and forth as we rushed. His shoes, which were patent, creaked unsuitably.

'Is it all-male?' I asked.

'No. Mixed,' he replied.

So that was why we hurried. To meet his wife at some appointed place. The hatred began to grow.

He did bring back the safety pin, but my superstition remained, because four straight pins with black rounded tops that had come off his new shirt were on my window ledge. He refused to take them. *He* was not superstitious.

Bad moments, like good ones, tend to be grouped together, and when I think of the dress occasion, I also think of the other time when we were not in utter harmony. It was on a street; we were searching for a restaurant. We had to leave my house because a friend had come to stay and we would have been obliged to tolerate her company. Going along the street – it was October and very windy – I felt that he was angry with me for having drawn us out into the cold where we could not embrace. My heels were very high and I was ashamed of the hollow sound they made. In a way I felt we were enemies. He looked in the windows of restaurants to see if any acquaintances of his were there. Two restaurants he decided against, for reasons best known to himself. One looked to be very attractive. It had orange bulbs inset in the walls and the light came through small squares of iron grating. We crossed the road to look at places on the opposite side. I saw a group of rowdies coming toward us, and for something to say – what with my aggressive heels, the wind, traffic going by, the ugly unromantic street, we had run out of agreeable conversation – I asked if he ever felt apprehensive about encountering noisy groups like that, late at night. He said that in fact a few nights before he had been walking home very late and saw such a group coming toward him, and before he even registered fear, he found that he had splayed his bunch of keys between his fingers and had his hand, armed with the sharp points of the keys, ready to pull out of his pocket should they have threatened him. I suppose he did it again while we were walking along. Curiously enough, I did not feel he was my protector. I only felt that he and I were two people, that there was in the world trouble, violence, sickness, catastrophe, that he faced it in one way and that I faced it – or to be exact, that I shrank from it – in another. We would always be outside one another. In the course of that melancholy thought the group went by, and my conjecture about violence was all for nothing. We found a nice restaurant and drank a lot of wine.

Later our lovemaking, as usual, was perfect. He stayed all night. I used to feel specially privileged on the nights he stayed, and the only little thing that lessened my joy was spasms of anxiety in case he should have told his wife he was at such and such a hotel and her telephoning there and not finding him. More than once I raced into an imaginary narrative where she came and discovered us and I acted silent and ladylike and he told her very crisply to wait outside until he was ready. I felt no pity for her. Sometimes I wondered if we would ever meet or if in fact we had already met on an escalator at some point. Though that was unlikely, because we lived at opposite ends of London.

Then to my great surprise the opportunity came. I was invited to a Thanksgiving party given by an American magazine. He saw the card on my mantelpiece and said, 'You're going to that, too?' and I smiled and said maybe. Was he? 'Yes,' he said. He tried to make me reach a decision there and then but I was too canny. Of course I would go. I was curious to see his wife. I would meet him in public. It shocked me to think that we had never met in the company of any other person. It was like being shut off . . . a little animal locked away. I thought very distinctly of a ferret that a forester used to keep in a wooden box with a sliding top, when I was a child, and of another ferret being brought to mate with it once. The thought made me shiver. I mean, I got it confused; I thought of white ferrets with their little pink nostrils in the same breath as I thought of him sliding a door back and slipping into my box from time to time. His skin had a lot of pink in it.

'I haven't decided,' I said, but when the day came I went. I took a lot of trouble with my appearance, had my hair set, and wore virginal attire. Black and white. The party was held in a large room with paneled walls of brown wood; blown-up magazine covers were along the panels. The bar was at one end, under a balcony. The effect was of shrunken barmen in white, lost underneath the cliff of the balcony, which seemed in danger of collapsing on them. A more unlikely room for a party I have never seen. There were women going around with trays, but I had to go to the bar because there was champagne on the trays and I have a preference for whiskey. A man I knew conducted me there, and en route another man placed a kiss on my back. I hoped that he witnessed this, but it was such a large room with hundreds of people around that I had no idea where he was. I noticed a dress I quite admired, a mauve dress with very wide crocheted sleeves. Looking up the length of the sleeves, I saw its owner's eyes directed on me. Perhaps she was admiring my outfit. People with the same tastes often do. I have no idea what her face looked like, but later when I asked a girl friend which was his wife, she pointed to this woman with the crocheted sleeves. The second time I saw her in profile. I still don't know what she looked like, nor do those eyes into which I looked speak to my memory with anything special, except, perhaps, slight covetousness.

Finally, I searched him out. I had a mutual friend walk across with me and apparently introduce me. He was unwelcoming. He looked strange, the flush on his cheekbones vivid and unnatural. He spoke to the mutual friend and virtually ignored me. Possibly to make amends he asked, at length, if I was enjoying myself.

'It's a chilly room,' I said. I was referring of course to his manner. Had I wanted to describe the room I would have used 'grim,' or some such adjective.

'I don't know about you being chilly but I'm certainly not,' he said with aggression. Then a very drunk woman in a sack dress came and took his hand and began to slobber over him. I excused myself and went off. He said most pointedly that he hoped he would see me again some time.

I caught his eye just as I left the party, and I felt both sorry for him and angry with him. He looked stunned, as if important news had just been delivered to him. He saw me leave with a group of people and I stared at him without the whimper of a smile. Yes, I was sorry for him. I was also piqued. The very next day when we met and I brought it up, he did not even remember that a mutual friend had introduced us.

'Clement Hastings!' he said, repeating the man's name. Which goes to show how nervous he must have been.

It is impossible to insist that bad news delivered in a certain manner and at a certain time will have a less awful effect. But I feel that I got my walking papers from him at the wrong moment. For one thing, it was morning. The clock went off and I sat up wondering when he had set it. Being on the outside of the bed, he was already attending to the push button.

'I'm sorry, darling,' he said.

'Did you set it?' I said, indignant. There was an element of betrayal here, as if he'd wanted to sneak away without saying goodbye.

'I must have,' he said. He put his arm around me and we lay back again. It was dark outside and there was a feeling – though this may be memory feeling – of frost.

'Congratulations, you're getting your prize today,' he whispered. I was being given an award for my announcing.

'Thank you,' I said. I was ashamed of it. It reminded me of being back at school and always coming first in everything and being guilty about this but not disciplined enough to deliberately hold back.

'It's beautiful that you stayed all night,' I said. I was stroking him all over. My hands were never still in bed. Awake or asleep, I constantly caressed him. Not to excite him, simply to reassure and comfort him and perhaps to consolidate my ownership. There is something about holding on to things that I find therapeutic. For hours I hold smooth stones in the palm of my hand or I grip the sides of an armchair and feel the better for it. He kissed me. He said he had never known anyone so sweet or so attentive. Encouraged, I began to do something very intimate. I heard his sighs of pleasure, the 'oy, oy' of delight when he was both indulging it and telling himself that he mustn't. At first I was unaware of his speaking voice.

'Hey,' he said jocularly, just like that. 'This can't go on, you know.' I thought he was referring to our activity at that moment, because of course it was late and he would have to get up shortly. Then I raised my head from its sunken position between his legs and I looked at him through my hair, which had fallen over my face. I saw that he was serious.

'It just occurred to me that possibly you love me,' he said. I nodded and pushed my hair back so that he would read it, my testimony, clear and clean upon my face. He put me lying down so that our heads were side by side and he began:

'I adore you, but I'm not in love with you; with my commitments I don't think I could be in love with anyone, it all started gay and lighthearted . . .' Those last few words offended me. It was not how I saw it or how I remembered it: the numerous telegrams he sent me saying, 'I long to see you,' or 'May the sun shine on you,' the first few moments each time when we met and were overcome with passion, shyness, and the shock of being so disturbed by each other's presence. We had even searched in our dictionaries for words to convey the specialness of our regard for each other. He came up with 'cense,' which meant to adore or cover with the perfume of love. It was a most appropriate word, and we used it over and over again. Now he was negating all this. He was talking about weaving me into his life, his family life . . . becoming a friend. He said it, though, without conviction. I could not think of a single thing to say. I knew that if I spoke I would be pathetic, so I remained silent. When he'd finished I stared straight ahead at the split between the curtains, and looking at the beam of raw light coming through, I said, 'I think there's frost outside,' and he said that possibly there was, because winter was upon us. We got up, and as usual he took the bulb out of the bedside lamp and plugged in his razor. I went off to get breakfast. That was the only morning I forgot about squeezing orange juice for him and I often wonder if he took it as an insult. He left just before nine.

The sitting room held the traces of his visit. Or, to be precise, the remains of his cigars. In one of the blue, saucer-shaped ashtrays there were thick turds of dark-gray cigar ash. There were also stubs, but it was the ash I kept looking at, thinking that its thickness resembled the thickness of his unlovely legs. And once again I experienced hatred for him. I was about to tip the contents of the ashtray into the fire grate when something stopped me, and what did I do but get an empty lozenge box and with the aid of a sheet of paper lift the clumps of ash in there and carry the tin upstairs. With the movement the turds lost their shape, and whereas they had reminded me of his legs, they were now an even mass of dark-gray ash, probably like the ashes of the dead. I put the tin in a drawer underneath some clothes.

Later in the day I was given my award – a very big silver medallion with my name on it. At the party afterward I got drunk. My friends tell me that I did not actually disgrace myself, but I have a humiliating recollection of beginning a story and not being able to go ahead with it, not because the contents eluded me, but because the words became too difficult to pronounce. A man brought me home, and after I'd made him a cup of tea, I said good night overproperly; then when he was gone I staggered to my bed. When I drink heavily I sleep badly. It was still dark outside when I woke up and straightaway I remembered the previous morning and the suggestion of frost outside, and his cold warning words. I had to agree. Although our meetings were perfect, I had a sense of doom impending, of a chasm opening up between us, of someone telling his wife, of souring love, of destruction. And still we hadn't gone as far as we should have gone. There were peaks of joy and of its opposite that we should have climbed to, but the time was not left to us. He had of course said, 'You still have a great physical hold over me,' and that in its way I found degrading. To have gone on making love when he had discarded me would have been repellent. It had come to an end. The thing I kept thinking of was a violet in a wood and how a time comes for it to drop off and die. The frost may have had something to do with my thinking, or rather, with my musing. I got up and put on a dressing gown. My head hurt from the hangover, but I knew that I must write to him while I had some resolution. I know my own failings, and I knew that before the day was out I would want to see him again, sit with him, coax him back with sweetness and my overwhelming helplessness.

I wrote the note and left out the bit about the violet. It is not a thing you can put down on paper without seeming fanciful. I said if he didn't think it prudent to see me, then not to see me. I said it had been a nice interlude and that we must entertain good memories of it. It was a remarkably controlled letter. He wrote back promptly. My decision came as a shock, he said. Still, he admitted that I was right. In the middle of the letter he said he must penetrate my composure and to do so he must admit that above and beyond everything he loved me and would always do so. That of course was the word I had been snooping around for, for months. It set me off. I wrote a long letter back to him. I lost my head. I oversaid everything. I testified to loving him, to sitting on the edge of madness in the intervening days, to my hoping for a miracle.

It is just as well that I did not write out the miracle in detail, because possibly it is, or was, rather inhuman. It concerned his family.

He was returning from the funeral of his wife and children, wearing black tails. He also wore the white silk scarf I had seen him with, and there was a black mourning tulip in his buttonhole. When he came toward me I snatched the black tulip and replaced it with a white narcissus, and he in turn put the scarf around my neck and drew me toward him by holding its fringed ends. I kept moving my neck back and forth within the embrace of the scarf. Then we danced divinely on a wooden floor that was white and slippery. At times I thought we would fall, but he said, 'You don't have to worry, I'm with you.' The dance floor was also a road and we were going somewhere beautiful.

For weeks I waited for a reply to my letter, but there was none. More than once I had my hand on the telephone, but something cautionary – a new sensation for me – in the back of my mind bade me to wait. To give him time. To let regret take charge of his heart. To let him come of his own accord. And then I panicked. I thought that perhaps the letter had gone astray or had fallen into other hands. I'd posted it, of course, to the office in Lincoln's Inn where he worked. I wrote another. This time it was a formal note, and with it I enclosed a postcard with the words YES and NO. I asked if he had received my previous letter to kindly let me know by simply crossing out the word which did not apply on my card, and send it back to me. It came back with the NO crossed out. Nothing else. So he had received my letter. I think I looked at the card for hours. I could not stop shaking, and to calm myself I took several drinks. There was something so brutal about the card, but then you could say that I had asked for it by approaching the situation in that way. I took out the box with his ash in it and wept over it, and wanted both to toss it out of the window and to preserve it forevermore.

In general I behaved very strangely. I rang someone who knew him and asked for no reason at all what she thought his hobbies might be. She said he played the harmonium, which I found unbearable news altogether. Then I entered a black patch, and on the third day I lost control.

Well, from not sleeping and taking pep pills and whiskey, I got very odd. I was shaking all over and breathing very quickly, the way one might after witnessing an accident. I stood at my bedroom window, which is on the second floor, and looked at the concrete underneath. The only flowers left in bloom were the hydrangeas, and they had faded to a soft russet, which was much more fetching than the harsh pink they were all summer. In the garden next door there were frost hats over the fuchsias. Looking first at the hydrangeas, then at the fuchsias, I tried to estimate the consequences of my jumping. I wondered if the drop were great enough. Being physically awkward I could only conceive of injuring myself fatally, which would be worse, because I would then be confined to my bed and imprisoned with the very thoughts that were driving me to desperation. I opened the window and leaned out, but quickly drew back. I had a better idea. There was a plumber downstairs installing central heating – an enterprise I had embarked upon when my lover began to come regularly and we liked walking around naked eating sandwiches and playing records. I decided to gas myself and to seek the help of the plumber in order to do it efficiently. I am aware – someone must have told me – that there comes a point in the middle of the operation when the doer regrets it and tries to withdraw but cannot. That seemed like an extra note of tragedy that I had no wish to experience. So I decided to go downstairs to this man and explain to him that I *wanted* to die, and that I was not telling him simply for him to prevent me, or console me, that I was not looking for pity – there comes a time when pity is of no help – and that I simply wanted his assistance. He could show me what to do, settle me down, and – this is absurd – be around to take care of the telephone and the doorbell for the next few hours. Also to dispose of me with dignity. Above all, I wanted that. I even decided what I would wear: a long dress, which in fact was the same color as the hydrangeas in their russet phase and which I've never worn except for a photograph or on television. Before going downstairs, I wrote a note which said simply: 'I am committing suicide through lack of intelligence, and through not knowing, not learning to know, how to live.'

You will think I am callous not to have taken the existence of my children into account. But, in fact, I did. Long before the affair began, I had reached the conclusion that they had been parted from me irrevocably by being sent to boarding school. If you like, I felt I had let them down years before. I thought – it was an unhysterical admission – that my being alive or my being dead made little difference to the course of their lives. I ought to say that I had not seen them for a month, and it is a shocking fact that although absence does not make love less, it cools down our physical need for the ones we love. They were due home for their mid-term holiday that very day, but since it was their father's turn to have them, I knew that I would only see them for a few hours one afternoon. And in my despondent state that seemed worse than not seeing them at all.

Well, of course, when I went downstairs the plumber took one look at me and said, 'You could do with a cup of tea.' He actually had tea made. So I took it and stood there warming my child-sized hands around the barrel of the brown mug. Suddenly, swiftly, I remembered my lover measuring our hands when we were lying in bed and saying that mine were no bigger than his daughter's. And then I had another and less edifying memory about hands. It was the time we met when he was visibly distressed because he'd caught those same daughter's hands in a motorcar door. The fingers had not been broken but were badly bruised, and he felt awful about it and hoped his daughter would forgive him. Upon being told the story, I bolted off into an anecdote about almost losing *my* fingers in the door of someone's Jaguar. It was pointless, although a listener might infer from it that I was a boastful and heartless girl. I would have been sorry for any child whose fingers were caught in a motorcar door, but at that moment I was trying to recall him to the hidden world of him and me. Perhaps it was one of the things that made him like me less. Perhaps it was then he resolved to end the affair. I was about to say this to the plumber, to warn him about so-called love often hardening the heart, but like the violets, it is something that can miss awfully, and when it does two people are mortally embarrassed. He'd put sugar in my tea and I found it sickly.

'I want you to help me,' I said.

'Anything,' he said. I ought to know that. We were friends. He would do the pipes tastefully. The pipes would be little works of art and the radiators painted to match the walls.

'You may think I will paint these white, but in fact they will be light ivory,' he said. The whitewash on the kitchen walls had yellowed a bit.

'I want to do myself in,' I said hurriedly.

'Good God,' he said, and then burst out laughing. He always knew I was dramatic. Then he looked at me, and obviously my face was a revelation. For one thing I could not control my breathing. He put his arm around me and led me into the sitting room and we had a drink. I knew he liked drink and thought, It's an ill wind that doesn't blow some good. The maddening thing was that I kept thinking a live person's thoughts. He said I had so much to live for. 'A young girl like you – people wanting your autograph, a lovely new car,' he said.

'It's all . . .' I groped for the word. I had meant to say 'meaningless,' but 'cruel' was the word that came out.

'And your boys,' he said. 'What about your boys?' He had seen photographs of them, and once I'd read him a letter from one of them. The word 'cruel' seemed to be blazing in my head. It screamed at me from every corner of the room. To avoid his glance, I looked down at the sleeve of my angora jersey and methodically began picking off pieces of fluff and rolling them into a little ball.

There was a moment's pause.

'This is an unlucky road. You're the third,' he said.

'The third what?' I said, industriously piling the black fluff into my palm.

'A woman farther up; her husband was a bandleader, used to be out late. One night she went to the dance hall and saw him with another girl; she came home and did it straightaway.'

'Gas?' I asked, genuinely curious.

'No, sedation,' he said, and was off on another story about a girl who'd gassed herself and was found by him because he was in the house treating dry rot at the time. 'Naked, except for a jersey,' he said, and speculated on why she should be attired like that. His manner changed considerably as he recalled how he went into the house, smelled gas, and searched it out.

I looked at him. His face was grave. He had scaled eyelids. I had never looked at him so closely before. 'Poor Michael,' I said. A feeble apology. I was thinking that if he had abetted my suicide he would then have been committed to the memory of it.

'A lovely young girl,' he said, wistful.

'Poor girl,' I said, mustering up pity.

There seemed to be nothing else to say. He had shamed me out of it. I stood up and made an effort at normality – I took some glasses off a side table and moved in the direction of the kitchen. If dirty glasses are any proof of drinking, then quite a lot of it had been done by me over the past few days.

'Well,' he said, and rose and sighed. He admitted to feeling pleased with himself.

As it happened, there would have been a secondary crisis that day. Although my children were due to return to their father, he rang to say that the older boy had a temperature, and since – though he did not say this – he could not take care of a sick child, he would be obliged to bring them to my house. They arrived in the afternoon. I was waiting inside the door, with my face heavily made up to disguise my distress. The sick boy had a blanket draped over his tweed coat and one of his father's scarves around his face. When I embraced him, he began to cry. The younger boy went around the house to make sure that everything was as he had last seen it. Normally I had presents for them on their return home, but I had neglected it on this occasion, and consequently they were a little downcast.

'Tomorrow,' I said.

'Why are there tears in your eyes?' the sick boy asked as I undressed him.

'Because you are sick,' I said, telling a half-truth.

'Oh, Mamsies,' he said, calling me by a name he had used for years. He put his arms around me and we both began to cry. I felt he was crying for the numerous unguessed afflictions that the circumstances of a broken home would impose upon him. It was strange and unsatisfying to hold him in my arms, when over the months I had got used to my lover's size – the width of his shoulders, the exact height of his body, which obliged me to stand on tiptoe so that our limbs could correspond perfectly. Holding my son, I was conscious only of how small he was and how tenaciously he clung.

The younger boy and I sat in the bedroom and played a game which entailed reading out questions such as 'A river?' 'A famous footballer?' and then spinning a disk until it steadied down at one letter and using that letter as the first initial of the river or the famous footballer or whatever the question called for. I was quite slow at it, and so was the sick boy. His brother won easily, although I had asked him to let the invalid win. Children are callous.

We all jumped when the heating came on, because the boiler, from the basement just underneath, gave an almighty churning noise and made the kind of sudden erupting move I had wanted to make that morning when I stood at the bedroom window and tried to pitch myself out. As a special surprise and to cheer me up, the plumber had called in two of his mates, and among them they got the job finished. To make us warm and happy, as he put it when he came to the bedroom to tell me. It was an awkward moment. I'd avoided him since our morning's drama. At teatime I'd even left his tea on a tray out on the landing. Would he tell other people how I had asked him to be my murderer? Would he have recognized it as that? I gave him and his friends a drink, and they stood uncomfortably in the children's bedroom and looked at the little boy's flushed face and said he would soon be better. What else could they say!

For the remainder of the evening, the boys and I played the quiz game over and over again, and just before they went to sleep I read them an adventure story. In the morning they both had temperatures. I was busy nursing them for the next couple of weeks. I made beef tea a lot and broke bread into it and coaxed them to swallow those sops of savory bread. They were constantly asking to be entertained. The only thing I could think of in the way of facts were particles of nature lore I had gleaned from one of my colleagues in the television canteen. Even with embellishing, it took not more than two minutes to tell my children: of a storm of butterflies in Venezuela, of animals called sloths that are so lazy they hang from trees and become covered with moss, and of how the sparrows in England sing different from the sparrows in Paris.

'More,' they would say. 'More, more.' Then we would have to play that silly game again or embark upon another adventure story.

At these times I did not allow my mind to wander, but in the evenings, when their father came, I used to withdraw to the sitting room and have a drink. Well, that was disastrous. The leisure enabled me to brood; also, I have very weak bulbs in the lamps and the dimness gives the room a quality that induces reminiscence. I would be transported back. I enacted various kinds of reunion with my lover, but my favorite one was an unexpected meeting in one of those tiled, inhuman, pedestrian subways and running toward each other and finding ourselves at a stairway which said (one in London actually does say), TO CENTRAL ISLAND ONLY, and laughing as we leaped up those stairs propelled by miraculous wings. In less indulgent phases, I regretted that we hadn't seen more sunsets, or cigarette advertisements, or something, because in memory our numerous meetings became one long uninterrupted state of lovemaking without the ordinariness of things in between to fasten those peaks. The days, the nights with him, seemed to have been sandwiched into a long, beautiful, but single night, instead of being stretched to the seventeen occasions it actually was. Ah, vanished peaks. Once I was so sure that he had come into the room that I tore off a segment of an orange I had just peeled, and handed it to him.

But from the other room I heard the low, assured voice of the children's father delivering information with the self-importance of a man delivering dogmas, and I shuddered at the degree of poison that lay between us when we'd once professed to love. Plagued love. Then, some of the feeling I had for my husband transferred itself to my lover, and I reasoned with myself that the letter in which he had professed to love me was sham, that he had merely written it when he thought he was free of me, but finding himself saddled once again, he withdrew and let me have the post-card. I was a stranger to myself. Hate was welling up. I wished multitudes of humiliation on him. I even plotted a dinner party that I would attend, having made sure that he was invited, and snubbing him throughout. My thoughts teetered between hate and the hope of something final between us, so that I would be certain of his feelings toward me. Even as I sat in a bus, an adver-tisement which caught my eye was immediately related to him. It said, DON'T PANIC, WE MEND, WE ADAPT, WE REMODEL. It was an advertisement for pearl stringing. I would mend and with vengeance.

I cannot say when it first began to happen, because that would be too drastic, and anyhow, I do not know. But the children were back at school, and we'd got over Christmas, and he and I had not exchanged cards. But I began to think less harshly of him. They were silly thoughts, really. I hoped he was having little pleasures like eating in restaurants, and clean socks, and red wine the temperature he liked it, and even – yes, even ecstasies in bed with his wife. These thoughts made me smile to myself inwardly, the new kind of smile I had discovered. I shuddered at the risk he'd run by seeing me at all. Of course, the earlier injured thoughts battled with these new ones. It was like carrying a taper along a corridor where the drafts are fierce and the chances of it staying alight pretty meager. I thought of him and my children in the same instant, their little foibles became his: my children telling me elaborate lies about their sporting feats, his slight puffing when we climbed steps and his trying to conceal it. The age difference between us must have saddened him. It was then I think that I really fell in love with him. His courtship of me, his telegrams, his eventual departure, even our lovemaking were nothing compared with this new sensation. It rose like sap within me, it often made me cry, the fact that he could not benefit from it! The temptation to ring him had passed away.

His phone call came quite out of the blue. It was one of those times when I debated about answering it or not, because mostly I let it ring. He asked if we could meet, if, and he said this so gently, my nerves were steady enough. I said my nerves were never better. That was a liberty I had to take. We met in a café for tea. Toast again. Just like the beginning. He asked how I was. Remarked on my good complexion. Neither of us mentioned the incident of the postcard. Nor did he say what impulse had moved him to telephone. It may not have been impulse at all. He talked about his work and how busy he'd been, and then relayed a little story about taking an elderly aunt for a drive and driving so slowly that she asked him to please hurry up because she would have walked there quicker.

'You've recovered,' he said then, suddenly. I looked at his face. I could see it was on his mind.

'I'm over it,' I said, and dipped my finger into the sugar bowl and let him lick the white crystals off the tip of my finger. Poor man. I could not have told him anything else, he would not have understood. In a way it was like being with someone else. He was not the one who had folded back the bedspread and sucked me dry and left his cigar ash for preserving. He was the representative of that one.

'We'll meet from time to time,' he said.

'Of course.' I must have looked dubious.

'Perhaps you don't want to?'

'Whenever you feel you would like to.' I neither welcomed nor dreaded the thought. It would not make any difference to how I felt. That was the first time it occurred to me that all my life I had feared imprisonment, the nun's cell, the hospital bed, the places where one faced the self without distraction, without the crutches of other people – but sitting there feeding him white sugar, I thought, I now have entered a cell, and this man cannot know what it is for me to love him the way I do, and I cannot weigh him down with it, because he is in another cell confronted with other difficulties.

The cell reminded me of a convent, and for something to say, I mentioned my sister the nun.

'I went to see my sister.'

'How is she?' he asked. He had often inquired about her. He used to take an interest in her and ask what she looked like. I even got the impression that he had a fantasy about seducing her.

'She's fine,' I said. 'We were walking down a corridor and she asked me to look around and make sure that there weren't any other sisters looking, and then she hoisted her skirts up and slid down the banister.'

'Dear girl,' he said. He liked that story. The smallest things gave him such pleasure.

I enjoyed our tea. It was one of the least fruitless afternoons I'd had in months, and coming out he gripped my arm and said how perfect it would be if we could get away for a few days. Perhaps he meant it.

In fact, we kept our promise. We do meet from time to time. You could say things are back to normal again. By normal I mean a state whereby I notice the moon, trees, fresh spit upon the pavement; I look at strangers and see in their expressions something of my own predicament; I am part of everyday life, I suppose. There is a lamp in my bedroom that gives out a dry crackle each time an electric train goes by, and at night I count those crackles because it is the time he comes back. I mean the real he, not the man who confronts me from time to time across a café table, but the man that dwells somewhere within me. He rises before my eyes – his praying hands, his tongue that liked to suck, his sly eyes, his smile, the veins on his cheeks, the calm voice speaking sense to me. I suppose you wonder why I torment myself like this with details of his presence, but I need it, I cannot let go of him now, because if I did, all our happiness and my subsequent pain – I cannot vouch for his – will all have been nothing, and nothing is a dreadful thing to hold on to.

Number Ten

Everything began to be better for Mrs. Reinhardt from the moment she started to sleepwalk. Every night her journey yielded a fresh surprise. First it was that she saw sheep – not sheep as one sees them in life, a bit sooty and bleating away, but sheep as one sees them in a dream. She saw myriads of white fleece on a hilltop, surrounded by little lambs frisking and suckling to their heart's content.

Then she saw pictures such as she had not seen in life. Her husband owned an art gallery and Mrs. Reinhardt had the opportunity to see many pictures, yet the ones she saw at night were much more satisfying. For one thing she was inside them. She was not an outsider looking in, making idiotic remarks, she was part of the picture: an arm or a lily or the grey mane of a horse. She did not have to compete, did not have to say anything. All her movements were preordained. She was simply aware of her own breath, a soft, steady, sustaining breath.

In the mornings her husband would say she looked a bit frayed or a bit intense, and she would say, 'Nonsense,' because in twenty years of marriage she had never felt better. Her sleeping life suited her and, of course, she never knew what to expect. Her daily life had a pattern to it. Weekday mornings she spent at home, helping or supervising Fatima, the Spanish maid. She gave two afternoons a week to teaching autistic children, two afternoons were devoted to an exercise class, and on Fridays she shopped in Harrods and got all the groceries for the weekend. Mr. Reinhardt had bought a farm two years before, and weekends they spent in the country, in their newly renovated cottage. In the country she did not sleep-walk, and Mrs. Reinhardt wondered if it might be that she was inhibited by the barbed-wire fence that skirted their garden. But there are gates, she thought, and I should open them. She was a little vexed with herself for not being more venturesome.

Then one May night, back in her house in London, she had an incredible dream. She walked over a field with her son – in real life he was at university – and all of a sudden, and in unison, the two of them knelt down and began scraping the earth up with their bare hands. It was a rich red earth and easy to crumble. They were so eager because they knew that treasure was about to be theirs. Sure enough, they found bits of gold, tiny specks of it which they put in a handkerchief, and then to crown her happiness Mrs. Reinhardt found the loveliest little gold key, and held it up to the light while her son laughed and in a baby voice said, 'Mama.'

Soon after this dream Mrs. Reinhardt embarked on a bit of spring cleaning. Curtains and carpets for the dry cleaners, drawers depleted of all the old useless odds and ends that had been piling up. Her husband's clothing, too, she must put in order. A little rift had sprung up between them and was widening day by day. He was moody. He got home later than usual and, though he did not say so, she knew that he had stopped at the corner and had a few drinks. Once that spring he had pulled her down beside him on the living-room sofa and stroked her thighs and started to undress her within hearing distance of Fatima, who was in the kitchen chopping and singing. Always chopping and singing or humming. For the most part, though, Mr. Reinhardt went straight to the liquor cabinet and gave them both a gin, pouring himself a bigger one because, as he said, all her bloody fasting made Mrs. Reinhardt light-headed.

She was sorting Mr. Reinhardt's shirts – T-shirts, summer sweaters, thick crew-neck sweaters – and putting them each in a neat pile, when out of his seersucker jacket there tumbled a little gold key that caused her to let out a cry. The first thing she felt was a jet of fear. Then she bent down and picked it up. It was exactly like the one in her sleepwalk. She held it in her hand, promising herself never to let it go. What fools we are to pursue in daylight what we should leave for nighttime.

Her next sleepwalking brought Mrs. Reinhardt out of her house into a waiting taxi and, some distance away, to a mews house. Outside the mews house was a black and white tub filled with pretty flowers. She simply put her hand under a bit of foliage and there was the latchkey. Inside was a little nest. The wallpaper in the hall was the very one she had always wanted for their house, a pale gold with the tiniest white flowers – mere suggestions of flowers, like those of the wild strawberry. The kitchen was immaculate. On the landing upstairs was a little fretwork bench. The cushions in the sitting room were stiff and stately, and so was the upholstery, but the bedroom – ah, the bedroom.

It was everything she had ever wanted their own to be. In fact, the bedroom was the very room she had envisaged over and over again and had described to her husband down to the last detail. Here it was – a brass bed with a little lace canopy above it, the entire opposite wall a dark metallic mirror in which dark shadows seemed to swim around, a light-blue velvet chaise longue, a hanging plant with shining leaves, and a floor lamp with a brown-fringed shade that gave off the softest of light.

She sat on the edge of the bed, marvelling, and saw the other things that she had always wanted. She saw, for instance, the photo of a little girl in First Communion attire; she saw the paper-weight that when shaken yielded a miniature snowstorm; she saw the mother-of-pearl tray with the two champagne glasses – and all of a sudden she began to cry because her happiness was so immense. Perhaps, she thought, he will come to me here, he will visit, and it will be like the old days and he won't be irritable and he won't be tapping with his fingers or fiddling with the lever of his fountain pen. He will smother me with hugs and kisses and we will tumble about on the big bed.

She sat there in the bedroom and she touched nothing, not even the two white irises in the tall glass vase. The little key was in her hand and she knew it was for the wardrobe and that she had only to open it to find there a nightdress with a pleated top, a voile dance dress, a silver-fox cape, and a pair of sling-back shoes. But she did not open it. She wanted to leave something a secret. She crept away and was home in her own bed without her husband being aware of her absence. He had complained on other occasions about her cold feet as she got back into bed, and asked in Christ's name what was she doing – making tea or what? That morning her happiness was so great that she leaned over, unknotted his pyjamas, and made love to him very sweetly, very slowly, and to his apparent delight. Yet when he wakened he was angry, as if a wrong had been done him.

Naturally, Mrs. Reinhardt now went to the mews house night after night, and her heart would light up as she saw the pillar of the house with its number, ten, lettered in gold edged with black. The naught was a little slanted. Sometimes she got into the brass bed and she knew it was only a question of time before Mr. Reinhardt followed her there.

One night as she lay in the bed, a little breathless, he came in very softly, closed the door, removed his dressing gown, and took possession of her with such a force that afterward she suspected she had a broken rib. They used words that they had not used for years. She was young and wild. A lovely fever took hold of her. She was saucy while he kept imploring her to please marry him, to please give up her independence, to please be his – adding that even if she said no he was going to whisk her off. Then to prove his point he took possession of her again. She almost died, so deep and so thorough was her pleasure, and each time as she came back to her senses she saw some little object or trinket that was intended to add to her pleasure – once it was a mobile in which silver horses chased one another around, once it was a sound as of a running stream. He gave her some champagne and they drank in utter silence.

But when she wakened from this idyll she was in fact in her own bed and so was he. She felt mortified. Had she cried out in her sleep? Had she moaned? There was no rib broken. She reached for the hand mirror and saw no sign of wantonness on her face, no tossed hair, and the buttons of her nightdress were neatly done up to the throat.

He was a solid mass of sleep. He opened his eyes. She said something to him, something anxious, but he did not reply. She got out of bed and went down to the sitting room to think. Where would it all lead to? Should she tell him? She thought not. All morning she tried the key in different locks, but it was too small. In fact, once she nearly lost it because it slipped into a lock and she had to tease it out with the prong of a fork. Of course she did not let Fatima, the maid, see what she was doing.

It was Friday, their day to go to the country, and she was feeling reluctant about it. She knew that when they arrived they would rush around their garden and look at their plants to see if they'd thrived, and look at the rose leaves to make sure there were no green fly. Then, staring out across the fields to where the cows were, they would tell each other how lucky they were to have such a nice place, and how clever. The magnolia flowers would be fully out and she would stand and stare at the tree as if by staring at it she could imbue her body with something of its whiteness.

The magnolias were out when they arrived – like little white china eggcups, each bloom lifted to the heavens. Two of the elms definitely had the blight, Mr. Reinhardt said, as the leaves were withering away. The elms would have to be chopped, and Mr. Reinhardt estimated that there would be enough firewood for two winters. He would speak to the farm manager, who lived down the road, about this. They carried in the shopping, raised the blinds, and switched on the central heating. The little kitchen was just as they had left it, except that the primroses in the jar had faded and were like bits of yellow skin. She unpacked the food they had brought, put some things in the fridge, and began to peel the carrots and potatoes for the evening meal. Mr. Reinhardt hammered four picture hangers into the wall for the new prints that he had brought down. From time to time he would call her to ask what order he should put them in, and she would go in, her hands covered with flour, and rather absently suggest a grouping.

She had the little key with her in her purse and would open the purse from time to time to make sure that it was there. Then she would blush.

At dusk she went out to get a branch of apple wood for the fire, in order to engender a lovely smell. A bird chirped from a tree. It was more sound than song. She could not tell what bird it was. The magnolia tree was a mass of white in the surrounding darkness. The dew was falling and she bent for a moment to touch the wet grass. She wished it were Sunday, so that they could be going home. In London the evenings seemed to pass more quickly and they each had more chores to do. She felt in some way she was deceiving him.

They drank some red wine as they sat by the fire. Mr. Reinhardt was fidgety but at the very same time accused her of being fidgety. He was being adamant about the Common Market. Why did he expound on the logistics of it when she was not even contradicting him? He got carried away, made gestures, said he loved England, loved it passionately, that England was going to the dogs. When she got up to push in a log that had fallen from the grate, he asked her for God's sake to pay attention.

She sat down at once, and hoped that there was not going to be one of those terrible, unexpected, meaningless rows. But blessedly they were distracted. She heard him say, 'Crikey!' and then she looked up and saw what he had just seen. There was a herd of cattle staring in at them. She jumped up. Mr. Reinhardt rushed to the phone to call the farm manager, since he himself knew nothing about country life, certainly not how to drive away cattle.

She grabbed a walking stick and went outside to prevent the cows from falling in the swimming pool. It was cold out of doors and the wind rustled in all the trees. The cows looked at her, suspicious. Their ears pricked. She made tentative movements with the stick, and at that moment four of them leaped over the barbed wire and back into the adjoining field. The remaining cow began to race around. From the field the four cows began to bawl. The fifth cow was butting against the paling. Mrs. Reinhardt thought, I know what you are feeling – you are feeling lost and muddled and you have gone astray.

Her husband came out in a frenzy because when he had rung the farm manager no one was there. 'Bloody never there!' he said. His loud voice so frightened the poor cow that she made a leap for it and got stuck in the barbed wire. Mrs. Reinhardt could see the barb in her huge udder and thought what a place for it to have landed. They must rescue her. Very cautiously they both approached the animal, and the intention was that Mr. Reinhardt would hold the cow while Mrs. Reinhardt freed the flesh. She tried to be gentle. The cow's smell was milky, and soft compared with her roar, which was beseeching. Mr. Reinhardt caught hold of the hindquarters and told his wife to hurry up. The cow was bucking. As Mrs. Reinhardt lifted the bleeding flesh away, the cow took a high jump and was over the fence and down the field, where she hurried to the river to drink.

The others followed her and suddenly the whole meadow was the scene of bawling and mad commotion. Mr. Reinhardt rubbed his hands and let out a sigh of relief. He suggested that they open a bottle of champagne. Mrs. Reinhardt was delighted. Of late he had become very thrifty and did not permit her any extravagances. In fact he had been saying that they would soon have to give up wine because of the state of the country. As they went indoors he put an arm around her. And back in the room she sat and felt like a mistress as she drank the champagne, smiled at him, and felt the stuff coursing through her body. The champagne put them in a nice mood and they linked as they went up the narrow stairs to bed. Nevertheless, Mrs. Reinhardt did not feel like any intimacy; she wanted it reserved for the hidden room.

They returned to London on Sunday evening, and that night Mrs. Reinhardt did not sleep. Consequently she walked nowhere in her dreams. In the morning she felt fidgety. She looked in the mirror. She was getting old. After breakfast, as Mr. Reinhardt was hurrying out of the house, she held up the little key.

'What is it?' she said.

'How would I know?' he said. He looked livid.

She called and made an appointment at the hairdresser's. She addressed herself. She must not get old. Later, when her hair was set she would surprise him – she would drop in at his gallery and ask him to take her to a nice pub. On the way she would buy a new scarf and knot it at the neck and she would be youthful.

When she got to the gallery, Mr. Reinhardt was not there. Hans, his assistant, was busy with a client from the Middle East. She said she would wait. The new secretary went off to make some tea. Mrs. Reinhardt sat at her husband's desk, brooding, and then idly she began to flick through his desk diary, just to pass the time. Lunch with this one and that one. A reminder to buy her a present for their anniversary – which he had done. He had bought her a beautiful ring with a sphinx on it.

Then she saw it – the address that she went to night after night. Number ten. The digits danced before her eyes as they had danced when she drove up in the taxi the very first time. All her movements became hurried and mechanical. She gulped her tea, she gave a distracted handshake to the Arab gentleman, she ate the ginger biscuit and gnashed her teeth, so violently did she chew. She paced the floor, she went back to the diary. The same address – three, four, or five times a week. She flicked back to see how long it had been going on. It was no use. She simply had to go there.

At the mews, she found the key in the flower tub. In the kitchen were eggshells and a pan in which an omelette had been cooked. There were two brown eggshells and one white. She dipped her finger in the fat; it was still warm. Her heart went ahead of her up the stairs. It was like a pellet in ber body. She had her band on the doorknob, when all of a sudden she stopped in her tracks and became motionless. She crept away from the door and went back to the landing seat.

She would not intrude, no. It was perfectly clear why Mr. Reinhardt went there. He went by day to keep his tryst with her, be unfaithful with her, just as she went by night. One day or one night, if they were very lucky, they might meet and share their secret, but until then Mrs. Reinhardt was content to leave everything just as it was. She tiptoed down the stairs and was pleased that she had not acted rashly, that she had not broken the spell.

Mrs. Reinhardt

Mrs. Reinhardt had her routes worked out. Blue ink for the main roads, red when she would want to turn off. A system, and a vow. She must enjoy herself, she must rest, she must recuperate, she must put on weight, and perhaps blossom the merest bit. She must get over it. After all the world was a green, a sunny, an enchanting place. The hay was being gathered, the spotted cows so sleek they looked like Dalmatians and their movements so lazy in the meadows that they could be somnambulists. The men and women working in the fields seemed to be devoid of fret or haste. It was June in Brittany, just before the throngs of visitors arrived, and the roads were relatively clear. The weather was blustery but as she drove along the occasional patches of sunlight illumined the trees, the lush grass and the marshes. Seeds and pollen on the surface of the marshes were a bright mustard yellow. Bits of flowering broom divided the roadside, and at intervals an emergency telephone kiosk in bright orange caught her attention. She did not like that. She did not like emergency and she did not like the telephone. To be avoided.

While driving, Mrs. Reinhardt was occupied and her heart was relatively serene. One would not know that recently she had been through so much and that presently much more was to follow. A lull. Observe the roadside, the daisies in the fields, the red and the pink poppies, and the lupins so dozey like the cows; observe the road signs and think if necessary of the English dead in the last war whose spectres floated somewhere in these environments, the English dead of whom some photograph, some relic or some crushed thought was felt at that moment in some English semi-detached home. Think of food, think of shellfish, think of the

French for blueberries, think of anything, so long as the mind keeps itself occupied.

It promised to be a beautiful hotel. She had seen photos of it, a dovecote on the edge of a lake, the very essence of stillness, beauty, sequesteredness. A place to re-meet the god of peace. On either side of the road the pines were young and spindly but the cows were pendulous, their udders shockingly large and full. It occurred to her that it was still morning and that they had been only recently milked so what would they feel like at sundown! What a nuisance that it was those cows' udders that brought the forbidden thought to her mind. Once in their country cottage, a cow had got caught in the barbed-wire fence and both she and Mr. Reinhardt had a time of it trying to get help, and then trying to release the creature, causing a commotion among the cow community. Afterwards they had drunk champagne intending to celebrate something. Or was it to hide something? Mr. Reinhardt had said that they must not grow apart and yet had quarrelled with her about the Common Market and removed her glasses while she was reading a story of Flaubert sitting up in bed. The beginning of the end as she now knew, as she then knew, or did she, or do we, or is there such a thing, or is it another beginning to another ending and on and on.

'Damnation,' Mrs. Reinhardt said, and speeded just as she came to where there were a variety of signs with thick arrows and names in navy blue. She had lost her bearings. She took a right and realised at once that she had gone to the east town rather than the main town. So much for distraction. Let him go. The worst was already over. She could see the town cathedral as she glanced behind, and already was looking for a way in which to turn right.

The worst was over, the worst being when the other woman, the girl really, was allowed to wear Mrs. Reinhardt's nightdress and necklace. For fun. 'She is young,' he had said. It seemed she was, this rival or rather this replacement. So young that she shouted out of car windows at other motorists, that she carried a big bright umbrella, that she ate chips or cough lozenges on the way to one of these expensive restaurants where Mr. Reinhardt took her. All in all she was gamine.

Mrs. Reinhardt drove around a walled city and swore at a system of signs that did not carry the name of the mill town she was looking for. There were other things, like a clock, and a bakery and a few strollers and when she pulled into the tree-lined square there was a young man naked to the waist in front of an easel, obviously sketching the cathedral. She spread the map over her knees and opened the door to get a puff of air. He looked at her. She smiled at him. She had to smile at someone. All of a sudden she had an irrational wish to have a son, a son who was with her now, to comfort her, to give her confidence, to take her part. Of course she had a son but he was grown up and had gone to America and knew none of this and must not know any of this.

The man told her that she need never have gone into the cathedral town but as she said herself she had seen it, she had seen the young man painting, she had given a Utile smile and he had smiled back and that was something. For the rest of the journey she remained alert, she saw trees, gabled houses, a few windmills, she saw dandelions, she passed little towns, she saw washing on the line, and she knew that she was going in the right direction.

Her arrival was tended with magic. Trees, the sound of running water, flowers, wild flowers and a sense of being in a place that it would take time to know, take time to discover. To make it even more mysterious the apartments were stone chalets scattered at a distance throughout the grounds. It was a complex really but one in which nature dominated. She went down some steps to where it said 'Reception' and having introduced herself was asked at once to hurry so as to be served lunch. Finding the dining room was an expedition in itself – up steps, down more steps, and then into a little outer salon where there were round tables covered with lace cloths and on each table a vase of wild flowers. She bent down and smelt some pansies. A pure sweet silken smell, with the texture of childhood. She felt grateful. Her husband was paying for all this and what a pity that like her he was not now going down more steps, past a satin screen, to a table laid for two by an open window, to the accompaniment of running water. She had a half bottle of champagne, duck pâté and a flat white grilled fish on a bed of thin strips of boiled leek. The hollandaise sauce was perfect and yellower than usual because they had added mustard. She was alone except for the serving girl and an older couple at a table a few yards away. She could not hear what they said. The man was drinking Calvados. The serving girl had a pretty face and brown curly hair tied back with a ribbon. One curl had been brought onto her forehead for effect. She radiated innocence and a dream. Mrs. Reinhardt could not look at her for long and thought she has probably never been to Paris, never even been to Nantes but she hopes to go and will go one day. That story was in her eyes, in the curls of her hair, in everything she did. That thirst.

After lunch Mrs. Reinhardt was escorted to her room. It was down a dusty road with ferns and dock on either side. Wild roses of the palest pink tumbled over the arch of the door and when she stood in her bedroom and looked through one of the narrow turret windows it was these roses and grassland that she saw, while from the other side she could hear the rush of the water and the two images reminded her of herself and of everybody else that she had known. One was green and hushed and quiet and the other was torrential. Did they have to conflict with the other? She undressed, she unpacked, she opened the little refrigerator to see what delights were there. There was beer and champagne and miniatures of whiskey and Vichy water and red cordial. It was like being a child again and looking into one's little toy house. She had a little weep.

For what did Mrs. Reinhardt weep – for beauty, for ugliness, for herself, for her son in America, for Mr. Reinhardt who had lost his reason. So badly did Mr. Reinhardt love this new girl, Rita, that he had made her take him to meet all her friends so that he could ask them how Rita looked at sixteen, and seventeen, what Rita wore, what Rita was like as a debutante, and why Rita stopped going to art school and had made notes of these things. Had made an utter fool of himself. Yes she cried for that, and as she cried it seemed to her the tears were like the strata of this earth, had many levels and many layers, and that those layers differed and that now she was crying for more than one thing at the same time, that her tears were all mixed up. She was also crying about age, about two grey ribs in her pubic hair, crying for not having tried harder on certain occasions as when Mr. Reinhardt came home expecting excite-ment or repose and getting instead a typical story about the non-arrival of the gas man. She had let herself be drawn into the weary and hypnotising whirl of domesticity. With her the magazines had to be neat, the dust had to be dusted, all her perfectionism had got thrown into that instead of something larger, or instead of Mr. Reinhardt. Where do we go wrong? Is not that what guardian angels are meant to do, to lead us back by the hand?

She cried too because of the night she had thrown a platter at him, and he sat there catatonic, and said that he knew he was wrecking her life and his, but that he could not stop it, said maybe it was madness or the male menopause or anything she wanted to call it, but that it was, what it was, what it was. He had even appealed to her. He told her a story, he told her that very day when he had gone to an auction to buy some pictures for the gallery, he had brought Rita with him and as they drove along the motorway he had hoped that they would crash, so terrible for him was his predicament, and so impossible for him was it to be parted from this girl whom he admitted had made him delirious, but Happy, but Happy as he kept insisting.

It was this helplessness of human beings that made her cry most of all and when long after, which is to say at sunset, Mrs. Reinhardt had dried her eyes, and had put on her oyster dress and her Chinese necklace she was still repeating to herself this matter of helplessness. At the same time she was reminding herself that there lay ahead a life, adventure, that she had not finished, she had merely changed direction and the new road was unknown to her.

She sat down to dinner. She was at a different table. This time she looked out on a lake that was a tableau of prettiness – trees on either side, overhanging branches, green leaves with silver undersides and a fallen bough where ducks perched. The residents were mostly elderly except for one woman with orange hair and studded sunglasses. This woman scanned a magazine throughout the dinner and did not address a word to her escort.

Mrs. Reinhardt would look at the view, have a sip of wine, chew a crust of the bread that was so aerated it was like communion wafer. Suddenly she looked to one side and there in a tank with bubbles of water within were several lobsters. They were so beautiful that at first she thought they were mannequin lobsters, ornaments. Their shells had beautiful blue tints, the blue of lapis lazuli, and though their movements had at first unnerved her she began to engross herself in their motion and to forget what was going on around her. They moved beautifully and to such purpose. They moved to touch each other, at least some did, and others waited, were the recipients so to speak of this reach, this touch. Their movements had all the grandeur of speech without the folly. But there was no mistaking their intention. So caught up was she in this that she did not hear the pretty girl call her out to the phone and in fact she had to be touched on the bare arm which of course made her jump. Naturally she went out somewhat flustered, missed her step and turned but did not wrench her ankle. It was her weak ankle, the one she always fell on. Going into the little booth she mettled herself. Perhaps he was contrite or drunk, or else there had been an accident, or else their son was getting married. At any rate it was crucial. She said her 'Hello' calmly but pertly. She repeated it. It was a strange voice altogether, a man asking for Rachel. She said who is Rachel. There were a few moments of heated irritation and then complete disappointment as Mrs. Reinhardt made her way back to her table trembling. Stupid girl to have called her! Only the lobsters saved the occasion.

Now she gave them her full attention. Now she forgot the mistake of the phone and observed the drama that was going on. A great long lobster seemed to be lord of the tank. His claws were covered with black elastic bands but that did not prevent him from proudly stalking through the water, having frontal battles with some but chiefly trying to arouse another: a sleeping lobster who was obviously his heart's desire. His appeals to her were mesmerising. He would tickle her with his antennae, he would put claws over her, then edge a claw under her so that he levered her up a fraction and then he would leave her be for an instant only to return with a stronger, with a more telling assault. Of course there were moments when he had to desist, to ward off others who were coming in her region and this he did with the same determination facing them with eyes that were vicious yet immobile as beads. He would lunge through the water and drive them back or drive them elsewhere and then he would return as if to his love and to his oracle. There were secondary movements in the tank of course but it was at the main drama Mrs. Reinhardt looked. She presumed it was a him and gave him the name of Napoleon. At times so great was his sexual plight that he would lower a long antennae under his rear and touch the little dun bibs of membrane and obviously excite himself so that he could start afresh on his sleeping lady. Because he was in no doubt but that she would succumb. Mrs. Reinhardt christened her the Japanese Lady, because of her languor, her refusal to be roused, by him, or by any of them, and Mrs. Reinhardt thought, Oh what a sight it will be when she does rise up and give herself to his embraces, oh what a wedding that will be! Mrs. Reinhardt also thought that it was very likely that they would only be in this tank for a short number of hours and that in those hours they must act the play of their lives. Looking at them, with her hands pressed together, she hoped the way children hope for a happy ending, to this courtship.

She had to leave the dining room while it was still going on, but in some way she felt with the lights out, and visitors gone, the protagonists safe in their tank, secured by air bubbles, secretly would find each other. She had drunk a little too much, and she swayed slightly as she went down the dusty road to her chalet. She felt elated. She had seen something that moved her. She had seen instinct, she had seen the grope and she had seen the will that refuses to be refused. She had seen tenderness.

In her bedroom she put the necklace into the heart-shaped wicker box and hid it under the bolster of the second bed. She had robbed her husband of it – this beautiful choker of jade. It had been his mother's. It was worth ten thousand pounds. It was her going-away present. She had extracted it from him. Before closing it in the box she bit on the beads as if they were fruits.

'If you give me the necklace I will go away.' That was what she had said and she knew that in some corner she was thereby murdering his heart. It was his family necklace and it was the one thing in which he believed his luck was invested. Also he was born under the sign of Cancer and if he clung, he clung. It was the thing they shared, and by taking it she was telling him that she was going away forever, and that she was taking some of him, his most important talisman, relic of his mother, relic of their life together. She had now become so involved with this piece of jewellery that when she wore it she touched her throat constantly to make sure that it was there, and when she took it off she kissed it, and at night she dreamed of it, and one night she dreamt that she had tucked it into her vagina for safety, and hidden it there. At other times she thought how she would go to the casino and gamble it away, his luck and hers. There was a casino nearby and on the Saturday there was to be a cycling tournament, and she thought that one night, maybe on the Saturday she would go out, and maybe she would gamble and maybe she would win. Soon she fell asleep.

On the third day Mrs. Reinhardt went driving. She needed a change of scene. She needed sea air and crag. She needed invigoration. The little nest was cloying. The quack-quack of the ducks, the running water were all very well but they were beginning to echo her own cravings and she did not like that. So after breakfast she read the seventeenth-century Nun's Prayer, the one which asked the Lord to release one from excessive speech, to make one thoughtful but not moody, to give one a few friends and to keep one reasonably sweet. She thought of Rita. Rita's bright blue eyes, sapphire eyes and the little studs in her ears that matched. Rita was ungainly like a colt. Rita would be the kind of girl who could stay up all night, swim at dawn and then sleep like a baby all through the day even in an unshaded room. Youth. Yet it so happened that Mrs. Reinhardt had found an admirer. The Monsieur who owned the hotel had paid her more than passing attention. In fact she hardly had to turn a corner but he was there, and he could find some distraction to delay her for a moment, so as he could gaze upon her. First it was a hare running through the undergrowth, then it was his dog following some ducks, then it was the electricity van coming to mend the telephone cable. The dreaded telephone. She was pleased that it was out of order. She was also pleased that she was still striking and there was no denying but that Mrs. Reinhardt could bewitch people.

It was when judging a young persons' art exhibition that he met Rita. Rita's work was the worst, and realising this she had torn it up in a tantrum. He came home and told Mrs. Reinhardt and said how sorry he had felt for her but how plucky she had been. It was February the twenty-second. The following day two things happened – he bought several silk shirts and he proposed they go to Paris for a weekend.

'If only I could turn the key on it and close the door and come back when I am an old woman, if only I could do that.' So Mrs. Reinhardt said to herself as she drove away from the green nest, from the singing birds and the hovering midges, from the rich hollandaise sauces and the quilted bed, from the over-whelming comfort of it all. Indeed she thought she may have suffocated her husband in the very same way. For though Mrs. Reinhardt was cold to others, distant in her relationships with men and women, this was not her true nature, this was some-thing she had built up, a screen of reserve to shelter her fear. She was sentimental at home and used to do a million things for Mr. Reinhardt to please him, and to pander to him. She used to warm his side of the bed while he was still undressing, or looking at a drawing he had just bought, or even pacing the room. The pacing had grown more acute. When she knit his socks in cable stitch she always knit a third sock in case one got torn, or ruined. While he was fishing or when he hunted in Scotland in August, she went just to be near him though she dreaded these forays. They were too public. House parties of people thrown in upon each other for a hectic and sociable week. There was no privacy. Some of the women would go as beaters, while some would sit in one of the drawing rooms swapping recipes or discussing face lifts, good clothes or domestic service bureaus. The landscape and the grouse were the same wonderful colour – that of rusted metal. The shot birds often seemed as if they had just lain down in jest so un-dead did they seem. Even the few drops of blood seemed unreal, theatrical. She loved the moors, the rusted colour of farm and brushwood She loved the dogs and the excitement but she baulked at the sound of the shots. A sudden violence in those untouched moors and then the glee as the hunters went in search of their kill. He might wink at her once or pass her a cup of bouillon when they sat down but he didn't include her in conversation. He didn't have to. She often thought that the real secret of their love was that she kept the inside of herself permanently warm for him like someone keeping an egg under a nest of straw. When she loved, she loved completely, rather like a spaniel. Her eyes were the same yellow-brown. As a young girl she was using a sewing machine one day and by accident put the needle through her index finger, but she did not call out to her parents who were in the other room, she waited until her mother came through. Upon seeing this casualty her mother let out a scream. Within an instant her father was by her side and with a jerk of the lever he lifted the thing out and gave her such a look, such a loving look. Mrs. Reinhardt was merely Tilly then, an only daughter, and full of trust. She believed that you loved your mother and father, that you loved your brother, that eventually you loved your husband and then most of all that you loved your children. Her parents had spoilt her, had brought her to the Ritz for birthdays, had left gold trinkets on her pillow on Christmas Eve, had comforted her when she wept. At twenty-one, they had had an expensive portrait done of her and hung it on the wall in a prominent position so that as guests entered they would say 'Who is that! Who is that!' and a rash of compliments would follow.

When she turned thirty, her husband had her portrait painted and it was in their sitting room, at that very moment, watching him and Rita, unless he had turned it around, or unless Rita had splashed house paint over it. Rita was unruly it seemed. Rita's jealousy was more drastic than the occasional submarines of jealousy Mrs. Reinhardt had experienced in their seventeen years of marriage – then it was over women, roughly her own age, women with poise, women with husbands, women with guile, women who made a career of straying but were back in their own homes by six o'clock. Being jealous of Rita was a more abstract thing – they had only met once and that was on the steps of a theatre. Rita had followed him there, run up the steps, handed him a note and run off again. Being jealous of Rita was being jealous of youth, of freedom and of spontaneity. Rita did not want marriage or an engagement ring. She wanted to go to Florence, she wanted to go to a ball, to go to the park on roller skates. Rita had temper. Once at one of her father's soirées she threw twenty gold chairs out of the window. If they had had a daughter things might now be different. And if their son lived at home, things might now be different. Four people might have sat down at a white table, under a red umbrella, looked out at a brown lake, whose colour was dimmed by the cluster of trees and saplings. There might be four glasses, one with Coca-Cola, one or maybe two with whiskey and hers with white wine and soda water. A young voice might say 'What is that?' pointing to a misshapen straw basket on a wooden plinth in the middle of the lake and as she turned her attention to discern what it was, and as she decided that it was either a nest for swans or ducks the question would be repeated with a touch of impatience – 'Mam, what is that?' and Mrs. Reinhardt might be answering. Oh, my yes the family tableau smote her.

So transported back was she, to the hotel and a united family, that Mrs. Reinhardt was like a sleepwalker traversing the rocks that were covered with moss, and then the wet sand between the rocks. She was making her way towards the distant crags. On the sand there lay caps of seaweed so green, and so shaped like the back of a head that they were like theatrical wigs. She looked down at one, she bent to pore over its greenness and when she looked up, he was there. A man in his mid-twenties in a blue shirt with lips parted seemed to be saying something pleasant to her, though perhaps it was only hello, or hi there. He had an American accent. Had they met in a cocktail bar or at an airport lounge it is doubtful that they would have spoken but here the situation called for it. One or other had to express or confirm admiration for the sea, the boats, the white houses on the far side, the whiteness of the light, the vista; and then quite spontaneously he had to grip her wrist and said, 'Look, look,' as a bird dived down into the water, swooped up again, re-dived until he came up with a fish.

'A predator,' Mrs. Reinhardt said, his hand still on her wrist, casually. They argued about the bird, she said it was a gannet and he said it was some sort of hawk. She said sweetly that she knew more about wildlife than he did. He conceded. He said if you came from Main Street, Iowa, you knew nothing, you were a hick. They laughed.

As they walked back along the shore he told her how he had been staying further up with friends and had decided to move on because one never discovers anything except when alone. He'd spend a night or two and then move on and eventually he would get to Turkey. He wasn't doing a grand tour or a gastronomic tour he was just seeing the wild parts of Brittany and had found a hotel on the other side that was hidden from everybody. 'The savage side,' he said.

By the time she had agreed to have a crepe with him they had exchanged those standard bits of information. He confessed that he didn't speak much French. She confessed that she'd taken a crammer course and was even thinking of spending three months in Paris to do a cookery course. When they went indoors she removed her headscarf and he was caught at once by the beauty of her brown pile of hair. Some hidden urge of vanity made her toss it, as they looked for a table.

'Tell me something,' he said, 'are you married or not?'

'Yes and no . . .' She had removed her wedding ring and put it in the small leather box that snapped when one shut it.

He found her reply intriguing. Quickly she explained that she had been but was about not to be. He reached out but did not touch her and she thought that there was something exquisite in that,

that delicate indication of sympathy. He said quietly how he had missed out on marriage and on kids. She felt that he meant it. He said he had been a wild cat and whenever he had met a nice girl he had cheated on her, and lost her. He could never settle down.

'I'm bad news,' he said and laughed and there was something so impish about him that Mrs. Reinhardt was being won over.

On closer acquaintance she had to admit that his looks were indeed flawless. So perhaps his character was not as terrible as he had made out. She used to press him to tell her things, boyish things like his first holiday in Greece, or his first girl, or his first guitar and gradually she realised she was becoming interested in these things although in them there was nothing new. It was the warmth really and the way he delighted in telling her these things that made Mrs. Reinhardt ask for more stories. She was like someone who has been on a voyage and upon return wants to hear everything that has happened on land. He told her that he had made a short film that he would love her to see. He would fly home for it that night if only he could! It was a film about motor-cycling and he had made it long before anyone else had made a film about it, or written a book about it. He told her some of the stories. Scenes at dusk in a deserted place when a man gets a puncture and says 'What the hell does it matter . . .' as he sits down to take a smoke. She sensed a purity in him alongside everything else. He loved the desert, he loved the prairie but yes he had lived on women, and he had drunk a lot and he had slept rough and he had smoked every kind of weed under the sun, and he wished he had known Aldous Huxley, that Aldous Huxley had been his dad.

'Still searching,' he said.

'It's the fashion now,' she said a little dryly.

'Hey, let's get married,' he said, and they clapped hands and both pretended it was for real. Both acted a little play and it was the very same as if someone had come into the room and said 'Do it for real, kids.' In jest, their cheeks met, in jest, their fingers interlocked, in jest, their knuckles mashed one another's and in jest they stood up, moved onto the small dance area and danced as closely as Siamese twins might to the music from the jukebox. In jest, or perhaps not, Mrs. Reinhardt felt through the beautiful folds of her oyster dress the press of his sexuality and round and round and round they danced, the two jesting betrothed people, who were far from home and who had got each other into such a spin of excitement. How thrilling it was and how rejuvenating to dance round and round and feel the strength and the need of this man pushing closer and closer to her while still keeping her reserve. On her face the most beautiful ecstatic smile. She was smiling for herself. He did slide his other hand on her buttock, but Mrs. Reinhardt just shrugged it off. The moment the dancing stopped they parted.

Soon after they sat down she looked at her tiny wrist-watch, peered at it, and at once he flicked on his blue plastic lighter so that she could read the tiny black insectlike hands. Then he held the lighter in front of her face to admire her, to admire the eyes, the long nose, the sensual mouth, the necklace.

'Real,' he said, picking up the green beads that she herself had become so involved with, and had been so intimate with.

'Think so,' she said and regretted it instantly. After all the world did abound in thieves and rogues and ten thousand pounds was no joke to be carrying around. She had read of women such as she, who took up with men, younger men or older men, only to be robbed, stripped of their possessions, bled. She curdled within and suddenly invented for herself a telephone call back at the hotel. When she excused herself he rose chivalrously, escorted her through the door, down the steps and across the gravel path to the car park. They did not kiss good night.

In the morning the world was clean and bright. There had been rain and everything got washed, the water mills, the ducks, the roses, the trees, the lupins and the little winding paths. The little winding paths of course were strewn with white, pink and pale blue blossoms. The effect was as of seeing snow when she opened the windows, leaned out and broke a rose that was still damp and whose full smell had not been restored yet. Its smell was smothered by the smell of rain and that too was beautiful. And so were her bare breasts resting on the window ledge. And so was life, physical well-being, one's own body, roses, encounter, promise, the dance. She drew back quickly when she saw that there Monsieur was down below, idly hammering a few nails into a wall. He seemed to be doing this to make a trellis for the roses but he was in no hurry as he looked in her direction. He had a knack of finding her no matter where she was. The night before as she drove back late he was in the car park to say that they had kept her a table for dinner. He had brought a spare menu in his pocket. The big black dog looked up too. Somehow her own whiteness and the milk-likeness of her breasts contrasted with the blackness of the dog and she saw them detached, yet grouped together in a very beautiful painting, opposites, one that was long and black with a snout, and one that was white and global like a lamp. She liked that picture and would add it to the pictures that she had seen during the years she sleepwalked. She sleepwalked no longer. Life was like that, you dreamed a lot, or you cried a lot, or you itched a lot, and then it disappeared and something else came in its place.

Mrs. Reinhardt dawdled. She put on one dress then another, she lifted a plate ashtray and found a swarm of little ants underneath, she took sparkling mineral water from the refrigerator, drank it, took two of her iron tablets and by a process of association pulled her lower eyelid down to see if she was still anaemic. She realised something wonderful. For whatever number of minutes it had been she had not given a thought to Mr. Reinhardt and this was the beginning of recovery. That was how it happened, one forgot for two minutes and remembered for twenty. One forgot for three minutes and remembered for fifteen but as with a pendulum the states of remembering and the states of forgetting were gradually equalised and then one great day the pendulum had gone over and the states of forgetting had gained a victory. What more did a woman want. Mrs. Reinhardt danced around the room, leapt over her bed, threw a pillow in the air and felt as alive and gay as the day she got engaged and knew she would live happily ever after. What more did a woman want. She wanted this American although he might be a bounder. He might not. She would have him but in her own time and to suit her own requirements. She would not let him move into her hotel apartment because the privacy of it was sacred. In fact she was beginning to enjoy herself. Think of it, she could have coffee at noon instead of at nine-thirty, she could eat an éclair, she could pluck her eyebrows, she could sing high notes and low notes, she could wander.

'Freedom!' Mrs. Reinhardt told the lovely supple woman in the flowered dressing gown who smiled into the long mirror while the other Mrs. Reinhardt told the lovely woman that the mirabelle she had drunk the night before was still swishing through her brain.

After breakfast she walked in the woods. Crossing a little plaited bridge she took off her sandals and tiptoed so as not to disturb the sounds and activities of nature. It was the darkest wood she had ever entered. All the trees twined overhead so that it was a vault with layer upon layer of green. Ferns grew in wizard abundance and between the ferns other things strove to be seen while all about were the butterflies and the insects. Mushrooms and toadstools flourished at the base of every tree and she knelt down to smell them. She loved their dank smell. The air was pierced with birdsong of every note and every variety as the birds darted across the ground, or swooped up into the air. This fecundity of nature, this chorus of birds and the distant cooing of the doves from the dovecote thrilled her and presently something else quickened her desires. The low, suggestive, all-desiring whistle of a male reached her ears. She had almost walked over him. He could see her bare legs under her dress. She drew back. He was lying down with his shirt open. He did not rise to greet her.

'You,' she said.

He put up his foot in salutation. She stood over him trying to decide whether his presence was a welcome or an intrusion.

'Amazing,' he said and held his hands out acceding to the abundance of nature about him. He apologised for his presence but said that he had cycled over to see her just to say hello, he had brought her some croissants hot from the oven but that upon hearing she was sleeping he decided to have a ramble in the woods. He had fed the croissants to the birds. He used some French words to impress her and she laughed and soon her petulance was washed away. After all, they were not her woods, and he had not knocked on her bedroom door, and she would have been disappointed if he had cycled off without seeing her. She spread her dress like a cushion underneath her and sat folding her legs to the other side. It was then they talked. They talked for a long time. They talked of courage, the different courage of men and women. The courage when a horse bolts, or the car in front of one just crashes, the draining courage of every day. She said men were never able to say *finito.'* 'Damn right,' he said and the jargon struck her as comic compared with the peace and majesty of the woods.

'You smell good,' he would sometimes say and that too belonged to another environment but for the most part he impressed her with his sincerity and with the way he took his time to say the thing he wanted to say. Before the week was out she would lead him to her bed. It would be stark and it would be unexpected, an invitation tossed at the very last minute as when someone takes a flower or a handkerchief and throws it into the bullring. She would be unabashed, as she had not been for years. They stayed for about an hour, talking, and at times one or the other would get up, walk or ran towards the little bridge and pretend to take a photograph. Eventually they got up together and went to find his bicycle. He insisted that she cycle. After the first few wobbles she rode down the path and could hear him clapping. Then she got off, turned round and rode back towards him. He said that next time she would have to stay on the bicycle while turning around and she biffed him and said she had not ridden for years. Her face was flushed and bicycle oil had got on her skirt. For fun he sat her on the bar of the bicycle, put his leg across and they set off down the avenue at a dizzying speed, singing, 'Daisy, Daisy, give me your answer do, I'm half crazy all for the love of you . . . .'

He would not stop even though she swore that she was going to fall off any minute.

'You're O.K. . . .' he'd say as he turned the next corner. In a while she began to stop screaming and enjoyed the butterflies in her stomach.

Mrs. Reinhardt stood in the narrow shower, the disc of green soap held under one armpit when she saw a rose branch being waved into the room. As in a mirage the petals randomly fell. Which of them was it? Him or Monsieur? She was feeling decidedly amorous. He climbed in through the window and came directly to her. He did not speak. He gripped her roughly, his own clothing still on, and he was so busy taking possession of her that he did not realise that he was getting drenched. The shower was full on, yet neither of them bothered to turn it off. The zip of his trousers hurt her but he was mindless of that. The thing is he had desired her from the very first, and now he was pumping all his arrogance and all his cockatooing into her and she was taking it gladly, also gluttonously. She was recovering her pride as a woman, and much more as a desirable woman. It was this she had sorely missed in the last ten months. Yet she was surprised by herself, surprised by her savage need to get even with life, or was it to get healed. She leaned against the shower wall, wet and slippery all over, and lolled so that every bit of her was partaking of him. She did not worry about him, though he did seem in quite a frenzy both to prove himself and please her, and he kept uttering the vilest of words calling her sow and dog and bitch and so forth. She even thought that she might conceive so radical was it and the only other thought that came to her was of the lobsters and the lady lobster lying so still while all the others sought her.

When he came, she refused to claim to be satisfied and with a few rough strokes insisted he fill her again and search for her every crevice. This all happened without speech except for the names he muttered as she squeezed from him the juices he did not have left to give. She was certainly getting her own back.

Afterwards she washed and as he lay on the bathroom floor out of breath she stepped over him and went to her room to rest. She felt like a queen and lying on her bed her whole body was like a ship decked out with beauty. A victory! She had locked the bedroom door. Let him wait, let him sweat. She would join him for dinner. She had told him so in French knowing it would doubly confound him. She went to sleep ordering herself pleasant dreams, coloured dreams, the colours of sunlight and of lightning, yellow sun and saffron lightning.

He kept the dinner appointment. Mrs. Reinhardt saw him from a landing, down in the little salon where there were lace-covered tables and vases of wild flowers. She remembered it from her first day. He was drinking a Pernod. It was almost dark down there except for the light from the table candles. It was a somewhat sombre place. The drawings on the wall were all of monks or ascetics and nailed to a cross of wood was a bird, it seemed to be a dead pheasant. He was wearing green, a green silk dinner jacket – had she not seen it somewhere? Yes, it had been on display in the little hotel showcase where they also sold jewellery and beachwear.

The moment she went to his table she perceived the change in him. The good-natured truant boy had given way to the slightly testy seducer and he did not move a chair or a muscle as she sat down. He called to Michele, the girl with the curly hair, to bring another Pernod, in fact to bring two. Mrs. Reinhardt thought that it was just a ruse and that he was proving to her what a man of the world he was. She said she had slept well.

'Where's your loot?' he said, looking at her neck. She had left it in her room and was wearing pearls instead. She did not answer but merely held up the paperback book to show that she had been reading.

'You read that?' he said. It was D. H. Lawrence.

'I haven't read that stuff since I was twelve,' he said. He was drunk. It augured badly. She wondered if she should dismiss him there and then but as on previous occasions when things got very bad Mrs. Reinhardt became very stupid, became inept. He gave the waitress a wink and gripped her left hand where she was wearing a bracelet. She moved off as languidly as always.

'You're a doll,' he said.

'She doesn't speak English,' Mrs. Reinhardt said.

'She speaks my kind of English,' he said.

It was thus in a state of anger, pique and agitation that they went in to dinner. As he studied the four menus he decided on the costliest one and said it was a damn good thing that she was a rich bitch.

'Rich bitch,' he said and laughed.

She let it pass. He said how about taking him to Pamplona for the bullfights and then went into a rhapsody about past fights and past bullfighters.

'Oh, you read it in Ernest Hemingway,' she said unable to resist a sting.

'Oh, we've got a hot and cold lady,' he said as he held the velvet-covered wine list in front of him. The lobster tank was gapingly empty. There were only three lobsters in there and those lay absolutely still. Perhaps they were shocked from the raid and were lying low, not making a stir, so as not to be seen. She was on the verge of tears. He ordered a classic bottle of wine. It meant the girl getting Monsieur, who then had to get his key and go to the cellar and ceremoniously bring it back and show the label and open it and decant it and wait. The waitress had changed clothes because she was going to the cycle tournament. Her black pinafore was changed for a blue dress with colours in the box pleats. She looked enchanting. Ready for showers of kisses and admiration.

'How would you like me to fuck you?' he said to the young girl who watched the pouring of the wine.

'You have gone too far,' Mrs. Reinhardt said, and perhaps fearing that she might make a scene he leaned over to her and said:

'Don't worry, I'll handle you.'

She excused herself, more for the waitress than for him, and hurried out. Never in all her life was Mrs. Reinhardt so angry. She sat on the hammock in the garden and asked the stars and the lovely hexagonal lamps and the sleeping ducks to please succour her in this nightmare. She thought of the bill, and the jacket, as she realised, also on her bill, and she cried like a very angry child who was unable to tell anyone what had happened. Her disgrace was extreme. She swung back and forth in the hammock cursing and swearing, then praying for patience. The important thing was never to have to see him again. She was shivering and in a state of shock by the time she went to her room. She really went to put on a cardigan and to order a sandwich or soup. There he was in her dressing gown. He had quit dinner he said being as she so rudely walked away. He too was about to order a sandwich. The fridge door was open and as she entered he clicked it closed. Obviously he had drunk different things and she could see that he was wild.

He was not giving this up, this luxury, this laissez faire. He rose up and staggered.

'Round one,' he said and caught her.

'Get out of here,' she said.

'Not me, I'm in for the licks.'

Mrs. Reinhardt knew with complete conviction that she was about to be the witness of, and participant in the most sordid kind of embroil. Alacrity took hold of her and she thought, coax him, seem mature, laugh, divert him. But seeing the craze in his eyes, instinct made her resort to stronger measures and the scream she let out was astounding even to her own ears. It was no more than seconds until Monsieur was in the room grappling with him. She realised that he had been watching all along and that he had been prepared for this in a way that she was not. Monsieur was telling him in French to get dressed and to get lost. It had some elements of farce.

'O.K., O.K.,' he was saying. 'Just let me get dressed, just let me get out of this asshole.'

She was glad of the language barrier. Then an ugly thing happened, the moment Monsieur let go of him he used a dirty trick. He picked up the empty champagne bottle and wielded it at his opponent's head. Suddenly the two of them were in a clench and Mrs. Reinhardt searched in her mind to know what was best to do. She picked up a chair but her action was like someone in slow motion because while they were each forcing each other onto the ground she was holding the chair and not doing anything with it. It was the breaking bottle she dreaded most of all. By then her hand had been on the emergency bell and as they both fell to the floor the assistant chef came in with a knife. He must have dashed from the kitchen. The two men were of course able to master the situation and when he got up he was shaking his head like a boxer who has been badly punched.

Monsieur suggested that she leave and go over to Reception and wait there. As she left the room he gave her his jacket. Walking

down the little road her body shook like jelly. The jacket kept slipping off. She was conscious of just having escaped indescribable
horror. Horror such as one reads of. She realised how sheltered her
life had been but this was no help. What she really wanted was to
sit with someone and talk about anything. The hotel lounge was
propriety itself. Another young girl, also with a rose in her hair,
was slowly preparing a tray of drinks. A party of Dutch people
sat in a corner, the dog snapped at some flies and from the other
room came the strains of music as there was a wedding in progress.
Mrs. Reinhardt sat in a deep leather chair and let all those pleasant
things lap over her. She could hear speeches and clapping and then
the sweet and lovely strains of the accordion and though she could
not explain to herself why these sounds made her feel enormously
safe, made her feel as if perhaps she was getting married and she
realised that that was the nice aftermath of shock.

The principal excitement next morning was the birth of seven
baby ducks. The little creatures had been plunged into the brown
rushing water while a delighted audience looked on. Other ducks
sat curled up on stones, sulking perhaps since they were so ignored
in favour of a proud mother and these little daft naked creatures.
The doves too fanned their tails in utter annoyance while everyone
looked towards the water and away from them. She sat and sipped
coffee. Monsieur sat a little away from her dividing his admiration
between her and the baby ducks. He flaked bread between his
hands then opened the sliding door and pitched it out. Then he
would look at her and smile. Speech was beyond him. He had
fallen in love with her, or was infatuated, or was pretending to be
infatuated. One of these things. Maybe he was just salvaging her
pride. Yet the look was genuinely soft, even adoring. His swallow
was affected, his cheeks were as red as the red poppies, and he did
little things like wind his watch or rearrange the tops of his socks
all for her benefit. Once he put his hand on her shoulder to alert

her to some new minutiae of the ducks' behaviour and he pressed achingly on her flesh.

If Madame were to find out! she thought and her being shuddered at the prospect of any further unpleasantness. She did not ask about the bounder but she did ask later for a glance at her bill and there indeed was the *veston*, the gentleman's *veston* for sixteen hundred francs. After breakfast she sat out on the lawn and observed the behaviour of the other ducks. They pass their time very amiably she thought, they doze a lot, then scratch or clean themselves, then re-doze, then have a little waddle and perhaps stretch themselves but she doubted that a duck walked more than a furlong throughout its whole life. Then on beautiful crested hotel notepaper she wrote to her son. She deliberately wrote a blithe letter, a letter about ducks, trees, and nature. Two glasses with the sucked crescent of an orange in each one were laid in an alcove in the wall and she described this to him and thought that soon she would be indulgent and order a champagne cocktail. She did not say 'Your father and I have separated.' She would say it later when the pain was not quite so acute, and when it did not matter so much. When would that be? Mrs. Reinhardt looked down at the cushion she was sitting on, and saw that it was a hundred per cent Fibranne, and as far as she was concerned that was the only thing in the world she could be absolutely sure of.

Going back to her room before lunch, she decided to put on a georgette dress and her beads. She owed it to Monsieur. She ought to look nice even if she could not smile. She ought to pretend to and by pretending she might become that person. All the burning thoughts and all the recent wounds might just lie low in her and she could appear to be as calm and unperturbed as a summer lake with its water-lily leaves and its starry flowers. Beneath the surface the carp that no one would cast down for. Monsieur's tenderness meant a lot to her, it meant she was still a person to whom another person bestowed attention, even love.

Poor lobsters, she thought and remembered those beseeching moves. When she opened the heart-shaped box in which the beads were hidden Mrs. Reinhardt let out a shriek. Gone. Gone. Her talisman, her life insurance, her last link with her husband Harold gone. Their one chance of being reunited. Gone. She ran back the road to the Reception. She was wild. Madame was most annoyed at being told that such a valuable thing had been so carelessly left lying around. As for theft she did not want to hear of such a thing. It was a vulgarity, was for a different kind of premises altogether, not for her beautiful three-star establishment. She ran a perfect premises which was her pride and joy and which was a bower against the outside world. How dare the outside world come into her province. Monsieur's face dissolved in deeper and deeper shades of red and a most wretched expression. He did not say a word. Madame said of course it was the visitor, the American gentleman, and there was no knowing what else he had taken. As far as Madame was concerned the scum of the earth had come into her nest and though it was a small movement it was a telling one, when she picked up a vase of flowers, put them down in another place, and put them down so that the water splashed out of them and stained the account she was preparing. This led to greater vexation. It was a moment of utter terseness and poor Monsieur could help neither of them. He pulled the dog's ear. Mrs. Reinhardt must ring her husband. She had to. There in full view of them, while Madame scratched figures onto the page and Monsieur pulled the dog's ear Mrs. Reinhardt said to her husband Harold in England that her beads had been stolen, that his beads had been stolen, that their beads had been stolen, and she began to cry. He was no help at all. He asked if they could be traced and she said she doubted it.

'A case of hit and run,' she said, hoping he would know what she meant. Perhaps he did because his next remark was that she seemed to be having an eventful time. She said she was in a bad way and she prayed to God that he would say 'come home.' He didn't. He said he would get in touch with the insurance people.

'Oh fuck the insurance people,' Mrs. Reinhardt said and slammed the phone down. Monsieur turned away. She walked out the door. There was not a friend in the world.

Mrs. Reinhardt experienced one of those spells that can unsettle one forever. The world became black. A blackness permeated her heart. It was like rats scraping at her brain. It was pitiless. Phrases such as 'how are you,' or 'I love you,' or 'dear one' were mockery incarnate. The few faces of the strange people around her assumed the masks of animals. The world she stood up in, and was about to fall down in, was green and pretty but in a second it would be replaced by a bottomless pit into which Mrs. Reinhardt was about to fall for eternity. She fainted.

They must have attended to her, because when she came to, her court shoes were removed, the buttons of her blouse were undone and there was a warm cup of *tisane* on a stool beside her. A presence had just vanished. Or a ghost. Had just slipped away. She thought it was a woman and perhaps it was her mother anointing her with ashes and she thought it was Ash Wednesday. 'Because I do not hope to live again,' she said but fortunately no one seemed to understand. She sat up, sipped the hot tea, apologised about the necklace and about the scene she had made. She was uncertain how far she had gone. King Lear's touching of the robe of Cordelia sprang to mind and she asked God if the dead could in fact live again, if, if she could witness the miracle that the three apostles witnessed when they came and saw the stone rolled away from Christ's grave. 'Come back,' she whispered and it was as if she were taking her own hand and leading herself back to life. The one that led was her present self and the one that was being led was a small child who loved God, loved her parents, loved the trees, and the countryside, and had never wanted anything to change. Her two selves stood in the middle, teetering. These were extreme moments for Mrs. Reinhardt and had she succumbed to them she would have strayed indeed. She asked for water. The tumbler she was holding went soft beneath her grip and the frightened child in her felt a memory as of shedding flesh, but the woman in her smiled and assured everyone that the crisis had passed which indeed it had. She lay back for a while and listened to the running water as it dashed and re-dashed against the jet-black millstone and she resolved that by afternoon she would go away and bid good-bye to this episode that had had in it enchantment, revenge, shame, and the tenderness from Monsieur.

As she drove away he came from behind the tree house bearing a small bunch of fresh pansies. They were multicoloured but the two predominant colours were yellow and maroon. They smelt like young skin and had that same delicacy. Mrs. Reinhardt thanked him and cherished the moment. It was like an assuage. She smiled into his face, their eyes met, for him too it was a moment of real happiness, fleeting but real, a moment of good.

The new hotel was on a harbour and for the second time in four days she walked over boulders that were caked with moss. At her feet the bright crops of seaweed that again looked like theatre wigs but this time she saw who was before and behind her. She was fully in control. What maddened her was that women did as she did all the time and that their pride was not stripped from them, nor their jewellery. Or perhaps they kept it a secret. One had to be so cunning, so concealed.

Looking out along the bay at the boats, the masts and the occasional double sails, she realised that now indeed her new life had begun, a life of adjustment and change. Life with a question mark. Your ideal of human life is? she asked herself. The answer was none. It had always been her husband, their relationship, his art gallery, their cottage in the country and plans. One thing above all others came to her mind and it was the thousands of flower petals under the hall carpet which she had put there for pressing. Those pressed flowers were the moments of their life and what would happen to them – they would lie there for years or else they would be swept away. She could see them there, thousands of sweet bright petals, mementos of their hours. Before her walk she had been reading Ruskin, reading of the necessary connection between beauty and morality but it had not touched her. She wanted someone to love. As far as she was concerned Ruskin's theories were fine sermons but that is not what the heart wants. She must go home soon, and get a job. She must try. Mrs. Reinhardt ran, got out of breath, stood to look at the harbour, re-ran and by an effort of will managed to extricate herself from the rather melancholy state she was in.

During dinner the headwaiter would come, between each of the beautiful courses, and ask how she liked them. One was a fish terrine, its colours summery white, pink, green, the colours of flowers. She would love to learn how to make it. Then she had dressed crab, and even the broken-off claws had been dusted with flour and baked for a moment so that the effect was the same as of smelling warm bread. Everything was right and everything was bright. The little potted plant on the table was a bright cherry pink, robins darted in and out of the dark trees and the ornamental plates in a glass cupboard had patterns of flowers and trelliswork.

'A gentleman to see you,' the younger waiter said. Mrs. Reinhardt froze, the bounder was back. Like a woman ready for battle, she put down her squashed napkin and stalked out of the room. She had to turn a corner to enter the main hall and there sitting on one of the high-backed Spanish-type chairs was her husband, Mr. Reinhardt. He stood up at once and they shook hands formally like an attorney and his client at an auspicious meeting. He has come to sue me, she thought, because of the necklace. She did not say 'Why have you come?' He looked tired. Mrs. Reinhardt flinched when she heard that he had taken a private plane. He had been to the other hotel and had motored over. He refused a drink and would not look at her. He was mulling over his attack. She was convinced that she was about to be shot when he put his hand in his pocket and drew the thing out. She did not mind being shot but thought irrationally of the mess on the beautiful Spanish furniture.

'They found it,' he said as he produced the necklace and laid it on the table between them. It lay like a snake as in a painting, coiled in order to spring. Yet the sight of it filled her with tears and she blubbered out about the bounder, and how she had met him and how he had used her and suddenly she realised that she was telling him something that he had no inkling of.

'The maid took them,' he said and she saw the little maid with the brown curly hair dressed for the tournament and now she could have plucked her tongue out for having precipitated the tale of the bounder.

'Was she sacked?' she asked.

He did not know. He thought not.

'Fine place they have,' he said referring to the lake and the windmills.

'This also is lovely,' she said and went on to talk about the view from the dining room, and the light which was so telling, so white, so unavoidable. Just like their predicament. In a minute he would get up and go. If only she had not told him about the bounder. If only she had let him say why he had come. She had closed the last door.

'How have you been?' he said.

'Well,' she said, but the nerve in her lower jaw would not keep still and without intending it and without in any way wanting it to happen Mrs. Reinhardt burst into tears, much to the astonishment of the young waiter who was waiting to take an order as he thought, for a drink.

'He tried to blackmail me,' she said and then immediately denied it.

Her husband was looking at her very quietly and she was not sure if there was any sympathy left in him. She thought, If he walks out now it will be catastrophic, and again she thought of the few lobsters who were left in the tank and who were motionless with grief.

'There is us and there is people like him,' Mr. Reinhardt said and though she had not told the whole story he sensed the gravity of it. He said that if she did not mind he would stay and that since he was hungry and since it was late might they not go in to dinner. She looked at him and her eyes were probably drenched.

'Us and people like him!' she said.

Mr. Reinhardt nodded.

'And Rita?' Mrs. Reinhardt said.

He waited. He looked about. He was by no means at ease.

'She is one of us,' he said and then qualified it. 'Or she could be, if she meets the right man.'

His expression warned Mrs. Reinhardt to pry no further. She linked him as they went into dinner.

The wind rustled through the chimney and some soot fell on a bouquet of flowers. She saw that. She heard that She squeezed his arm. They sat opposite. When the wind roars, when the iron catches rattle, when the very windowpanes seem to shiver, then wind and sea combine, then dogs begin to howl and the oncoming storm has a whiff of the supernatural. What does one do, what then does a Mrs. Reinhardt do? One reaches out to the face that is opposite, that one loves, that one hates, that one fears, that one has been betrayed by, that one half knows, that one longs to touch and be reunited with, at least for the duration of a windy night. And by morning who knows? Who knows anything anyhow.

The Mouth of the Cave

There were two routes to the village. I chose the rougher one, to be beside the mountain rather than the sea. It is a dusty ill-defined stretch of road littered with rocks. The rocks that have fallen from the cliff are a menacing shade of red once they have split open. On the surface the cliff appears to be gray. Here and there on its gray and red face there are small clumps of trees. Parched in summer, tormented by winds in winter, they nevertheless survive, getting no larger or no smaller.

In one such clump of green, just underneath the cliff, I saw a girl stand up. She began to tie her suspenders slowly. She had bad balance because when drawing her knickers on she lost her footing more than once. She put her skirt on by bringing it over her head, and lastly her cardigan, which appeared to have several buttons. As I came closer she walked away. A young girl in a maroon cardigan and a black skirt. She was twenty or thereabouts. Suddenly, and without anticipating it, I turned toward home so as to give the impression that I'd simply been having a stroll. The ridiculousness of this hit me soon after and I turned around again and walked toward the scene of her secret. I was trembling, but these journeys have got to be accomplished.

What a shock to find that nothing lurked there, no man, no animal. The bushes had not risen from the weight of her body. I reckoned that she must have been lying for quite a time. Then I saw that she, too, was returning. Had she forgotten something? Did she want to ask me a favor? Why was she hurrying? I could not see her face, her head was down. I turned and this time I ran toward the private road that led to my rented house. I thought, Why am I running, why am I trembling, why am I afraid? Because she is a woman and so am I. Because, because? I did not know.

When I got to the courtyard I asked the servant, who had been fanning herself, to unchain the dog. Then I sat outdoors and waited. The flowering tree looked particularly dramatic, its petals richly pink, its scent oppressively sweet. The only tree in flower. My servant had warned me about those particular flowers; she had even taken the trouble to get the dictionary to impress the word upon me – *Venodno*, poison, poison petals. Nevertheless I had the table moved in order to be nearer that tree, and we steadied it by putting folded cigarette cartons under two of its legs. I told the servant to lay a place for two. I also decided what we would eat, though normally I don't, in order to give the days some element of surprise. I asked that both wines be put on the table, and also those long sugar-coated biscuits that can be dipped in white wine and sucked until the sweetness is drained from them and redipped and resucked, indefinitely.

She would like the house. It had simplicity despite its grandeur. A white house with green shutters and a fanlight of stone over each of the three downstairs entrances. A sundial, a well, a little chapel. The walls and the ceilings were a milky blue, and this, combined with the sea and sky, had a strange hallucinatory effect, as if sea and sky moved indoors. There were maps instead of pictures. Around the light bulbs pink shells that over the years had got a bit chipped, but this only added to the informality of the place.

We would take a long time over supper. Petals would drop from the tree; some might lodge on the stone table, festooning it. The figs, exquisitely chilled, would be served on a wide platter. We would test them with our fingers. We would know which ones when bitten into would prove to be satisfactory. She, being native, might be more expert at it than I. One or the other of us might bite too avidly and find that the seeds, wet and messy and runny and beautiful, spurted over our chins. I would wipe my

chin with my hand. I would do everything to put her at ease. Get
drunk if necessary. At first I would talk, but later show hesitation
in order to give her a chance.

I changed into an orange robe and put on a long necklace made
of a variety of shells. The dog was still loose in order to warn me.
At the first bark I would have him brought in and tied up at the
back of the house, where even his whimpering would be unheard.

I sat on the terrace. The sun was going down. I moved to
another chair in order to get the benefit of it. The crickets had
commenced their incessant near-mechanical din and the lizards
began to appear from behind the maps. Something about their
deft, stealthlike movements reminded me of her, but everything
reminded me of her just then. There was such silence that the
seconds appeared to record their own passing. There were only
the crickets and, in the distance, the sound of sheep bells, more
dreamlike than a bleat. In the distance, too, the lighthouse, faithfully signaling. A pair of shorts hanging on a hook began to flutter
in the first breeze, and how I welcomed it, knowing that it
heralded night. She was waiting for dark, the embracing dark, the
sinner's dear accomplice.

My servant waited out of view. I could not see her, but I was
conscious of her the way one sometimes is of a prompter in the
wings. It irritated me. I could hear her picking up or laying down
a plate, and I knew it was being done simply to engage my attention. I had also to battle with the smell of lentil soup. The smell,
though gratifying, seemed nothing more than a bribe to hurry the
proceedings, and that was impossible. Because, according to my
conjecture, once I began to eat the possibility of her coming was
ruled out. I had to wait.

The hour that followed had an edgy, predictable, and awful
pattern – I walked, sat on various seats, lit cigarettes that I quickly
discarded, kept adding to my drink. At moments I forgot the
cause of my agitation, but then recalling her in dark clothes and

downcast eyes, I thrilled again at the pleasure of receiving her. Across the bay the various settlements of lights came on, outlining towns or villages that are invisible in daylight. The perfection of the stars was loathsome.

Finally, the dog's food was brought forth, and he ate as he always does, at my feet. When the empty plate skated over the smooth cobbles – due to my clumsiness – and the full moon, so near, so red, so oddly hospitable, appeared above the pines, I decided to begin, taking the napkin out of its ring and spreading it slowly and cere-moniously on my lap. I confess that in those few seconds my faith was overwhelming and my hope stronger than it had ever been.

The food was destroyed. I drank a lot.

Next day I set out for the village, but took the sea road. I have not gone the cliff way ever since. I have often wanted to, especially after work, when I know what my itinerary is going to be: I will collect the letters, have one Pernod in the bar where retired colo-nels play cards, sit and talk to them about nothing. We have long ago accepted our uselessness for each other. New people hardly ever come.

There was an Australian painter whom I invited to supper, having decided that he was moderately attractive. He became offensive after a few drinks and kept telling me how misrepre-sented his countrymen were. It was sad rather than unpleasant, and the servant and I had to link him home.

On Sundays and feast days girls of about twenty go by, arms around each other, bodies lost inside dark commodious garments. Not one of them looks at me, although by now I am known. She must know me. Yet she never gives me a sign as to which she is. I expect she is too frightened. In my more optimistic moments I like to think that she waits there, expecting me to come and search her out. Yet I always find myself taking the sea road, even though I most desperately desire to go the other way.

Green Georgette

Thursday

Mama and I have been invited to the Coughlans. It is to be Sunday evening at seven o'clock. I imagine us setting out in good time, even though it is a short walk to the village where they live and Mama calling out to me to lift my shoes so that the high wet grass won't stain the white patent. I expect that Rita, the maid, will admit us and we will be ushered in to the room where the piano is. It is a black piano. I saw it the day the Coughlans moved here, saw four men drag it in, sweating and swearing, and when it was put down it emitted a little sound of its own, a ghostly broken tune.

They have been here almost four months. Mr Coughlan works in the bank and though they have a car, he walks to work each morning, setting out punctually at twenty minutes to nine and carrying a lizard-skin attaché case. He probably walks for the exercise, as he is somewhat podgy, and there are always beads of perspiration on his forehead. He is slightly bald. Adjacent to the bank is the River Graney, and faithfully he leans over the stone bridge to look down at the brown, porter-coloured water, or perhaps at the little fish, perches and minnows, that are carried along in the swift current. He ignores most people, giving a mere nod to one or two notables. He is not popular. His wife, on the other hand, is the cynosure of all. She is like a queen. There is not one woman who is not intrigued by her finery, her proud carriage, and her glacial smile. Every Sunday when she comes in to mass, people gawp and nudge, as she goes up the aisle to sit as near as possible to the altar. She has a variety of smart fitted costumes and oodles of accessories and brooches. When they first came it was

February and she wore a teddy bear coat that had brown leather buttons with cracks in them. They looked like fallen horse chestnuts. Soon after that, she wore a brown bouclé coat that came almost to her ankles and she wore it open so as to reveal a contrasting coloured dress in muted orange. She has a butterfly brooch, an amber brooch with a likeness of a beetle, a long-leafed marcasite brooch, and a turquoise wreathed with little seed pearls. Her first name is Drew. Her sister Effie lives with them and she is far plainer, with only two outfits, both tweed. She wore a fox collar some Sundays, and the glassy eyes of the fox staring out looked quite sinister. She was in a convent, but left before taking her final vows and for reasons that remain muddied. She prays very stead-fastly, eyes shut tight, and she keeps kissing her metal crucifix. Drew on the other hand looks straight ahead at the altar, as if she is perceiving some mystery in it. I try to manoeuvre a seat in front of her, so that I can turn round and stare at her, and take note of her little habits and how often she swallows. She blinks with such languor.

Mama says that we will have a scone before setting out, as we are not certain if we are invited for eats. We might go in by the side entrance, where there is a damp path under a canopy of tarpaulin and a lawn roller that is never moved. It depends if there is somebody already looking from behind the window. My father has not been invited, so it seems that it is an occasion for ladies only. It will probably be Drew, Effie, Mama and me. The little daughters are away at boarding school. They are twins, Colette and Cissy, and I am glad that they are absent, as I might be put in a separate room with them, banished from the company of the grown-ups. I will not say a word. I will not need to.

Our being invited is a miracle and came about in an accidental way. The Coughlans were having a supper party. The whole parish knew about it. They were having prawn cocktail to start, then suckling pig with apple sauce, followed by chocolate éclairs and cream. Rita boasted of it in the butchers, the hardware, and the three grocery shops. The guests were other banking people from far afield and a hunting lady separated from her husband and known as a bit of a card. Yet on the day of their supper party, calamity struck. The cream in the creamery had turned sour. It seems the vats had not been scalded properly and all the contents had to be thrown out. Rita went to the various shops and all she could get was one tin of cream, with a picture of a red carnation on the label. Mrs Coughlan was livid. She said one does not give tinned cream to people of note and that fresh cream must be found. Rita thought of us. She knew us well and used to come the odd Saturday to help my mother, but once she went to them she did not want to know us and looked the other way if ever we met. Nevertheless, she arrived with a jug and a half a crown in her hand and Mama said coldly, 'Hello stranger.' Rita said that they were in a terrible pickle, not being able to get fresh cream, and might Mama, in the goodness of her heart, help out. Mama did not say yes at once. She took Rita to task for being a turncoat and for not telling us that she would no longer come of a Saturday to scrub. Rita was very flustered, said she knew she had done wrong, that she was awake nights over it and was biting her nails. She showed her nails, which were certainly bitten down to the quick. Mama then got the white jug. It was a lovely long slender jug, with a picture of a couple in sepia, standing, modestly, side by side. There were three large pans of cream put to settle in the dairy and with the tips of her fingers, Mama skimmed the cream into the jug. She did it perfectly, making sure that no milk got in. The separated milk was a bluish white in colour, not like the butter yellow colour of the cream. She refused the money. Having been tart with Rita, she had now melted and gave her a bag of cooking apples in case they were short.

We heard that the party went off wonderfully. There were four cars with different registrations parked in the street outside and a sing-song after dinner. One lady guest could be heard in the public house across the road singing, 'There's a bridle hanging on the wall and a saddle in a lonely stall', screeching it, as the men in the pub attested to.

Mama says I am to wear my green knitted dress with the scalloped angora edging and carry my cardigan in case it gets chilly on the way home. It is about a half a mile's walk. She herself is going to wear her tweedex suit – a fawn, flecked with pink, one that she knitted for an entire winter. I know in her heart that she hopes the conversation will get around to the fact of her knitting it. Indeed, if it is admired, she will probably offer to knit one for Mrs Coughlan. She is like that. Certainly she will make Drew a gift of a wallet, or a rug, as she goes to the new technical school at night to master these skills. Nothing would please her more than that they would become friends, the Coughlans coming to us and a big spread of cakes and buns and sausage rolls and caramel custards in their own individual ramekins. She says that we are not to mention anything about our lives, the geese that got stolen up by the river at Christmas time, my father's tantrums, or above all, his drinking sprees, which blessedly have tapered off a bit. My father will insist that his supper be prepared before we leave and a kettle kept simmering on the stove, so that he can make a pot of tea. We will have put the hens and chickens in their hatches and, being still bright, we are bound to have trouble in coaxing them in. Quite soon after we arrive, it will be evident whether or not there are to be refreshments. There will be a smell from the kitchen, or Rita bustling, or Effie going in and out to oversee things.

Monday

We went. Effie greeted us and saw us into the drawing room, where Mrs Coughlan sat upright on a two-seater sofa with gilt-edged side arms. She wore green georgette and a long matching scarf which swathed her neck and part of her chin. The picture instantly brought to mind was one I had seen in a book at school, featuring an English lady, swathed in white robes and crossing the desert. She let out a light, brittle laugh and her hand, when it took mine, was weightless as a feather. 'Such pretty ringlets,' she said, and laughed again. I was hearing her voice for the very first time, and it was like sound coming from a music box, sweet and tinkling. Turning to Mama, she said how much she had been looking forward to the visit and how terribly kind it was to give her that delicious cream. Instantly, they had a topic. They discussed whether cream should be whipped with a fork or with a beater, and they agreed that a beater in the hands of a mopey girl, no names mentioned, could lead to having a small bowl of puddiny butter.

There was a fire in the room, with an embroidered screen placed in front of it. The various lit lamps had shades of wine red, with masses of a darker wine fringing. It was like a room in a story, what with the fire, the fire screen, the fenders and fire irons gleaming, and the picture above the black marble mantelpiece of a knight on horseback breaching a storm. I sat on a low leather pouffe, looking at Drew and then looking out the window at the setting sun, from which thin spokes of golden light irradiated down, then back on her, whose perfume permeated the room, and despite her bemused smile and the different and affecting swivel of hand and wrist, her eyes looked quite sad. I could not understand why she was swathed in that scarf, unless it was for glamour, as the room was quite warm. Effie was extremely nervy – she would begin a sentence but not finish it and from time to time slap herself smartly and mutter, much to the irritation of her sister. It struck me then that she probably had to leave the convent on account of her nerves. Moreover, she seemed on the verge of tears, even though she was telling us how well they had settled in, how they loved the canal and the boating, loved their walks in the wood road, and had made friends with a few people.

'Hugh doesn't love it,' Mrs Coughlan said, adding that he was too much of a loner. This gave Mama another opening in the conversation, admitting that after she had come back from America – something she was most anxious to be let known – she, too, had felt herself to be an outsider. Mrs Coughlan exclaimed and said, 'But why ever did you come home?' Mama explained that she had merely come on a holiday, and had got engaged, and soon after got married. A little sigh escaped them both. Mrs Coughlan said that Hugh would not be joining us, since he was painfully shy and a bad mixer. I expect he was in his own den doing figures, or maybe reading. She then uncrossed her legs and lifted the folds of green georgette a fraction, so that to my heart's content I was able to see her beautiful shoes. They were cloth shoes of a silver filigree, with purple thread running through the silver, and there was a glittery buckle on the instep. I could have knelt at them. Effie then excused herself, looking more teary than ever. Mama welcomed that, because I felt that she wanted to get confidential with Mrs Coughlan and to share views about marriage, childbearing, and the change of life.

'It's not a bed of roses, by any means,' Mama starkly announced, and Mrs Coughlan concurred. She even became a little indiscreet, said that on her wedding day three unfortunate things happened – the edge of her veiling got caught on the church railing as they posed for the photographs, the handle of the knife broke in the wedding cake as she cut it, and an old aunt swore that she saw a fat mouse move across the dining room of the hotel floor and went into hysterics. Then, casually, she mentioned that she had been married off in her twenties. I reckoned that she was about thirty-five or six. She said that small towns were stifling and that bank folk only talked shop. Moreover, every few years Hugh got transferred to another town, so they could never put down roots and it was all ghastly. Mama sympathised, said she had once been in the same place for many years, but now loved her farm, her kitchen garden and her house, and would not be parted from them. Then she slipped in the fact that she hoped Mrs Coughlan would feel free to call on us, whenever she wished and this was met with tepid, absent-minded gratitude. Things were not going brilliantly. There was no ripple to it and there was no excitement. There were times when it seemed as if Mrs Coughlan had literally floated away from us, not listening, not seeing, lost in her own world-weary reverie.

A trolley was wheeled in. The china tea set was exquisite, with matching slop bowl, sugar bowl, and jug. The teapot was like a little kettle and had a cane handle. But the eats were not that thrilling. The sandwiches looked rough, obviously made by Rita, and I could swear that it was a shop cake. It had pink icing with a glacé cherry on top, not like Mama's cakes, which were dusted with caster sugar or a soft-boiled icing that literally melted on the tongue. There were also shop biscuits. Drew urged us to tuck in, as she refrained from food and kept feeling her throat through the layers of green folded georgette. Effie's hand trembled terribly as she passed us the cup and saucer, and Drew told her for goodness sake to get the nesting tables open so that we could at least have something to balance on.

Wanting desperately to show gratitude, Mama said that if ever they needed cream, fresh eggs, cabbage, or cooking apples they had only to ask. Normally she was reserved but her yearning to form a friendship had made her over-accommodating.

All of a sudden Drew got up and rushed to look in the oval mirror that had two candlesticks affixed to it, the white candles unlit, and unwinding the georgette scarf she sighed, saying to Effie to come and look, that the rash was much worse. Effie rushed to her, felt her glands, and said yes, that her lip had also swollen up. To our eyes there was no swelling at all, just a slightly chapped lip and a cold sore. Effie said they would ring the doctor at once, but Mrs Coughlan tut-tutted, said that was too much of an imposition and that they would go there instead. My heart sank. Mama's must have sank, too. Mama agreed with Effie that they should send for him and that he would come and bring several medicines in his doctor's bag. Drew was adamant and told Effie to run and get her fur coatee. She kept touching her lip and her glands with her forefinger, and Mama wondered aloud if perhaps it was some allergy, that maybe she had been gardening and touched nettles or some other plant, to which there came the distinct and crisp answer of 'Nouh'. Mama could not find the right thing to say.

Effie was back, all solicitude, putting the coatee around her sister's shoulders as they went out. We stood in the hall door to see them off, and Effie, who had only recently learned to drive, set out at a reckless speed. She could have killed someone. We debated as to what we should do, but the truth was we did not want to go home so early. Mama looked down at the perforated rubber mat that allowed for muck and wet to fall through and vowed that when she had a bit of money she would invest in one, so as not to be down on her knees scrubbing the kitchen floor and hall three times a week. It was not yet dark. Men were sitting on a bench across the road, drinking and talking quietly among themselves. They recognised us but did not call across, as by being in the Coughlan house we had somehow placed ourselves above them. Mama said that yes, the sitting room was nice, but it did not have a very salubrious view. It was a hushed night and there was a smell of flowers, especially night-scented stock from Mrs McBride's garden next door. Mrs McBride was a fanatic gardener and was forever wheeling different pots with flowering plants onto her front porch. We had heard that there was a rift between her and the Coughlans, as both had allotments at the back of their houses and there was argument about the boundary fence – so much so that a guard had had to be called to keep the peace.

We went back into the room and surprised Mr Coughlan, who was wolfing the sandwiches. The moment he saw us he made some apologetic murmur and bolted. Mama whispered to me that there was a strong smell of drink off him and said that no one ever knew the skeletons that lurked in other people's cupboards. She removed the fire screen and out of habit poked the fire and put a sod on it, and then she vetted the contents of the room more carefully, estimated the cost of all the furnishings, and said if she could have one item it would be the tea trolley and perhaps the mirror with the little candelabras on either side, but that she would not give tuppence for the piano. Then, as if I were absent, she said aloud to herself that there was no swelling and no rash, and that for a woman to wish to go to the doctor at that hour of evening was fishy, decidedly fishy.

'I adored her silver shoes,' I said, trying to sound grown up.

'Did you darling,' she said, but she was too busy cogitating matters such as how much did he drink, did husband and wife get on, and why were very young children in a boarding school, and why did the sister, the ex-nun, live with them.

The doctor was something of a ladies' man, and though Mama did not refer to it, it was known that he kissed young nurses in the grounds of the hospital and had taken a student nurse once to Limerick to the pictures, where they stayed canoodling for the second showing, much to the annoyance of the usherette. She conceded that though the green georgette dress and the shoes were the height of fashion, it was not the kind of attire to wear when going to a doctor. At that very moment and like a lunatic, I imagined Drew lying on the doctor's couch, he leaning in over her, patting her lip, perhaps with iodine, she flinching, her complexion so soft, a little flushed, and how both, as in a drama, had a sudden urge to kiss each other, but did not dare to. We sat for a bit and helped ourselves to some biscuits.

When they got back they showed real surprise at our being still there. I even think that Drew was irked.

'Nothing serious I hope,' Mama said, and Effie flinched and said that Drew had been given an ointment and also a tonic, because she was very run down. He had, it seems, checked her eyelids for anaemia. Drew looked different, as if something thrilling had happened to her, and was gloating over the fact that the doctor and his wife were on first names with her, as if they'd all known one another for an age. It seems they had to wait in the hall as the doctor was tending to an epileptic child, and while they were waiting, his wife came through and chatted with them, offered them a sherry and insisted that they call her Madeleine. Mama's hopes were thus dashed. The doctor's wife used to know us, used to visit us, which was such an honour and meant that we were people of note. Mama did things for her, like sew and knit and bake, and always kept a baby gin in a hidden drawer so that she could be given a tipple, unbeknownst to my father, when she came. Then she stopped coming, and much to Mama's bewilderment – we were never given a reason, and there had been no coolness and no argument. Months later, we heard that she told the draper's wife that our milk had a terrible smell and that she would not be visiting again. It had so happened that on one occasion when she came, the grass was very rich and hence the milk did smell somewhat strong, but being a town person she would not know the reason.

Effie then said that Drew should go straight to bed, and Mama concurred and asked if we might be excused. She was too conciliatory, even though she was rattled within.

'So glad you could both come,' Mrs Coughlan said, but it lacked warmth – it was like telling us that we were dull and lustreless and that we were not people of note.

'Well now I can say I met the grand Mrs Coughlan,' Mama said tartly as we walked home, and she repeated her old adage about old friends and new friends – when you make new friends, forget not the old, for the new ones are silver, but the old ones are gold.

We were in a gloom. The grass was heavy with dew, cattle lying down, munching and wheezing. She did not warn me to lift my

feet in order to preserve my white shoes, as she was much preoccu-
pied. There was no light from the kitchen window, which signified
that my father had gone up to bed and that we would have to bring
him a cup of tea and humour him, as otherwise he would be testy
on the morrow.

I had this insatiable longing for tinned peaches, but Mama
said it would be an extravagance to open a tin at that hour, while
promising that we would have them some Sunday with an orange
soufflé, which she had just mastered the recipe for. Mixed in with
my longing was a mounting rage. Our lives seemed so drab, so
uneventful. I prayed for drastic things to occur – for the bullocks
to rise up and mutiny, then gore one another, for my father to die
in his sleep, for our school to catch fire, and for Mr Coughlan to
take a pistol and shoot his wife, before shooting himself.

'Oft in the Stilly Night'

IT IS A SMALL SOMNOLENT VILLAGE with a limestone rock that sprawls irregularly over the village green, where sprouts a huge beech tree along with incidental saplings that meander out of it. Picturesque, you might say. Life has a quiet hum to it. You are passing through, on your way to somewhere livelier. You would never dream that so many restless souls reside here, dreaming of a different destiny. As you enter you see a stone, Roman-type church, one of the oldest in the land, a graveyard adjoining it and, on the tombstones, huge white lozenges of lichen that look bold, if not to say comic. In contrast a ball alley next door is green and oozes damp from years of rain. This is a rainy hamlet, being on the Gulf Stream. You would rarely come across anyone playing handball, except perhaps on Sundays, when a few youths, having trampled over grave plots and flower domes, take it into their heads to give themselves another bit of diversion by pegging a ball or some stones at the green lamenting cement. However, they soon tire of that and move on to amuse themselves with old cars or old motorcycles.

The effect when you first enter is of a backwater where souls and bodies have fallen prey to a stubborn tedium. You will find dogs, many of them mongrels, chasing each other over the ample green or snoozing in the sun. In the grocery shop the prevailing smell will be of flour and grain stuff and if you are lucky you might find bananas or grapes but most likely you will have to settle for apples. You could be tempted by a wide open-faced biscuit, like the face of a clock, studded with dark brown raisins. You would not suspect that in the big house with the wrought-iron gateway and the winding overgrown avenue a wife went a little peculiar, lost her marbles. It is said that it was her sister's fault, her sister, Angela. After spending many years in a convent, Angela to the chagrin of her order and her relatives upped and left, and came to live with Margaret in the big house. At first she hid, even from Margaret's husband, but gradually when her hair grew she emerged from her bedroom and eventually ventured down to the drawing room, to give a tinkle on the piano. It is said that it was there the husband, Ambrose, first saw her in a secular outfit, because of course he had seen her as a nun. Ambrose, who was something of a fop, was immediately captivated by her beauty and the slenderness of her frame inside a long brown velvet dress that buttoned down the centre and had a flare. Anything can happen to three people who languish in a house, a big house, a damp house, a house with gongs on the kitchen wall and many dank passages which could do with a lick of paint but for a chronic shortage of money. People can drive each other mad in such circumstances. Angela ate like a bird, gardened and played the piano in the evenings. Also she sang. She sang 'Oft In The Stilly Night' and 'There's A Bridle Hanging On The Wall'. In the summer evenings, with the bow window open, her voice could be heard by children or people milking in the fields nearby and it was thought to be rather screeching. The gardener who went there once a week to do a bit of scything stole their gooseberries and refused to oil the hinges of the lych-gate or do any extra favours because they never invited him indoors or offered him a cup of tea, being too stuck-up. Neighbours said he had every right to take the gooseberries and plagued him for a little can for themselves. They were very sweet gooseberries, yellow, translucent.

The sisters, Angela and Margaret, quarrelled a lot; at times so bitterly that Angela's belongings were flung out the window – dresses, a corset, her prayer book and beads, and the fur tippet which she wore at Mass and which sported the narrow and knowing face of a little fox. Ambrose, however, always intervened and Angela was dragged back from the avenue or even beyond the gate if she had ventured so far. No one knew or could imagine how peace was restored, what strategies of sweetness or authority Ambrose had had to resort to. What was rumoured was that he and Angela cuddled in the kitchen garden. Many people had seen them or had boasted about seeing them, and many wondered why his wife did not throw him out, since it was she who owned the house. Ambrose was something of a gentleman and shunned work. Soon as he married Margaret – the plainer sister – he rented out the land for grazing and spent his time on more dilatory pursuits, such as keeping bees and making elderflower wine. Ambrose knew so little about country matters that he was the butt of a standing joke. He had a sick beast which was too feeble to stir from its manger. He called on some locals, hoping to save himself the expense of a veterinary surgeon, and they simply turned the beast around to see if a bit of exercise might help. Ambrose, re-entering the manger after a suitable interval, said to the two men, 'Her eyes are brighter,' whereas in fact he was contemplating her rear. The two men drank liberally on the joke and, as time went by, embellished it.

Not long after Angela came to live there, tales of the unhappy trio began to trickle out and speculation was rife indeed, some locals even promising to steal over the high wall into the kitchen garden to get a gawk through the drawing room window. No one ever visited there, because Margaret was fiendishly thrifty and often returned to the shop with a package of bacon, to say there was one rasher short. Luck was not on their side. Angela grew ill, got thinner, was obliged to see a specialist and learned that she was struck down with a wasting disease. Sympathies changed quite drastically, and her good points – her singing, her devoutness at Mass and her taste in dressing – were now promulgated. She died in June and had a quite presentable funeral. Her brother-in-law followed her before a month was out and this, of course, substantiated the clandestine love story. Margaret became an object of pity, received gifts of jam and shortbread and was invited to card games which she did not attend. Margaret herself was an invalid a few years later, crippled with rheumatoid arthritis. At first she could move about with a stick and in the post office many were eager to discuss the pain with her and to suggest cures, all of which were useless. Eventually she was house-bound.

The jubilee nurse called once a week and let herself in by the back kitchen door, which was on the latch. It was she who reported that Margaret had repaired to the bridal room, where a dormant love for her husband burgeoned and was reaching fantastic proportions. His name was constantly on her lips, stories about their courtship, the food he liked and the idealization of her until the day of his death. Local women also called but Margaret could not hear the knocker, which was rusty, and so she remained banished in that bridal room with the baize-covered shutters, unable to admit the visitors that she longed for, muttering prayers, saying her husband's name and at times getting confused in the day of the week, wondering if the jubilee nurse was due or not.

You would not know, either, that in the main street, in the row of imitation Georgian houses, many fracas lurk. There is an unfortunate woman who scrubs and cleans for a living while her husband skulks in woods to assault girls and women. Some he does not have to assault, some wanton ones it is said go there, dally and allow themselves to be hauled into thickets or bracken or verdure. A kindly girl, Oonagh, takes in washing, starches sheets and tablecloths to such a stiffness that they are like boards. Her clothes-line is never free of sheets, tablecloths, serviettes and even more private garments. Nearby a lady who has the audacity to keep tinkers actually admits them into her house and allows them up to her bedrooms, five or six to a room. Her hallway smells foul, and no wonder. Many a Monday morning she is shaking bedspreads and eiderdowns from a top window and neighbours shout caustic things, not directly to her, but to each other so that she can hear. The Flea Hotel is the nickname of her crumbling premises.

A respectable lady who lives in the cut stone house with the bow window was the victim of one of those tinkers, who stole her shoes. They were tan brogue shoes which she had decided to dye brown. While they were drying, a hussy had come begging but was not received despite incessant knocking and pleading about the babe in her arms. In pique she helped herself to the shoes.

She was caught not long after, found by the sergeant at some sort of regatta where she was telling fortunes, squatting down on a bit of red velvet, giving the impression of an Eastern sage and wearing the shoes. In the court, her accuser, a married woman dressed in a black coat with Persian lamb trimming down the front, lost her heart for retribution, remembered somehow her own childhood, her dire poverty, her ancestors having been evicted from the fertile plains and having to flee to a mountain abode, repented having reported the thing at all and asked the judge in tearful tones to overlook it and to exercise clemency. The judge, who did not like this sort of interruption on a busy day – there was an anteroom full of people with cases waiting to be heard – asked her tetchily to be a little more circumspect in the future about clemency and to save her contrition for the confessional. As the shoes were handed over, the married woman begged that the tinker woman be let keep them, but of course such a request was impossible and she left the court carrying them in her hand limply, as if she would drop them the moment she got outside. The tinker woman was given a sentence of seven days and nights in the county gaol, which could be reprieved if she paid a fine of fifty pounds. This of course was impossible and sent all the tinkers on a wild binge around the town, cursing and vowing ructions.

In another house a nervous priest who has been defrocked sits most of the day. The scandal is so great it can hardly be mentioned.

His nerves are cited as the reason, but one who has travelled far has come back with a murky secret, in short, claiming that the priest had an eye for the ladies. Anyhow, he cannot say Mass, does not even serve at High Masses, and is seen on the hospital roads on Sundays walking with his mother. They gather branches to decorate their living room. They are the only people who call it by that name, as all others say parlour or drawing room and they are the only people who put flowers and branches indoors. One small clemency meted to the young priest is that insanity runs in the family since a cousin hanged himself from a tree, years back.

Yes, you would pass houses where there are drunks, where husbands on the day they get their pay packets do not come home till well after midnight, their wives accosting them on the top of the stairs or at the bottom of the stairs or wherever; and there are houses with bachelors whose rooms have never had a woman's hand to them and hence are dusty and somewhat inhospitable. You will pass various families with young children and another family which keeps horses and ponies and has had the misfortune to have one of its horses bolt out into the main road and be killed by a motorist, who then set out to sue the family for negligence.

'Spliced her in half,' the young son of the family is fond of saying, as a pathetic re-enactment of the restless mare and her mad bolting is described again and again.

You will find a former music teacher who no longer takes pupils but still keeps the sheet music on her piano to prove her former prowess, and who allows her little bantam hens the run of her house. Not far away, you will find a gentleman who was for a time like any common convict in Australia doing penal servitude, but has now returned to his roots. His crime was that he fired a shot at a barmaid who refused to serve him a drink after hours, and unfortunately he was a good shot and killed her. He no longer drinks but lives in semi-solitude, playing patience in the evening. There is a doting couple too, because of course every village has a doting couple. These are a childless pair who make their own butterscotch and resort to the most extreme endearments at all hours, even at breakfast-time. When the husband goes to work in the forestry his wife stealthily follows soon after on her bicycle, stationing herself behind the high limestone wall at the edge of the forest to make sure that her husband does not talk or mingle with any of these passing young girls or women.

There is too, in the house with the gorgeous geraniums on the porch, a budding beauty, plump, not too plump, eyes navy and limpid, eye sockets like inkwells in which this enticing navy stuff swills about, eyes ready for love. She reads magazines and cuts out the tips about hair and beauty and figure and so forth. There are children galore, housed in the school most of the time and utter nuisances during holiday time. There is a saddler's from whose doorway the pleasant smell of new leather and linseed oil drifts out, and not far away a shoemaker with the more fetid smell of sweat and old leather. That place is a jumble of old shoes heaped in an immemorial pyre. Then three mornings a week there is the heartening smell of fresh bread, when a van comes from the big city and trays of loaf bread, rock buns and tea cakes are carried into the shop. Hunger grips the village – women in the middle of washing or ironing hurry across, often with their aprons still on, often without the money, eager to collar one of those long soft loaves that are the food of life.

'I'll pay you later' or 'I'll pay you Friday' is often heard as they hasten back to their own kitchens to devour the sacramental fare. In the snug room of the bar, there are already at that hour one or two early topers drinking slowly, methodically, recognizing that the day has just begun, and here too gossip is rife, but in more measured tones. In this dark precinct that smells of porter, old porter and freshly drawn porter, the light is dim because of the fawn blind being permanently drawn, for privacy's sake, and the men, when they at length do decide to address each other, try to escape small matters of their own environment and discuss world topics from items they have gleaned in the newspapers. The furniture here is brown, the counter traced again and again with the circle of the glasses, circles that loop into one another like the circles in the core of a tree.

The loaves of bread that have been snapped up are devoured by housewives at home who lather them with jam or pickles or whatever, anything to give the morning a bit of zest, and soon it's time to put on the dinner and women hurry into their back gardens to cut a head or two of cabbage, then wash it to free it of clay and slugs and put it on to boil for the dinner, which is served midday, usually with bacon. Nice big greasy dinners for some, for others, scraps. Children in front gardens eating bits of bread and sugar, mild activity around lunch-time, people to-ing and fro-ing and the dogs on the village green yelping over a bone or territory or some distemper. Then a lull until tea-time. Older people dozing and from the school window, if it is open, the chants from the children either yelling or reciting in unison.

In the evenings the smell of the yew trees and the pine trees seems to be more pronounced, especially after rain. These grow in profusion in the church grounds, some that were planted many years ago and some that have seeded themselves. Across the road from the church you will see a two-storey stone house, you cannot avoid it. It was once painted blue but is now a dim replica of that colour. The garden is a disgrace. Everything is rampant: trees, shrubs, briars all meshed together in some mad knot, not only obscuring the path, but travelling right up along the windows, so that no one can see in. In there is Ita. Ita was once a paragon in this hamlet, the most admired devout person there. Along with looking after her brother and having a few hens and chickens and milking the cows, she looked after the church; she was the sacristan. The church was at once her sanctuary and her flower garden.

Outside, and due to the inclemency of the weather, the blue cut stone may have imparted a lugubriousness to passersby, but inside all was gleaming, as befits a place which houses God. The sanctuary lamp, perpetually alight, was of Paduan silver hanging low on lattice chains, its bowl pierced with holes containing the inner red bowl in which the sacred oil first glugged, then swayed; here too floated the wick with its tongue of sacred flame bespeaking the presence of Christ. Each time that Ita McNamara stepped inside she not only genuflected, she fell in front of the altar and prayed to God to sweeten her bitter cup, and God did.

It is many years now, but the memory of it is lasting. The missioners were due. The altar had to be sumptuously decked. She did not despair, she knew she would not have to resort to bits of evergreen and shrub because the Protestant spinsters would leave a sheaf of flowers in the porch, ample as a sheaf of corn. They were the only people who gardened, others had not the time or the will for such fal-lalling; others grew potatoes, cabbages and turnips but not flowers or flowering trees; maybe a bit of wild honeysuckle might be found threading its way through the eaves or a few devil's pokers defying the sodden aspect of a forlorn front garden, but a profusion of flowers, no. People had too much to do, trying to keep body and soul together, to eke out an existence. It was June when the catastrophe happened to Ita. 'Satan's net', it was fancifully christened by the cookery teacher who reminded the shocked faithful that many mystics in the Middle Ages had shown such symptoms, and that Ita could have been saved had there been a sensible doctor in the place. Before her downfall, her rhapsody. The flowers that she had been expecting were indeed in the chapel porch, and a prodigal bunch it was. She ran back to her own house to get extra vases, possibly uttering a prayer for the poor heathens, hoping a bolt of lightning would strike them, as it did Saul of Tarsus. Her fears for their damnation were no secret. She confessed once that her own flesh scorched at the thought, that she itched under the armpits and in her joints, it was as if live coals had been placed there, off a tongs. She often asked people to remember them in their prayers, so that they would not be perpetually lost, banished behind the gates of Hell, among the self-loathing, howling hordes.

Ita's brother, who was then alive, saw her pick up three empty jam jars, dump the remains of marmalade that had fungus on it from another jar, rinse it, then pick out the artificial flowers from the rainbow-spiralled vase and run. She took a long time decking the altar. She put the blue and the purple flowers on the altar steps, reserving the white lilies, Mary's flowers, for the altar itself, placing them on either side of the gold-crested tabernacle. The orange flaggers being too flagrant were put in the outer porch near the holy-water font. She stood enraptured, surveying things – the altar cloth like a frosted banner, the white flowers spectral, satin, the pristine beeswax candles, and then other flowers along the steps, where alas those imps of altar boys could kick them or trample on them as they bustled about. She liked none of those boys, infidels at heart, making fun of the parish priest, trying on his vestments, imitating his sing-song voice and the way his eyes rolled upwards of their own accord.

Next day she scrubbed the tiled floor, waxed the woodwork, even waxing the seats where people would plonk their backsides and their wet drapery. Not a cobweb remained in the high corners of the ceiling or in the window casements, no dust along the rim of the confessional doors and ledges and the church doors wide open to let the fresh air pour through. Later, she hauled across the two buckled stepladders, put a plank along the top, rested a chair on that and climbed up, in order to fill the sanctuary lamp with oil. Even her brother feared that she might have a seizure. He insisted that she rest, but no, she had a last chore. She had to make a sponge cake for the missioner, even though she did not know his taste in eats. The missioner the previous year had been elderly and had left them with a dire imprimatur, which was that when in bed they were to fold their arms in the form of a cross and recite:

> 'I must die, I do not know when, nor how,
> Nor where; but if I die in mortal sin
> I am lost for ever;
> Oh, Jesus, have mercy on me.'

Yes, everything was at the ready, the chapel spick and span, the altar seraphic, the sponge cake filled with lemon curd, sprinkled with sugar, propped on a cake plate and Ita with her long hair drawn back and held with a tortoiseshell slide. If she had any worry, it was the desecration, as such, that the local people would do to the church. She resented them trooping in, enjoying the sight of the flowers, soaking up the missioner's words, lingering afterwards to have a word with him. Many of the farmers smelt awful, smelt of cow-dung and things, but many of the town girls smelt worse, smelt of sin, and Ita knew it. If she had her way she would take these girls, lock them in a dark room, beat them and then starve them to death. One such hussy had the audacity to ask if Ita wanted any help with the altar or if she could perhaps wash the linen. The linen! Her lewd hands touching it, her scrubbing board party to it, a scrubbing board on which filth had been pummelled. Ita slapped her face, slapped her smartly on both cheeks, so much so that word went round that Ita McNamara had gone insane, had lost her marbles.

She went to the parish priest's house after dark, knocked on the side door and spoke to a grump of a maid who did an 'Indeed' as she went down the hall calling 'Father – Father.' The priest met Ita without his stiri collar and was obviously nettled at being disturbed. There were crumbs on his lips, yellow cake crumbs. He listened to her explanation and accepted her offer for a Mass to be said as propitiation. It was a large donation, the money she had put aside to go to Dublin one day. She did not regret it. Her joy in her work was utter, and on the evening before the mission she knelt for a moment surveying her little palace, yielding to a moment of ecstasy. A child who was kneeling in the back of the chapel said she saw Ita McNamara wobble, then she saw her stagger as she held on to the altar rails, then she heard her talk either to herself or to Our Lord or to someone.

So perhaps it had begun then, although others insisted that it began the moment she laid eyes on the missioner himself. He was a young man and came upon her by surprise. He had come into the chapel softly, scarcely making any tread, in his thonged, well-worn sandals. He smiled when he saw what she was doing. From a glass perfume spray, Ita was bathing the faces of the flowers. This thin, delicate-looking priest introduced himself as Father Bonaventure and congratulated her on the beauty of the chapel. He said that one might be at Chartres or Lourdes, so exalting were the surroundings. She thanked him and shuffled away, having registered his rimless spectacles with a half-moon of thicker glass at the bottom of each lens, his commodious robes the colour of bullrushes and his voice gentle yet so incisive, like a diamond cutter.

His sermon on the first evening of the mission began gently, ruminatively; yet no one was misled by that gentleness, least of all the wayward young girls, who sensed the sternness in his being, or the young men, who bristled at his scrutiny as he asked them to lift the veil and look into their souls and consider if by evil ways or evil thoughts they were crucifying afresh their loving Saviour, putting through the most holy soul of Mary the shaft of a sword, a shaft similar to that which passed through her in the hours of the Passion. His voice carried. It issued through the open windows, so that the Protestants doing a bit of gardening could hear it, as could the dumb beasts, the braying donkeys with gnats clotted on their eyelids, as could the little tufts of cowslips or primroses and every growing thing.

It was Ita who tended to him later, got some glucose and a glass of water. It seems he slumped on a bench in the sacristy, beads of sweat on his lips and on his temples accusing himself of not having moved the faithful enough. He resembled some great performer who feared that he had lost his touch with his audience. His assistant, a far younger priest, Father Finbar, was outside in the chapel grounds, bidding the people good night. Father Finbar, who had pinkish skin rather like a girl's, did not of course give sermons, but would be called on to assist at the Rosary and the Benediction and would probably hear some of the confessions. Later the two priests left together, their horn rosaries swaying against the folds of their brown robes and their hoods pulled up because it had begun to spatter with rain. They walked in silence over the path where the trod-on berries from the yew trees were like drops of blood, and then they went along the main road that was deserted now because of all the people having gone home. Ita watched them, and some children who were playing hide-and-seek saw what she did, then tattled about it. She picked up a cake box that was inside the gate to her house and ran after them, at a gallop. They had stopped at a bend on the road to look at a herd of fawn cattle, in a field. She thrust the box into Father Bonaventure's hands and came away blushing. She put her finger to her lips by way of exacting secrecy from the children, and gave them a penny between them.

Confessions were heard each morning and the entire parish was enjoined to go. Ita watched them like a hawk each year because some were bound to cheat. A wicked or a cunning person could go up, kneel down, but at the last moment refuse the Host and yet return with eyes devoutly closed, as if the Host were dissolving. Just after the first two people had gone in to confess, an incident occurred. A girl by the name of Nancy fainted, fainted in high operatic manner, so that her arms slapped onto those next to her and her missal with all its contents scattered over the aisle; holy pictures with far from holy inscriptions were seen and read by several. The upshot was that this girl Nancy could not go in to confess, had to be carried to the harness-maker's nearby and be given a spoon of tonic wine in hot water. Ita, sensing foul play, commandeered the girl's younger sister, Della, brought Della out to the chapel grounds and quizzed her inordinately about her sister's behaviour. Was Nancy out late at night? Was Nancy seeing some boy? Was Nancy off her food in the morning and complaining of nausea? In short, was Nancy in a state of mortal sin and possibly having a baby? Another blight on their village.

The little girl Della got so frightened at this inquisition that to divert things she put the palm of her hand on the spear of the railing and threatened to gouge herself, to do penance for the whole world, her sister included. Ita gave her a sound thumping then and sent her back into the church. Many overheard it and wondered why Ita had become so officious. She quarrelled with several local people, but particularly with the parish priest's house-keeper, since the missioners were staying there, tackled her about menus, told her to buck up and give them something better than packet soup and synthetic jelly set with boiled milk to give it a bit of fuzz. Later people were quick to insist that yes, they had noticed it then but they had thought it was a temporary aberration.

She spent far more hours than was necessary in the church, laying out several vestments for the priest, separating each of the altar breads in such a manner that when they were put in the chalice the priest could pick each one up separately and easily. She used the excuse to be in the church all the time by polishing the floor again and again, so much so that people skeetered over it, and once she was heard humming to herself and it was not a hymn, more like a refrain. Because of the crush in the church for the evening sermons – all were obliged to go and mostly all did – people had to be accommodated behind the altar rails, lined up along the altar steps, and usually it was children who were put there and usually it was the sacristan who organized it. No longer.

Ita selected who would go in there and then sat among them, directly gazing up at the priest, catching the words, the incendiary words as they formed in his mouth just before he uttered them. Father Bonaventure, who had been gentle on the first evening, grew fiercer with each sermon, expatiating on the fires of Hell, the loss of the sight of God, the absence of grace, and reminding them of their last, perhaps their very last chance for redemption. At certain moments he foamed. He spared no one. He paused between words and sentences, to look into faces, the faces of those clustered around him including Ita, the gnarled faces of the older people in the pews with their heads bent, the shamed faces of the men standing at the back, and to each of them, it was as if he spoke directly and clairvoyantly. Then, fearing he had gone too far, he appealed to them. He softened his words and reminded them that if they persisted in their mortifications God would respond, and His pent-up fountain of love and mercy would burst open to grant their wishes.

Emotion was rampant. People quaked with terror, others made vows out loud, others thumped their chests, others moaned, all except Ita, who gazed at him, glorious, beatific, triumphant, no longer the awkward creature, but now an almost presentable woman with a beret which she wore at an angle. People had remarked about this because Ita had always worn a headscarf and pulled it so far forward that it shelved on either side of her face. But here she was, inside the altar rails, gazing at the priest, her black angora beret at an angle, her cheeks adorned with rouge. At least some swore it was rouge though others said it was flush from the blaze of the candles.

At his last sermon, so fervid was he, so resonant the vibrations of his words, that a lily, a white flute, fell stealthily off its stalk, onto the altar cloth. The people shivered, all hearkening to his strictures. The 'terrene affections', as he called them, had to be crushed in favour of the love of the Almighty and the camaraderie of Christ. Many saw the lily, its white skin shrivelling in the heat, its yellow stamen specking the altar cloth, but then it was just a lily, a fallen inert thing.

When the faithful had gone, Ita had many tasks to do. She had to put away the cruets and the silver for the next year's mission, throw out the withered flowers and put the good ones on the tiled floor of the sacristy, far away from the fumes of the quenched candles. Moreover, people were pestering her with requests to have a word with Father Bonaventure, alone. Some thought that a private word with him would grant them unheard-of indulgences. The little nitwit Della asked if she could have her autograph book signed, and for her impertinence got a biff. All the while Father Bonaventure was behind the screen changing from his embroidered vestments into the brown robes of his order. Sometime during that bustle, Ita must have taken the lily flute and put it in her pocket; maybe she thought to place it under her pillow, in the way that young girls put the crumbs of a wedding cake there, to dream of their betrothed. Della swears that Ita was crying, but then the mission made many people cry as they came face to face with the gravity of things. No one actually saw her and Father Bonaventure say goodbye. Many are divided about the hour of his departure. Some say he dallied, while others insist that he left almost immediately. The stall owners, who had tents outside the chapel gates, had already gone, and the mother-of-pearl rosaries, the fulsome leaflets, the blessed scapulars and all the other sacred impedimenta were in boxes, waiting to be despatched to the seaside town where Father Bonaventure was due to preach.

Ita went home, and as her dismayed brother was later to attest, she behaved quite normally. He admitted to having been rather ratty with her on account of her being so late, he himself had driven a few crippled people home from the mission and was still back half an hour before she appeared. The fire was out, as he said, and he had to coax it back to life with newspaper and paraffin. She seemed to him no different than usual except that she refused to eat, vowing that she would be fasting from now on. Those hours mark the divide between the Ita that everyone knew and the lunatic that was to emerge and be dragged out of there at cockcrow.

Villagers were sunk in sleep, even dogs that barked and marauded on the green had quietened down, when a roar followed by a volley of roars shook the village. It being summertime, most people had their windows open. Ita's brother heard it, of course, as did the nearest neighbours, who jumped out of their beds believing there was a robbery or that the tinkers were on the rampage again. People with coats or cardigans flung over them were seen running, and soon they were in Ita's room witnessing the crazed sight of her sitting up in bed, her nightdress bundled up around her middle as she wept copiously. Her brother asked if it was bats, as he lit a stump of a candle. Often on the summer nights bats came in, cleaved to the ceiling or the rim of a ewer, and then swooped about once it was dark. 'Not bats . . . not bats,' she said, pointing to the lily, which was the cause of her dementia. It lay beside her on the bed, close to the calf of her leg, which was full of scratches. It had moved. It had taken flesh. It was dirty. They must get Father Bonaventure, because only he could exorcise it.

'Keep back . . . keep back,' she said as her brother tried to pluck it from her. She had now withdrawn to the head of the bed, her black hair splayed on the wrought iron. Her eyes were wild too. She got it into her head that they were all against her, and cursed them from the fortress of her bed. The cookery teacher tried to calm her, told her how much they all loved her and asked if she would like a cup of tea. Then she reminded everyone of Ita's Trojan work during the mission and said that most likely she was exhausted. The praise softened her ire, and breaking into a childlike smile Ita blessed herself and said, 'Blessed is he that is not scandalized in me.' They knew now that it was in earnest and that she was talking heresy. Her moods altered between states of near beatitude and begging to be beaten, to be scourged alive. Her

brother said that was what was needed and dashed out of the
room to get his ash plant but the neighbours remonstrated with
him, said she must have the priest because she was possessed.

While he was gone, Ita treated them to some strange tales and
used swear words that they did not know were in her vocabulary.
She described the assault of the lily, how it ran out from under the
pillow, crawled all over her like a hairy Molly and was impervious
to grasp. Yes, it was the Devil, she knew that. Then she expressed
a doubt and said it was not the Devil; then she tore at her flesh
again, which was already full of cuts, and asked them to pray that
she could be redeemed. Yet when Father Bonaventure arrived she
acted like a courtesan, put her hand out to welcome him, said to
excuse her 'deshabille', adding that her stockings were in flitters.
Then she asked to be left alone with him and spoke in a whisper.
She made mention of their days together, the promises they had
made, and how they were going abroad as a team to convert
heathens. Each time he accused her of imagining things she flared
up and asked him to look at her body, to look at where Satan had
been, to drive the serpent away, to crush it with his thumbs or
his sandalled foot or his beads. He did not wish to look at her
body. With one hand she grabbed him and with the other held
the candleholder slant-wise over the thin matt of greying hair
and asked did he not see it? She said he must see it. It was there. It
was a blister of blood, Christ's blood, and had blood as its essence.
She had been with Christ. Oh yes, he knew, but he was jealous,
wanting her for himself. Who now was the culprit clinging to
'terrene affections', begging for her love? Who now but him?
Immediately he began to pray rapidly and summoned the others
in from the landing to pray with him, and so great was her rage at
his calling for witnesses that she put the candle first to the sleeve of
her nightdress, then to the matt of hair where she had been taken
in adultery. But who were they to throw stones? Quick to smell
the scorching, a youngster came from the kitchen with a pitcher of

water which was poured over her. Ita laughed and said she felt like a little girl, remembered her youth, the daisy chains she had made and a game she played tracing a penny onto a page.

Very early, she was brought to the asylum, where she spent the best part of a year and took to sucking in her cheeks, refusing to speak to anyone and having to be barred from the chapel because the sight of flowers drove her into a frenzy. She took up smoking too, and the authorities indulged her in that, thinking it would take her mind off her troubles. She cadged cigarettes off visitors and told some very tall tales about travels she had made in the Far East, where she was a nursing sister and where she had contracted malaria. In about a year, when she was calm with tablets and shock treatment, they brought her home, and from then on she avoided people, growling at anyone who spoke to her, even the priest or the doctor. Being alone now, she does the farm work and has taken to wearing her brother's old clothes and Wellington boots. She is always forking manure, or washing out the cow house, or carrying buckets of feed and water up the hills to the store cattle. 'There goes the one with the roastings,' people say. She is like a landmark, one bucket in either hand, either going up the hill or returning to have them refilled. Children say that she curses them, and those who knock on her door are likely to be met with a pitchfork or a saucepan of hot stirabout.

Now I ask you, what would you do? Would you comfort Ita, would you tell her that her sins were of her own imagining; then might you visit the budding beauty and set her dreaming of the metropolis, would you loiter with the drunkards and laugh with the women gorging the white bread, would you perhaps visit the grave to say an Ave where Angela, her sister and the errant husband lie close together, morsels for the maggots, or would you drive on helter-skelter, the radio at full blast. Perhaps your own village is much the same, perhaps everywhere is, perhaps pity is a luxury and deliverance a thing of the past.

What a Sky

THE CLOUDS – DARK, MASSED AND PURPOSEFUL – raced across the sky. At one moment a gap appeared, a vault of blue so deep it looked like a cavity into which one could vanish, but soon the clouds swept across it like trailing curtains, removing it from sight. There were showers on and off – heavy showers – and in some fields the water had lodged in shallow pools where the cows stood impassively, gaping. The crows were incorrigible. Being inside the car, she could not actually hear their cawing, but she knew it very well and remembered how long ago she used to listen and try to decipher whether it denoted death or something more blithe.

As she mounted the granite steps of the nursing home, her face, of its own accord, folded into a false, obedient smile. A few old people sat in the hall, one woman praying on her big black horn rosary beads and a man staring listlessly through the long rain-splashed window, muttering, as if by his mutters he could will a visitor, or maybe the priest, to give him the last rites. One of the women tells her that her father has been looking forward to her visit and that he has come to the front door several times. This makes her quake, and she digs her fingernails into her palms for fortitude. As she crosses the threshold of his little bedroom, the first question he fires at her is 'What kept you?', and very politely she explains that the car ordered to fetch her from her hotel was a little late in arriving.

'I was expecting you two hours ago,' he says. His mood is foul and his hair is standing on end, tufts of grey hair sprouting like Lucifer's.

'How are you?' she says.

He tells her that he is terrible and complains of a pain in the back from the shoulder down, a pain like the stab of a knife. She asks if it is rheumatism. He says how would he know, but whatever it is, it is shocking, and to emphasize his discomfort he opens his mouth and lets out a groan. The first few minutes are taken up with showing him the presents that she has brought, but he is too disgruntled to appreciate them. She coaxes him to try on the pullover, but he won't. Suddenly he gets out of bed and goes to the lavatory. The lavatory adjoins the bedroom; it is merely a cupboard with fittings and fixtures. She sits in the overheated bedroom listening, while trying not to listen. She stares out of the opened window; the view is of a swamp, while above, in a pale untrammelled bit of whey-coloured sky, the crows are flying at different altitudes and cawing mercilessly. They are so jet they look silken, and listening to them, while trying not to listen to her father, she thinks that if he closes the lavatory door perhaps all will not be so awful; but he will not close the lavatory door and he will not apologize. He comes out with his pajamas streeling around his legs, his walk impaired as he goes towards the bed, across which his lunch tray has been slung. His legs like candles, white and spindly, foreshadow her own old age, and she wonders with a shudder if she will end up in a place like this.

'Wash your hands, Dad,' she says as he strips the bedcovers back. There is a second's balk as he looks at her, and the look has the dehumanized rage of a trapped animal, but for some reason he concedes and crosses to the little basin and gives his hands, or rather his right hand, a cursory splash. He dries it by laying the hand on the towel that hangs at the side of the basin. It is a towel that she recognizes from home – dark blue with orange splashes. Even this simple recollection pierces: she can smell the towel, she can remember it drying on top of the range, she can feel it without touching it. The towel, like every other item in that embattled house, has got inside her brain and remained there like furniture inside a room. The white cyclamen that she has brought is staring at her, the flowers like butterflies and the tiny buds like pencil tips, and it is this she obliges herself to see in order to generate a little cheerfulness.

'I spent Christmas Day all by myself.'

'No, Dad, you didn't,' she says, and reminds him that a relative came and took him out to lunch.

'I tell you, I spent Christmas Day all by myself,' he says, and now it is her turn to bristle.

'You were with Agatha. Remember?' she says.

'What do you know about it?' he says, staring at her, and she looks away, blaming herself for having lost control. He follows her with those eyes, then raises his hands up like a supplicant. One hand is raw and red. 'Eczema,' he says almost proudly. The other hand is knobbly, the fingers bunched together in a stump. He says he got that affliction from foddering cattle winter after winter. Then he tells her to go to the wardrobe. There are three dark suits, some tweed jackets, and a hideous light-blue gabardine that a young nun made him buy before he went on holiday to a convent in New Mexico. He praises this young nun, Sister Declan, praises her good humour, her buoyant spirit, her generosity and her innate sense of sacrifice. As a young girl, it seems, this young nun preferred to sit in the kitchen with her father, devising possible hurley games, or discussing hurley games that had been, instead of gallivanting with boys. He mentions how the nun's father died suddenly, choked to death while having his tea, but he shows no sign of pity or shock, and she thinks that in some crevice of his scalding mind he believes the nun has adopted him, which perhaps she has. The young nun has recently been sent away to the same convent in New Mexico, and the daughter thinks that perhaps it was punishment, perhaps she was getting too fond of this lonely, irascible man. No knowing.

'A great girl, the best friend I ever had,' he says. Wedged among the suits in the cupboard is the dark frieze coat that belongs to the bygone days, to his youth. Were she to put her hand in a pocket, she might find an old penny or a stone that he had picked up on his walks, the long walks he took to stamp out his ire. He says to look in the beige suitcase, which she does. It is already packed with belongings, summer things, and gallantly he announces that he intends to visit the young nun again, to make the journey across the sea, telling how he will probably arrive in the middle of the night, as he did before, and Sister Declan and a few of the others will be waiting inside the convent gate to give him a regal welcome.

'I may not even come back,' he says boastfully. On the top shelf of the wardrobe are various pairs of socks, and handkerchiefs – new handkerchiefs and torn ones – empty whiskey bottles, and two large framed photographs. He tells her to hand down one of those photographs, and for the millionth time she looks at the likeness of his mother and father. His mother seems formidable, with a topknot of curls, and white laced bodice that even in the faded photograph looks like armour. His father, who is seated, looks meeker and more compliant.

'Seven years of age when I lost my mother and father, within a month of each other,' he says, and his voice is now like gravel. He grits his teeth.

What would they have made of him, his daughter wonders. Would their love have tamed him? Would he be different? Would she herself be different?

'Was it very hard?' she asks, but without real tenderness.

'Hard? What are you talking about?' he says. 'To be brought out into a yard and put in a pony and trap and dumped on relations?'

She knows that were she to really feel for him she would enquire about the trap, the cushion he sat on, if there was a rug for his knees, what kind of coat he wore, and the colour of his hair then; but she does not ask these things. 'Did they beat you?' she asks, as a form of conciliation.

'You were beaten if you deserved it,' he says, and goes on to talk about their rancour and how he survived it, how he developed his independence, how he found excitement and sport in horses and was a legend even as a young lad for being able to break any horse. He remembers his boarding school and how he hated it, then his gadding days, then when still young – too young, he adds – meeting his future wife, and his daughter knows that soon he will cry, and talk of his dead wife and the marble tombstone that he erected to her memory, and that he will tell how much it cost and how much the hospital bill was, and how he never left her, or any one of the family, short of money for furniture or food. His voice is passing through me, the daughter thinks, as is his stare and his need and the upright sprouts of steel-coloured hair and the over-pink plates of false teeth in a glass beer tumbler. She feels glued to the spot, feels as if she has lost her will and the use of her limbs, and thinks, This is how it has always been. Looking away to avoid his gaze, her eyes light on his slippers. They are made of felt, green and red felt; there are holes in them and she wishes that she had bought him a new pair. He says to hand him the brown envelope that is above the washbasin. The envelope contains photographs of himself taken in New Mexico. In them, he has the air of a suitor, and the pose and look that he has assumed take at least thirty years off his age.

At that moment, one of the senior nuns comes in, welcomes her, offers her a cup of tea, and remarks on how well she looks. He says that no one looks as well as he does and proffers the photos. He recounts his visit to the States again – how the steward-esses were amazed at his age and his vitality, and how everyone danced attendance on him. The nun and the daughter exchange a look. They have a strategy. They have corresponded about it, the nun's last letter enclosing a greeting card from him, in which he begged his daughter to come. From its tone she deduced that he had changed, that he had become mollified; but he has not, he is the same, she thinks.

'Now talk to your father,' the nun says, then stands there, hands folded into her wide black sleeves, while the daughter says to her father, 'Why don't you eat in the dining room, Dad?'

'I don't want to eat in the dining room,' he says, like a corrected child. The nun reminds him that he is alone too much, that he cries too much, that if he mingled it would do him some good.

'They're ignorant, they're ignorant people,' he says of the other inmates.

'They can't all be ignorant,' both the nun and the daughter say at the same moment.

'I tell you, they're all ignorant!' he says, his eyes glaring.

'But you wouldn't be so lonely, Dad,' his daughter says, feeling a wave of pity for him.

'Who says I'm lonely?' he says roughly, sabotaging that pity, and he lists the number of friends he has, the motorcars he has access to, the bookmakers he knows, the horse trainers that he is on first names with, and the countless houses where he is welcome at any hour of day or night throughout the year.

To cheer him up, the nun rushes out and shouts to a little girl in the pantry across the way to bring the pot of tea now and the plate of biscuits. Watching the tea being poured, he insists the cup be so full that when the milk is added it slops over onto the saucer, but he does not notice, does not care.

'Thank you, thank you, Sister,' he says. He used not to say thank you and she wonders if perhaps Sister Declan had told him that courtesy was one way to win back the love of recalcitrant ones. He mashes the biscuits on his gums and then suddenly brightens as he remembers the night in the house of some neighbours when their dog attacked him. He had gone there to convalesce from shingles. He launches into a description of the dog, a German shepherd, and his own poor self coming down in the night to make a cup of tea, and this dog flying at him and his arm going up in self-defence, the dog mauling him, and the miracle that he was not eaten to death.

He charts the three days of agony before he was brought to the hospital, the arm being set, being in a sling for two months, and the little electric saw that the county surgeon used to remove the plaster.

'My God, what I had to suffer!' he says. The nun has already left, whispering some excuse.

'Poor Dad,' his daughter says. She is determined to be nice, admitting how wretched his life is, always has been.

'You have no idea,' he says, as he contrasts his present abode, a dungeon, with his own lovely limestone house that is going to ruin. He recalls his fifty-odd years in that house – the comforts, the blazing fire, the mutton dinners followed by rice pudding that his wife served. She reminds him that the house belongs to his son now and then she flinches, remembering that between them, also, there is a breach.

'He's no bloody good,' he says, and prefers instead to linger on his incarceration here.

'No mutton here; it's all beef,' he says.

'Don't they have any sheep?' she says, stupidly.

'It's no life for a father,' he says, and she realizes that he is about to ask for the guarantee that she cannot give.

She takes the tea tray and lays it on the hallway floor, then praises the kindness of nuns and of nurses and asks the name of the matron, so that she can give her a gift of money. He does not answer. In that terrible pause, as if on cue, one crow alights on a dip of barbed wire outside the window and lets out a series of hoarse exclamations. She is about to say it, about to spring the pleasant surprise. She has come to take him out for the day. That is her plan. The delay in her arrival at the nursing home was due to her calling at a luxurious hotel to ask if they did lunches late. When she got here from London, late the previous night, she had stayed in a more commercial hotel in the town, where she was kept awake most of the night by the noise of cattle. It was near an abattoir, and in the very early hours of the morning she could hear the cattle arriving, their bawling, their pitiful bawling, and then their various slippings and slobberings, and the shouts of the men who got them out of the trailers or the lorries and into the pens, and then other shouts, indeterminable shouts of men. She had lain in the very warm hotel room and allowed her mind to wander back to the time when her father bought and sold cattle, driving them on foot to the town, sometimes with the help of a simpleton, often failing to sell the beasts and having to drive them home again, with the subsequent wrangling and sparring over debts. She thinks that indeed he was not cut out for a life with cattle and foddering but that he was made for grander things, and it is with a rush of pleasure that she contemplates the surprise for him. She had already vetted the hotel, admitting, it is true, a minor disappointment that the service did not seem as august as the gardens or the imposing hallway with its massive portraits and beautiful staircase. When she visited to enquire about lunch, a rather vacant young boy said that no, they did not do lunches, but that possibly they could manage sandwiches, cheese or ham. Yet the atmosphere would exhilarate him, and sitting there in the nursing home with him now, she luxuriates in her own bit of private cheer. Has she not met someone, a man whose very voice, whose crisp manner fill her with verve and happiness? She barely knows him, but when he telephoned and imagined her surrounded by motley admirers, she did not disabuse him of his fantasy. She recalls, not without mischief, how that very morning in the market town she bought embroidered pillowcases and linen sheets, in anticipation of the day or the night when he would cross her bedroom doorway. The thought of this future tryst softens her towards the old man, her father, and for a moment the two men revolve in her thoughts like two halves of a slow-moving apparition. As for the new one, she knows why she bought pillowslips and costly sheets: because she wants her surroundings not only to be beautiful for him but to carry the vestiges of her past, such sacred things as flowers and linen, and all of a sudden, with unnerving clarity, she fears that she wants this new man to partake of her whole past – to know it in all its pain and permutations.

The moment has come to announce the treat, to encourage her father to get up and dress, to lead him down the hallway, holding his arm protectively so that the others will see that he is cherished, then to humour him in the car, to ply him with cigarettes, and to find in the hotel the snuggest little sitting room – in short, to give him a sense of well-being, to while away a few hours. It will be a talking point with him for weeks to come, instead of the eczema or the broken arm. Something is impeding her. She wants to do it, indeed she will do it, but she keeps delaying. She tries to examine what it is that is making her stall. Is it the physical act of helping him to dress, because he will, of course, insist on being helped? No, a nun will do that. Is it the thought of his being happy that bothers her? No, it is not that; she wants with all her heart to see him happy. Is it the fear of the service in the hotel being a disappointment, sandwiches being a letdown when he would have preferred soup and a meat course? No, it is not that, since, after all, the service is not her responsibility. What she dreads is the intimacy, being with him at all. She fears that something awful will occur. He will break down and beg her to show him the love that he knows she is withholding; then, seeing that she cannot, will not, yield, he will grow furious, they will both grow furious, there will be the most terrible showdown, a slanging match of words, curses, buried grievances, maybe even blows. Yes, she will do it in a few minutes; she will clap her hands, jump up off the chair, and in a sing-song voice say, 'We're late, we're late, for a very important date.' She is rehearsing it, even envisaging the awkward smile that will come over his face, the melting, and his saying, 'Are you sure you can afford it, darling?', while at the same moment ordering her to open the wardrobe and choose his suit.

Each time she moves in her chair to do it, something gets between her and the nice gesture. It is like a phobia, like being too terrified to enter the water but standing at its edge. Yet she knows that if she were to succumb, it would not only be a delight for him, it would be for her some enormous leap. Her heart has been hardening now for some time, and when moved to pity by something she can no longer show her feelings – all her feelings are for the privacy of her bedroom. Her heart is becoming a stone, but this gesture, this reach will soften her again and make her, if not the doting child, at least the eager young girl who brought home school reports or trophies that she had won, craving to be praised by him, this young girl who only recited the verses of 'Fontenoy' in place of singing a song. He had repeatedly told her that she could not sing, that she was tone-deaf.

Outside, the clouds have begun to mass for another downpour, and she realizes that there are tears in her eyes. She bends down, pretending to tie her shoe, because she does not want him to see these tears. She saw that it was perverse not to let him partake of this crumb of emotion, but also saw that nothing would be helped by it. He did not know her; he couldn't – his own life tore at him like a mad dog. Why isn't she stirring herself? Soon she will. He is talking non-stop, animated now by the saga of his passport and how he had to get it in such a hurry for his trip to America. He tells her to fetch it from the drawer, and she does. It is very new, with only one official entry, and that in itself conveys to her more than his words ever could: the paucity and barrenness of his life. He tells how the day he got that passport was the jolliest day he ever spent, how he had to go to Dublin to get it, how the nuns tut-tutted, said nobody could get a passport in that length of time because of all the red tape, but how he guaranteed that he would. He describes the wet day, one of the wettest days ever, how Biddy the hackney driver didn't even want to set out, said they would be marooned, and how he told her to stop flapping and get her coat on. He relives the drive, the very early morning, the floods, the fallen boughs, and Biddy and himself on the rocky road to Dublin, smoking fags and singing,

Biddy all the while teasing him, saying that it is not a passport that he is going for but a mistress, a rendezvous.

'So you got the passport immediately,' the daughter says, to ingratiate herself.

'Straightaway. I had the influence – I told the nuns here to ring the Dáil, to ring my TD, and by God, they did.'

She asks the name of the TD, but he has no interest in answering, goes on to say how in the passport office a cheeky young girl asked why he was going to the States, and how he told her he was going there to dig for gold. He is now warming to his tale, and she hears again about the air journey, the nice stewardesses, the two meals that came on a little plastic tray, and how when he stepped out he saw his name on a big placard, and inside the convent gate, three nuns with big smiles waiting to receive him, the youngest with her hand up, in salutation. 'Kindest creature ever born,' he says with emphasis.

Suddenly she knows that she cannot take him out; perhaps she will do it on the morrow, but she cannot do it now and so she makes to rise in her chair.

He senses it, his eyes now hardening. 'You're not leaving?' he says.

'I have to; the driver could only wait an hour,' she says feebly.

He gets out of bed, says he will at least see her to the front door, but she persuades him not to. He stares at her as if he is reading her mind, as if he knows the generous impulse that she has defected on. In that moment she dislikes herself even more than she has ever disliked him. Tomorrow she will indeed visit, before leaving, and they will patch it up, but she knows that she has missed something, something incalculable, a moment's reconciliation. The downpour has stopped the clouds swept away, the sky an immensity of grey, like a grey sieve, sieving a greater greyness. As she rises to leave, she feels that her heart is in shreds, all over that room. She has left it in his keeping, but he is wildly, helplessly looking for his own.

Brother

BAD CESS TO HIM. Thinks I don't know, that I didn't smell a
rat. All them bachelors swaggering in here, calling him out to
the haggart in case I twigged. 'Tutsy this and Tutsy that.' A few
readies in it for them, along with drives and big feeds. They
went the first Sunday to reconnoitre, walk the land and so forth.
The second Sunday they went in for refreshments. Three married
sisters, all gawks. If they're not hitched up by now there must be
something wrong; hare lip or a limp or fits. He's no oil painting, of
course. Me doing everything for him; making his porridge and
emptying his worshipful po, for God knows how many years. Not
to mention his lumbago, and the liniment I rubbed in.

'I'll be good to you, Maisie,' he says. Good! A bag of toffees on
a holy day. Takes me for granted. All them fly-boys at threshing
time trying to ogle me up into the loft for a fumble. Puckauns. I'd
take a pitchfork to any one of them; so would he if he knew. I
scratched his back many's the night and rubbed the liniment on it.
Terrible aul smell. Eucalyptus.

'Lower . . . lower,' he'd say. 'Down there.' Down to the puddingy
bits, the lupins. All to get to my Mary. He had a Mass said in the
house after. Said he saw his mother, our mother; something on her
mind. I had to have grapefruit for the priest's breakfast, had to
de-pip it. These priests are real gluttons. He ate in the breakfast
room and kept admiring things in the cabinet, the china bell and
the bog-oak cabin, and so forth. Thought I'd part with them. I
was running in and out with hot tea, hot water, hot scones; he ate
enough for three. Then the big handshake; Matt giving him a
tenner. I never had that amount in my whole life. Ten bob on
Fridays to get provisions, including sausages for his breakfast.

Woeful the way he never consulted me. He began to get hoity-
toity, took off that awful trousers with the greasy backside from
all the sweating and lathering on horseback, tractor and bike;
threw it in the fire cavalierlike. Had me airing a suit for three
days. I had it on a clothes-horse, turning it round every quarter of
an hour, for fear of it scorching.

Then the three bachelors come into the yard again, blabbing
about buying silage off him. They had silage to burn. It stinks the
countryside. He put on his cap and went out to talk to them. They
all leant on the gate, cogitating. I knew 'twas fishy, but it never
dawned on me it could be a wife. I'd have gone out and sent them
packing. Talking low they were, and at the end they all shook
hands. At the supper he said he was going to Galway Sunday.

'What's in Galway?' I said.

'A greyhound,' he said.

First mention of a greyhound since our little Deirdre died. The
pride and joy of the parish she was. Some scoundrels poisoned her.
I found her in a fit outside in the shed, yelps coming out of her,
and foam. It nearly killed him. He had a rope that he was rumi-
nating with, for months. Now this bombshell. Galway.

'I'll come with you, I need a sea breeze,' I said.

'It's all male, it's stag,' he said and grinned.

I might have guessed. Why they were egging him on I'll never
know, except 'twas to spite me. Some of them have it in for me; I
drove bullocks of theirs off our land, I don't give them any haults
on bonfire night. He went up to the room then and wouldn't
budge. I left a slice of griddle bread with golden syrup on it outside
the door. He didn't touch it. At dawn I was raking the ashes and
he called me, real soft-soapy, 'Is that you Maisie, is that you?' Who
in blazes' name did he think it was – Bridget or Mary of the gods!
'Come in for a minute,' he said, 'there's a flea or some goddamn
thing itching me, maybe it's a tick, maybe they've nested.' I strip
the covers and in th'oul candlelight he's like one of those saints

that they boil, thin and raky. Up to then I only ventured in the dark, on windy nights when he'd say he heard a ghost and I had to go to him. I reconnoitre his white body while he's muttering on about the itch, says, 'Soldiers in the tropics minded itch more than combat.' He read that in an almanac.

'Maisie,' he says in a watery voice, and puts his hand on mine and steers me to his shorthorn. Pulled the stays off of me. Thinking I don't know what he was after. All pie. Raving about me being the best sister in the wide world and I'd give my last shilling and so forth. Talked about his young days when he hunted with a ferret. Babble, babble. His limbs were like jelly, and then the grunts and him burying himself under the red flannel eiderdown, saying God would strike us.

The next Sunday he was off again. Not a word to me since the tick mutiny, except to order me to drive cattle or harness the horse. Got a new pullover, a most unfortunate colour, like piccalilli. He didn't get home that Sunday until all hours. I heard the car door banging. He boiled himself milk, because the saucepan was on the range with the skin on it. I went up to the village to get meal for the hens and everyone was gassing about it. My brother had got engaged for the second time in two weeks. First it was a Dymphna and now it was a Tilly. It seemed he was in their parlour – pictures of cows and millstreams on the wall – sitting next to his intended, eating cold ox-tongue and beetroot, when he leans across the table, points to Tilly and says, 'I think I'd sooner her.'

Uproar. They all dropped utensils and gaped at him, thinking it a joke. He sticks to his guns, so much so that her father and the bachelors drag him out into the garden for a heart-to-heart. Garden. It seems it's only high grass and an obelisk that wobbles. They said, 'What the Christ, Matt?' He said, 'I prefer Tilly, she's plumper.' Tilly was called out and the two of them were told to walk down to the gate and back, to see what they had in common.

In a short time they return and announce that they understand one another and wish to be engaged. Gink. She doesn't know the catastrophe she's in for. She doesn't know about me and my status here. Dymphna had a fit, shouted, threw bits of beetroot and gizzard all about and said, 'My sister is a witch.' Had to be carried out and put in a box-room, where she shrieked and banged with a set of fire-irons that were stored there. Parents didn't care, at least they were getting one cissy off their hands. Father breeds French herds, useless at it. A name like Charlemagne. The bachelors said Matt was a brave man, drink was mooted. All the arrangements that had been settled on Dymphna were now transferred to Tilly. My brother drank port wine and got maudlin. Hence the staggers in the yard when he got home and the loud octavias. Never said a word at the breakfast. I had to hear it in the village. She has mousey hair and one of her eyes squints, but instead of calling it a squint the family call it a 'lazy eye'. It is to be a quiet wedding. He hasn't asked me, he won't. Thinks I'm too much of a gawk with my gap teeth, and that I'd pass remarks and say, 'I've eaten to my satisfaction and if I ate any more I'd go flippety-floppety,' a thing he makes me say here to give him a rise in the wet evenings.

All he says is 'There'll be changes, Maisie, and it's for the best.' Had the cheek to ask me to make an eiderdown for the bed, rose-coloured satin. I'll probably do it, but it will only be a blind. He thinks I'm a softie. I'll be all pie to her at first, bringing her the tea in bed and asking her if she'd like her hair done with the curling tongs. We'll pick elderflowers to make jelly. She'll be in a shroud before the year is out. To think that she's all purty now, like a little bower bird, preening herself. She won't even have the last rites. I've seen a photo of her. She sent it to him for under his pillow. I'll take a knife to her, or a hatchet. I've been in Our Lady's once before, it isn't that bad. Big teas on Sundays and fags. I'll be out in a couple of years. He'll be so morose from being all alone, he'll welcome me back with open arms. It's human nature. It stands to reason. The things I did for him, going to him in the dark, rubbing in that aul liniment, washing out at the rain barrel together, mother-naked, my bosoms slapping against him, the stars fading and me bursting my sides with the things he said – 'Dotey'. Dotey no less. I might do for her out of doors. Lure her to the waterfall to look for eggs. There're swans up there and geese. He loves the big geese eggs. I'll get behind her when we're on that promontory and give her a shove. It's very slippery from the moss. I can just picture her going down, yelling, then not yelling, being swept away like a newspaper or an empty canister. I'll call the alarm. I'll shout for him. If they do smell a rat and tackle me, I'll tell them that I could feel beads of moisture on my brother's poll without even touching it, I was that close to him. There's no other woman could say that, not her, not any woman. I'm all he has, I'm all he'll ever have. Roll on, nuptials. Daughter of death is she.

The Widow

Bridget was her name. She played cards like a trooper, and her tipple was gin-and-lime. She kept lodgers, but only select lodgers: people who came for the dapping, or maybe a barrister who would come overnight to discuss a case with a client or with a solicitor.

The creamery manager was the first guest to be more or less permanent. After a few months it was clear he wasn't going to build the bungalow that he had said he would, and after a few more months he was inviting girls to the house as if it were his own. Oh the stories, the stories! Card parties, drink, and God knows what else. No one dared ask expressly. Gaudy women, with nail varnish, and lizard handbags and so forth, often came, sometimes staying for the weekend. Bridget had devoted the sitting room to him and his guests, choosing to say that whatever they wanted to do was their business.

She worked in the daytime, in a local shop, where she was a bookkeeper. She kept herself very much to herself – sat in her little office with its opaque beaded-glass panelling, and wrote out the bills and paid for commodities, and rarely, if ever, came out to the shop to serve customers. The owner and she got on well. He called her Biddy, short for Bridget, which meant, of course, that they were good friends. Occasionally she would emerge from her glass booth to congratulate a young mother on having a baby or to sympathize with someone over a death, but this, as people said, was a formality, a mere gesture. No one had been invited to her new pebble-dash house, and the twin sisters who called un-announced were left standing on the doorstep, with some flimsy excuse about her distempering the kitchen ceiling. She was determined to remain aloof, and as if to emphasize the point she had Venetian blinds fitted.

You may ask, as the postmistress had asked – the postmistress her sworn enemy – 'Why have Venetian blinds drawn at all times, winter and summer, daylight and dark? What is Bridget trying to hide?' What went on there at night, after she strolled home, carrying a few tasties that the owner of the shop had given her, such as slices of bacon or tins of salmon? It was rumoured that she changed from her dark shop overall into brighter clothes. A child had seen her carrying in a scuttle of coal. So there was a fire in the parlour, people were heard to say.

Parties began to take place, and many a night a strange car or two, or even three, would park outside her driveway and remain there till well near dawn. Often people were heard emerging, singing 'She'll be comin' 'round the mountain when she comes, when she comes.' Such frivolities inevitably lead to mishaps, and there came one that stunned the parish. A priest died in the house. He was not a local priest but had arrived in one of those strange cars with strange registration numbers. The story was that he went up to the bathroom, missed a step as he came out, and then, of course – it could happen to anyone – tripped and fell. He fell all the way down the fifteen steps of stairs, smashed his head on the grandfather clock that was at the bottom, and lay unconscious on the floor. The commotion was something terrible, as Rita, a neighbour, reported. There were screams from inside the house. The creamery manager, it seems, staggered to his car, but was too inebriated to even start the engine; then a young lady followed, drove off, and shortly after the local curate arrived at the house with the viaticum. An hour later, the ambulance brought the priest to the hospital, but he was already dead.

Bridget put a brave face on it. Instead of hiding her understandable guilt, she acknowledged it. She spoke over and over again of the fatal night, the fun that had preceded the tragedy, the priest, not touching a drop, regaling them with the most wonderful account of being admitted to the Vatican – not for an audience, as he had thought, but to see the treasures. 'Thousands of pounds' worth of treasures . . . thousands of pounds' worth of treasures!' he had apparently said as he described a picture or a sculpture or a chalice or vestments. Then Bridget would go on to describe how they had all played a game of forty-five and before they knew where they were it was three in the morning and Father So-and-So rose to return home, going upstairs first. He had had, as she said, glass after glass of lemonade. Then the terrible thud, and their not believing what it was, and the creamery manager getting up from the table and going out to the hall, and then a girl going out, and then the screams. Bridget made it known that she would never forgive herself for not having had a stronger bulb on the landing. At the High Mass for the priest's remains, she wore a long black lace thing, which she had not taken out since her beloved husband had died.

Her husband had been drowned years before, which is why she was generally known as the Widow. They had been married only a few months and were lovebirds. They had lived in another house then – a little house with a porch that caught the sun, where they grew geraniums and begonias and even a few tomatoes. Her despair at his death was so terrible it was legendary. Her roar, when the news was broken to her, rent the parish, and was said to have been heard in distant parishes. Babies in their cots heard it, as did old people who were deaf and sitting beside the fire, as did the men working out in the fields. When she was told that her husband had drowned she would not believe it: her husband was not dead; he was a strong swimmer; he swam down at the docks every evening of his life before his tea. She rebelled by roaring. She roared all that evening and all that night. Nobody in the village could sleep. When they found his body in the morning with reeds matted around it, her cries reached a gargantuan pitch. She could not be let to go to the chapel. Women held her down to keep her from going berserk.

Then, some days after he was buried, when the cattle began to trample over the grave and treat it as any old grave, she stopped her keening. Soon after, she put on a perfectly calm, cheerful, resigned countenance. She told everyone that she was a busy woman now and had much to do. She had to write to thank all the mourners, and thank the priests who officiated at the High Mass, and then decide what to do about her husband's clothes. Above all, she was determined to sell her house. She was advised against it, but nothing would deter her. That house was for Bill and herself – 'Darling Bill', as she called him – and only by leaving it would the memory, the inviolate memory, of their mornings and their evenings and their nights and their tête-à-têtes remain intact.

She sold the house easily, though far too cheaply, and went back to the country to live with her own folks – a brother and a deaf-mute sister. No one in the village heard of her until a few years later, when her brother died and her sister went to an institution. Unable to manage the tillage and foddering, Bridget sold the farm and moved back to the town. She was a changed woman when she came back – very much more in charge of herself. Very much more the toff, as people said. She got a job as a bookkeeper in the shop and started to build a house, and while it was being built many conjectured that she had a second husband in mind. There were rumours about bachelors seen talking to her, and especially one who came from America and took her to the dog track in Limerick a few Saturday nights in a row and bought her gins. The news of her drinking soon spread, and the verdict was that she could bend the elbow with any man. Hence, being installed in her new house was not the neighbourly affair it might have been. There was no housewarming, for instance; no little gifts of cream or homemade black puddings or porter cake; no good-luck horseshoe on her door. In short, the people ostracized her. She seemed not to mind, having always kept to herself anyway. She had a good wardrobe, she had a good job, and as soon as she started to keep select boarders – only two, or at the most three – everybody remarked that she was getting above herself. Her house was sarcastically called the Pleasure Dome, and sometimes, more maliciously, she was coupled with the song 'Biddy the Whore, who lived in a hotel without any door'.

Her first two guests were strangers – men who were doing some survey for the land commission, and whom all the farmers suspected of being meddlesome. They and Bridget became the best of friends – sat outside on deck chairs and were heard laughing; went to Mass together, the last Mass on Sundays; and in the evening imbibed, either at home or in the hotel. When they left, the creamery manager arrived – a big man with wide shoulders and a large, reddish face. He was voluble, affectionate. He touched people's lapels, particularly women's, and he was not shy about asking for a kiss. A few of the girls professed to have spurned him. The old maids, who mistrusted him, watched him when he left the creamery at half past five in the evening to see if he would go straight to his lodgings or across to the town to have a pint or two. They would lie in wait behind walls, or behind the windows of their sitting rooms. He rarely mentioned Bridget by name but referred to her as the Landlady, often adding how saucy she was, and what a terrific cook. He was especially fond of her lamb stew, which, as people said, was really mutton stew.

Soon the creamery manager, whose name was Michael, acquired a steady girlfriend called Mea. Mea was a bank clerk from the city, and she came in her car at weekends and stayed two nights. He would splash himself with eau de cologne on the evenings she was expected, and was to be seen traipsing in front of the house, so eager was he to see her. They never kissed on the steps but always went inside and left some of the local snoopers, especially the women, demented with curiosity as to what happened next. She could, as Bridget told the shopkeeper, who then told it to everyone else, twist Michael around her little finger. She was subject, it seemed, to the most fitful moods – sometimes bright as a hummingbird, other times professing to have a headache or a sinus or a stomach ache, and refusing even to speak to him. Once, she locked herself in her bedroom and did not come out for the whole evening. She ate like a bird, bleached her hair with egg yolk and lemon, and cut a great dash at Mass or devotions, always managing to have a different hat or a different headscarf each Sunday. It was noticed that she hardly prayed at all – that she looked around, summing up the people, sneering at them – and that she was not certain when were the times to stand and when were the times to kneel, but would look around to gauge what others were doing.

'Ah, it's her sweet mystery . . . her sweet mystery,' Michael had told Bridget, who had told the shopkeeper, who had, of course, told others. Before long, Mea and Michael were engaged, and Mea was coming not only two nights a week but three nights a week, and driving all around with him to see if there were any uninhabited houses or bungalows, because of course they would want their own place. Each week, as well, she bought some item of furniture, usually something bulky – a mirror or a wardrobe or a whatnot or a bureau – and he was heard to say that she was furniture-mad. In jest he would ask the men why he was putting a rope around his neck.

They were to be married in June, but one evening early in May there was a rift. Michael broke it off. It happened at the hotel, just as the crowd was wishing them well and making innuendos about the patter of little feet. Michael was very drunk – his drinking had got heavy over the past few weeks – and suddenly he turned to Mea and said, very candidly and almost tearfully, that he could not go through with it. She was to keep the ring; he wanted every-thing to end in good faith. She slapped him, there and then, three times on the cheek in front of everyone. 'How dare you,' she said with the acerbity of a governess, and then she ran out and he followed, and soon they drove off down the Shannon Road – no doubt to patch things up, as people said. But Michael was adamant. The engagement was broken off.

She left that night, and Michael hid for three days. He went back to the creamery, drawn and unshaven, and on that Friday he learned of her suit for breach of promise by reading of it in the weekly newspaper. There were photos of him and Mea, mention of some little lovey-dovey exchanges, and even a photo of Bridget, who Mea said had had too much influence over him and was probably responsible for the rift. Mea also talked about her broken heart, the several plans she had made, the house that she envis-aged, the little rose garden, then discussed her bottom drawer, which was full of linen and lavender sachets and so on. Above all, she bemoaned the fact that her romantic future with any other man was out of the question; in short, that her life was destroyed. Michael received a solicitor's letter, consulted his local solicitor, and was said to have paid her a hefty compensation. Then he went on the batter for a few weeks and was carted to the Cistercian monastery, and finally came home looking thinner and much more subdued. 'A gold-digger, a gold-digger, that's what she was,' Bridget would say whenever Mea's name was mentioned, and in time the matter was forgotten.

It was perceived – first by the postmistress, then by another woman, who spoke about it to several others – that Bridget and the creamery manager were flirting openly. Soon after, they were seen holding hands as they took a walk down the Chapel Road after Benediction. They had lingered in the chapel, allowing the others to leave. It was the sacristan who saw them, and ran and told it in the town, once she had recovered from her fright. People asked if she was certain, or if she had not imagined it. 'That I may drop dead if it's not true,' she said, putting her hand to the grey wool cardigan that covered her sunken bosom.

The inappropriateness of this was more than they could stomach. After all, she was a widow, and she was a woman in her forties, who ought to know better. Neighbours began to watch more carefully, especially at night, to see how many lights went on in the upstairs rooms – to see if they had separate bedrooms or were living in mortal sin. The less censorious said it was a flash in the pan and soon he would have another beauty in tow, so that all, all were flabbergasted the morning Bridget stood in the doorway of the shop and announced her engagement. To prove it, a lozenge of blue shimmered on her finger, and her eyes were dancing as the people gaped at her.

Before long, Bridget bought a car, and Michael gave her driving lessons on the Dock Road, the very road where her husband had walked to his death. He stopped soliciting young girls, even the young buttermaker in the creamery, and told strangers how happy he was, and that up to now all the women he had known were mere bonbons, and that this was *It*.

Her happiness was too much for people to take; they called her a hussy, they predicted another breach of promise, they waited for the downfall. Some of the older women went to the parish priest about it, but when they arrived the parish priest was in such a grump about the contributions towards a new altar that he told them to pull their socks up and try to raise money by selling cakes and jellies and things at a bazaar. He suspected why they had come, because the creamery manager had gone to him alone, and stayed an hour, and no doubt gave him a substantial offering for Masses.

To put a good complexion on the engagement period, a young-ster was brought to Bridget's house from the country, a boy so daft that he dug up the tubers of the irises in mistake for onions – in short, no chaperon. They were to be married in December, which left Bridget two months to pack up her job and prepare her trousseau. She was always to be seen flying in her red car now, a menace to pedestrians and cattle that strayed on the roadside. To ingratiate herself, as they said, she offered people lifts to the city, or offered to do errands for them. Some, being weak, accepted these favours, but not the diehards. A few of the men, it is true, praised her, said what spunk she had. She was much older than Michael, and moreover, she had got him off the booze; he drank only wine now – table wine.

A week before the wedding, the pair went to the local pub, which they had got out of the habit of doing, and stood drinks to everyone. The shopkeeper, proposing the toast, said he knew that Biddy and Michael had everyone's blessing. People clapped, then someone sang. Then Biddy, being a little tipsy, tapped her glass with her engagement stone and said she was going to give a little recitation. Without further ado, she stood up, smiled that sort of urchin smile of hers, ran her tongue over her lips, another habit, and recited a poem entitled 'People Will Talk'. It was a lunge at all those mischievous, withered people who begrudged her her little flourish. It may have been – indeed, many people said that it was – this audacious provocation that wreaked the havoc of the next weeks. Had she confided in a few local women, she might have been saved, but she did not confide; she stood aloof with her man, her eyes gleaming, her happiness assured.

It never came to light who exactly had begun it, but suddenly the word went round, the skeleton that had been lurking for years – that her husband had not drowned by accident, he had taken his own life. His predicament, it was said, was so grinding that he saw no way out of it. He went down to the docks that evening, after yet another hideous row with her, pen and paper in his pocket, and wrote his farewell note. It was in his trousers pocket before they handed it to her. Why else had she roared for three days, they asked, and why was she unfit to attend her own husband's funeral or the High Mass? Why else did she recover so soon, but that she was a wicked, heartless harlot? The creamery manager, they predicted, would be a scapegoat once the marriage vows were exchanged. First one person whispered it, then another, and then another; the story slipped from house to house, from mouth to mouth, and before long it reached Bridget's appalled ears. As if that were not shock enough, she received one morning an anonymous letter saying that her husband-to-be would know of her skeleton shortly. She flung the letter into the stove, then tried in vain to retrieve it. Luckily, Michael was still upstairs, asleep in his own room. It was then that she made her first mistake – she ran around trying to bribe people, asking them not to mention this terrible rumour, not to tell the creamery manager, for God's sake not to tell. The more she tried to quash the talk, the more people concluded her guilt. She lost all composure. She could be seen in her bare feet or in her nightgown running up the road to meet the postman, to ward off any other dreadful bulletins.

After that morning, she dared not let Michael go anywhere alone, in case someone told him. She knew, or at least clung to the belief, that no one at work would risk telling him, for fear of being fired on the spot. But in the street or on the way to Mass or at the pub – these were the danger zones, and for weeks she followed him everywhere, so that he began to show signs of impatience and said that she was a hairy Molly, clinging to him. Her looks, which had improved since the engagement, took a turn for the worse, and she was what she once had been – a scraggy older woman, with thin hair and skin that was much too yellow.

Michael saw that she was distraught, but did not understand it. It seems he told the young buttermaker that his missus had got the jitters and the sooner they got married the better. Even while he was saying this, his missus-to-be was grasping at any straw. She confided in the shopkeeper, who advised her to tell Michael, but she broke down and even flared up, mistrusting her one friend. 'Why not take the bull by the horns and tell him straight out?' he had said. She couldn't. He would jilt her. Had he not already jilted a younger and comelier girl, and was she, Bridget, not haunted by that same prospect? It was then that she remembered the old woman who had lived across the road from her husband and herself and had later moved back to the country. She would go to find this woman, who would swear that she had never heard a voice raised, and that in fact Bridget and her first husband used to sit in the sun porch in the evening, among the geraniums and the begonias, whispering, holding hands, canoodling.

Then a little respite came. Michael decided to go home to his own folks for a week, and that was a godsend. They would then meet in Limerick, with a small sprinkling of relatives, and there they would be married in the Augustinian church. One of the friars was a friend of Michael's, and he had already made the arrangements. Because of the breach-of-promise episode, it was going to be a very hushed-up affair.

Before leaving, Michael tackled her. He sat her in the little armchair by the kitchen stove, where they had often, so often, joked and cuddled. He asked her if perhaps she was having second thoughts about things, if perhaps she did not love him. Her eyes filled up with tears. She said, 'No, no, Michael . . . no.' She was so in love, she confessed, that she was afraid that it would go wrong. Then he kissed her and reproved her for being a daft little hen of a woman, and they waltzed around the kitchen, promising things that they would do when they were married, like putting a skylight in the kitchen, and getting a new range so that she did not have to dirty her fingers with the ashes and clinkers. He loved her little hands, he said, and he kissed them. 'Num, num.' he said, as if he were eating them, as if they were jam tarts.

As she told the shopkeeper later, they had a blissful farewell. He tried to coax out of her what she was planning to wear at the wedding, but she sang dumb. 'I sang dumb,' she said, and described how she ran upstairs to get the old fox collar, with its little foxy snout and beady eyes, and threatened him with it, went 'Yap, yap, yap.' They played hide-and-seek, they laughed, they teased one another, but on no account would she allow him into the room where her trousseau was stored – her voile gown and her satin shoes, and her piles of new undies, and the fleecy bed jacket. Their farewell was so tender that Michael even debated if he should cancel his journey. 'God blast it, I'm over twenty-one,' he said. But she persuaded him to go, insisted. She knew it was essential that he be away from this place, where any mischief-maker could say, 'I believe your intended wife drove her first husband to his death.' She could not risk it. There was something about Michael, although she never told him this, that reminded her of her first husband. They were both childlike and affectionate, and they both had gruff tempers but were quick to apologize – to lay a bar of chocolate or a hanky on the pillow as an appeasement. She loved them in much the same way – the same gushing, bubbly, childish way that she had loved at twenty – and miraculously, her love was reciprocated.

The day after he left, Bridget set out to see the old woman. She was cheerful in the town when she stopped to buy petrol. She even told the young attendant that she was thinking of throwing a party, and asked if he would like to come. 'Deffo,' was what he claimed to have said.

No one of us ever knew what ensued with the old woman, because it was on the way back that it happened. It was a treacherous bit of road, always known to be; it twisted, then straightened, and then forked suddenly and ridged under a thick canopy of beech trees. Lorries and cars had crashed there so often that people said there was a curse on that stretch. A witch had once lived nearby – a witch who defied the hierarchy and concocted pagan cures from herbs. People wondered if the aftermath of this witch was not the cause of all these disasters, and holy water had been sprinkled there many a time by the priests.

It was after dark when the accident happened. Bridget had gone to the old woman, and afterwards had gone to a hotel in the nearest town and treated herself to a drink. It may have been that she went to the hotel to celebrate, to taste for the first time the joy, as well as the certainty, of her future. Maybe the old woman had said, 'I'll tell them how happy you and Bill were,' or had cried, remembering that other time, when she was not old, when she did not have cataracts in her eyes, when the nice young couple invited her across the road for a glass of stout or a cup of tea. Or maybe the old woman had forgotten almost everything and just shook and stared. Whatever took place was never known, but in the hotel where Bridget drank the gin-and-lime and bought the crisps she chattered with the owner and asked him for his card, saying that she would be coming back there with her husband for a dinner. The locality, she said, was lucky for her, and she felt she owed it a little recompense. Half an hour later, she was around a tree, the car up on its hind legs, like an animal, her face on the dashboard, askew, her eyes wide open.

Some workmen who had been tarring the road heard the screech of the crash, and ran from a little caravan where they were cooking supper. None of them knew her. Two stayed while the third went to a lodge of a big house to ask to use the telephone. The woman in the gate lodge was a bit strange and did not want to let them in, so they had to go up to the big house, and quite a long time passed before the ambulance and the guards came. But the consensus was that she had died on the spot. She was brought back to the local hospital, where a young nurse laid her out in white. The mourners who came the next day were surprised, even aghast, that her face was so beautifully smooth, without cuts or gashes. It was makeup, they claimed, perfect makeup, and what a scandalous thing to adorn a corpse.

Michael knelt beside her and roared intemperately, as she had once roared, leaving no one in doubt that he loved her passionately. At the grave he tried to talk to her, tried to stop them from lowering the coffin. He knew everything now; he knew her plight and was helpless to do anything about it. She had quite a large funeral, but beneath the prayers and the murmurs were the whispers of how drunk she had been when she got into that car. They said her face had been disfigured, but that some silly nurse had made her look presentable, had doctored the truth, sent her to her maker with this monstrous camouflage – some chit of a nurse, as dissolute as Bridget herself had been.

Storm

THE SUN GAVE TO THE BARE FIELDS the lustre of ripened hay. That is why people go, for the sun and the scenery – ranges of mountains, their peaks sparkling, an almost cloudless sky, the sea a variety of shades of blue, ceaselessly flickering like a tray of jewels. Yet Eileen wants to go home; to be more precise, she wishes that she had never come. Her son Mark, and his girlfriend, Penny, have become strangers to her and, though they talk and go to the beach and go to dinner, there is between them a tautness. She sees her age and her separateness much more painfully here than when at home, and she is lost without the props of work and friends. She sees faults in Penny that she had not noticed before. She is irked that a girl of twenty can be so self-assured, irked at the languid painstaking way that Penny applies her suntan oil, making sure that it covers each inch of her body, then rolling onto her stomach imploring Mark to cover her back completely. At other times Penny is moody, her face buried in a large paperback book with a picture of a girl in a gauze bonnet on the cover. There are other things, too: when they go out to dinner Penny fiddles with the cutlery or the salt-and-pepper shakers, she is ridiculously squeamish about the food, and offers Mark tastes of things as if he were still a baby.

On the third night, Eileen cannot sleep. On impulse she gets out of bed, dons a cardigan and goes out on the terrace to plan a strategy. A mist has descended, a mist so thick and so opaque that she cannot see the pillars and has to move like a sleepwalker to make her way to the balustrade. Somewhere in this sphere of milky white the gulls are screaming, and their screams have a whiff of the supernatural because of her not being able to see their shapes. A few hours earlier, the heavens were a deep, a hushed blue, studded with stars; the place was enchanting, the night balmy and soft. In fact, Penny and Mark sat on the canvas chairs looking at the constellations while waiting and hoping for a falling star so that they could make a wish together. Eileen had sat a little apart from them, lamenting that she had never been that young or that carefree. Now, out on the terrace again, staring into the thicket of mist and unnerved by the screaming gulls, she makes herself a firm promise to go home. She invents a reason, that she has to do jury duty; then, like a sleepwalker, she gropes her way back to bed.

But next day she finds herself lying on the beach near them, smarting beneath a merciless sun. There is a little drama. Penny has lost a ring and Mark is digging for it in the sand. He scrapes and scrapes, as a child might, and then he gets a child's shovel which has been left behind and digs deep, deeper than is necessary. He retraces where he has already scraped. Penny is crying. It was a ring Mark gave her, an amethyst. Eileen would like to help, but he says he knows where he has already searched and it is best to leave it to him. Penny dangles her long, elegant fingers and recalls how the ring slipped off. He jokes a little and says what a pity that she hadn't called out at the very moment, because then they could trace it. Others watch, some supposing that it is money that is lost. Penny begs him to give up, saying that obviously it was meant and alluding to possible bad luck. He goes to a different spot.

'It can't be there,' Penny says, almost crisp. Eileen sees that he is smiling. She does not see him pick anything up, but soon after he stands over Penny, bends down and re-enacts the ritual of putting on an engagement ring. Penny cries out with joy and disbelief, says she can't believe it, and a great ripple of warmth and giddiness overtakes them. Mark is fluent now with stories of life at university, fights he got into, scrapes he got into, being stopped by the police on his motorcycle and so on, as if the relief of finding the ring has put to rest any unspoken difference between them.

In the late afternoon they drive back to the villa and discuss where they should go for dinner. Penny decides to cut her fringe and stations herself at the kitchen table wielding a huge pair of scissors, the only pair in the house, while Mark holds a small, shell-shaped mirror in front of her. Sometimes in jest Penny puts the point of the scissors to his temple or nips a little hair from above his ear and they joke as to who is the bigger coward. Afterwards, the shreds of cut blond hair lie on the table, but Penny makes no attempt to sweep them up. They have drinks and the bits of hair are still there, dry now and exquisitely blond. Eileen eventually sweeps them up, resenting it, even while she is doing it.

When they arrive for dinner they are bundled out onto a terrace and told they must wait.

'*Aspetta . . . aspetta*,' the waiter keeps saying, although his meaning is already clear. Eileen notices everything with an awful clarity, as if a gauze has been stripped from her brain – the metal chairs glint like dentist's chairs, a pipe protruding from underneath the terrace is disgorging sewage into the sea, while a little mongrel dog barks at the sewage with untoward glee. The waiter brings three tall glasses filled with red Campari and soda.

'It's just like mouthwash,' Penny says, wiggling one of the straws between her lips. Eileen is doing everything to be pleasant, but inside she feels that she will erupt. First she counts backwards from one to a hundred, then she takes a sip from her glass, not using a straw, then resumes counting and wonders if they, too, are aware of the estrangement. She is meaning to tell them she will go home earlier than planned, but each time she is on the point of saying it, there is some distraction, Penny asking for a fresh straw, or the mongrel now at their table, or two people identically dressed and with similar haircuts, their gender a mystery.

As they drive back to the villa after dinner, it happens. Its suddenness is stunning. Eileen does not understand how it happens except that it does: a sharp word, then another, then another, then the eruption.

'Are you all right in the back?' he asks.

'Fine,' Eileen says.

'We're not going too fast for you?' he asks.

'If Penny were driving too fast I'd tell her to slow down.'

'Huh . . . it wouldn't make any difference,' Penny says. 'I'd tell you to hitch.' Eileen bristles. She infers in this insolence, dislike, audacity. Suddenly she is speaking rapidly, gracelessly, and she hears herself saying cruel things, mentioning their moodiness, cut hairs, the cost of the villa, the cost of the very car they are driving in, and even as she says this she is appalled. In contrast they are utterly still, and the only change she sees is Mark's hand laid over Penny's. Eventually Eileen becomes silent, her outburst spent, and they drive without saying a word. When they arrive home, they stagger out of the car and she sees them walk towards the villa with an air of exhaustion and defeat. She hurries, to try and salvage things.

'We must talk,' she says to Mark, and touches his sleeve. He flings her off as if she were vermin. It is his turn to explode. His rage is savage and she realizes that a boy who has been mild and gentle all his life is cursing her, vehemently. Penny clings to him as if he were a mast, begging him not to be angry, and there is such terrifying contrast between the tender appeal of her sobs and the rabidness of his words as he denounces his mother. She, too, looks at him, begging him to stop, and sees that the whites of his eyes are the colour of freshly shed blood. He has passed sentence on her forever. A thousand memories pass through her as she begs to be allowed to explain herself. He will not hear of it. When he finishes his exhortation, he leads Penny towards the open door and they go out, down the steps and up the path to the gateway. Eileen knows that to call after them is useless, and yet she does. They disappear from sight, and turning round in the kitchen, she does something that she knows to be absurd: she dons an apron and goes to the sink to wash the glasses that have been there since before they went out. She washes them in soapy water, rinses them under the hot tap, then under the cold tap, and dries them until they are so dry that she can hear the whoosh of the cloth on the dry glass.

Soon the kitchen is utterly silent. She can hear the lap of water through the open window and the clatter from the rigging of the few boats that bob back and forth in the breeze. She is waiting both for the sound of the car to start up or for their return. She combs her hair, walks around her bedroom, consults her bedside clock and listens for them. After an hour she undresses and turns out her light in the belief that the dark house and the knowledge that she has gone to bed will bring them back. Lying there, praying – a thing she has not done for years – she hears them come in on tiptoe, and without any premeditation she rushes out to the passage and in one burst apologizes and says some madness possessed her. Idiotically she mentions sunstroke, and they look at each other with blanched and mortified faces.

In the morning they all rise earlier than usual and she can see that, like her, they did not sleep. They are quiet; they are utterly thoughtful and polite, but they are embarrassed. She asks a favour of them. She reminds them that for days they had planned to go sailing and she wonders if they could go today, as she would welcome the day to herself. They are relieved and, as she can see, quite glad, and without even touching their breakfast they get up and start to gather a few things – towels, bathing suits, suntan oil and bottled water in case, as Mark says, they are marooned! She waves goodbye to them as they drive off. When they have gone she comes back into the house, makes another pot of tea and sits by the table, moping. Later she makes her bed and then closes the door of their bedroom, not daring, or wanting, to venture in. The floor of their room is strewn with clothes – a pink chiffon dress, silver shoes, a sun hat and, most wrenching of all, a threadbare teddy bear belonging to Penny.

Eileen gathers up the large bottles that had contained seltzer water and walks to the little local supermarket with them to collect a refund. She is carrying a dictionary in order to make the transaction easier. In the little harbour a few children are bathing and paddling while their mothers sit on large, brightly-coloured towels, talking loudly and occasionally yelling at the children. It is not a beach proper, just a harbour with a few fishing boats and a pathetically small strip of sand. After she has exchanged the bottles she comes and sits next to the local mothers, not understanding a word of what they are saying. Everywhere there are children: children darting into the water, children coming out and begging to be dried, children with plastic bubbles like eggs strapped to their backs to enable them to swim, children wet and slippery as eels, teeth chattering. Two small boys in red seersucker bathing suits are arguing over a piece of string, and as she follows the line of the string with her eyes she sees a kite, high above, fluttering in the air. The fine thread sustaining the kite suggests to her that thin thread between mother and child and it is as if the full meaning of motherhood has been revealed to her at last. Although not a swimmer, she decides to go in the water. She thinks that it will calm her, that her agitation is only caused by the heat. She rushes home to fetch a bathing suit and towel, and on the way there convinces herself that Mark and Penny have come back.

'Yoo-hoo,' she says as she enters the kitchen, and then goes towards their bedroom door and knocks cautiously. As there is no answer, she goes inside and starts to make their bed. She pulls the cover off in one rough gesture, pummels the mattress and then very slowly and patiently makes the bed, even folding back the top sheet the way it is done in hotels. She then picks up the various garments from the floor and starts to hang them in the already crammed closet. She notices that Mark has brought two dark suits, a cream suit, sports jackets and endless pairs of leather shoes. She wonders what kind of vacation he had envisioned and suddenly realizes that for them, too, the holiday must seem a fiasco. Her mood veers between shame and anger. They should have understood, should have apologized, should have been more sympathetic. She is alone, she has recently been jilted, she has dreamed of her lover on a swing with his wife, both of them moving through the air, charmed, assured creatures. Great copious tears run down her face onto her neck, and as they reach her breastbone she shivers. These tears blind her so that the red tiles of the floor appear to be curving, the roses on the bedspread float as if on a lake, and the beaded eyes of the teddy bear glint at her with malice. She will swim, or she will try to swim; she will dispel this frenzy.

At the harbour she lifts her dress off shyly, and then with considerable shame she reaches for her water wings. They are blue plastic and they carry a flagrant advertisement for a suntan lotion. Standing there in the water is a boy of about eighteen holding a football and letting out the most unseemly and guttural sounds. He is a simpleton. She can tell by the way he stares. She tries to ignore him, but sees the ball come towards her as she makes her intrepid passage through the water. The ball hits her shoulder, so she loses her balance, wobbles and takes a second to stand up straight again. The simpleton is staring at her and trying to speak, a foam of spittle on his lips. Drawing off her wings, she looks into the distance, pretending that she is not aware of him. He moves towards her, puts a hand out and tries in vain to catch hold of her, but she is too quick. She hurries out of the water, positions herself against a rock and cowers inside a huge brown fleecy towel. He follows. He is wearing a chain around his neck, attached to it a silver medal with a blue engraving of the Virgin Mary. His skin is mahogany colour. He comes close to her and is trying to say something or suggest something, and trembling inside the big brown towel, she tells him in his language to go away, to get lost. 'Vamoose,' she says, and flicks the back of her hand to confirm that she is serious. Then one of the local women yells abuse at him and he goes off silently into the water, tossing the ball to no one in particular.

At home, forcing herself to have lunch, Eileen begins to admit the gravity of things. She realizes now that Mark and Penny have left. She pictures them looking at a cheap room on some other part of the island, or perhaps buying a tent and deciding to sleep on the beach. On her plate colonies of ants are plundering the shreds of yellow and pink flesh that have adhered to a peach pit, and their assiduousness is so utter that she has to turn away.

She hurries out, takes a short cut across a field, through some scrubland to the little white church on the hill. It is like a beehive, and she thinks, as she goes toward it, that somehow her anguish will lessen once she gets inside, once she kneels down and prostrates herself before her Maker. The door is locked yet she tries turning the black iron knob in every direction. She walks around to find that the side door is also locked, and then, attempting to climb the pebble wall in order to look in the window, she loses her grip halfway and grazes her knee. She looks apologetically in case she has been seen, but there is no one there. There is simply a ragged rosemary bush and some broken bottles – the relics of a recent binge. She breaks off a few sprigs of rosemary to put in their bedroom.

'I am doing things as if they are coming back,' she says as she searches for wildflowers. Walking down from the chapel she is again assailed by the sight of children, children refreshed from their siestas, pedalling furiously on tricycles and bicycles, children on a rampage through the street, followed by a second gang with feathers in their hair, wielding bows and arrows. Mindlessly she walks, and her steps carry her away from the town towards a wood. It is a young wood and the pine trees have not grown to any reasonable height, but their smell is pleasant and so is the rustle of the russet needles. She listens from time to time for a chorus of birds but realizes that there are none and hears instead the distant sough of the sea. Some trees have withered, are merely grey, shorn stumps, dry and leafless. They remind her of her anger and once again she recalls last night's scene, that snapshot glued to her retina.

Three youths on motorcycles enter the wood and come bounding across as if intent on destroying themselves and every growing thing. They are like a warring clan, and they shout as they come towards her. She runs into a thicket and, crouching, hides under the trees out of their sight. She can hear them shouting and she thinks that they are calling to her, and now on hands and knees she starts to crawl through the underbrush and make her way by a hidden route back to the town. Scratches do not matter, nor does the fact that her clothing is ripped; her one concern is to get back among people, to escape their ravages and her escalating madness. It is while she is making her way back that the light changes and the young trees begin to sway, like pliant branches. A wind has risen and in the town itself the houses are no longer startling white but a dun colour, like houses robbed of their light. Dustbin lids are rolling along the street and not a child or an adult is in sight. All have gone indoors to avoid the storm. On the water itself boats are like baubles, defenceless against the brewing storm. On the terrace, the canvas chairs have fallen over, and so, too, has her little wooden clothes-horse with its tea towels. As she crosses to retrieve them the umbrella table keels forward and clouts her. Her mind can jump to only one conclusion – she sees Mark and Penny in a sail-boat, Penny exclaiming, Mark jumping and tugging at the sails, trying in vain to steer them to safety. She does not know where

Penny's parents live and at once runs to their bedroom to look for her passport. The beautiful childlike face that looks out at her from the passport photograph seems to be speaking to her, begging, asking for clemency. She sees them in the middle of the ocean, flung apart by the waves, like ill-starred lovers in a mythological tale. The next moment she tells herself that Mark is a capable sailor and will lead them to safety. Then she is asking aloud where she will bury them, forgetting that they are lost at sea.

'Nonsense . . . nonsense,' a voice that is her own shouts, insisting that islanders would not rent a sailing boat on such a day. She runs from room to room, closing doors and windows against a gale that rampages like a beast. Suddenly there is a knock, and putting on a semblance of composure, she runs to open the door, only to find that there is no one there. She stares out in the pitch-black and believes the keening wind to be a messenger of death.

The hours drag on, and in those hours she knows every shade of doubt, of rallying, of terror and eventually of despair. She remembers a million things, moments of her son's childhood, his wanting to pluck his long curved eyelashes and give them to her, a little painted xylophone he had had, stamps that he collected and displayed so beautifully under single folds of yellow transparent paper. She sees Penny tall and stalklike in her tight jeans and pink T-shirt with pearl droplets stitched to the front, her eyes flashing, dancing on his every whim.

At seven she sets out for a restaurant, believing that by doing so she will hasten their return. A note of optimism grips her. They will be back, and what is more, they will be famished. The restaurant is empty, so that she has a choice of tables. She chooses one near the window and looks out over the sea, which is no longer churning but is grey and scowling in the aftermath of the storm. In fact, she realizes that she cannot look at the sea, so she quickly changes tables. The owner and his daughter, who are laying out other tables, give each other a shrug. She is not welcome. For one thing, she has come too early and for another she is being stroppy about tables. She orders a bottle of the best wine. The daughter brings it with a dish of green olives. At moments, hearing footsteps, Eileen half rises to welcome Mark and Penny, but those who enter are other waiters arriving for work, removing jackets as they cross the floor. Soon the restaurant takes on a festive appearance. The daughter folds the napkins into shapes that look like fezzes and she carries them on a tray, along with vases each containing a single rose. The guitar music is much too harsh, and Eileen asks for it to be put lower, but her request is ignored. Yes, she does admit that Penny and Mark are thoughtless to have stayed out so long and not to be back for pre-dinner drinks, yet she will not scold them, she will make a big fuss over them. She has already asked if there is lobster and has asked for three portions to be put aside. 'But suppose they don't come,' she asks aloud, as if addressing another person. The daughter, who decidedly does not like her, hears this and mutters something to her father. Eileen now asks herself irrational questions, such as if they have not arrived by eight, or at the latest by eight thirty, should she eat, and if they do not arrive at all, will she be obliged to pay for the lobsters? She opens her purse and looks at the mauve-tinted cheques, flicking her finger along each one, wondering if she has enough money to defray the expenses that most certainly will be hers.

No sooner has she finished the first glass of wine than the tears start up and the owner, who until then has disliked her, comes over to the table to enquire what is the matter.

'*Morto,*' she says as she looks up at him, and now he becomes solicitous and asks her in broken English to explain to him what the matter is.

'*Il mare,*' she says, and he nods and describes the fury of the storm by puffing out his cheeks and making awesome gulping sounds. Upon hearing her story, he pushes away the wine bottle and tells his daughter, Aurora, to bring cognac. Eileen realizes that it must be grave indeed, because of his ordering the cognac. He recalls a drowning in their little village, the grief and horror, the darkness that descended, and although she cannot understand everything that he is saying, she gets the gist of it and wrings her hands in terror. He crosses to the counter and quickly dials the phone, all the time looking in her direction in case she does an injury to herself. Then as soon as the phone is picked up at the other end, he turns away and talks hurriedly, leaving her to assume the worst. He comes back proudly twirling his moustache and in halting English tells her that no news of a sailing accident has been reported to the lifeboat people.

'Courage, courage, courage,' he says, confident that the anguish will turn to laughter before long. By about nine she decides to go back to the house and he assures her that a table will be kept for the hungry ones. Then he dashes to the counter and takes from a jug two roses, which he gallantly gives her, along with his card.

The villa is dark, dark as a tomb, and she runs in and switches on all the lights.

'They'll come in the next five minutes,' she says, quite convinced, and even dares to stare up at the wall clock with its spider-like hands. They do not come. They will not come. The patron of the restaurant is her one friend. He will help her with the formalities, he will talk to the police for her, he will see to it that the divers go down. But what then? What then? she asks, her voice quivering. With each fresh admission she feels that the measure of her delirium is heaped full and that she cannot bear it, yet mind and body dart to the next awful minute. She walks all around the table touching its surface, then into the bathroom and out again, and back and around the table, and then into the two bedrooms, first her own, then theirs, and draws back the covers ceremoniously as if for a honeymoon couple. The clock and woodcuts on the wall are askew and she sets about straightening them. Then she commences a letter to the owner of the villa, who lives in Madrid, explaining why she has had to leave sooner than expected. By doing this she is admitting the worst. She is very calm now and her handwriting clear as a child's. She thinks of Penny's parents, whom she has never met, foresees their grief, their shock, their rage, their disbelief. How could they lose such a daughter, Penny, Penelope, the embodiment of cheer and sunniness? Her father, being an army man, will probably take it better, but what of her mother, the overweight woman whom Penny described as being psychic? Maybe she already knows, has seen her daughter in the depths of the ocean, among the preying fishes. Then, with a grief too awful to countenance, she sees Mark with the bloodshot eyes and recalls his renunciation of her.

There is a beam of headlights in her drive and immediately she rallies, concluding that it is the police, but as she rises she hears the small friendly hoot that is their signal. All of a sudden she feels ridiculous. They come in, bright, tousled and brimming with news. They tell how they met an Englishman with a metal detector who took them on a tour of the island, showed them old ruins and burial grounds, and how later they went to a hotel and swam in the pool but had to hide underwater each time a waiter went by. They are giddy with happiness.

'Did you sail?' she asks Mark.

'We did, but it got a bit dangerous,' Mark says, guessing how she must have panicked. Together he and Penny tell her of a beautiful restaurant where they have been; tables tucked away in corners, the cloths, the flowers, the music and above all, the scrumptious food – sweet mutton, zucchini and potatoes cooked with mint and butter.

'We're going to take you tomorrow night,' Penny says with a smile. It is the first time they have looked at each other since the outburst and Eileen now feels that she is the younger of the two and by far the more insecure. Penny has forgiven her, has forgotten it. The day has brought her closer to Mark and she is all agog.

'We've booked a table,' Mark says and wags a finger at Eileen to indicate that they are taking her, that it is to be their treat.

'I think I should go home,' she says, lamentably.

'Don't be silly,' he says and the look that he gives her is full of both pity and dread. She is on the point of telling him about the day, the scrubland, the youths, the storm, her frenzy, but his eyes, now grave and moist, beg her not to. His eyes ask her to keep this pain, this alarm, to herself.

'What did you do?' he asks nevertheless.

'Oh, lots of jolly things,' she says, and the lie has for her, as well as for him, all the sweetness and freshness of truth. For the remainder of the vacation they will behave as if nothing has happened, but of course, something has. They have each looked into the abyss and drawn back, frightened of the primitive forces that lurk there.

'Tomorrow . . .' he says and smiles his old smile.

'Tomorrow . . .' she says, as if there was no storm, no rift, as if the sea outside was a cradle lulling the world to a sweet, guileless sleep.

Long Distance

AH, THE SNUG LITTLE HIDEAWAY with its cushions and its inscrutable Buddha, dim lights like scalloped stars in various niches and the gleam of the fire on the red-brown leather upholstery. So warm, so mischievous. Winter was almost upon them. Yet, the glow of the fire and that boyish smile on his newly shaven face, smiling the smile of infancy and boyhood and puberty and manhood, eating the nuts, the salt occasionally on his lips like a bit of frost which he licked as he would have licked her hands gladly. How long was it? He probably had forgotten. A party, a chance thing had brought them together again. Ah, that first time. Vertigo at the top of the staircase in a ponderous London club with portraits everywhere of gouty faces, faces bespeaking lust and disgust, and how they whispered though they were strangers. 'Swift as the lightning in the collied night,' she had said to him. Such a peculiar thing to say but he saw it as an anthem. Now he was telling her that he had learned a proverb, it was this: that the eyes are in the fingertips. He had learned it in the Far East: he often went. He worked all over the world designing hotels and airports and helicopter launches and he employed God knows how many, but he still had a boyish quality and was saying 'Is that dress new?' as if they had met just yesterday or at most last week. There wasn't a trace of bitterness in his voice or in his eyes, the grey eyes with the tenderest flinch. He had probably quite forgotten how it had ended, forgotten the late-night calls, the mad curses she had visited on him, the cold rodent glances he gave her when they met once at a summer party. He was conscious again, as if for the first time, of her radiance, this woman in a black dress, composed and at the same time reeking wildness. Of course much was concealed. There was behind that composed face of hers, with its high patch of blush, another being, in some ways more beautiful, in some ways more ugly and certainly more hungry, sucking him in, drawing him in, in, in, if only for the moment, if only for that hour while they were together. He would have whisked her away anywhere, given her anything; he was her slave through and through. What was he telling her? Yes, how he had learned to ski and how exhilarating it was, a new thing, and now he had two hobbies instead of one; his boats and the ski slopes. Oh yes, and he had named his boat after a saint. He did not say if she had crossed his mind in the intervening years but she must have, an image now and then, a thread of vexation about the bitter bilious letter she had sent to his home and was read, oh yes, read, and the nicer moment too, at a house party, at dusk in a grand house, all the ladies weighted with jewels, and catching sight of someone just like her with a flower in her hair, a bit of bougain-villea picked off a tree; or being alone in a strange city and looking out onto a harbour with its necklace of lights, lights glinting – so many eyes stuck into the mountain of night – and wishing she would appear by his side. Oh yes, he would have thought of her, not often but at those tenderest of moments when he forgot work and forgot ambition and put aside the little gnawing dream he had to run the world and listened to his truer self.

She, too, had of course remembered him but gradually stamped upon it, foot upon foot, grinding it zealously into any piece of earth or street she stood upon, burying it, burying him, clothes, shoes, braces, wallet and all. He had come in dreams, always retrans-ported to her original terrain, always alone, on a wall or a headland or standing on a pathway under a tree, a priestly figure waiting to chastise her, not quite welcoming her but not dismissing her either.

'Did you ever dream of me?' she asked lightly, in a bantering way.

'All the time,' he said in the softest of voices. Now what did that mean? What was he saying? Were they good dreams, bad dreams, crowded dreams? In those dreams were they united or were they apart like those Japanese figures on a plate in which the lovers are perpetually divided by cruel waters? She also wanted to ask if, when he dreamt of her, he saw her in her happy guise, all aglow, or with a pulpy, tear-stained, supplicant face. It meant so much to her to know that little thing, the consistency of the image of her that roamed his mind. She didn't ask.

How had she spent the summer? In every question and every remark tossed back and forth between lovers who have not played out the last fugue, there is one question and it is this – 'Is there someone new?' The old entanglements, of course, remain like milestones and can be countenanced, but someone new can make an upheaval. That someone new might be the one to put a sledge-hammer to those milestones, reduce them to rubble. She was telling about her holiday, the grandeur of it, a bay of course, yachts, canny people who talked always of hobbies and resorts, things they could share out in the open, never talking about the things they had in their vaults, their jewellery or their money or their savage secrets. She was describing it: her own little bungalow and a personal maid called Lupa who became so devoted to her that when she scrubbed the floors and made the bed and stacked it with a compilation of pillows and chenille, sausage-shaped cushions, she lingered. Then what did Lupa do next? She took to washing the faces of the flowers outside, washing each face as if it was a baby's face, first with a damp cloth and then with a less damp cloth and then a dry cloth, pulling off dead leaves as she went, putting them into a pile, and then going and getting a dustpan to shovel up the dead leaves, sweeping slowly, slowly, reluctant to go. What she did not tell him was that on one of those days, during one of those several sweepings, she had shed tears, many tears. They had simply gushed out of her in a huge flow, like a blood flow. Were they for him? Partly. But they were also for life, its heartlessness, and her qualms about losing something incarnate in herself. Lupa, who was hovering, saw these tears, crossed and stood in front of her, pulling down the lower lid of one of her own eyes to emphasize that she understood. Maybe she was saying that it was no joke to be a maid, irking to be fated to work for people who only spoke three or four words and these three or four words were 'Breakfast', 'Immediately', 'Iron', 'Wash', a maid whose wardrobe was not silk and satin but broom and mop made of cut-up rags. The moment had etched itself. There were three urns with plumbago flowers, water making fretful shadows on a bit of white wall, a lizard clinging to it, inanimate as a piece of jade. The maid was disappointed in her, yes, truly; tears were for the starving, not for ladies who had bowls of fruit to gorge from and a four-poster ornamented with porcupine quills.

He did not have to order the next drink. They came quietly, surreptitiously, the previous undrained glasses carried away. What a lovely time she was having, almost as enchanting as the first except that she was a little braver now, and a little warier, and much more assured and determined to tell him those light-hearted tales about her travels, about seeing men one night chase a butterfly because it was not lucky, stamp on it, and a drive home through lonely countryside with all the houses shuttered up, the jalousies closed to give the appearance of dolls' houses, the inmates asleep and the mountain itself girdled in white mist, like a presence it was, so that one thought of a Santa Claus roaming about. Then she found herself describing the beautiful painting, red and gold, the colours still seeming moist, seeming to seep though it was centuries old. It was of the Last Supper, the faces at the table grave, shrewd and austere, and not necessarily devout, and then a distance away – the supper table was outdoors – a woman with half-torn garb, also red, but muddied; a prostitute on the ground with a baby in her arms. Had someone thrown her out there, or had she come back to supplicate, or had she chosen that position for herself in order to debase herself in front of those grave, shrewd, austere faces? Or was it that at last she had given up because disease had struck her?

It was not what he and she were saying that mattered, it was what they were thinking. They were merely skimming the surface of the years, hiding all the urgent parts of themselves, she hiding the vengeances that indeed she had conceived because she had been jilted, and he believing that she had betrayed him with that bilious letter. She would insist that her betrayal was because of his betrayal and so on. Tit-for-tat. Maybe that was why she thought of that painting, that above any other, a woman cast aside by judicious men. Luckily he was not able to read her thoughts because he had begun to describe a hotel in Thailand, where he had recently stayed. He went on about the beauty, the harmony, the uncanny way in which people served without seeming servile.

'You can get anything . . . anything,' he said, conveying his own amazement.

'Even love?' she said, picking up the cue. He smiled. He had wanted to get her to that word and had achieved it so easily; so insouciantly had he steered her to it.

'Love . . . you have to bring yourself,' he said in a teasing way. It only took a minute – or was it five minutes – to tell her that he was going back there soon and he was going alone and nothing would please him more than to take her and to show her the city. For one who was not over-lyrical, he went on about the flowers, flowers in the trees, flowers in the drinks, and then the flower-coloured floating dresses that the women wore. The streets she could picture too, narrow and with little vehicles, little tuk-tuks that people travelled around in, and, of course, the vivid colours and the all-prevailing courtesy. Yes, it would be charming and she knew it. He would be at his best. They would meet there. He would meet her off the plane, he in a light suit, a different suit, and he would help her into a car, or maybe those little tut-tut machines, but probably a car, and point out things as they drove along, then take her to the hotel and up to a suite that was spacious and they would stand in that big room, timid, timid as flowers, virgin lovers, in that land of flowers, everything ordained. Every bit of her wanted to say yes. Her eyes said it and the eyes at the tip of her fingertips said it and the flesh at the back of her throat ached at the thought of these new sensations. It was a place she had always wanted to visit, as if self-discovery awaited her there. The women, she believed, had something to teach her, a vein of patience perhaps. It beckoned. She was weakening. The image that floated into her head was a field of grass overwhelmed by wind, each blade veering in the same direction, powerless. He was taking out his diary. It was an invitation to take her own out because, after all, she was a busy woman too. His touch on her knee was like a little electric shock, but pleasant. If only they could go there and then. If only he stood up and carried her. Yet her answer was firm. She knew what she must say. The little beads of ecstasy in her throat were turning to tears, salt tears. It came back in a blinding guttural flash, the pain when he had left, the savagery of it, his deafness to her pleas, his refusal even at Christmas to answer a telephone call, his forgetting her address, the address at which he had called in daylight and in dark and had once flung clay up at her window; he had forgotten that address, simple as it was. How she hated these thoughts rearing up in her, but she had no control over them; they consumed her. It was not that she hated him; she did not hate him, but that old grudge, like a bit of flint in the ground, had come up to confront her. His eyes were so soft, his face so pale and gentle, his manner so suppliant that she longed to say yes, yes.

'It's not possible,' she said, but in a tone of voice so suggestive and so laden with innuendo that it really was saying 'There is another, whom I cannot leave.'

'Even if you tried?' he said, his eyes smarting now because he couldn't abide the merest rejection. Also, he was taken aback.

'Even if I tried, it wouldn't be possible,' she said, and a whole landscape of flowers and silk saris and tuk-tuk machines passed before her like dizzying images seen from a speeding train. He leaned over to the table beside them and took the plate of nuts and began to eat ravenously. She wanted to take his hand and tell him why. It would have saved everything. She put her hand on the sofa and at that moment he drew back his, his white fingers curling away from her like the tail of a white mouse receding into wainscoting. He had come with this gift, this offering, these days wrenched from his life and she had spat on it. He looked around as he always did when he became irate, and said they hadn't done a damn thing to the room in years, they hadn't even given it a lick of paint.

'Let's have another drink,' she said.

'You can have one,' he said as he rose, adding that he did not see why he should sit around and have her tell him why she did not want to go away with him. She must redeem it, she must. She jumped up and saw that he was cold now, disapproving like those disciples in the paintings.

'But you see why I can't go,' she said openly.

'No, I don't see,' he said, even more irritable.

'Because I would have to come back … *we* would have to come back,' she said, no longer afraid of her emotions, no longer raving about bays and bougainvillea, but reaching right down to the root of the love or the lingering love that was there, hauling him out of himself, shedding the lies and the little pretences, forsaking the wobbly balustrade that had been theirs.

'We're getting carried away again,' she said, and shook her head solemnly to make him understand. He felt it. His hand on hers, now so gentle, like condensation, a hand which she longed to hold on to forever, a keepsake. Never were they so near as at this moment of parting. But they were parting properly, decently, as they should have done years ago, and now she loved him in a way that she had not loved him before.

Outside the light was unsettling insofar as it was still bright, but all the street lights had come on. People in cars, people walking hand in hand, posters on the facings of cable boxes, torn faces, torn half-faces, the red glow of the traffic signals in the distance like heated moons, drivers with set jaws taking issue with God, a white-shirted waiter listlessly hailing a cab, and in the park now – because she had gone in there – the treetops all close together, snuggling, whispering, the hexagonals of light beneath them, haloed by both leaf and drizzle. There was a drizzle that pattered onto the leaves and onto her face, and the fallen leaves bristled like taffeta as she stepped over them.

'What now, what now?' she asked, and walked with pointless vigour, unable to exorcise the sight of him in his old tweed over-coat, moving away from her, somewhat downcast, somewhat melancholy, but not showing the full hurt. That overcoat must be ten or fifteen years old. She was touched by the thought that he had not bought another, something more plush. Only love makes one notice a thing like that, love, that bulwark between life and death. Love, she thought, is like nature but in reverse; first it fruits, then it flowers, then it seems to wither, then it goes deep, deep down into its burrow, where no one sees it, where it is lost from sight and ultimately people die with that secret buried inside their souls.

Paradise

In the harbor were the four boats. Boats named after a country, a railroad, an emotion, and a girl. She first saw them at sundown. Very beautiful they were, and tranquil, white boats at a distance from each other, cosseting the harbor. On the far side a mountain. Lilac at that moment. It seemed to be made of collapsible substance so insubstantial was it. Between the boats and the mountain a lighthouse, on an island.

Somebody said the light was not nearly so pretty as in the old days when the coast guard lived there and worked it by gas. It was automatic now and much brighter. Between them and the sea were four fields cultivated with fig trees. Dry yellow fields that seemed to be exhaling dust. No grass. She looked again at the four boats, the fields, the fig trees, the suave ocean; she looked at the house behind her and she thought, It can be mine, mine, and her heart gave a little somersault. He recognized her agitation and smiled. The house acted like a spell on all who came. He took her by the hand and led her up the main stairs. Stone stairs with a wobbly banister. The undersides of each step bright blue. 'Stop,' he said, where it got dark near the top, and before he switched on the light.

A servant had unpacked for her. There were flowers in the room. They smelled of confectionery. In the bathroom a great glass urn filled with talcum powder. She leaned over the rim and inhaled. It caused her to sneeze three times. Ovaries of dark-purple soap had been taken out of their wrapping paper, and for several minutes she held one in either hand. Yes. She had done the right thing in coming. She need not have feared; he needed her, his expression and their clasped hands already confirmed that.

They sat on the terrace drinking a cocktail he had made. It was of rum and lemon and proved to be extremely potent. One of the guests said the angle of light on the mountain was at its most magnificent. He put his fingers to his lips and blew a kiss to the mountain. She counted the peaks, thirteen in all, with a plateau between the first four and the last nine.

The peaks were close to the sky. Farther down on the face of the mountain various juts stuck out, and these made shadows on their neighboring juts. She was told its name. At the same moment she overheard a question being put to a young woman, 'Are you interested in Mary Queen of Scots?' The woman, whose skin had a beguiling radiance, answered yes overreadily. It was possible that such radiance was the result of constant supplies of male sperm. The man had a high pale forehead and a look of death.

They drank. They smoked. All twelve smokers tossing the butts onto the tiled roof that sloped toward the farm buildings. Summer lightning started up. It was random and quiet and faintly theatrical. It seemed to be something devised for their amusement. It lit one part of the sky, then another. There were bats flying about also, and their dark shapes and the random fugitive shots of summer lightning were a distraction and gave them something to point to. 'If I had a horse I'd call it Summer Lightning,' one of the women said, and the man next to her said, How charming. She knew she ought to speak. She wanted to. Both for his sake and for her own. Her mind would give a little leap and be still and would leap again; words were struggling to be set free, to say something, a little amusing something to establish her among them. But her tongue was tied. They would know her predecessors. They would compare her minutely, her appearance, her accent, the way he behaved with her. They would know better than she how important she was to him, if

it were serious or just a passing notion. They had all read in the
gossip columns how she came to meet him; how he had gone to have
an X-ray and met her there, the radiographer in white, committed
to a dark room and films showing lungs and pulmonary tracts.

'Am I right in thinking you are to take swimming lessons?' a
man asked, choosing the moment when she had leaned back and
was staring up at a big pine tree.

'Yes,' she said, wishing that he had not been told.

'There's nothing to it, you just get in and swim,' he said.

How surprised they all were, surprised and amused. Asked
where she had lived and if it was really true.

'Can't imagine anyone not swimming as a child.'

'Can't imagine anyone not swimming, period.'

'Nothing to it, you just fight, fight.'

The sun filtered by the green needles fell and made play on the
dense clusters of brown nuts. They never ridicule nature, she
thought, they never dare. He came and stood behind her, his hand
patting her bare pale shoulder. A man who was not holding a
camera pretended to take a photograph of them. How long would
she last? It would be uppermost in all their minds.

'We'll take you on the boat tomorrow,' he said. They cooed.
They all went to such pains, such excesses, to describe the cruiser.
They competed with each other to tell her. They were really
telling him. She thought, I should be honest, say I do not like
the sea, say I am an inland person, that I like rain and roses in a
field, thin rain, and through it the roses and the vegetation, and
that for me the sea is dark as the shells of mussels, and signifies
catastrophe. But she couldn't.

'It must be wonderful' was what she said.

'It's quite, quite something,' he said shyly.

At dinner she sat at one end of the egg-shaped table and he at the
other. Six white candles in glass sconces separated them. The

secretary had arranged the places. A fat woman on his right wore a lot of silver bracelets and was veiled in crepe. They had cold soup to start with. The garnishings were so finely chopped that it was impossible to identify each one except by its flavor. She slipped out of her shoes. A man describing his trip to India dwelt for an unnaturally long time on the disgustingness of the food. He had gone to see the temples. Another man, who was repeatedly trying to buoy them up, threw the question to the table at large: 'Which of the Mediterranean ports is best to dock at?' Everyone had a favorite. Some picked ports where exciting things had happened, some chose ports where the approach was most beguiling, harbor fees were compared as a matter of interest; the man who had asked the question amused them all with an account of a cruise he had made once with his young daughter and of how he was unable to land when they got to Venice because of inebriation. She had to admit that she did not know any ports. They were touched by that confession.

'We're going to try them all,' he said from the opposite end of the table, 'and keep a logbook.' People looked from him to her and smiled knowingly.

That night behind closed shutters they enacted their rite. They were both impatient to get there. Long before the coffee had been brought they had moved away from the table and contrived to be alone, choosing the stone seat that girdled the big pine tree. The seat was smeared all over with the tree's transparent gum. The nuts bobbing together made a dull clatter like castanets. They sat for as long as courtesy required, then they retired. In bed she felt safe again, united to him not only by passion and by pleasure but by some more radical entanglement. She had no name for it, that puzzling emotion that was more than love, or perhaps less, that was not simply sexual, although sex was vital to it and held it together like wires supporting a broken bowl. They both had had many breakages and therefore loved with a wary superstition.

'What you do to me,' he said. 'How you know me, all my vibrations.'

'I think we are connected underneath,' she said quietly. She often thought he hated her for implicating him in something too tender. But he was not hating her then.

At length it was necessary to go back to her bedroom, because he had promised to get up early to go spearfishing with the men.

As she kissed him goodbye she caught sight of herself in the chrome surface of the coffee flask which was on his bedside table – eyes emitting satisfaction and chagrin and panic were what stared back at her. Each time as she left him she expected not to see him again; each parting promised to be final.

The men left soon after six; she heard car doors because she had been unable to sleep.

In the morning she had her first swimming lesson. It was arranged that she would take it when the others sat down to breakfast. Her instructor had been brought from England. She asked if he'd slept well. She did not ask where. The servants disappeared from the house late at night and departed toward the settlement of low-roofed buildings. The dog went with them. The instructor told her to go backward down the metal stepladder. There were wasps hovering about and she thought that if she were to get stung she could bypass the lesson. No wasp obliged.

Some children, who had been swimming earlier, had left their plastic toys – a yellow ring that craned into the neck and head of a duck. It was a duck with a thoroughly disgusted expression. There was as well a blue dolphin with a name painted on it, and all kinds of batdeships. They were the children of guests. The older ones, who were boys, took no notice of any of the adults and moved about, raucous and meddlesome, taking full advantage of every aspect of the place – at night they watched the lizards patiently and for hours, in the heat of the day they remained in the water, in the early morning they gathered almonds, for which they received from him a harvesting fee. One black flipper lurked on the bottom of the pool. She looked down at it and touched it with her toe. Those were her last unclaimed moments, those moments before the lesson began.

The instructor told her to sit, to sit in it, as if it were a bath. He crouched and slowly she crouched, too. 'Now hold your nose and put your head under water,' he said. She pulled the bathing cap well over her ears and forehead to protect her hairstyle, and with her nose gripped too tightly she went underneath. 'Feel it?' he said excitedly. 'Feel the water holding you up?' She felt no such thing. She felt the water engulfing her. He told her to press the water from her eyes. He was gentleness itself. Then he dived in, swam a few strokes, and stood up, shaking the water from his gray hair. He took her hands and walked backward until they were at arm's length. He asked her to lie on her stomach and give herself to it. He promised not to let go of her hands. Each time, on the verge of doing so, she stopped: first her body, then her mind refused. She felt that if she was to take her feet off the ground the unmentionable would happen. 'What do I fear?' she asked herself. 'Death,' she said, and yet, it was not that. It was as if some horrible experience would happen before her actual death. She thought perhaps it might be the fight she would put up.

When she succeeded in stretching out for one desperate minute, he proclaimed with joy. But that first lesson was a failure as far as she was concerned. Walking back to the house, she realized it was a mistake to have allowed an instructor to be brought. It put too much emphasis on it. It would be incumbent upon her to conquer it. They would concern themselves with her progress, not because they cared, but like the summer lightning or the yachts going by, it would be something to talk about. But she could not send the instructor home. He was an old man and he had never been abroad before. Already he was marveling at the scenery. She had to go on with it. Going back to the terrace, she was not sure of her feet on land, she was not sure of land itself; it seemed to sway, and her knees shook uncontrollably.

When she sat down to breakfast she found that a saucer of almonds had been peeled for her. They were sweet and fresh, reinvoking the sweetness and freshness of a country morning. They tasted like hazelnuts. She said so. Nobody agreed. Nobody disagreed. Some were reading papers. Now and then someone read a piece aloud, some amusing piece about some acquaintance of theirs who had done a dizzy, newsworthy thing. The children read the thermometer and argued about the penciled shadow on the sundial. The temperature was already in the eighties. The women were forming a plan to go on the speedboat to get their midriffs brown. She declined. He called her into the conservatory and said she might give some time to supervising the meals because the secretary had rather a lot to do.

Passion-flower leaves were stretched along the roof on lifelines of green cord. Each leaf like the five fingers of a hand. Green and yellow leaves on the same hand. No flowers. Flowers later. Flowers that would live a day. Or so the gardener had said. She said, 'I hope we will be here to see one.' 'If you want, we will,' he said, but of course he might take a notion and go. He never knew what he might do; no one knew.

When she entered the vast kitchen, the first thing the servants did was to smile. Women in black, with soft-soled shoes, all smiling, no complicity in any of those smiles. She had brought with her a phrase book, a notebook, and an English cookery book. The kitchen was like a laboratory – various white machines stationed against the walls, refrigerators churtling at different speeds, a fan over each of the electric cookers, the red and green lights on the dials faintly menacing, as if they were about to issue an alarm.

There was a huge fish on the table. It had been speared that morning by the men. Its mouth was open; its eyes so close together that they barely missed being one eye; its lower lip gaping pathetically. The fins were black and matted with oil. They all stood and looked at it, she and the seven or eight willing women to whom she must make herself understood. When she sat to copy the recipe from the English book and translate it into their language, they turned on another fan. Already they were chopping for the evening meal. Three young girls chopped onions, tomatoes, and peppers. They seemed to take pleasure in their tasks; they seemed to smile into the mounds of vegetable that they so diligently chopped.

There were eight picnic baskets to be taken on the boat. And armfuls of towels. The children begged to be allowed to carry the towels. He had the zip bag with the wine bottles. He shook the bag so that the bottles rattled in their surrounds of ice. The guests smiled. He had a way of drawing people into his mood without having to say or do much. Conversely he had a way of locking people out. Both things were mesmerizing. They crossed the four fields that led to the sea. The figs were hard and green. The sun played like a blow lamp upon her back and neck. He said that she would have to lather herself in suntan oil. It seemed oddly hostile, his saying it out loud like that, in front of the others. As they got nearer the water she felt her heart race. The water was all shimmer. Some swam out, some got in the rowboat. Trailing her hand in the crinkled surface of the water she thought, It is not cramp, jellyfish, or broken glass that I fear, it is something else. A ladder was dropped down at the side of the boat for the swimmers to climb in from the sea. Sandals had to be kicked off as they stepped inside. The floor was of blond wood and burning hot. Swimmers had to have their feet inspected for tar marks. The boatman stood with a pad of cotton soaked in turpentine ready to rub the marks. The men busied themselves – one helped to get the engine going, a couple put awnings up, others carried out large striped cushions and scattered them under the awnings. Two boys refused to come on board.

'It is pleasant to bash my little brother up under water,' a young boy said, his voice at once menacing and melodious.

She smiled and went down steps to where there was a kitchen and sleeping quarters with beds for four. He followed her. He looked, inhaled deeply, and murmured.

'Take it out,' she said, 'I want it now, now.' Timorous and whim mad. How he loved it. How he loved that imperative. He pushed the door and she watched as he struggled to take down his shorts but could not get the cord undone. He was the awkward one now. How he stumbled. She waited for one excruciating moment and made him wait. Then she knelt, and as she began he muttered between clenched teeth. He who could tame animals was defenseless in this. She applied herself to it, sucking, sucking, sucking, with all the hunger that she felt and all the simulated hunger that she liked him to think she felt. Threatening to maim him, she always just grazed with the edges of her fine square teeth. Nobody intruded. It took no more than minutes. She stayed behind for a decent interval. She felt thirsty. On the window ledge there were paperback books and bottles of sun oil. Also a spare pair of shorts that had names of all the likely things in the world printed on them – names of drinks and capital cities and the flags of each nation. The sea through the porthole was a small, harmless globule of blue.

They passed out of the harbor, away from the three other boats and the settlement of pines. Soon there was only sea and rock, no reedy inlets, no towns. Mile after mile of hallucinating sea. The madness of mariners conveyed itself to her, the illusion that it was land and that she could traverse it. A land that led to nowhere. The rocks had been reduced to every shape the eye and the mind could comprehend. Near the water there were openings that had been forced through by the sea – some rapacious, some large enough for a small boat to slink in under, some as small and unsettling as the sockets of eyes. The trees on the sheer faces of these rocks were no more than the struggle to be trees. Birds could not perch there, let alone nest. She tried not to remember the swimming lesson, to postpone remembering until the afternoon, until the next lesson.

She came out and joined them. A young girl sat at the stern, among the cushions, playing a guitar. She wore long silver spatula-shaped earrings. A self-appointed gypsy. The children were playing I Spy but finding it hard to locate new objects. They were confined to the things they could see around them. By standing she found that the wind and the spray from the water kept her cool. The mountains that were far away appeared insubstantial, but those that were near glinted when the sharp stones were pierced by the sun.

'I find it a little unreal,' she said to one of the men. 'Beautiful but unreal.' She had to shout because of the noise of the engine.

'I don't know what you mean by unreal,' he said.

Their repertoire was small but effective. In the intonation the sting lay. Dreadfully subtle. Impossible to bridle over. In fact, the unnerving thing about it was the terrible bewilderment it induced. Was it intended or not? She distinctly remembered a sensation of once thinking that her face was laced by a cobweb, but being unable to feel it with the hand and being unable to put a finger on their purulence felt exactly the same. To each other, too, they transmitted small malices and then moved on to the next topic. They mostly talked of places they had been to and the people who were there, and though they talked endlessly, they told nothing about themselves.

They picnicked on a small pink strand. He ate very little, and afterward he walked off. She thought to follow him, then didn't.

The children waded out to sea on a long whitened log, and one of
the women read everybody's hand. She was promised an illness.
When he returned he gave his large yellowish hand reluctantly.
He was promised a son. She looked at him for a gratifying sign
but got none. At that moment he was telling one of the men about
a black sloop that he had loved as a child. She thought, What is it
that he sees in me, he who loves sea, sloops, jokes, masquerades,
and deferment? What is it that he sees in me who loves none of
those things?

Her instructor brought flat white boards. He held one end, she the
other. She watched his hands carefully. They were very white
from being in water. She lay on her stomach and held the boards
and watched his hands in case they should let go of the board. The
boards kept bobbing about and adding to her uncertainty. He said
a rope would be better.

The big fish had had its bones removed and was then pieced
together. A perfect decoy. Its head and its too near eyes were
gone. On her advice the housekeeper had taken the lemons out
of the refrigerator, so that they were like lemons now rather than
bits of frozen sponge. Someone remarked on this and she felt
childishly pleased. Because of a south wind a strange night exhilaration arose. They drank a lot. They discussed beautiful evenings.
Evenings resurrected in them by the wine and the wind and a
transient goodwill. One talked of watching golden cock pheasants
strutting in a back yard; one talked of bantams perched on a gate
at dusk, their forms like notes of music on a blank bar; no one
mentioned love or family, it was scenery or nature or a whippet
that left them with the best and most serene memories. She relived
a stormy night with an ass braying in a field and a blown bough
fallen across a road. After dinner various couples went for walks,
or swims, or to listen for children. The three men who were single

went to the village to reconnoiter. Women confided the diets they were on, or the face creams that they found most beneficial. A divorcée said to her host, 'You've *got* to come to bed with me, you've simply *got* to,' and he smiled. It was no more than a pleasantry, another remark in a strange night's proceedings where there were also crickets, tree frogs, and the sounds of clandestine kissing. The single men came back presently and reported that the only bar was full of Germans and that the whiskey was inferior. The one who had been most scornful about her swimming sat at her feet and said how awfully pretty she was. Asked her details about her life, her work, her schooling. Yet this friendliness only reinforced her view of her own solitude, her apartness. She answered each question carefully and seriously. By answering she was subscribing to her longing to fit in. He seemed a little jealous, so she got up and went to him. He was not really one of them, either. He simply stage-managed them for his own amusement. Away from them she almost reached him. It was as if he were bound by a knot that maybe, maybe, she could unravel, for a long stretch, living their own life, cultivating a true emotion, independent of other people. But would they ever be away? She dared not ask. For that kind of discussion she had to substitute with a silence.

She stole into their rooms to find clues to their private selves – to see if they had brought sticking plaster, indigestion pills, face flannels, the ordinary necessities. On a dressing table there was a wig block with blond hair very artfully curled. On the face of the block colored sequins were arranged to represent the features of an ancient Egyptian queen. The divorcée had a baby's pillow in a yellow muslin case. Some had carried up bottles of wine and these though not drunk were not removed. The servants only touched what was thrown on the floor or put in the wastepaper baskets. Clothes for washing were thrown on the floor. It was one of the house rules, like having cocktails on the terrace at evening time.

Some had written cards which she read eagerly. These cards told nothing except that it was all super.

His secretary, who was mousy, avoided her. Perhaps she knew too much. Plans he had made for the future.

She wrote to her doctor:

> *I am taking the tranquillizers but I don't feel any more relaxed. Could you send me some others?*

She tore it up.

Her hair got tangled by the salt in the sea air. She bought some curling tongs.

One woman, who was pregnant, kept sprinkling baby powder and smoothing it over her stomach throughout the day. They always took tea together. They were friends. She thought, If this woman were not pregnant would she be so amiable? Their kind of thinking was beginning to take root in her.

The instructor put a rope over her head. She brought it down around her middle. They heard a quack-quack. She was certain that the plastic duck had intoned. She laughed as she adjusted the noose. The instructor laughed, too. He held a firm grip of the rope. She threshed through the water and tried not to think of where she was. Sometimes she did it well; sometimes she had to be brought in like an old piece of lumber. She could never tell the outcome of each plunge; she never knew how it was going to be or what thoughts would suddenly obstruct her. But each time he said, 'Lovely, lovely,' and in his exuberance she found consolation.

A woman called Iris swam out to their yacht. She dangled in the water and with one hand gripped the sides of the boat. Her nail varnish was exquisitely applied and the nails had the glow of a rich imbued pearl. By contrast with the pearl coating, the half-moons were chastely white. Her personality was like that, too – full of glow. For each separate face she had a smile, and a word or two for those she already knew. One of the men asked if she was in love. Love! she riled him. She said her good spirits were due to her breathing. She said life was a question of correct breathing. She had come to invite them for drinks but he declined because they were due back at the house. His lawyer had been invited to lunch. She chided him for being so busy, then swam off toward the shore, where her poodle was yapping and waiting for her. At lunch they all talked of her. There was mention of her past escapades, the rows with her husband, his death, which was thought to be a suicide, and the unpleasant business of his burial, which proved impossible on religious grounds. Finally, his body had to be laid in a small paddock adjoining the public cemetery. Altogether an unsavory story, yet preening in the water had been this radiant woman with no traces of past harm.

'Yes, Iris has incredible willpower, incredible,' he said.

'For what?' she asked, from the opposite end of the table.

'For living,' he said tartly.

It was not lost on the others. Her jaw muscle twitched.

Again she spoke to herself, remonstrated with her hurt: 'I try, I try, I want to fit, I want to join, be the someone who slips into a crowd of marchers when the march has already begun, but there is something in me that I call sense and it balks at your ways. It would seem as if I am here simply to smart under your strictures.' Retreating into dreams and monologue.

She posed for a picture. She posed beside the sculptured lady. She repeated the pose of the lady. Hands placed over each other and laid on the left shoulder, head inclining toward those hands. He took it. Click, click. The marble lady had been the sculptor's wife and had died tragically. The hands with their unnaturally long nails were the best feature of it. Click, click. When she was not looking he took another.

She found the account books in a desk drawer and was surprised at the entries. Things like milk and matches had to be accounted for. She thought, Is he generous at the roots? The housekeeper had left some needlework in the book. She had old-fashioned habits and resisted much of the modern kitchen equipment. She kept the milk in little pots, with muslin spread over the top. She skimmed the cream with her fat fingers, tipped the cream into small jugs for their morning coffee. What would they say to that! In the evenings, when every task was done, the housekeeper sat in the back veranda with her husband, doing the mending. They had laid pine branches on the roof, and these had withered and were tough as wire. Her husband made shapes from soft pieces of new white wood, and then in the dark put his penknife aside and caroused with his wife. She heard them when she stole in to get some figs from the refrigerator. It was both poignant and untoward.

The instructor let go of the rope. She panicked and stopped using her arms and legs. The water was rising up over her. The water engulfed her. She knew that she was screaming convulsively. He had to jump in, clothes and all. Afterward they sat in the linen room with a blanket each and drank brandy. They vouched to tell no one. The brandy went straight to his head. He said in England it would be raining and people would be queueing for buses, and his eyes twinkled because of his own good fortune at being abroad.

More than one guest was called Teddy. One of the Teddys told her that in the mornings before his wife wakened he read

Proust in the dressing room. It enabled him to masturbate. It was no more than if he had told her he missed bacon for breakfast. For breakfast there was fruit and scrambled egg. Bacon was a rarity on the island. She said to the older children that the plastic duck was psychic and had squeaked. They laughed. Their laughing was real, but they kept it up long after the joke had expired. A girl said, 'Shall I tell you a rude story?' The boys appeared to want to restrain her. The girl said, 'Once upon a time there was a lady, and a blind man came to her door every evening for sixpence, and one day she was in the bath and the doorbell rang and she put on a gown and came down and it was the milkman, and she got back in the bath and the doorbell rang and it was the bread man, and at six o'clock the doorbell rang and she thought, I don't have to put on my gown it is the blind man, and when she opened the door the blind man said, "Madam, I've come to tell you I got my sight back."' And the laughter that had never really died down started up again, and echoed. No insect, no singing bird was heard on that walk. She had to watch the time. The children's evening meal was earlier. They ate on the back veranda and she often went there and stole an anchovy or a piece of bread so as to avoid getting too drunk before dinner. There was no telling how late dinner would be. It depended on him, on whether he was bored or not. Extra guests from neighboring houses came each evening for drinks. They added variety. The talk was about sailing and speeding, or about gardens, or about pools. They all seemed to be intrigued by these topics, even the women. One man who followed the snow knew where the best snow surfaces were for every week of every year. That subject did not bore her as much. At least the snow was nice to think about, crisp and blue like he said, and rasping under the skis. The children could often be heard shrieking, but after cocktail hour they never appeared. She believed that it would be better once they were married and had children. She would be accepted by courtesy of them. It was a swindle really, the fact that small creatures, ridiculously easy to beget, should solidify a relationship, but they would. Everyone hinted how he wanted a son. He was nearing sixty. She had stopped using contraceptives and he had stopped asking. Perhaps that was his way of deciding, of finally accepting her.

Gulls' eggs, already shelled, were brought to table. The yolks a very delicate yellow. 'Where are the shells?' the fat lady, veiled in crepe, asked. The shells had to be brought. They were crumbled almost to a powder but were brought anyhow. 'Where are the nests?' she asked. It missed. It was something they might have laughed at, had they heard, but a wind had risen and they were all getting up and carrying things indoors. The wind was working up to something. It whipped the geranium flowers from their leaves and crazed the candle flames so that they blew this way and that in the glass sconces. That night their lovemaking had all the sweetness and all the release that earth must feel with the long-awaited rain. He was another man now, with another voice – loving and private and incantatory. His coldness, his dismissal of her hard to believe in. Perhaps if they quarreled, their quarrels, like their lovemaking, would bring them closer. But they never did. He said he'd never had a quarrel with any of his women. She gathered that he left his wives once it got to that point. He did not say so, but she felt that must have been so, because he had once said that all his marriages were happy. He said there had been fights with men but that these were decent. He had more rapport with men; with women he was charming but it was a charm devised to keep them at bay. He had no brothers, and no son. He had had a father who bullied him and held his inheritance back for longer than he should. This she got from one of the men who had known him for forty years. His father had caused him to suffer, badly. She did not know in what way and she was unable to ask him, because it was information she should never have been given a hint of.

After their trip to the Roman caves the children came home ravenous. One child objected because the meal was cold. The servant, sensing a certain levity, told her master, and the story sent shrieks of laughter around the lunch table. It was repeated many times. He called to ask if she had heard. He sometimes singled her out in that way. It was one of the few times the guests could glimpse the bond between them. Yes, she had heard. 'Sweet, sweet,' she said. The word occurred in her repertoire all the time now. She was learning their language. And fawning. Far from home, from where the cattle grazed. The cattle had fields to roam, and a water tank near the house. The earth around the water tank always churned up, always mucky from their trampling there. They were farming people, had their main meal in the middle of the day, had rows. Her father vanished one night after supper, said he was going to count the cattle, brought a flashlamp, never came back. Others sympathized, but she and her mother were secretly relieved. Maybe he drowned himself in one of the many bog lakes, or changed his name and went to a city. At any rate, he did not hang himself from a tree or do anything ridiculous like that.

She lay on her back as the instructor brought her across the pool, his hand under her spine. The sky above an innocent blightless blue, with streamers where the jets had passed over. She let her head go right back. She thought, If I were to give myself to it totally, it would be a pleasure and an achievement, but she couldn't.

Argoroba hung from the trees like blackened banana skins. The men picked them in the early morning and packed them in sacks for winter fodder. In the barn where these sacks were stored there was a smell of decay. And an old olive press. In the linen room next door a pleasant smell of linen. The servants used too much bleach. Clothes lost their sharpness of color after one wash. She used to sit in one or another of these rooms and read. She went to the library for a book. He was in one of the Regency chairs that was covered with ticking. As on a throne. One chair was real and one a copy, but she could never tell them apart. 'I saw you yesterday, and you nearly went under,' he said. 'I still have several lessons to go,' she said, and went as she intended, but without the book that she had come to fetch.

His daughter by his third marriage had an eighteen-inch waist. On her first evening she wore a white trouser suit. She held the legs out, and the small pleats when opened were like a concertina. At table she sat next to her father and gazed at him with appropriate awe. He told a story of a dangerous leopard hunt. They had lobster as a special treat. The lobster tails, curving from one place setting to the next, reached far more cordially than the conversation. She tried to remember something she had read that day. She found that by memorizing things she could amuse them at table.

'The gorilla resorts to eating, drinking, or scratching to bypass anxiety,' she said later. They all laughed.

'You don't say,' he said, with a sneer. It occurred to her that if she were to become too confident he would not want that, either. Or else he had said it to reassure his daughter.

There were moments when she felt confident. She knew in her mind the movements she was required to make in order to pass through the water. She could not do them, but she knew what she was supposed to do. She worked her hands under the table, trying to make deeper and deeper forays into the atmosphere. No one caught her at it. The word 'plankton' would not let go of her. She saw dense masses of it, green and serpentine, enfeebling her fingers. She could almost taste it.

His last wife had stitched a backgammon board in green and red. Very beautiful it was. The fat woman played with him after dinner. They carried on the game from one evening to the next. They played very contentedly. The woman wore a different arrangement of rings at each sitting and he never failed to admire and compliment her on them. To those not endowed with beauty he was particularly charming.

Her curling tongs fused the entire electricity system. People rushed out of their bedrooms to know what had happened. He did not show his anger, but she felt it. Next morning they had to send a telegram to summon an electrician. In the telegram office two men sat, one folding the blue pieces of paper, one applying gum with a narrow brush and laying thin borders of white over the blue and pressing down with his hands. On the white strips the name and address had already been printed. A motorcycle was indoors, to protect the tires from the sun, or in case it might be stolen. The men took turns when a telegram had to be delivered. She saved one or the other of them a journey because a telegram from a departed guest arrived while she was waiting. It simply said 'Adored it, Harry.' Guests invariably forgot something and in their thank-you letters mentioned what they had forgotten. She presumed that some of the hats stacked into one another and laid on the stone ledge were hats forgotten or thrown away. She had grown quite attached to a green one that had lost its ribbons.

The instructor asked to be brought to the souvenir shop. He bought a glass ornament and a collar for his dog. On the way back a man at the petrol station gave one of the children a bird. They put it in the chapel. Made a nest for it. The servant threw it nest and all into the wastepaper basket. That night at supper the talk was of nothing else. He remembered his fish story and he told it to the new people who had come, how one morning he had to abandon his harpoon because the lines got tangled and next day, when he went back, he found that the shark had retreated into the cave and had two great lumps of rock in his mouth, where obviously he had bitten to free himself. That incident had a profound effect on him.

'Is the boat named after your mother?' she asked of his daughter. Her mother's name was Beth and the boat was called *Miss Beth*. 'He never said,' the daughter replied. She always disappeared after lunch. It must have been to accommodate them. Despite the heat they made a point of going to his room. And made a point of inventiveness. She tried a strong green stalk, to excite him, marveling at it, comparing him and it. He watched. He could not endure such competition. With her head upside down and close to the tiled floor she saw all the oils and ointments on his bathroom ledge and tried reading their labels backward. Do I like all this lovemaking? she asked herself. She had to admit that possibly she did not, that it went on too long, that it was involvement she sought, involvement and threat.

They swapped dreams. It was her idea. He was first. Everyone was careful to humor him. He said in a dream a dog was lost and his grief was great. He seemed to want to say more but didn't, or couldn't. Repeated the same thing, in fact. When it came to her turn, she told a different dream from the one she had meant to tell. A short, uninvolved little dream.

In the night she heard a guest sob. In the morning the same guest wore a flame dressing gown and praised the marmalade, which she ate sparingly.

She asked for the number of lessons to be increased. She had three a day and she did not go on the boat with the others. Between lessons she would walk along the shore. The pine trunks were pale, as if a lathe had been put to them. The winds of winter the lathe. In winter they would move; to catch up with friends, business meetings, art exhibitions, to buy presents, to shop. He hated suitcases, he liked clothes to be waiting wherever he went, and they were. She saw a wardrobe with his winter clothes neatly stacked, she saw his frieze cloak with the black astrakhan collar, and she experienced such a longing for that impossible season, that impossible city, and his bulk inside the cloak as they set out in the cold to go to a theater. Walking along the shore, she did the swimming movements in her head. It had got into all her thinking. Invaded her dreams. Atrocious dreams about her mother, her father, and one where lion cubs surrounded her as she lay on a hammock. The cubs were waiting to pounce the second she moved. The hammock, of course, was unsteady. Each time she wakened from one of those dreams she felt certain that her cries were the repeated cries of infancy, and it was then she helped herself to the figs she had brought up.

He put a handkerchief, folded like a letter, before her plate at table. On opening it she found some sprays of fresh mint, wide-leafed and cold. He had obviously put it in the refrigerator first. She smelled it and passed it around. Then on impulse she got up to kiss him and on her journey back nearly bumped into the servant with a tureen of soup, so excited was she.

Her instructor was her friend. 'We're winning, we're winning,' he said. He walked from dawn onward, walked the hills and saw the earth with dew on it. He wore a handkerchief on his head that he knotted over the ears, but as he approached the house, he removed this headdress. She met him on one of these morning walks. As it got nearer the time, she could neither sleep nor make love. 'We're winning, we're winning.' He always said it no matter where they met.

They set out to buy finger bowls. In the glass factory there were thin boys with very white skin who secured pieces of glass with pokers and thrust them into the stoves. The whole place smelled of wood. There was chopped wood in piles, in corners. Circular holes were cut along the top of the wall between the square grated windows. The roof was high and yet the place was a furnace. Five kittens with tails like rats lay bunched immobile in a heap. A boy, having washed himself in one of the available buckets of water, took the kittens one by one and dipped them in. She took it to be an act of kindness. Later he bore a hot blue bubble at the end of a poker and laid it before her. As the flame subsided it became mauve, and as it cooled more, it was almost colorless. It had the shape of a sea serpent and an unnaturally long tail. Its color and its finished appearance were an accident, but the gift was clearly intentioned. There was nothing she could do but smile. As they were leaving she saw him waiting near the motorcar, and as she got in, she waved wanly. That night they had asparagus, which is why they went to the trouble to get finger bowls. These were blue with small bubbles throughout, and though the bubbles may have been a defect, they gave to the thick glass an airiness.

There was a new dog, a mongrel, in whom he took no interest. He said the servants got new dogs simply because he allotted money for that. But as they were not willing to feed more than one animal, the previous year's dog was either murdered or put out on the mountain. All these dogs were of the same breed, part wolf; she wondered if when left on the mountain they reverted to being wolves. He said solemnly to the table at large that he would never allow himself to become attached to another dog. She said to him directly, 'Is it possible to know beforehand?' He said, 'Yes.' She could see that she had irritated him.

*

He came three times and afterward coughed badly. She sat with him and stroked his back, but when the coughing took command he moved her away. He leaned forward, holding a pillow to his mouth. She saw a film of his lungs, orange shapes with insets of dark that boded ill. She wanted to do some simple domestic thing like give him medicine, but he sent her away. Going back along the terrace, she could hear the birds. The birds were busy with their song. She met the fat woman. 'You have been derouted,' the woman said, 'and so have I.' And they bowed mockingly.

An archaeologist had been on a dig where a wooden temple was discovered. 'Tell me about your temple,' she said.

'I would say it's 400 B.C.,' he said, nothing more. Dry, dry.

A boy who called himself Jasper and wore mauve shirts received letters under the name of John. The letters were arranged on the hall table, each person's under a separate stone. Her mother wrote to say they were anxiously awaiting the good news. She said she hoped they would get engaged first but admitted that she was quite prepared to be told that the marriage had actually taken place. She knew how unpredictable he was. Her mother managed a poultry farm in England and was a compulsive eater.

Young people came to ask if Clay Sickle was staying at the house. They were in rags, but it looked as if they were rags worn on purpose and for effect. Their shoes were bits of motor tire held up with string. They all got out of the car, though the question could have been asked by any one of them. He was on his way back from the pool, and after two minutes' conversation he invited them for supper. He throve on new people. That night they were the ones in the limelight – the three unkempt boys and the long-haired girl. The girl had very striking eyes, which she fixed on one man and then another. She was determined to compromise one of them. The boys described their holiday, being broke, the trouble they had with the car, which was owned by a hire purchase firm in

London. After dinner an incident occurred. The girl followed one of the men into the bathroom. 'Want to see what you've got there,' she said, and insisted on watching while the man peed. She said they would do any kind of fucking he wanted. She said he would be a slob not to try. It was too late to send them away, because earlier on they'd been invited to spend the night and beds were put up, down in the linen room. The girl was the last to go over there. She started a song, 'All around his cock he wears a tricolored rash-eo,' and she went on yelling it as she crossed the courtyard and went down the steps, brandishing a bottle.

In the morning, she determined to swim by herself. It was not that she mistrusted her instructor, but the time was getting closer and she was desperate. As she went to the pool, one of the youths appeared in borrowed white shorts, eating a banana. She greeted him with faltering gaiety. He said it was fun to be out before the others. He had a big head with closely cropped hair, a short neck, and a very large nose.

'Beaches are where I most want to be, where it all began,' he said. She thought he was referring to creation, and upon hearing such a thing he laughed profanely. 'Let's suppose there's a bunch of kids and you're all horsing around with a ball and all your sensory dimensions are working . . .'

'What?' she said.

'A hard-on . . .'

'Oh. . .'

'Now the ball goes into the sea and I follow and she follows me and takes the ball from my hand and a dense rain of energy, call it love, from me to her and vice versa, reciprocity in other words . . .'

Sententious idiot. She thought, Why do people like that have to be kept under his roof? Where is his judgment, where? She walked back to the house, furious at having to miss her chance to swim.

Dear Mother: It's not that kind of relationship. Being unmarried installs me as positively as being married, and neither installs me with any certainty. It is a beautiful house, but staying here is quite a strain. You could easily get filleted. Friends do it to friends. The food is good. Others cook it, but I am responsible for each day's menu. Shopping takes hours. The shops have a special smell that is impossible to describe. They are all dark, so that the foodstuffs won't perish. An old woman goes along the street in a cart selling fish. She has a very penetrating cry. It is like the commencement of a song. There are always six or seven little girls with her, they all have pierced ears and wear fine gold sleepers. Flies swarm around the cart even when it is upright in the square. Living off scraps and fish scales, I expect. We do not buy from her, we go to the harbor and buy directly from the fishermen. The guests – all but one woman – eat small portions. You would hate it. All platinum people. They have a canny sense of self-preservation; they know how much to eat, how much to drink, how far to go; you would think they invented somebody like Shakespeare, so proprietary are they about his genius. They are not fools – not by any means. There is a chessboard of ivory and it is so large it stands on the floor. Seats of the right height are stationed around it.

Far back – in my most distant childhood, Mother – I remember your nightly cough; it was a lament really and I hated it. At the time I had no idea that I hated it, which goes to show how unreliable feelings are. We do not know what we feel at the time and that is very perplexing. Forgive me for mentioning the cough, it is simply that I think it is high time we spoke our minds on all matters. But don't worry. You are centuries ahead of the people here. In a nutshell, they brand you as idiot if you are harmless. There are jungle laws which you never taught me; you couldn't, you never knew them. Ah well!

I will bring you a present. Probably something suede. He says the needlework here is appalling and that things fall to pieces, but you can always have it remade. We had some nice china jelly molds when I was young. Whatever happened to them? Love.

Like the letter to the doctor, it was not posted. She didn't tear it up or anything, it just lay in an envelope and she omitted to post it from one day to the next. This new tendency disturbed her. This habit of postponing everything. It was as if something vital had first to be gone through. She blamed the swimming.

The day the pool was emptied she missed her three lessons. She could hear the men scrubbing, and from time to time she walked down and stood over them as if her presence could hurry the proceedings and make the water flow in, in one miracle burst. He saw how she fretted, he said they should have had two pools built. He asked her to come with them on the boat. The books and the suntan oil were as she had last seen them. The cliffs as intriguing as ever. 'Hello, cliff, can I fall off you?' She waved merrily. In a small harbor they saw another millionaire with his girl. They were alone, without even a crew. And for some reason it went straight to her heart. At dinner the men took bets as to who the girl was. They commented on her prettiness though they had hardly seen her. The water filling the pool sounded like a stream from a faraway hill. He said it would be full by morning.

Other houses had beautiful objects, but theirs was in the best taste. The thing she liked most was the dull brass chandelier from Portugal. In the evenings when it was lit, the cones of light tapered toward the rafters and she thought of woodsmoke and the wings of birds endlessly fluttering. Votive. To please her he had a fire lit in a far-off room simply to have the smell of woodsmoke in the air.

The watercress soup that was to be a specialty tasted like salt water. Nobody blamed her, but afterward she sat at the table and wondered how it had gone wrong. She felt defeated. On request he brought another bottle of red wine, but asked if she was sure she ought to have more. She thought, He does not understand the workings of my mind. But then, neither did she. She was drunk. She held the glass out. Watching the meniscus, letting it tilt from side to side, she wondered how drunk she would be when she stood up. 'Tell me,' she said, 'what interests you?' It was the first blunt question she had ever put to him.

'Why, everything,' he said.

'But deep down,' she said.

'Discovery,' he said, and walked away.

But not self-discovery, she thought, not that.

A neurologist got drunk and played jazz on the chapel organ. He said he could not resist it, there were so many things to press. The organ was stiff from not being used.

She retired early. Next day she was due to swim for them. She thought he would come to visit her. If he did they would lie in one another's arms and talk. She would knead his poor worn scrotum and ask questions about the world beneath the sea where he delved each day, ask about those depths and if there were flowers of some sort down there, and in the telling he would be bound to tell her about himself. She kept wishing for the organ player to fall asleep. She knew he would not come until each guest had retired, because he was strangely reticent about his loving.

But the playing went on. If anything, the player gathered strength and momentum. When at last he did fall asleep, she opened the shutters. The terrace lights were all on. The night breathlessly still. Across the fields came the lap from the sea and then the sound of a sheep bell, tentative and intercepted. Even a sheep recognized the dead of night. The lighthouse worked faithfully as a heartbeat. The dog lay in the chair, asleep, but with his ears raised. On other chairs were sweaters and books and towels, the remains of the day's activities. She watched and she waited. He did not come. She lamented that she could not go to him on the night she needed him most.

For the first time she thought about cramp.

In the morning she took three headache pills and swallowed them with hot coffee. They disintegrated in her mouth. Afterward she washed them down with soda water. There was no lesson because the actual swimming performance was to be soon after breakfast. She tried on one bathing suit, then another; then, realizing how senseless this was, she put the first one back on and stayed in her room until it was almost time.

When she came down to the pool they were all there ahead of her. They formed quite an audience: the twenty house guests and the six complaining children who had been obliged to quit the pool. Even the housekeeper stood on the stone seat under the tree, to get a view. Some smiled, some were a trifle embarrassed. The pregnant woman gave her a medal for good luck. It was attached to a pin. So they were friends. Her instructor stood near the front, the rope coiled around his wrist just in case. The children gave to the occasion its only levity. She went down the ladder backward and looked at no face in particular. She crouched until the water covered her shoulders, then she gave a short leap and delivered herself to it. Almost at once she knew that she was going to do it. Her hands, no longer loath to delve deep, scooped the water away, and she kicked with a ferocity she had not known to be possible. She was aware of cheering but it did not matter about that. She swam, as she had promised, across the width of the pool in the shallow end. It was pathetically short, but it was what she had vouched to do. Afterward one of the children said that her face was tortured. The rubber flowers had long since come off her bathing cap, and she pulled it off as she stood up and held on to the ladder. They clapped. They said it called for a celebration. He said nothing, but she could see that he was pleased. Her instructor was the happiest person there.

When planning the party they went to the study, where they could sit and make lists. He said they would order gypsies and flowers and the caviar would be served in glass swans packed with ice. None of it would be her duty. They would get people to do it. In all, they wrote out twenty telegrams. He asked how she felt. She admitted that being able to swim bore little relation to not being able. They were two unreconcilable feelings. The true thrill, she said, was the moment when she knew she would master it but had not yet achieved it with her body. He said he looked forward to the day when she went in and out of the water like a knife. He did the movement deftly with his hand. He said next thing she would learn was riding. He would teach her himself or he would have her taught. She remembered the chestnut mare with head raised, nostrils sniffing the air, and she herself unable to stroke it, unable to stand next to it without exuding fear.

'Are you afraid of nothing?' she asked, too afraid to tell him specifically about the encounter with the mare, which took place in his stable.

'Sure, sure.'

'You never reveal it.'

'At the time I'm too scared.'

'But afterward, afterward . . .' she said.

'You try to live it down,' he said, and looked at her and hurriedly took her in his arms. She thought, Probably he is as near to me as he has been to any living person and that is not very near, not very near at all. She knew that if he chose her they would not go in the deep end, the deep end that she dreaded and dreamed of. When it came to matters inside himself, he took no risks.

She was tired. Tired of the life she had elected to go into and disappointed with the man she had put pillars around. The tiredness came from inside, and like a deep breath going out slowly, it tore at her gut. She was sick of her own predilection for tyranny. It seemed to her that she always held people to her ear, the way her mother held eggs, shaking them to guess at their rottenness, but unlike her mother she chose the very ones that she would have been wise to throw away. He seemed to sense her sadness, but he said nothing; he held her and squeezed her from time to time in reassurance.

Her dress – his gift – was laid out on the bed, its wide white sleeves hanging down at either side. It was of openwork and it looked uncannily like a corpse. There was a shawl to go with it, and shoes and a bag. The servant was waiting. Beside the bath her book, an ashtray, cigarettes, and a little book of soft matches that were hard to strike. She lit a cigarette and drew on it heartily. She regretted not having brought up a drink. She felt like a drink at that moment, and in her mind she sampled the drink she might have had. The servant knelt down to put in the stopper. She asked that the bath should not be run just yet. Then she took the biggest towel and put it over her bathing suit and went along the corridor and down by the back stairs. She did not have to turn on the lights; she would have known her way blindfolded to that pool. All the toys were on the water, like farm animals just put to bed. She picked them out one by one and laid them at the side near the pile of empty chlorine bottles. She went down the ladder backward.

She swam in the shallow end and allowed the dreadful thought to surface. She thought, I shall do it or I shall not do it, and the fact that she was of two minds about it seemed to confirm her view of the unimportance of the whole thing. Anyone, even the youngest child, could have persuaded her not to, because her mind was without conviction. It just seemed easier, that was all, easier than the strain and the incomplete loving and the excursions that lay ahead.

'This is what I want, this is where I want to go,' she said, restraining that part of herself that might scream. Once she went deep, and she submitted to it, the water gathered all around in a great beautiful bountiful baptism. As she went down to the cold and thrilling region she thought, They will never know, they will never, ever know, for sure.

At some point she began to fight and thresh about, and she cried, though she could not know the extent of those cries.

She came to her senses on the ground at the side of the pool, all muffled up and retching. There was an agonizing pain in her chest, as if a shears were snipping at her guts. The servants were with her and two of the guests and him. The floodlights were on around the pool. She put her hands to her breast to make sure; yes, she was naked under the blanket. They would have ripped her bathing suit off. He had obviously been the one to give respiration, because he was breathing quickly and his sleeves were rolled up. She looked at him. He did not smile. There was the sound of music, loud, ridiculous, and hearty. She remembered first the party, then everything. The nice vagueness quit her and she looked at him with shame. She looked at all of them. What things had she shouted as they brought her back to life? What thoughts had they spoken in those crucial moments? How long did it take? Her immediate concern was that they must not carry her to the house, she must not allow that last episode of indignity. But they did. As she was borne along by him and the gardener, she could see the flowers and the oysters and the jellied dishes and the small roast piglets all along the tables, a feast as in a dream, except that she was dreadfully clearheaded. Once alone in her room she vomited.

For two days she did not appear downstairs. He sent up a pile of books, and when he visited her he always brought someone. He professed a great interest in the novels she had read and asked how the plots were. When she did come down, the guests were polite and offhand and still specious, but along with that they were cautious now and deeply disapproving. Their manner told her that it had been a stupid and ghastly thing to do, and had she succeeded she would have involved all of them in her stupid and ghastly mess. She wished she could go home, without any farewells. The children looked at her and from time to time laughed out loud. One boy told her that his brother had once tried to drown him in the bath. Apart from that and the inevitable letter to the gardener, it was never mentioned. The gardener had been the one to hear her cry and raise the alarm. In their eyes he would be a hero.

People swam less. They made plans to leave. They had ready-made excuses – work, the change in the weather, airplane bookings. He told her that they would stay until all the guests had gone and then they would leave immediately. His secretary was traveling with them. He asked each day how she felt, but when they were alone, he either read or played patience. He appeared to be calm except that his eyes blazed as with fever. They were young eyes. The blue seemed to sharpen in color once the anger in him was resurrected. He was snappy with the servants. She knew that when they got back to London there would be separate cars waiting for them at the airport. It was only natural. The house, the warm flagstones, the shimmer of the water would sometimes, no doubt, reoccur to her; but she would forget him and he would live somewhere in the attic of her mind, the place where failure lurks.

Lantern Slides

'MACHUSLA, MACHUSLA, MACHUSLA MACREE...' Someone would sing that refrain before the night was over; a voice slightly drunk, or maybe very drunk, would send those trenchant lines to all the swooning hearts who, by midnight, would not be nearly so suave or so self-possessed. At first it did not seem like a song that would be sung there, because this was a smart gathering in a select part of the outskirts of Dublin – full, as Mr Conroy said, of nobs.

There were people from the world of politics, the world of theatre, the racing world, and the world of rock music. No rock stars were present, but a well-known manager of one group was there and, as Mr Conroy said, maybe one of his besequinned protégés would storm in later on. As Miss Lawless and Mr Conroy squeezed into the big hall, she saw a mêlée of people, well togged, waiters wading about with trays and bottles, and in the big limestone grate, a turf fire blazing. The surround was a bit lugubrious, like a grotto, but this impression was forgotten as the flames spread and swagged into brazen orange banners. In the sitting room, a further galaxy of people – all standing except for a few elderly ladies, who sat on a chintz-covered banquette in the middle of the room. Here, too, was a fire, and here the hum of voices that presaged an evening that would be lively, maybe even hectic. The waiters, mostly young men, moved like altar boys among the panting throngs, and so immense was the noise that people asked from time to time how this racket could be quelled, because quelled it would have to be when the moment came, when the summons for silence came.

Reflected in everything around her were the signs of prosperity – hunting scenes in big gilt frames, low tables crammed with

ornaments, porcelain boxes, veined eggs and so forth – and the
chandeliers seemed to be chattering, so dense and busy and clustered were the shining pendants of glass. The big flower arrangements were all identical – pink and red carnations, as if these were
the only flowers to be found. Yet by looking through the window
Miss Lawless could see that lilac was just beginning to sprout, and
small white eggcups of blossom shivered on jet-black magnolia
branches. It was a nippy evening.

Mr Conroy, as he led her through the throng, beamed. He was
the one who pressed her to come, rang up and asked if he might
bring her. They had walked earlier that morning on Dollymount
Strand, had left their footprints on the sand that Miss Lawless had
described as being white as saltpetre. On the walk they had relived
several moments of their past. Mr Conroy had made her laugh
and then almost reduced her to tears. She laughed as he described
his love life, or, rather, his attempts at a love life – the coaxing and
wooing of women, especially women who came up from the
country and wanted a bit of an adventure. He spoke glowingly of
racing women, who were always good sports. Then, in quieter
tones, he talked of his first love, or, as he so gallantly put it, his first
shared love, because, as he added, Miss Lawless was the other half
of his heart's desire. Both Miss Lawless and a girl called Nicola
had a claim on his heart, though neither of them ever knew it. Mr
Conroy, who worked in a hotel, said it was amazing, unbelievable
altogether, the things that happened in a hotel, the little twists of
fate, and he went on to describe how one day, returning from a
weekend off, he was told there was a lady drinking heavily in
Room 68. He chastised the barman, said didn't he know they
didn't approve of female guests drinking in their rooms alone.
What he had to do then was ring the housekeeper and the two of
them went up on the pretext that the room was going to be
repapered shortly. Lo and behold, whom did he find but the
sweetheart he had not laid eyes on for twenty years, who was now

back in Dublin because her mother was dying, and who was, as he had to admit to Miss Lawless, blind drunk, her voice slurry and her face puffy.

'And what did you do?' Miss Lawless asked.

'I kissed her of course,' Mr Conroy said, and painted a picture of this girl as she once was, this vision who wore hats and veils and always put her hand out when she was introduced and repeated the person's name in a coquettish voice. Every man in Dublin had loved her, but she married a banker and emigrated to South Africa. She had come home only for her mother's funeral and, while she was there had died herself. At her own funeral all her former friends from the fashion world and the entertainment world convened, and, like Mr Conroy, they were desolated, bemoaning the untimely death of someone who had been so beautiful. Many made mention of her veils, and how she put an arm out when introduced to people and spoke in that unique voice, and all were shaken by the tragedy.

'We must commemorate her,' Mr Conroy had said, and all those gathered, moved by drink and grief, repeated his words and echoed his sentiments. It was decided that Mr Conroy would commission a bronze of Nicola to which they would all contribute. Alas, alas, when the bronze was delivered, months later, Mr Conroy indeed paid for it but did not receive the promised donations. It was, as he said, on his own mantelpiece, for himself alone.

But that was morning and it was night now – heady, breathless night – and Miss Lawless felt that something thrilling would happen to her. She did not feel like the peevish Miss Lawless who had put her stockings on in the hotel bedroom and given a little hiss as she saw a ladder starting from her big toe; and she did not feel like the Miss Lawless who feared that her black dress was a little too dressy because of a horseshoe-shaped diamanté buckle on one side, doing nothing in particular, just brazenly calling attention to itself. She saw now that her dress was perfect and, if anything, she was underdressed. The room was a pageant of fashion, and the combined perfume of the ladies, along with the aftershave of the men, drowned out the smell of carnations – that is, if they had any smell, because, as Miss Lawless reminded herself, shop flowers were not fragrant any more. Suddenly in her mind she saw old-fashioned climbing roses, their pink buds tight, compact, and herself getting on tiptoe to reach the branch in order to smell them, to devour them. This was followed by a flood of childhood evocations – a painted-cardboard doll's house with a little swivelled insert for a front door, which could be flicked open with a thumbnail; a biscuit barrel impregnated with the smell of ratafia essence, and a spoon with an enamelled picture of the Pope. Somehow the party had begun to trigger in her a host of things, memory upon memory, like hands placed on top of one another in a childhood game.

Meanwhile, coiffured and bejewelled, women looked around for the perfect spot in which to be seen, in which to appoint themselves, and their voices rose in a chorus of conjecture and alarm, repeating the selfsame remark: 'What is she going to do? I mean, is Betty going to faint?' Some were affirming that she would faint – those who were her dearest friends adding that they would faint with her, so excruciating was the suspense. They vied with each other as to this orgy of proposed fainting, and Miss Lawless saw bodies heaped on the sumptuous carpet, some in trouser suits with jangles of bracelets, others in ra-ra skirts, their gauze frills like the webbing of old-fashioned tea cosies, grazing their bare thighs, and still others in sedate, pleated costumes.

Mr Conroy was engaged in a bit of banter with two other men. Dr Fitz, a bachelor and long-standing friend of Betty's family, was assuring his two male companions that he had not put on weight because, like most modern men nowadays, he went to a gymnasium. Not only that, and he winked at Miss Lawless as he said this, but a good friend of his, a 'widda', had a Jacuzzi, and he availed himself of that whenever he dropped by.

'Oh, the floozy with the Jacuzzi,' Mr Conroy said, implying that he knew the widow. He then said that his weight never altered, simply because he never altered his diet, having a grape-fruit and a slice of toast in the morning, a salad at lunch, and a collation in the evening. He was one of the few people in the room who did not imbibe. Mr Gogarty was younger than these two men, lived in London, but hopped back and forth, as he said, to recharge the batteries, and, of course, wouldn't have missed the party for anything, as Betty was an old friend of his. With a glint in his eye, Mr Gogarty brought it to the attention of the two other men that the city they lived in was a very dirty city indeed. They did not blanch, knowing this was a preamble to some joke.

'Haven't we Ballsbridge?' he said, waiting for the gleam on their faces. 'And haven't we Dollymount?' he said, with further relish, hesitant before throwing in Sandymount and Stillorgan. He went on to say that innocent people visited these haunts and never registered their bawdy associations.

'I believe there's a Carnal Way somewhere,' Dr Fitz said, not wanting to be lacking in a reply, and he pulled at the shirtsleeve of Bill the Barrow Boy, who stood nearby. Bill knew all these places from his early days selling oranges with his mother.

Bill the Barrow Boy was no longer a barrow boy, of course. He now mixed with 'the cream', being a successful broker. But he still knew his Dublin, especially the back streets, and was able to say that Carnal Way was somewhere near Wine Tavern Street, and that all those places were full of antiquity, so much so that if the pavings were dug up it would be proved that Ireland surpassed every other country in ancientness and memorabilia. He spoke with a Dublin accent, had a broad handsome face and a broad contented smile. While he talked he did a couple of card tricks, both to amuse himself and to prepare himself for the entertain-ments that were bound to take place later.

'Fourteen of us children,' he said to Miss Lawless, and boasted they were never hungry. He praised his mother – her thrift, her intelligence, her stamina – and described how she made money boxes out of cardboard, covered them with fancy paper, and how faithfully, every Saturday night, there were contributions to the coal box, the food box, the meat box, the candle box and the odds-and-ends box, in case any of them ever got sick.

'Made dinners for us out of samphire and cockles,' he said proudly. Although Mr Conroy liked to reminisce, he did not think that this was an occasion for recounting hardship, and, after praising the fortitude of mothers, he went on to draw attention to the gala that they were privileged to be party to.

'I was in on the secret from the first instant,' Dr Fitz said, stressing that he was a bosom friend of Betty's and of her children. Undeterred, Bill the Barrow Boy pointed to his bride, Denise, and deemed her the most photogenic girl in the room. He described their happy and healthy life, how they never drank indoors, except at Christmastime, and how they rose at six and played a few rounds of tennis before breakfast.

'Jaysus, it's like living in a monastery,' Dr Fitz said, and added that he had never heard of an Irish house that didn't have drink in it. Bill the Barrow Boy corrected him, said yes, they did have drink, oodles of it, but only for the benefit of visitors.

'Pardon my taking the liberty,' Bill the Barrow Boy said, lifting the heavy gold pendant of Miss Lawless's necklace. She told him it was Mexican but he insisted on believing that it had been dug up in an Irish field, as it was redolent of Malachy's colour of gold. Then he took her to task, in a joking way, for having become an exile. 'She's here,' 'She's here,' 'She's here,' voices said, and the urgent signal travelled back through the room. Lights were quenched, and those nearest the door kept calling back to those at the rear of the room to 'for Christ's sake, shut up'. Everyone waited, expecting to hear a little applause out in the hall, because it was those people that Betty would encounter first; in fact, the very first person Betty would encounter was the mime artist who had been hired for the occasion. There he was at the doorway, on this bright spring evening, wearing a black suit – pale as a gargoyle, moving nothing but one red-painted eyebrow, which he wriggled to amuse the arrivals. Yes, Betty would see him first, and no doubt she would guess that a birthday celebration had been arranged in her absence. She had gone innocently to the races and had intended to come home and have supper in bed, but her friends and family had foxed her and devised this surprise party.

'False alarm!' someone shouted, and the crowd laughed and resumed drinking as the lights were put on again and the waiters were summoned more urgently than ever, for people reckoned there would be many more false alarms before the birthday girl showed up.

When Betty did arrive, she took it totally in her stride, walked through the entryway, it seems winked at the waiters, and told one of the staff that the hall fire was smoking. Loud cheers hailed her as she came into the sitting room – a youngish-looking woman with short brown hair and sallow skin, wearing a coral suit and a coral necklace. She stood as an accomplished actress might, her hands reaching out to welcome a group that she certainly had not been expecting. She waited a moment before singling out any one person, but soon friends rushed to her, especially those women who had vowed that they would faint. People were kissing her, handing her presents, others were pulling her to be introduced to this one and that one, including Miss Lawless.

Mr Conroy said to Miss Lawless that it was a good thing they had taken that walk by Dollymount in the morning, or otherwise he would never have thought of inviting her. She agreed. Seeing her after several years – a little aged, but still glowing – it occurred to Mr Conroy that maybe there dwelt in some secret crevice of her heart a soft spot for him. He had seen her through love affairs. Once he had taken her to a fortune-teller on the north side of the city, saw her come out crying. Soon after, he had rung up a lover on her behalf, a married man, only to be told by the man's wife that he did not wish to come to the phone. He had had to report those uncompromising words to Miss Lawless. 'He does not wish to come to the phone,' he had to say, and then witnessed the hour or two of dementia that ensued. To others, she might seem composed, but he sensed that inside a storm raged and all those attachments battered her.

Suddenly there was a loud call for dinner from the chief waiter, followed by cheers and whistles from waiters and guests alike. All were relieved. A few grumbled jokingly and blamed Betty for having taken so long to arrive. Mr Gogarty asked where in heaven's name she could have been from the time the races ended until she got to her own house.

'Mum's the word,' Dr Fitz said, but the glint in his eye betrayed his indiscretion. He knew that she had met her husband and had gone with him as his wife to get the trophy that he had won.

The dining room was temptingly lit, and red garlands dipped from the ceiling in loops. The tables were covered with pink cloths and lit with pink candles, and all over the walls there were blown-up photos of Betty in a bathing suit and a choker. At the far end of the room there was a dais, where the orchestra already sat and was playing soft, muted music. Balloons floated in the air – blue, yellow and silver orbs, moving with infinite hesitation. Miss Lawless was seated with the group she had already talked to, and Mr Conroy introduced her to the remaining few whom she had not met. There were Mr and Mrs Vaughan, a girl called Sinead and Dot the Florist. There was also one empty place. Dot the Florist was wearing a pink catsuit, so tight-fitting that she seemed to be trussed. Mrs Vaughan – Eileen, who was in a grey angora suit – made not the slightest attempt to be sociable. Mr Conroy whispered to Miss Lawless that Mr and Mrs Vaughan had not spoken for over a year, but that nevertheless Mrs Vaughan insisted on escorting him everywhere.

'Any windfalls?' Mr Conroy called across, knowingly, to Mr Vaughan. It was their code word for asking if Mrs Vaughan had at all thawed. By his look, Mr Vaughan seemed to be saying that hostilities were dire. Sinead, who was in a black strapless dress, told her fellow guests, for no reason, that she was in mourning for her life.

'Cut out the histrionics, Sinead,' Dr Fitz said, and glowered at her. They were courting, but, as she was quick to tell the present company, he was full of moods. To his chagrin, Bill the Barrow Boy was not seated with his bride, Denise, a thing he could scarcely endure. He allowed himself a moment of misery as he thought of the one blot on their nuptial bliss. Denise did not want a child. Her figure mattered to her too much. 'Later on' was what she said. Many's the time he slipped into the Carmelite chapel off Grafton Street and gave an offering for a votive candle to be lit.

'Isn't Denise a picture?' he said to the others, and Mr Conroy seized the moment to remark on Miss Lawless's beauty, to say that it was a medieval kind of beauty, and that he believed that she was a throwback, like that queen, Maire Ruadh, who lived in a castle at Corcomroe, and who when she had her fill of a lover had him dumped over the casement into the sea.

'Didn't Yeats set "The Dreaming of the Bones" at Corcomroe?' Mr Gogarty said, with a certain bookish authority. Bill the Barrow Boy said he wouldn't know, as he never read a 'buke' in his life, he let Denise do all the reading, and assured them that she could read any ordinary book in a sitting.

'Oh, river and stream,' Mr Conroy said, as plates were placed briskly on the table. Some said it was trout, others said it was salmon. In fact, things became rather heated at one moment, as

Dot the Florist insisted it was trout, said she had grown up on a river in Wicklow and that she knew one kind of fish from another, and Dr Fitz said that any fool could see it was salmon, its blush diminished by the subtle lighting. Miss Lawless put her fork in it, tasted it and said somewhat tentatively that yes, it was salmon in an aspic sauce. Dot the Florist pushed hers away and said she wasn't hungry and grabbed one of the waiters to ask for a vodka on the rocks. Dr Fitz said it was a crying shame to drink vodka when good table wines were being served, although, he added somewhat ruefully, not as good as they would be if the great man of the house were present. He boasted to Miss Lawless that they had often drunk two thousand pounds' worth of wine at an intimate dinner party in that very house.

'Now, now,' Sinead called to Dr Fitz, not wanting the missing – indeed the vagrant – husband to be given any mention. She was on Betty's side; Betty was her friend; she made it clear that Betty had poured her heart out to her often, and that she well knew the evenings Betty had supper alone on a tray in her bedroom, like many another jilted woman. Then, fearing that she might have betrayed a friendship, she commented on Betty's figure and, pointing to the various blown-up photos of Betty all over the room, she asked aloud, 'Why would any man leave a beautiful woman like that for a slut!' Why indeed? Dr Fitz told her to pipe down and not to talk about people she knew nothing about. Yet he was pleased to tell Miss Lawless in confidence one or two things about Betty's rival, a Danish woman called Clara. Miss Lawless somehow envisaged her as being blond with very long legs, and also as being very assured.

'Not a bit of it,' Dr Fitz said, and described a woman who was not at all svelte, who wore ordinary clothes, had never gone to a hairdresser or a beauty parlour in her life, and was overweight.

'So why did he run off with her?' Miss Lawless asked, genuinely mystified.

'She makes him feel good,' Dr Fitz said, and by the way he gulped a swig of wine he seemed to express a desire for such a woman and not the needful, tempestuous Sinead.

Mr Vaughan and Mr Conroy were in a pleasing exchange on the subject of Mr Conroy's tie. Nothing pleased Mr Conroy more than to relate yet again the story of how he came to get such a beautiful tie and what a double-edged gift it was. It had been given to him, he said, by a very generous lady, a rich lady whose baby he was godfather to. One day at the races, the tie was admired by a bloke and Mr Conroy heard himself saying rather gallantly, 'Oh, I'll get you one, Seamus,' thinking to himself that all he had to do was to go into Switzer's or Brown Thomas's and fork out fifteen quid and be in the good books of this man, Seamus, whom he had reason to want to befriend. Seamus used to do night work in Mr Conroy's hotel, but had been summarily dismissed because of incivility. Late at night, when guests from overseas arrived, he would tell them to 'feck off', as he was too lazy to get up from the stool and help with a suitcase or open a door. However, the fellow they got to replace him was even worse and an alcoholic, to boot, so they hoped to coax Seamus back. Lo and behold, as he confessed, the next day he scoured the shops, to find there was no tie like it, not even one approaching it. He finally had to ring the rich woman's secretary – the woman herself was always travelling – only to be told, 'Didn't you know? That's a very special tie. That's a Gucci tie.'

'Is that so?' he claims to have said, telling everyone at the table of his naivety, but meaning it for Miss Lawless in particular. He added that one label was the same as another to him, and he knew a fellow in England, a foreman who worked on a building site, and he sent the tie over for a duplicate to be bought. After a couple of weeks, back it came with its companion in a regal box, and, Christ, wasn't it forty-eight pounds fifty pence. A shocker altogether, as everyone agreed, and the other men now began to stare at the tie with incomprehension. Sinead and Dot looked at each other quite piqued, and Sinead announced that the ladies would like a bit of stimulating conversation – they had not come to a party to be treated like ornaments, as was the case with most women in Ireland. She added that though they were treated like pieces of china at a party, they were frequently 'knocked about' at home.

'Bollocks,' Dr Fitz said, and by the way he picked up a bottle of wine it appeared he might brain Sinead with it. His cheeks were getting flushed and he proceeded to loosen his tie.

'So set us an agenda,' Mr Gogarty, the aggrieved divorcé, said, also nettled by Sinead's remark. For some unfortunate reason, divorce was pounced upon as a subject, so the table became even more heated, with men and women shouting each other down. The men insisted that divorce was wrong, because of the way children suffer, while the women claimed vociferously that children suffered anyhow, because their fathers were always in the boozer or in the backs of motorcars necking with younger women. Mrs Vaughan was the sole female voice who took issue with the other women, adding that young girls nowadays were tramps in the way they dressed and the way they behaved.

'How do you know how we behave?' Sinead said tartly.

'What's right is right,' Eileen Vaughan said, pushing her plate away contemptuously and applying herself to cutting bread into infinitesimal pieces, which she did not touch.

Much against the advice of Dr Fitz, Sinead began to tell how she, as a young girl not yet thirty-five, had been the victim of a modern Irish marriage, and it was 'the pits'. She recalled coming into her own building one evening and actually finding the chain drawn on her door, then ringing the bell but receiving no answer, having to go to the apartment below and ask a neighbour to shelter her for the night, ringing the telephone number but not receiving an answer, and a few days later learning that the person he had had in the room when he had put the chain on was a call girl. When she tackled him about it, he said that he needed comfort because she had gone out and he was not sure if she was coming back.

'It's bloody ridiculous the way women have to kowtow,' she said directly to Eileen Vaughan, who looked like a weasel ready to hiss. Dr Fitz began to fume fearing above all else that the next thing Sinead would treat them to was an account of her husband's suicide, of the amount of pills he took in that hotel in the North, and of Dr Fitz being called, because he happened to be there on a fishing holiday. Worse, she would treat them to the long rigmarole about her miscarriage and her husband beating her brutally. He was right. She was off on her favourite target. The four days in the labour ward, other women screaming and groaning, but to some avail, since they did not lose their babies. Then the bit about her husband coming to collect her, her imagining a treat – lunch out, maybe, or coffee and biscuits in that smart pub off Grafton Street – but instead their going out the sea road, her heartening at the thought of a walk along the strand, with the dunes on one side and the sea on the other, returning to the spot where they had courted, as an appease-ment, a reward for all that she had been through. Hardly had they taken twenty paces along that littered seashore when he began to beat her up. Sinead became more hysterical as she described it, more dramatic – herself on the ground, her husband kicking her, first in silence, then his beginning to shout, to ask why had she lost the child, why had she been so bloody careless. His child – his, his. 'You're mad,' she recounted having said to him, and then told of standing up and feeling battered inside and out.

Bill the Barrow Boy leaned across the table and tried to stop her, but the other men turned from her in dismay and towards Dr Fitz, who was appraising the nose of a red wine that had just been brought in dome-shaped decanters. On the surface, the wine had a violet hue. The main course was also being served. It was duck with roast potatoes and apple sauce, which, as Mr Gogarty said, was far preferable to steak on a spring evening. The light had faded, and in the dining room, what with the balloons, the waving wings of yellow candle flame and the high-pitched voices, the atmosphere was fervid. Many were popping streamers from the little toy pistols that were on their side plates, and these coloured wisps of straw weaving and wandering from table to table, shoulder to shoulder, formed a web, uniting them in a carnival chain.

'Now, what is the difference between Northside girls and Southside girls?' Mr Gogarty asked with pride.

Answers were proffered, but in the end Mr Gogarty was pleased to tell them they were all dullards. 'Northside girls have real jewellery and fake orgasms,' he said, and laughed loudly while Eileen Vaughan repeatedly blessed herself and, as if it were a maggot, lifted the streamer that joined her to Mr Gogarty.

Mr Conroy, in order to bring harmony back to the proceedings, recounted the morning's walk that he and Miss Lawless had taken, gloated over what a sight it had been, what refreshment, the air so bracing, not a ruffle on the sea, the sand so white – or, as he said, white as saltpetre, to quote Miss Lawless.

Yes, Miss Lawless had asked him to take her there, but it was not so much to retrace her steps as to find them for the first time. Twenty-five years had gone by since that momentous occasion on the dunes. It was there she had surrendered herself to a man that she likened to Peter Abelard. He was tall and blond, with a stiff, almost wooden body – a sternness and yet a seducer's charm. The first time Miss Lawless had sighted him was in a newspaper office where she had gone to deliver a piece that she had written for a competition. Readers had been asked to describe a day by the sea. She could not remember precisely how she had described it then, but today, when she walked there with Mr Conroy, she saw patches of sea like diagonals of stained glass, the colours deepening as the water swerved from the shore to the Hill of Howth far beyond. Mr Conroy had said that if she waited a week or two more the rhododendrons would be in bloom over in Howth and they could go there for an excursion. She knew, just as Mr Conroy knew, that the red rhododendrons they conjured up were mostly in the mind – talismans, transfused with memory. On the walk, Mr Conroy often stopped in his tracks to draw breath, said he was getting on a bit and was easily winded, then pointed to his elastic stockings and spoke of varicose veins. But in telling the story to the guests at the table he spoke only of a glorious walk where they linked and strode together.

Yes, the traces of her and Abelard were there, because of course he had cropped up again in her mind. On the evening when she had first met him, when she took her little essay to the news-paper office, she had had a premonitory feeling that something was going to happen between them, just as this evening, sitting at that table, she felt that something was pending. She remembered clearly how Abelard had taken her essay, asked her where she worked, and how he diligently wrote down her address and her telephone number – as a formality, but from the way he smiled at her she knew that he had some personal interest. When her piece was featured in the paper as having placed first in the competition, the editor had got her name wrong, so the flush of her winning was a little dimmed. But Peter Abelard pursued her. They began to meet. She tasted her first gin and tonic and thought not much of it, but afterwards there was a floaty feeling inside her stomach, and then she took off her gloves and touched his hand and was not ashamed. One night they met far earlier than was usual for them, took a bus out to the sea, got off at Dollymount, walked over a bit of footbridge and then down a road and into the labyrinth and secrecy of the dunes, with the high swags of coarse grass and the sandy mounds serving as beds. It was there among those dunes that she gave herself to this Abelard. Although she knew she had, she could not remember it; it was like something experienced in a blur. It appalled her that she had in a sense detached herself at one of the more poignant and crucial moments in her whole life. Nor could she remember much of the hotel where they went later on, except that it was a dingy place near the railway station, and that the bathroom was out on the landing and, having no nightdress or dressing gown, she had to put Abelard's blazer on when she went out of the room. They were near and not near. He would embrace her but he did not want to know anything about her. She wanted dearly to tell him that this was the first time, although he must have known.

It was not long after that that he introduced her to his wife at some party, and his wife, maybe sensing that she was the type of girl her husband might like, or else feeling extremely lonely, invited her to come to their house for an evening, because her husband was going away to England on a job. She could remember clearly her visit to that house, and three children in ragged pyjamas refusing to go to bed. Then, later, her sitting downstairs in the big draughty kitchen with his wife, eating mashed potatoes and sausages and thinking what a lonely house it was, now the rowdiness had died down. They drank quite a lot of whiskey, and while they were drinking and talking about the mysticism of Gerard Manley Hopkins the telephone rang, and so great was the wife's excitement and alacrity that in jumping up from the table she turned her ankle and knocked over a lamp but still raced. She knew or hoped that the phone call would be from her husband, and indeed it was. She told him how their youngest son had bellowed his daddy's name all over the garden, bellowed for him to come home, and that at that very moment she and Miss Lawless were having a chin-wag. Miss Lawless had wanted to confess her wrong there and then to this woman, but she baulked. Instead, they continued to ramble and drink a bit, and later she kicked off her shoes and asked if by any chance she could sleep on the sofa.

In the very early morning when she wakened, she saw the garden through the long uncurtained window, saw clothes on a line and a tree with tiny shrunken apples that looked as if they had some sort of disease, some blight.

The secret affair with her Abelard ended, and in a welter of choked emotion Miss Lawless had spent half a week's earnings – she worked in a shop and was paid very little – purchasing a book of poems for him, a secondhand book. So determined was she to be discreet, and so certain was she that the good God would reward her for her discretion and her sense of sacrifice, that she slipped a little greeting card not into the book itself but between the brown paper cover and the frittered binding of the book. She felt sure that he would remove that cover and find the greeting, that he would be touched and immediately restored to her. He would come to the shop where she worked, he would whisk her away, maybe even take her to a restaurant. The lines she had copied onto the card were from one of James Stephens's poems:

> And we will talk until
> Talk is a trouble, too,
> Out on the side of the hill;
> And nothing is left to do,
>
> But an eye to look into an eye;
> And a hand in a hand to slip;
> And a sigh to answer a sigh;
> And a lip to find out a lip!

As it happened, her Abelard did not find that note for many years, but when he did find it he wrote to tell her, saying also that he had lately been dreaming of her, and that in one dream he cherished they were at the races together, and he wished he had never wakened from it. She had not answered that letter. She did not know exactly what to say. She believed that someday she might bump into him and then the right words would come.

Today, as she and Mr Conroy walked along the strand, she had in fact asked him how her Abelard was, and was a little disappointed to hear that he was almost blind now, and that he walked with a stick. Unthinkable. Much as Miss Lawless wanted to see him, she did not at all like the idea of meeting a blind man with a stick. Mr Conroy, who knew that she had had this fling, kept suggesting that she phone him. 'Or I'll phone him for you,' he said.

She said she would think it over. In another part of her mind she actually just wanted to find the spot where she had lain, as if finding the spot would redeem the years.

'Dollymount is ideal for courting couples,' Mr Gogarty said, as if reading her thoughts, yet winking at Mr Conroy, thereby implying they both had caroused there.

'I declare to God,' said Mr Conroy, 'I was with a girl out there at about one in the morning not so long ago when a geezer tapped the window and asked me for the right time. The pair of us jumped out of our skins and I told the blasted Peeping Tom where to go.'

'End of a lovely . . .' Mr Gogarty said, but did not finish the sentence, because of ladies being present. Eileen Vaughan suddenly exploded, thumped her husband, and said that never in her life had she been subjected to such smut.

'Ah, the Meat Baron,' Dr Fitz said, ignoring the tirade and pointing to a tall, bulky man who had come into the room. He was wearing a light suit and a very jazzy tie.

'Hawaiian,' Mr Gogarty said with a slight sneer, declaring how money betrays on a man's puss.

The Meat Baron looked around smiling, realizing that he was being alluded to. Dr Fitz told Miss Lawless that the man had a great brain – a brain that could be used for music or mathematics, could have succeeded at anything, but that it happened to be meat he got started on, because of going down to the knacker's yard as a young lad and buying hooves to make rosary beads with. Dr Fitz said that his admiration for self-made men was boundless; he said it showed real originality; he said that people who had inherited money were often scoundrels, drifters or drug addicts. Money, he attested, could either forge character or weaken it. He calculated that, now that the Meat Baron had arrived, and including the other various tycoons already present, there was easily billions of pounds' worth of money up for grabs in that room – enough money to support a Third World country. Bill the Barrow Boy leaned across and said that he would not want that kind of big money, that those people who had their own yachts and their own jets often came a cropper – went out in the morning in one of these yachts or one of these jets and by noon were in a Black Maria, stripped of every personal belonging even down to their Rolexes. The Meat Baron stopped for a moment, looked down at the uneaten duck on Dr Fitz's plate and said, 'She'll never fly over Loch Dan again,' and laughed. Dot the Florist pulled him by the sleeve, but he was already walking on and did not notice.

Dot had a plan of her own that night. She had vowed that before the night was over she would dance with one of the rich men, whichever one didn't have his wife with him. The bank was foreclosing on her. The little flower shop that she had opened a year before was still a treasure garden as far as she was concerned, but the novelty had gone and people went back to buying dull things like carnations and evergreen plants. Where else, she asked herself bitterly, would they find mallows and phlox and Canterbury bells; where else were birds' eggs and moss and miniature roses tucked into rush baskets; where else were the jugs of sweet peas like suspended butterflies? Where, but in her shop that was really half a shop? The other half was a newsagent's, and she could hear the ringing of their cash register all day long, while with her it was a question of people coming in and asking if she had any cheap flowers. It had been such a success in the beginning: she was written up, photographed in her little jalopy bedecked with boughs and branches, coming from the market. But now – that very afternoon, in fact – a cow of a woman had arrived in a jeep and bought half the shop, for next to nothing, asking if she could have a guarantee that these were not refrigerated flowers, that they would not wilt once she got them in her drawing room.

Dot eyed the Meat Baron; she had met him before, and felt that with enough vodka she could perhaps lure him. She would have to do it. Otherwise it was a 'For Rent' sign above the door, with the newsagent taking over the whole place. Galling. Galling. Some would say she was lucky to be there, that she was there only because of being a friend of Betty's daughter. But she believed she was still dishy and an asset at any party. A gypsy who had come to her shop had told her to make the most of her Mediterranean looks. When the time came for the ladies' choice, she would ask the Meat Baron up. 'Ah, the arms of Morpheus,' Mr Conroy said, nudging Miss Lawless as they both looked at Mr Vaughan, who had fallen fast asleep, his head on the table. Mr Conroy then began to whisper to Miss Lawless, describing Mr Vaughan's ghastly life. His wife hid packets of biscuits so that he could not find them; she put his dinner on a tray at six o'clock promptly each evening and left it there even if he was not home for days, so that the poor man had cold boiled potatoes and tough meat most of the time. Mr Vaughan, like many an Irishman, as Mr Conroy conceded, had an eye for the ladies and had met this beautiful lady – English, mark you – at Leopardstown races and assisted her, it seems, in stepping over a puddle. As a result, he repaired with her to the trainers' bar, and as a further result coaxed her to pay a visit in the fullness of time to a rural hotel in the South of Ireland. The English lady turned up with two suitcases, was given a suite, and later in the evening was visited by Mr Vaughan, who spent two nights with her, wining and dining her in the suite, having the occasional drive to the seaside with her to get a blow of air, and having cock-tails galore and even the little farewell gift of a Waterford rose bowl from the hotel boutique. Mr Vaughan naturally told the manager to send the damages to him, as he would pay the bill at the end of the month, when his wages came through. Mr Vaughan was a dealer in motorcars and was paid monthly. It was in his capacity as salesman that he had first met Betty – sold her a sports car. The manager, a religious man and a teetotaller, condoned the illicit weekend, chiefly on the grounds of Mr Vaughan's being married, as everyone knew, to a harridan.

'No problem,' the manager said, and passed on the instructions to the girl in Accounts, a snibby girl who at that time was plan-ning to leave the place and go to England to work in a health spa. The time came and Miss Snib, having paid no attention to the instructions she was given, sent the bill for the wining, the dining, the suite and the Waterford bowl to the English lady – Miss Beale by name. Miss Beale, it seems, was indeed taken aback at receiving it, and doubly taken aback at the huge amount that had accrued. But being a person who prided herself on her dignity – she worked in the City for a company of financiers – she paid the bill, then put pen to paper and sent Mr Vaughan a letter that was nicely balanced between umbrage and desire. She expressed mild surprise that he should prove to be so lacking in gentlemanly courtesy, but, being a sport, as she reminded him he had often called her, she decided that the cost was trifling compared with the pleasure, and she went into some very accurate and fulsome details about his hairy body on the peach cushions of her flesh, and luxuriated on the tussle waged between these two bodies – their all-night combat, and, as she said, his little black thing getting its way in the end, and then morning, which brought them not fatigue but fresh vigour, fortified as they were by a gigantic breakfast. She was glad to have paid for such a romp, she teasingly said in a postscript; she would pay again for it.

'*Mon Dieu!*' Mr Conroy said and looked up at the ceiling, where shoals of balloons were on their happy circuit.

The letter did reach Mr Vaughan safely, and, once over his shock – having rung the bookkeeper at the hotel and made a complaint – and maybe feeling nostalgic for Miss Beale, he put the letter in his suit pocket and went on a bit of a binge. He was away for several days and nights, seeing friends up and down the country, and returned to his own house and his wife, Eileen, a sickly man who had to spend two days in bed, with porridge and cups of weak tea. Unfortunately, when Mr Vaughan rose to resume work he was in something of a dither, having express word from his boss in Dublin that unless he got moving and got his act together and sold at least one foreign motorcar down in the windy hills of the Shannon Estuary he would be drawing the dole by the following Monday week. Mr Vaughan dressed hurriedly and set off with the zealousness of a missioner, even on the way composing a short rhyme that would further the sales of the car. There was going to be a display of these cars in a week, and he knew how to get the public interested. The rhyme he invented was borrowed from 'The Lake Isle of Innisfree' and went:

> I will arise and go down to Kinsale,
> Agog in my brand new Ford Fiesta;
> I will eat fresh oysters there
> And in the afternoon have a siesta.

In his haste, Mr Vaughan forgot to remove various items from the pockets of his other suit, and he was hardly at the crossroads one mile from his house before his wife, Eileen, was reading a description of his prowess, which, after eighteen years, came as a shock to her. She lost no time. She had the letter copied on the new machine in the post office, making sure that she oversaw the copying herself, and soon after all of his friends, plus his family, including his sister the nun, plus Eileen's family, plus his employers, were party to the ill-fated *billet doux*.

Soon after, Mr Vaughan suffered his first heart attack, going down the steps of a hotel, where he had presided over a sales conference that had boosted his standing – principally, it was rumoured, because of his versifying.

While she was listening, Miss Lawless suffered a slight shock. Before her very eyes there appeared a modern-day Abelard. It was eerie. He was wearing a black dress suit and a cream shirt with frills that reached all the way down the front, like jonquils. The suit seemed to be not of serge or wool but of silk, and the sleeves were wide like the sleeves of a woman's kimono. He was blond, with fair skin and blue eyes. The blue was like that glass that has been rinsed again and again and for some reason emanates a private history, a sorrow. He was obviously a man of note, because various people waved, trying to induce him to come and sit at their table, but he just stood and smiled, determined not to be stuck anywhere he did not want to be. 'There's a place here,' Miss Lawless said, but under her breath. She was not usually so flagrant; in fact, she prided herself on her reserve. Betty ran and kissed him, and Miss Lawless experienced a flicker of jealousy as she watched this newcomer squeeze Betty's cheeks while they laughed over some little private joke they had. Miss Lawless thought that, as he strolled with Betty, he had something of the quality of a panther. She felt that his shoes, which she could not see, were made of suede, or else they were slippers, because he seemed to walk so softly, he padded through that room. Mr Conroy suddenly referred to him, called him Reggie, and said how he knew him for the pup he was – chasing young girls, his wife hardly cold in the grave. There had been a drowning accident the year before, and this husband was swanning about in Italian-style clothes, getting sympathy off ladies for his tragedy, leading a game life of it, flying to London twice a week, where, it was rumoured, he had a flat.

Dr Fitz looked up and was not at all pleased at the attention Betty was giving to this Reggie.

'Too much of a blush in that woman's cheek,' Dr Fitz said, as he looked after them, and then he turned to Miss Lawless to tell her about the day Betty's husband had left her and how he, he was the one to hold her hand. A party of them were just getting on the jet to go to Spain when the husband – John was his name – suddenly said to Betty, 'You go on ahead. I've decided it would be better if we lived apart.' Here Dr Fitz hesitated in order for Miss Lawless to take in the brutal significance of the remark, which indeed she did. He then painted a picture of Betty, the pretty and ever-cheerful wife who dressed always as her prominent husband liked her to dress, which was smartly; who rode to hounds at her husband's wish; who rarely complained if he failed to turn up at a theatre or a concert; who organized lunches, dinners, breakfasts for fifty or more at the last minute; and who even overcame her fear of skiing – all for his sake. Betty, suddenly a husbandless, stranded woman. Dr Fitz dilated further on the pity of it, the shock the poor woman got, and how she went berserk on the little plane en route, going mad up there in the filtered atmosphere, with the pilot wondering whether he should turn back or keep going, or what.

'If I'd had an injection with me,' Dr Fitz said, lamenting even now how he had set out that day without his doctor's bag – a thing he had never done since. He described again the plane soaring through the cloudless upper atmosphere, having to undo the buttons of her blouse, having to undo her shoes, holding her down, telling her that the whole thing was a bad dream from which she would one day awaken.

'You two are like a pair at confession,' Sinead called across the table rather sneeringly. Dr Fitz went on talking to Miss Lawless, ignoring the gibe. Sinead, who hoped to marry Dr Fitz, had thought for a few weeks now that she was pregnant, and knew that if she were she would keep it a secret until it was no longer possible to abort. She would then use every trump card of sentiment and religion to make him ashamed of even the word 'abortion'. She believed she was doing good by keeping this pregnancy a secret. Marriage would steady him. He still had the schoolboy notion of winning over every new female, which he was now trying to do with Miss Lawless, for which Sinead could happily wring her white neck with its collar of gold. Yes, a baby would settle him, preferably a boy.

Miss Lawless did not look back after Abelard and Betty to see where he was being seated, as that would have been too notice-able. The fact that this stranger was in the room was enough for her and made her think, with a wan smile, how slender, how delicate, people's dreams are. Suddenly her lips, her fingers, the follicles of her hair began to tingle, and she knew that if she looked into her little tortoiseshell mirror the pupils of her eyes would be dark and glistening. That was how it always was when she admired someone, and she had not seen anyone she admired for a long time. Her excitement was utter.

'Your eyes are like rhinestones,' Mr Conroy said to her, but he believed it was the general gaiety that made her look like that. As for himself, he was thinking that, with the help of God, he would take her home, and on the way he would suggest that they have another sea breeze; out there, with the dark sea, the misty empti-ness, and the Hill of Howth, with its rhododendrons about to burgeon, who knew? He did not think she would go the whole hog, but he felt she would yield to a kiss, and to kiss Miss Lawless was a lifelong dream. Miss Lawless and Nicola had caused him many a sleepless night. He had a pinup of each of them in his mind, constantly, these opposite girls – Nicola so dazzling, with her veils and her husky voice; Nicola so sophisticated, and Miss Lawless so shy and so awkward, with that big crop of hair and a bosom that swelled under her shabby clothes, the man's dress scarf with the fringing, which she wore for glamour, and her always spouting snatches of poetry to layabouts and drunkards who had only the one interest in her. To kiss her would be the realization of a dream and, as he thought, maybe a disappointment at that. He well knew that emotions often blur pleasure, especially for a man. He had been married, but had buried his wife some years before. It had not been a happy marriage, and he often thought that an excess of emotions was at the root of it. 'Too much love,' he often said to those who sympathized with him on the untimely death.

Sinead, now quite tipsy, was becoming even more miffed with the Doctor for the way he concentrated so utterly on Miss Lawless, and so she piped up and asked him if he loved her.

'Never say soft things to a woman or it will be thrown back at you,' Dr Fitz shouted. Young Mr Gogarty had to agree. Mr Gogarty had his own reason to be disenchanted with the opposite sex. There he was, a divorced man, quite well off, taking women to the theatre, giving them *pâté de foie gras* picnics on luxury trains, taking them to Glyndebourne to hear opera, and all he got when he brought them home to their front doors at midnight was a peck.

'Jesus, there's the queer one,' Dot the Florist said, and they all looked up and saw standing in the doorway a strange creature who looked around, gaped, appearing to be deaf, blind and listless. The newcomer had cropped hair and was wearing a mini-skirt and a big woollen sweater. It was clear she had just come through the open front door, and Mr Gogarty remarked that it was shocking altogether that no member of the staff had impeded her. All eyes were on this strange girl, some even supposing that maybe she was invited as part of the entertainment. Miss Lawless felt pity for her. There was something so trusting about her, so simple, as she looked around with her big grey sheeplike eyes, mesmerized by the crowd and the balloons and the orchestra and, now, the huge bowls of pink confection that waitresses were carrying about, along with plates of sugared biscuits that were shaped like thumbs and caramelized at the edges. Why not give her one, Miss Lawless thought.

'It's a damn shame,' Dr Fitz said and castigated those outside who had let her in, because in his opinion she had put a kind of shadow on the room, as if she augured some trouble. Mr Conroy said they shouldn't worry unduly, because although the girl looked a bit odd she was no trouble at all; she often called at his hotel for a gaze, especially when any notables came to stay and the red carpet was out. She walked the city all day and half the night, but never begged and never said a brazen thing. He went on to say it was a tragedy, really, because the girl had come from a good family, and that her aunt had been a certain Madame Georgette, who made corsets and had a shop in Dame Street. It seems that the girl had been orphaned and the Sisters of Charity had taken her in, but that her particular quirk was to keep walking, always walking, as if looking for something. This sent a shiver through Miss Lawless. The strange girl stared into the room intensely and then made as if to move forward to join the party. A waiter stopped her. He was joined by two waitresses, who spoke to her quietly. Then the waiter reached up and took down a big silver kidney-shaped balloon and handed it to her, and she clutched it in her arms as if it were a baby as she moved off.

Once again Dr Fitz asked them to consider the pluck and individuality of Betty. He said that nobody would believe it, but that he could assure them, that that very afternoon Betty had stood beside her errant husband after his horse won and had accepted the trophy with him. He then leaned across and said that he could tell them something that would shake them. She had not only accepted the trophy with her husband but she had gone to the champagne bar with him to have a drink.

'You're not serious,' Mr Conroy said.

'God strike me dead, I saw them,' Dr Fitz said, whereupon Sinead tackled him, said she had not known he had been to the races and asked him in an inflamed manner to account for himself. Then it was why hadn't he taken her, why had he lied, why had he pretended to be doing his hospital rounds when in fact he was drinking and gallivanting. 'I'm not putting up with this,' she said, her voice cracking.

'No one's asking you to,' he said, but by his expression he was saying much else, such as do not humiliate me in front of these people and do not make a fool of yourself.

She was asking loudly if it was with Betty he went to the races, and now it was dawning on her that maybe Betty's friendship with her was also to be questioned, was another part of the grand deceit. Suddenly, unable to contain herself, she rooted in her crocodile handbag and flourished the first love letter that he had ever written to her. It was on ruled paper and had been folded over many times. The colour in his face was beetroot as he reached across and tried to grab the letter from her. They grappled for it, Sinead grasping the greater part of it as she rose and ran through the room crying.

'Ah, it's the hors d'oeuvres that's had her,' Bill the Barrow Boy said, meaning the nerves. But he was the one to get up and follow her, because he pitied her on account of the story she had told them about losing that baby. He caught up with her at the doorway and dragged her back onto the dance floor, where people were already dancing. Betty waltzed with the Meat Baron, her head lolling on his shoulder, and Dot the Florist feared that, after all, the Meat Baron might not be the one, that she might have to look elsewhere. Dr Fitz, feeling that it was necessary to apologize somewhat to the people at the table, said that Sinead had a good heart, and that all the beggars in Grafton Street knew her and chased after her, but that she should never touch drink. To himself he was thinking that, yes, admittedly he had befriended her after her husband's death, and it was true that he had fallen for that soft swaying bottom of hers and the plait of black shiny hair that she sucked on, but it was also true that she had changed and had got possessive, and now, as far as he was concerned, it was two evenings a week in bed and no questions asked.

All this time, Eileen Vaughan kept looking around the table wondering if at any moment someone would throw a word to her. None of them liked her, she knew that. Hard, hard was what they thought she was. Yet the day her world fell apart, the day she lost her last ounce of faith in her husband, what had she done? She had drawn the curtains in her bedroom, the mauve curtains that she had sewn herself; she had lain on the floor and cried out to her Maker, cursing not the errant husband but herself for being the sour, hard fossil of a woman that she was, for never throwing him a word of kindness, and for not being able to express an endearment except through gruffness. She had prayed with all her heart and soul for a seizure to finish her off, but she just grew thinner and thinner, and tighter and tighter, like a bottle brush.

At that very moment, Miss Lawless was picked up from her chair and swept away from her own group. One of the ladies who had picked her up told her that she was taking her to another table to meet an eligible bachelor. In fact, it was this new Abelard. He did not turn to greet Miss Lawless when she sat down, but she saw immediately that she was right about his eyes – they were a washed blue and they conveyed both coldness and hurt. His voice was very low and when he did turn to address her his manner was detached.

'I suppose you know my whole history,' he said, a little crisply. Miss Lawless lied and said that she did not, but Dublin being Dublin, he disbelieved her but began anyway to tell her how he had lost his wife less than a year before, and while listening to the story and falling a little under his spell Miss Lawless was also wondering if he was not a cold fish indeed. Although there were shades of her first Abelard, he was a more ruthless man, and she could see that he would be at home in any gathering – had sufficient a smile and sufficient a tan and sufficient savoir faire to belong anywhere. He recounted, with a candidness that made her shudder, the terrible accident and the celebrated funeral that he himself had arranged. It had happened over a year ago. It was winter, and his wife, who was always restless, had decided to go riding. There had been a heavy storm, and the fields were flooded and many boughs had fallen from the trees, but as soon as the storm lifted she had decided on this journey. He had rung her from his office and she had told him that she was about to set out with her friend. She went and, as he said, never came back. Mystery and conjecture naturally clouded the incident but, he was telling Miss Lawless, as far as he was concerned she and her friend had decided to ford a stream that normally would be shallow but owing to the storm had swelled to the proportions of a sea; that the horses had baulked; that one of the riders, her companion, was thrown and his wife had jumped down to try and rescue her. In their heavy gear, both women had been carried away. The horses, meanwhile, crossed the stream and galloped hither and thither over watery fields into other parts of the county and were not traced until nightfall. He said that he knew about it before he was actually told; felt creepy while driving across the wooden bridge that led to his house, going into his house, and finding two of his children watching television with as yet no signs of emergency. Then darkness fell and the groom came into the hallway in a great state to say riderless horses had been seen. It was like a ghost story. He became animated as he described the funeral, the dignitaries that came, a song that a famous singer had composed and sang in the church, and then the fabulous party that he threw afterwards. As he was telling her this,

Miss Lawless was thinking two opposite things. She thought about how grief sometimes makes people practical and frenetic arrangements keep them from losing their grip; but she also thought that he had dwelt unduly on the party, the dignitaries and the newly composed song. He told how he had not lost his composure – not once – and how at three in the morning he and a few close friends sat in the den and reminisced.

'Was she dark-haired?' Miss Lawless asked, unthinkingly.

'No. Fair, with freckles,' he said, summoning up a picture of a girl bright as a sunflower. He added that she liked the outdoors and was really a desert girl.

'And what do you feel about her now?' Miss Lawless asked.

'She was a good friend and a good lover,' he said quietly. It sent a chill through Miss Lawless, and yet his features were so fine, his manner so courteous and his eyes so sensitive that she found a way within herself to excuse him. Leaning very close to her, he said that he liked talking to her and that perhaps if she was staying on in Dublin, they might have a drink or a bite. That thrilled her. She believed his resemblance to the other Abelard to be significant and that, whatever happened between them, she would not be detached from it, she would not blot it out, she would hold it dear. She imagined going home with him and sitting in one of his rooms, which she deemed to be enormous, with grey, billowing curtains, like a gauze sea, and their talking quietly but ceaselessly. She wanted him to be human, to be marked by the tragic event. She wanted to peel off his mask – that is, if it was a mask. Now her imaginings were taking a liberty, and she thought that if they kissed, which they might, it would not be a treachery against his dead wife but somehow a remembrance of her, a consecration. She wanted to lie close to him and be aware of him dreaming. Foolish, really. It was the night – hectic, amorous, intoxicating night. She felt the better for it, felt better towards him, towards herself and all those people in the room. She was making her peace with the first Abelard now, because it was true that for these many years she had borne a grudge – angry with him for ignoring the significance of their affair, and with herself for allowing him to. What she thought now was not of the aftermath with that first Abelard, but of the excitement and freshness when it was beginning – the shy, breathless feeling they had each imparted when they met, realizing secretly that they were bewitched. She suddenly remembered little moments, such as having her hand in his overcoat pocket as they walked down a street, and looking up at the sky that was like navy nap, so soft and deep and dense was it.

Betty's was the first speech, and it was very witty and plucky. Betty said that being 'of a certain age' was not the worst time in a woman's life, and then she made some light references to previous parties when she was not nearly so spoiled. Taking the cue from Betty, Dr Fitz walked slowly to the dais and deliberated a bit before speaking. He said that while wanting to wish her well – indeed, wishing her well – he could not forget 'the terrible day' when he had been lucky enough to be by her side. Several voices tried to hush him, but he went on, insisting that it was all part of the tapestry of Betty's life, it proved Betty had guts, and that she could stand there tonight and knock the spots off all the other women in the room. People cheered, and Betty herself put two fingers between her teeth and let out a raunchy whistle. Another family friend recited a poem that he had written, which made several guests squirm. Miss Lawless felt uneasy, too. The speaker, however, seemed very proud of it and grew more and more emotional as he declaimed:

> When I look down at the soil in our troubled land,
> I see its forty shades of green
> And say to myself, Why isn't our fourth green field
> As green as the other three?

A few began to heckle and say it was songs they had come for and not drip stuff. Abelard left the table, but by a signal – indeed, a colluding wink – he indicated to Miss Lawless that he would be back. She assumed that he was going to phone someone and thought that possibly he was cancelling an arrangement. Even his absence from the table made her feel lonesome. He had that lit-up quality that gave off a glow even though his manner was cold. Mr Conroy, seeing her unattended, rushed across the room and asked her if she had had any advances from the playboy. Shaking her head, she asked in turn what the man's wife had been like. Mr Conroy described a thinnish woman who drank a bit, and who always seemed to be shivering at parties and having to borrow a jacket from one of the men. Meanwhile, the last verse of the poem was being heard and people were listening with some modicum of courtesy because they knew it was near the end.

> But when I look up in to the vast azure sky
> Irish politics and history recede from my mind,
> And in their place the glory of the Creator
> comes flooding through,
> And the sky and the stars give a promise of eternity.

Though the people were still cheering and letting out catcalls, they were also surging onto the floor to make sure that dancing would now continue, and to satisfy them the music was hotting up – in fact, it was deafening. This did not deter Mr Conroy from telling his rival, who had returned, that he had known Miss Lawless for many years, that he had driven her to beauty spots all over Ireland, and had copied out for her the words of the ballads that were so dear to her heart. Then he embarked on a story about how, a few years before, he had taken her for tea to a renowned hotel in the west. He had gone in search of the proprietress, Tildy, whom he found in the basement, ironing pillowslips. He told her how he had a lady friend upstairs in the lounge and wondered if Tildy could spare a moment to come up and welcome her.

'Oh, Mr Conroy, I'd love to but I haven't a minute,' he reported the proprietress as saying, and added that he went away a bit crushed, but hadn't mentioned it to Miss Lawless; and that later Tildy came up, in a sparkling blue gown, her glasses on a gold cord, and how she looked at Miss Lawless and said in a sort of sarcastic voice, 'Who do we have here, who is it?' Miss Lawless could see that Abelard had no interest in the story but was polite enough to suffer it. She felt that each of them intended to take her home, and she wished that it would be Abelard. Yet she could not refuse Mr Conroy; she had been invited by him. She hoped for some confusion, so that the threesome would be interrupted and Abelard might at least whisper something to her, alone.

At that moment, the lights were quenched and the guests treated to a fresh surprise. Miniature trees with tiny lights as thin as buds dropped from the ceiling, so that the room took on the wonder of a forest. The tiny evergreens suggested sleigh rides, the air fresh and piercing with the fall of snow. Then four waiters ceremoniously carried in a gigantic cake. It was iced in pink and decorated with angels, and crenulations surrounding Betty's name. They placed it in the centre of the room and Betty was led across to cut it, while two eager photographers rushed to capture the moment. The great clock in the hall outside struck midnight, but the pauses between the chimes seemed unnaturally long. Then a dog barked outside – a whole series of yelps, growing fiercer and fiercer, reaching a frothing crescendo, and then suddenly stopping as if overwhelmed. This dog, Tara, had never been known to be silenced by any but its master. Were a stranger now entering, the dog, even on its fetters, would be ungovernable. It must be its master. Who else could it be? Such were the words that people spoke, whether by a look or by expressing them directly.

'It would be awfully inconvenient now if it was John,' Betty said very loudly, the knife still poised in the big cake, the icing beginning to shed from the impact of the blade. And yet everyone hoped that it was John, the wandering Odysseus returned home in search of his Penelope. You could feel the longing in the room, you could touch it – a hundred lantern slides ran through their minds; their longing united them, each rendered innocent by this moment of supreme suspense. It seemed that if the wishes of one were granted, then the wishes of others would be fulfilled in rapid succession.

It was like a spell. Miss Lawless felt it, too – felt prey to a surge of happiness, with Abelard watching her with his lowered eyes, his long fawn eyelashes soft and sleek as a camel's. It was as if life were just beginning – tender, spectacular, all-embracing life – and she, like everyone, were jumping up to catch it. Catch it.

Shovel Kings

In one lapel was a small green and gold harp, and in the other a flying angel. His blue jacket had seen better days. He wore a black felt homburg hat, and his white hair fell in coils – almost to his shoulders. His skin was sallow, but his huge hands were a dark nut brown, and on the right hand he had a lopsided knuckle, obviously caused by some injury. Above it, on the wrist, he wore a wide black strap. He could have been any age, and he seemed like a man on whom a permanent frost had settled. He drank the Guinness slowly, lifting the glass with a measured gravity. We were in a massive pub named Biddy Mulligan's, in North London, on St Patrick's Day, and the sense of expectation was palpable. Great banners with HAPPY ST PATRICK draped the walls, and numerous flat television screens carried pictures of the homeland, featuring hills, dales, lakes, tidy towns, and highlights of famed sporting moments down the years. Little votive lamps, not unlike Sacred Heart lamps, were nailed in corners to various wooden beams and seemed talismanic on that momentous day. Only three people were there, the quiet man, a cracked woman with tangled hair gabbling away, and myself.

Adrian, the young barman, was chalking up the promised delights, large Jameson at less than half price, teeny dishes of Irish stew and apple cake for free. Moreover, the governor had left a box full of green woolly hats and green scarves that were reserved to be given to the regular customers. Adrian was young and affable, asking if I needed more coffee and wondering if the quiet man, whom he called Rafferty, would like a refill, in honour of the day. Much to the chagrin of Clodagh, the spry young assistant, Adrian indulged his nostalgia by playing 'Galway Shawl' on the jukebox, over and over again.

The coffee that I had been served was dire, but I lingered, because of being early for an appointment, and picked up a newspaper that was lying on the vacant table next to me. Disaster and scandals featured prominently. Further unrest was reported in a northern province of China; an actress was pictured being helped out of a nightclub in a state of inebriation; another photograph showed her arriving only a few hours earlier wearing a white clinging dress and perilously high heels. A hostage who had been released in some African bush after sixty-seven days in detention seemed dazed by the posse of journalists who surrounded him. I looked at the weather forecast for New York, where I had often spent St Patrick's Day and stood among milling crowds as they cheered floats and bands, feeling curiously alone in the midst of all that celebration.

My appointment was with a doctor whom I had been seeing for the best part of a year and who had just moved to this less salubrious part of London, leaving his rooms in Primrose Hill, probably because of the rents being exorbitant. This would be my first time at this new abode, and I dreaded it, partly because I had left, as I saw it, fragments of myself behind in that other room, with its stacks of books, an open fire, and an informality that was not customary between patient and analyst. Sitting there, with an eye on the wall clock, I kept checking on this new address and asked Adrian about such and such a road to make doubly sure that I had not gone astray. Yes, he knew the man, said he had been in several times, which I took to imply that my doctor liked a drink.

Meanwhile, Clodagh was bustling around in an emerald-green pinafore, reciting a verse for all to hear:

> Boxty on the griddle
> Boxty in the pan
> If you don't eat the boxty
> You'll never get your man.

The light from the leaded-glass panels danced on her shadow as she flitted from table to table, extolling the miracle of the boxty potato bread and dragging a duster over the round brown tables which bore the mottling of years and years of porter stains.

That done, she began to pipe green tincture onto the drawn pints of Guinness to simulate the emblem of the shamrock, something Rafferty observed with a quiet sufferance. A noisy group burst in, decked with leprechauns and green gewgaws of every description, led by a tall woman who was carrying fresh shamrock still attached to a clump of rich earth. In a slightly affected voice she described writing to her old uncle several times since Christmas, reminding him that the plant must not be detached from its soil and, moreover, he must remember to sprinkle it with water and post it in a perforated box filled with loam.

'Was it holy water by any chance?' the cracked woman shouted out.

'Shut your gob,' she was told, at which she raised a hectoring finger, claiming, 'I was innit before yous was all born.'

As the single sprigs of shamrock were passed around, they somehow looked a little forlorn.

A second group followed hot on the heels of the first group, all greeting each other heartily, spreading coats and bags on the various tables and commandeering quiet nooks in the alcoves, for friends whom they claimed were due. A cocky young man with sideburns, wearing a black leather jacket, walked directly to the fruit machine, where the lime-green and cherry-red lights flashed on and off, the lit symbols spinning at a tantalising speed. Two youngsters, possibly his brothers, stood by, gazing and gaping as he fed coin after coin into the machine, and as they waited in vain for the clatter of the payout money, the younger one held an open handkerchief to receive the takings. The elder, who was plump, consigned squares of chocolate into his mouth and sucked with relish, while his brother looked on with the woebegone expression of an urchin.

I had put the newspaper down and was jotting in a notebook one or two things that I might possibly discuss with my doctor when, to my surprise, Rafferty was standing above me and almost bashfully said, 'Do you mind if I take back my paper?' I apologised, offering him a drink, but he was already on his way, detached from the boisterous crowd, carrying himself with a strange other-worldly dignity as he raised his right hand to Adrian in salutation.

Three or four weeks passed before we exchanged a few words.

'What's the harp for?' I asked one morning when, as had become his habit, he made a little joke of offering me the newspaper.

'To prove that I'm an Irishman,' he replied.

'And the angel?'

'Oh that's the guardian angel . . . We all have one,' he said, with a deferential half smile.

About six months after our first meeting I came upon Rafferty unexpectedly, and we greeted each other like old friends. I was on the Kilburn High Road outside a second-hand furniture shop, where he was seated on a leather armchair, smiling at passers-by, like a potentate. He was totally at ease out in the open, big white lazy clouds sailing by in the sky above us, surrounded by chairs, tables, chests of drawers, fire irons, fenders, crockery, and sundry bric-à-brac.

Offering me a seat, he said that the owner believed his presence perked up an interest in business, because once, when he had been singing 'I'll Take You Home Again, Kathleen', passers-by had stopped to listen and, as he put it, had browsed. Nearby, a woman haggled over the price of a buckled sieve, and a young mother was in vain trying to get her son off the rocking horse to which he was affixed. The white paint was scraped in several places, and the golden mane a smudged brown, but to the boy his steed was noble.

Rafferty rolled a cigarette, folded his tobacco pouch, and, impelled by some inner recollection, began to tell me the story of coming to London forty years earlier, a young lad of fifteen arriving in Camden Town with his father and thinking that it was the strangest, sootiest place he had ever seen, that even the birds, the fat pigeons that waddled about, were man-made. Theirs was a small room, which his father had rented the year previous. It had a single iron bed, a thin mattress, a washbasin, and a little gas ring to boil a kettle.

The next morning at the Camden tube station, where lorries and wagons were parked and young men waited to be recruited, literally hundreds of them, hundreds of Irishmen, hoped for a job. A foreman eyed Rafferty up and down and said to his father that no way was that boy seventeen, but his father lied, insisting that he was. More heated words were exchanged, about effing cousins and so forth, but eventually Rafferty was told to climb onto the lorry, and he did. I believed (Rafferty said) that a great future lay ahead of me, but the look of despair on the lads left behind standing in that street was awful, and one I can never forget.

They were driven a few miles north to where a group of young men were digging a long trench, for the electricity cables to be put in later on. The paving stones were already taken up and stacked in piles. At his first sight of it, it was hard for him, as he said, not to imagine those men, young though they were, destined for all eternity to be kept digging some never-ending grave. He was handed a shovel and told to get to work. The handle of the shovel was short, shorter than the ones he had been used to at home when he dug potatoes or turnips, and the blade was square and squat. And so I was (he said) put to digging the blue clay of London, as it was then called, blue from leaking gas and sticky, so sticky you had to dip the shovel in a bucket of water every so often, then wedge it in under the soil to try and shift it. Lads in a line, stripped to the waist because it was so hot, each man given a certain number of yards to dig, four foot six inches wide and four foot six inches deep. The foreman in his green Wellingtons walking up and

down, putting the fear of God into us. A brute, and an Irish brute
at that. After an hour of digging, I was half asleep over the shovel
and only for Haulie, I would have been fired. He covered for me,
held me up. He was from Donegal, said the mountains and the
hilly roads made him wiry, and that I'd get used to it. Two
Connemara men nearby spoke only the Irish and didn't understand a word others were saying, but they understood the foreman
and the ruthlessness of him. I didn't feel hungry, only thirsty, and
the cup of milk at half past ten was a godsend. Tea was brewing
all day long in a big bucket, but Haulie said it tasted like senna.
Teaboy Teddy was in charge of the grub, and men were given
potatoes and cabbage for the dinner, except that I couldn't eat. By
the time the whistle went in the evening, my hands were bloodied
and my back was ready to break. In the room, I fell fast asleep at
the little table, and my father flung me onto the bed, boots and all,
and went out.

The same drudge every day (he continued), but they talked and
yarned to keep the spirits up. They would talk about everything
and anything to do with home. One lad caused riots of laughter
when, out of the blue, he announced that turnips needed the
frost to taste sweet. He got christened Turnip O'Mara instantly.
Nicknames meant for greater camaraderie, down there in the
trenches, a brotherhood, us against them, the bull of a foreman
and the contractors and subcontractors, who were merely brutes to
us, downright brutes. We might chance upon treasure. The legend
was that someone had found a Roman plate worth hundreds, and
someone else dug up a wooden box with three gold crosses, which
he pawned. All we found were the roots of trees, embedded and
sinewy, the odd coal bill, and rotten shells of gas piping that
German prisoners of war had laid in the forties. On Thursdays
a Cork man arrived in a green van to hand out the wages, his
bodyguard, also a Cork man, wielding a cricket bat in case of
robbery. Men felt like kings momentarily. I got four pounds, which

I had to hand over to my father, who also made me write a letter to my mother to say how happy I was and how easily I had settled in to life in London. So much so that she wrote and said she hoped I would not acquire an English accent, as that would be faithless.

I really knew nothing of London (Rafferty said, apologetically), nothing except the four walls of the room, the broken springs of the bed, the street that led to where the wagons and lorries picked men up, and the big white, wide chapel with three altars where the Irish priest gave thunderous sermons on a Sunday. I was full of fears, thought everything was a sin. If the Holy Communion touched my teeth I thought that was a mortal sin. After Mass we had a cup of tea in the sacristy and biscuits dusted with sugar. Sundays were awful, walking up and down the streets and looking at the dinginess of the shop fronts and dirty net curtains in upstairs windows, and the old brickwork daubed black. My father went off very early of a Sunday, but I never knew where to.

We had one book on the small shelf in our room. It was by Zane Grey. I must have read it dozens of times. I was so familiar with it that I could picture swathes of purple sage and cottonwood in Utah, outlaws, masked riders, and felons trailing each other in the big open ranges, one area peculiarly named Deception Pass. I think I swore that I would go there, because I missed the outdoors, missed roaming in the fields around home and hunting on Sundays with a white ferret. My poor mother was writing at least twice weekly, pleading with my father to come home, saying that she could not mind children, do farmwork, and take in washing, and, moreover, that she was suffering increasingly from dizziness. Eventually my father announced that he was going home, and shortly before he did, something happened. We were in the room, and the landlady called my father to the telephone, which was in the kitchen. I thought that maybe my mother had died, but no, he came back in whistling and smiling, handed me two and six and told me to go to the Italian restaurant on the high street and stay there until he picked me up. I lingered for three hours, but no sign of him. The place was shutting. They were putting chairs up on the tables, and a woman waited, the mop already sunk in a bucket of water, to wash the floor. When I got back, the bedroom door was locked. I knocked and waited and knocked, and my father shouted at me to go down the hall, into the back garden. Instead I went towards the hall door. Not long after, a tall, blonde woman, wearing a cape, emerged from our room. She was not a patch on my mother. The way she picked her steps, so high and haughty, I could see that she thought herself way above us. She threw me a strange condescending smile. My father went mad when he saw where I was standing. He said nothing, just drew me into the room by my hair, pulled my pants down and beat me savagely. He kept saying the same thing over and over again as he was belting me – 'I'll teach you . . . I'll teach you honour . . . and I'll teach you obedience . . . and I'll teach you to respect your elders. I'll teach you I'll teach you I'll teach you,' raving mad at having been found out.

A good bit after my father went home (Rafferty continued), I started going to the pub. I was feeling more independent then. I'd go to the Greek café that had been renamed Zorba and have rashers and eggs and fried bread. The kitchen was behind the counter, and the Irish lads had taught Zorba to forget the kebabs and stuffed vine leaves and master the frying pan. Then I'd go straight across to The Aran pub, pure heaven, the warmth, the red table lamps, the talking and gassing, getting a pint, sitting down on a stool, without even exchanging a word. Weeknights were quiet, but weekends were rough, always a fight, because everyone got drunk. The fights could be about anything, a girl, a greyhound, grudges, because a foreman had got rid of six men in order to hire men from his own parish, one wrong word, you know and the punches started. First inside the pub, then in the vestibule and finally out onto the street, the two heavyweights vowing murder and the crowd of us on either side of the pavement egging them on, not unlike the time of the gladiators. When things got really bad and they were near beat to a pulp, someone, usually the landlord, would call the cops. If two cops came on foot they did nothing. They stood by, because they wanted to see the Irish slaughter one another. They hated the Paddies. When the Black Maria pulled up, the two men with blood pouring out of them were just thrown into the back, to fight it out before they got to the station. That's what gave us a bad name, the name of hooligans.

You see (he said apologetically), you had to be tough, on the job and off the job, even if you were dying inside. That's how the sensitivity was knocked out of us. But it was still there, lurking. One night in the bar (and here his voice grew solemn) I saw grown men cry. It was like a wake. They were a gang from Hounslow, and they came in shaken and sat silent, like ghosts. Something catastrophic had happened, and they were all part of it, because they saw it with their own eyes. A young man by the name of Oranmore Joe was up on the digger when the hydraulic gave way and the lever slipped. He didn't realise it for some seconds, not until he saw the big steel bucket full of earth hurtling through the air and crashing on top of a fella that was standing underneath. Knocked him to the ground and cut the head off him. Bedlam. Foremen, building inspectors, cops, a blue plastic sheet put around the scene, and men told to go home and report for work the next morning. Not seeing it (Rafferty said), but hearing about it, at first haltingly and then in a burst, brought it to life, the awful spectacle of a severed head and the young man's eyes wide open, as one of them put it, like the eyes of a sheep's head in a pot. The worst of it was that Oranmore Joe and J.J., that was the young man's name, came from the same townland, and Joe had actually got him the job. Was like a brother to him. A collection was taken in the pub to send the remains home. Lads gave what they could. A pound was a lot in those days, but several pound notes were flung into the tweed cap that had been thrown onto the counter. From that night on (Rafferty

lamented), Oranmore Joe was a different man. He wouldn't get on
a machine again. The company bought a new machine, but he
wouldn't get up on it. He took ground work. He'd sit in the pub,
pure quiet, just staring. Lads would try to cheer him up and say,
'No problem Joe, no problem, it wasn't your fault.' Except he
believed it was. We'd see him thinking and thinking, and then one
evening he comes in, in the navy blue suit and the suitcase, whistling, walking around the pub like a man looking for his dog,
calling, ducking under the stools and the tables, and then we hear
what he's saying. He's saying, 'Come on J.J., we're going home,' and
we knew, we knew that he'd lost it, and we wouldn't be seeing him
again. A goner. 'Not one, but two lives lost,' Rafferty said gravely.

In the winter of 1962, two years after his father had gone, he
almost had to follow. The snow began to fall on St Stephen's Day
and continued unabated for weeks. All outdoor work ceased.
Roads and pavements were iced over, the ice so thick that it would
break any sledgehammer, and the trenches were heaped with
snow. Men were laid off without pay and many headed for the
boat. His landlady, a woman from Trinidad, gave him a few
weeks' grace, and as luck would have it, he met up with Moleskin
Muggavin in the pawnshop, where Rafferty was pawning a pair of
silver plated cufflinks, with a purple stone. Moleskin was looking
for men to do renovation on a hotel over in Kensington. The work
was altogether different. Feeding sand, gravel, cement, and water
into a hopper, the knack being to get the mixed concrete out before
it settled, while it was still fluid. He and Murph, a two-man band,
easier, as Rafferty said, than shovelling the blue clay of London
and no foreman. Moleskin was boss, walking around with a pencil
behind the ear, slipping out to the pub and the bookmaker's from
time to time, since he fancied himself a keen judge of bloodstock.
After work Rafferty accompanied Moleskin to a cocktail bar that
adjoined a casino. It was there, as he said, that he got the liking for
chasers. Moleskin was on first names with all sorts of notorious

people and, moreover, had a friendship with a divorcée who lived in a big white stucco house with steps up to it. Every evening around nine or ten they repaired there, with bottles of porter, and the divorcée, in peacock-coloured dresses and ropes of pearl, would be waiting for Moleskin. Pairs of brown felt slippers were inside the door, as their boots were crusted with snow and wet ice. The brown felt stuff (as he said) reminded him of a tea cosy they had at home, the same material, with a white thatched cottage embroidered on it. Large rooms, leading off one another, carpeted heavens. A party was always in full swing, people dancing and sitting on each other's laps, the cocktail cabinet thrown open and, as a particular feature, Moleskin standing by the piano, to give a rendering of 'I'm Burlington Bertie, I Rise At Ten Thirty'. At midnight, a girl dressed as a shepherdess would enter, ringing a glass bell, announcing supper. All sorts of Austrian delicacies, Wiener schnitzel, goulash, apple strudel with spicy jams, and, in deference to Ireland, boiled pigs' feet and cabbage.

The hotel work was expected to last at least nine months, but it unfortunately came to an abrupt end the day Moleskin socked Dudley, the boss's son, and flung him between the joists of a floor onto a bed of rubble. Dudley, in his Crombie coat and tartan scarf, would call unexpectedly to make sure we weren't slacking. He was a namby-pamby, always spouting about Daddy, every other word being Daddy. Daddy was a great man, a compassionate man. Daddy loved Ireland so much that he flew home every Thursday evening, so as to step on Irish soil and be reunited with wife and family. This particular day, when he said that Daddy deserved to have a plaque erected in his honour, alongside the liberator Daniel O'Connell and famous dead poets, Moleskin erupted and said to cut out the tripe.

After the fracas that ensued, he and Moleskin kept away from the London area for several weeks. Moleskin knew a man who kept a caravan above the beach at Hove, where they holed up, living on bread and sardines. Passing himself off as a landscape gardener, Moleskin got them piecework, and (Rafferty said) he was once more at the mercy of the shovel.

The last he saw of Moleskin was one evening in The Aran after the frozen ground had thawed and he was working for a different set of contractors, jumping on a blue wagon instead of a brown one (he said). Moleskin arrived in a green trench coat and announced that he was leaving London to attend on a lady in Lincolnshire, then proceeded to borrow from all before him and promised to invite them for a shooting weekend.

At times over the years, Rafferty was put to work out of London. Once near Birmingham, where they were building a motorway, and another time outside Sheffield, for the construction of a power plant. The men lived in huge camps, sleeping on straw mattresses and fending for themselves in a communal kitchen. But I always (he said, quite shyly) missed Camden. Camden was where I first came, and though I cried my eyes out in the beginning and walked those hopeless sullen streets, it was where I had put roots down. The odd thing was that you can be attached to a place, or a person, you don't particularly like, and he put it down to mankind's addiction to habit.

It was only when he took his leave of me that I realised that darkness had fallen. The white clouds of a few hours earlier had sallied off, and a star flickered wanly in the heavens. People on foot, in cars, and on bicycles were hurrying with that frenzied speed that seizes them at rush hour, and Rafferty had nothing more to impart. I suggested buying him a drink, but not then, nor at any time in the year that I would come to know him, would he accept hospitality. His last vestige of pride.

After Christmas, in the pub, Rafferty was buoyant. He had had a haircut and was sporting a maroon silk handkerchief in the top pocket of his jacket. He had been 'away', as he put it. Away was only a few miles north, but to him, confined to his own immediate

radius, any journey was an adventure. I knew a little of his movements by now. He drank the one pint in Biddy Mulligan's each
morning, returning in the evening to have his quota of two. In the
day he walked and, as he said, could be a census collector, if only
anyone would employ him. At noon he went to the Centre where
he, along with several others, were given a cooked dinner and
coffee. Roisin, the woman in charge, was a stalwart friend, and
every so often gave him a jacket or a pullover, as consignments of
clothes were sent from a Samaritan in Dublin, to help the down-
trodden Irish in London. Sometimes he helped out a bit in the
garden and was even enlisted by Roisin to give sound advice to
other young men who might be in danger of slipping.

Christmas he had spent with Donal and Aisling at their pub in
Burnt Oak. They were, he said, gallant friends. The pub shut early
on Christmas Eve so as to entertain the visitors, which included
him, Clare Mick, who lived over Fulham way, and Whisky Tipp,
who had had a stroke, but luckily his brain wasn't affected. Also
the lodgers upstairs, three Irishmen, a Mongolian, and a black.
Pure heaven, as he put it. Up behind the counter and pull your
own pint or whatever you wanted. The light in the pub dimmed,
the steel shutters drawn, carols on the radio – 'A partridge in a
pear tree' – bacon and cabbage for the Christmas Eve dinner, and
then, on Christmas Day, as he put it, a banquet. At the start of the
dinner, Donal plonked a bottle of champagne in front of each
guest, although he and Aisling never themselves touched a drop.
What with the roast goose, potato stuffing, sage and onion stuffing,
roast spuds, the children larking about, crackers, paper hats, jokes,
riddles, and gassing, these dinners were unadulterated happiness.
This was how you imagine a home could be, Rafferty said, his
voice surely belying the melancholy within it.

One appointment in March with my doctor had been switched to
evening. The night was dark and foggy when I got out, and the

warm lights of the pub were indeed inviting. The atmosphere was completely different from that of daytime. Such hub and gaiety that, as I entered, I already felt a little intoxicated. Moreover, it was packed. At a large round table a birthday party was in full swing, and a young, obese woman was literally submerged by bunches of flowers and basking in her role as guest of honour. I made my way to the counter where Rafferty was standing and ordered a glass of white wine. Once I had been served, he moved me along to a second counter, where no one was drinking, to avoid the crush. For a while we did not exchange a word. Instead, we studied the array of bottles that were stacked on the top shelf, with their proud labels in gold or black or russet, scored with ornate lettering and coats of arms, testaments to their long lineage. On the lower shelf were the bottles placed upside down, their necks fluting into the clear plastic optics. Every pub, Rafferty said, gave a different measure, and Biddy's was popular because they gave five millimetres extra on a small whisky or vodka. Pondering this for a moment, he said that with drink the possibilities were endless, you could do anything or thought you could. Moreover, time got swallowed up, or more accurately, as he put it, got lost.

A few years after his father went home, his mother died. His father, as he believed, had killed her, had worn her out. The telegram came with the sad news, and he set out, as he said, for Victoria Station, to catch Slattery's coach that fetched passengers to the boat at Holyhead. Never made it. Went on benders along the way in various pubs, lads sympathising with him and saying maudlin things, until the day had turned to night and the coach had left. I'll always regret that I didn't go, he said.

It was quite a while after that the drink got a hold on him, but he knew it was all connected, all part of the same soup. He'd work for six weeks and then booze. Then he'd work the odd day, get a few bob to buy cider, and before long, he was loafing. Mattresses under the bridges, men from every corner of Ireland, gassing at night, talking big in their cups, then arguing and puking in the morning, delirium tremens, seeing rats and snakes, sucking on empty bottles.

One morning (Rafferty continued), I crawled out from under a quilt to go and get a fix. Usually a few people were in the streets going to work or coming from night work, and they'd give you something, especially the women, the women had softer hearts. On the other side of the street I saw a woman in a belted white raincoat looking across at me. It was Madge, who'd married Billy.

She came over, and I can still see her thinking it but not saying it, 'You should see yourself, Rafferty, your dignity gone, your teeth half-gone, your beautiful black hair gone grey, and your eyes glazed.'

I said, 'How's Billy?' and she said, 'Billy's dead and gone,' and her eyes filled up with tears. I could hardly believe it, Accordion Bill that had been such a swank, the two of them such swanks on the dance floor, winning medals and drinking rosé wine. Billy had left the building work after they got the franchise of a pub over in St Martin's Lane, which, as she said, was the ruination of him, of them. Then all of a sudden, she pulled a little notepad from her pocket and thrust it into my hand. This was the chance encounter he believed she had been waiting for, to meet someone from the old days, so that she could show it. Her history, jotted down at different times, often a scrawl and with several coloured inks.

Badly beaten up again. Internal bleeding, rushed to hospital and nearly lost the baby.

Bill not home for three days and three nights, searched up and down the high street, found him in an allotment with other blokes drinking cheap cider, didn't even recognise me, brought him home, cleaned him up, washed him, shaved him, promised to get him new clothes when I got my pay packet.

Billy wept in my arms half the night and I plucked up the courage and I asked him why did he drink like that and his answer was to blank things. I said what things. He said something happened, and that's all he'd say. Something happened. Took it to his grave he did.

Another time I wakened, and he was stuffing pills and whisky down my neck, half unconscious at the time. He wanted to be dead and he wanted us to go together because we loved one another. 'Go together,' I shouted, 'and two young children in the very next room.'

His mother was an Aries. On her seventieth birthday I got him the ticket to go home. I said have a drink, have a few drinks, but promise me you won't get blotto, if you love me, promise me that, and he did and we hugged. He got to his sister's house very early in the morning, and the little niece was pulling at him to put on a CD, and his sister went into the kitchen to put on the kettle when he collapsed in the doorway. Never wakened again.

I handed it back, and she said, 'I still love him . . . Will you tell me why I still love him, Rafferty?' I couldn't. As she ran to catch the bus she turned back and shouted, 'No one is given a life just to throw it away.' It done something to me. I went back to the tiny room beyond Holloway that a priest had got for me. I rarely set foot in it, because I preferred being under the bridges with the bums, but I went that morning. There was a mirror I got off a ship and seeing how I had fallen, I turned its face to the wall. I started to clean up, emptied things, worn tubes of toothpaste, eye lotion, old socks, and jumpers and put them all in a bin bag. Then I got the Hoover from under the stairs and hoovered, and I poured bleach into a can of water and scrubbed the windowsills and the woodwork. Standing in the shower, watching the pictures of little black umbrellas on the plastic curtain, I made this pact with myself. I couldn't quit the drink. You could say that I half won and I half lost. I set myself a goal, one pint in the morning and two pints at night and not a drop more, ever, except maybe for a toast at a wedding.

'A woman,' he said, looking at me almost bashfully, 'a woman can do something to a man that cuts deep. Madge did it, and so did my mother.'

The night before I left home for good (he went on) my mother decided that we would pick fraughans for a pie. They are a berry the colour of the blueberry, but more tart, and they grew in secret places far up in the woods. It was one of those glorious summer evenings, the woods teeming with light, with life, birds, bees, grasshoppers, a sense that the days would never be grey or rainy again. We were lucky. We filled two jugs to the brim, our hands dyed a deep indigo. For some reason my mother daubed her face with her hands and then so did I, and there we were, two purple freaks, like clowns, laughing our heads off. Maybe the laughing, or maybe the recklessness emboldened her, but my mother squeezed my knuckles and said she had something to tell me, she loved me more than anything on this earth, more than her hot-tempered husband and her two darling daughters. It was too much. It was too much to be told at that young age, and I going away forever.

At times, he said after a long silence, he had toyed with the idea of going home, to visit the grave, when he saw Christmas decorations in the shop windows and raffles for Christmas cake, or got the cards from his sisters, who were now grown up and had married young and moved away. Except that he never went. 'If I went home I would have had to kill him,' he said, his sad grey eyes looking into mine, unflinchingly.

One Sunday in summer I was enlisted to help at a car-boot sale in a warehouse outside London. Adrian had organised it, so as to collect money to send deprived children to the seaside for a week's holiday. I was assigned to the bookstall – mostly tattered paperbacks with their covers torn off, a few novels, and a book about trees and plants indigenous to the Holy Land, pictures with panoramic views accompanied by beautiful quotations from the Bible. Rafferty was impresario, steering people to the various folding tables, to ransack for bargains. The offerings were motley – winter and summer dresses, worn blankets, quilts, men's shirts, crockery, car tyres, and stacks of old records.

A young nun, her blue nylon veiling fluttering down her back, did brisk business selling cakes, pies, loaves of bread, and homemade jams that had been, as she proudly said, made in the mother house of her order. The other stand that drew a crowd was a litter of young pups in a deep cardboard box, mewling and scampering to get out. They were spaniel and some other breeds. One child, whose birthday it was, lifted his favourite one out, a black and white puppy with a single russet gash on the prow of its head, and as the father handed over two coins, numerous children clamoured for a pet.

Though business was not great, Adrian pronounced it an outand-out success. We packed the unsold stuff and swept up to give some semblance of cleanliness to the place. As we were being driven back to London in a van, Rafferty asked courteously if I would care for a drink before setting out for home. We got dropped off in a part of London that neither of us was familiar with and that was anything but inviting. Blocks of tall, dun-coloured flats veered towards the sky. They were of such deliberate ugliness their planners must have determined that those who would live in them would do so in unmitigated gloom. A scarlet kite flew above them, sailing in its desultory way, now and then flurrying, as if a sudden swell of wind had overtaken it, and we could not but express the hope that it would never return to the ugly ravine from whence someone, perhaps a child, had dispatched it. Nearby was a playground, more like a yard, bordered with a line of young poplars, beyond which youths yelled and shouted at one another as they played different ball games, the taller ones converged around a basketball net. Dogs ran around, barking ceaselessly.

We could see the sign for a pub, but the entrance eluded us. It was tucked in between a Catholic church, which we recognised by the cross on its grey-blue spire, and a community centre for youths, but though we went up and down several flights of concrete steps and under dark, foul-smelling concrete archways, we kept returning to the same spot. A young Irishman in shorts offered to be of assistance, but said we must first have a peep in the window of the Catholic church, because the altar, brought from Europe centuries previous, was priceless. The church was locked, as evening mass had been said. We looked through a long stained-glass window and saw an empty room with only a few pews. The altar, set back from the wall, had intricate sprays of gold leaf and was flanked with stout gold pillars. He was a most talkative young man, and pointing to the vista of flats, he listed the crimes that were rife there. He was a community worker and helped the local priest, whom he pronounced his hero. With ebullience, he produced a map of the area, where, with green drawing pins, he had highlighted the scene of three murders, all connected with drugs. Then he descanted, as might an aficionado, on the type of drugs that were being sold, their quality, and the astronomical prices they fetched. He asked us to guess how many languages were current in the neighbourhood and then answered for us, more than twenty languages, and the Irish no longer in the majority, many having gone home and many others having become millionaires.

We thanked him for conveying us, but he was already off on another tangent about some delinquent who passed himself off as blind and was actually a brilliant pickpocket. Inside the pub we had the greatest difficulty getting rid of him and only after Rafferty whispered that we had an important matter to discuss did he take his leave of us, but not before he gave us his business card, printed with his name, a degree in ecology, and his availability as a tour guide of the area.

The place was completely empty. The faint straggling rays of the setting sun came through the long, low window, and fiddle music filtered from the kitchen area. Tapping one foot, Rafferty listened, listening so intently he seemed to be hearing it there and then, and also hearing it from a great distance, rousing tunes that ushered him back to the neon purlieu of the Galtymore Dance Hall in Cricklewood, where they had modern and fiddle. Saturday nights. Admission two shillings and sixpence. Scores of young men, including him, togged out in the navy suit, white shirt, and savvy tie, standing at the edge of the dance floor, gauging the form. One girl was called Grania, after a pirate queen. Other girls wore bright flashy frocks or skirts with stiffened petticoats, but Grania had on a black dress with a white collar and inlaid white bib, giving the appearance of being a nurse. As he learned later, she was a seamstress in a shop on Oxford Street, making curtains and doing alterations. What first struck him, apart from her pure white skin and thick brown hair, with hues of red and gold like an autumn bogland, was how down-to-earth she was. Between dances she would sit, fling off her shoes, and mash her feet to ready herself for the next bout on the floor. Up at the mineral bar, other men would be buying her lemonade and pressing her for the next dance, and the one after that, and she was always saucy with them. He himself never got on the floor, because of an unconquerable shyness. Six months or more passed before she threw him a word, and as long again before she allowed him to walk her home. She lodged three miles beyond Cricklewood, near Holloway Fields. He recalled standing outside her digs till one or two in the morning, hearing her soft voice as she bewitched him with stories. Listening to her was like being transported. Her father was a tailor who also had a pub and grocery, where people drank, mulled over the latest bit of gossip. She herself preferred when one of the old people, from up the country, happened to come in and told stories of the long ago, cures and curses, warts removed by being rubbed with black stones taken out of the bed of the river, and the wonders of Biddy Early the witch who, by gazing into her blue bottle, reached second sight.

He would drink in the week evenings, but kept himself fairly sober on the Saturdays, to gaze at Grania, to buy her the minerals and walk her home. One night when they were parting she handed him a gift in a sheet of folded paper and whispered a few words in Irish. This was her way of saying she was his.

Next morning he studied the gift again and again. It was a smooth flattened seashell, the ribs on the underside, bone white, curving out into a fan, and in the interstices, tiny vermilion shadings like brush strokes, as if someone had painted them on.

They found a little flat above a hardware shop that was many miles from Camden. Friends donated things, sheets, bolsters, and a jam dish with a hanging spoon that carried a coloured likeness of His Holiness the Pope. Soon he learned what a fine cook Grania was, but she was also very particular. For their Sunday walk, she would not let him out with a crease in his shirt, having already cleaned the clay under his nails with a crochet needle. The thing was (as he ruefully put it) Grania could drink any man under the table, but she knew when to stop. In the evenings when he got home, two glasses of milk would be on the table, to have with the dinner. But he was missing the pub, the noise, the gas, and before long he would be dropped off at The Aran and have a few drinks and arrive home late. Then later. Soon he pretended he was on overtime, and would not be home till midnight. A row would often follow, or else Grania would have gone to bed, his dinner, with a plate over it, on a rack above the gas cooker. One night he got back and found a note on the kitchen table – 'You can have your overtime, now and forever,' was all it said. He thought she would be back the next evening, or the next, but she wasn't.

'She took nothing, not even the jam dish with the hanging spoon and the likeness of the Pope,' he said, then broke off abruptly. One of the dogs from the playground had come in and was staring up at us, panting wildly. Rafferty put his hand on its snout and kept it there until the animal's breathing had quieted, and in the silence, I was conscious for the first time of a ticking wall clock.

Considering the plethora of crimes we'd been warned of, I suggested taking a minicab and offered to drop Rafferty home.

'Most kind,' he said, which I knew to be his way of declining, followed by his raising the large hand, with the black, wide wristband.

We were out of doors, sitting, as it happened, on a bench, in a graveyard that was anything but morose. A wide bordered path ran from a gateway to another at the opposite entrance, allowing a shortcut for pedestrians and cyclists, so that it was as much a haunt of the living as of the dead. The graves were neatly tended, the grass bank on the far side newly mowed, and there was the added gaiety of springtime in London. Borders of simmering yellow tulips, front gardens and back gardens surpassing each other in bounteous displays, the wisteria a feast in itself, masses of it falling in fat folds, the blue so intense, it lent a blueness to the eyes themselves. Adrian had said that Rafferty would love a few moments with me if it was possible and hinted that he had super-duper news.

He could not contain his joy. He was going home. For good. No more bills. No more hassle. Then he took the letter from his leather wallet that was worn and crinkled, but hesitated before handing it to me, since he needed to explain the circumstances. A benefactor, who had begun life digging, but who had bettered himself and accrued great riches, had contacted the Centre, asking for someone of good character to come home to Ireland and take care of an elderly relative. Roisin, being the stalwart she was, had suggested Rafferty, and after a ream of letters, his credentials, etcetera, passed on, he was accepted. Moreover, she had given him a new tweed suit and pullover, since a fresh consignment had come from the Samaritan.

The house, the dream house or bungalow to where he was going, would be shared with the elderly man, but a woman was coming in every day to do the dinner and keep an eye on the elderly man's needs, since he suffered from diabetes, something which he contracted later in life. Rafferty must have read the benefactor's letter dozens of times, as it had been folded again and again. Forty years previously, when he left Ireland, his mother, his lovely mother, had packed his things in a brown suitcase, and he had taken his belongings out, except for three sacred things: a missal, a crucifix, which she had had blessed, and striped pyjamas, which he never wore, but had kept in case he had to go to hospital. He was lucky to have escaped that, because many of his mates were struck down with chronic illnesses, asthma, lung diseases, skin diseases, and injuries of every kind. He said he would humour the elderly relative, whom he guessed would sleep half of the day, or at least doze. He would play cards with him, or maybe do crosswords. With a vigour, he contemplated picking up a shovel again and getting a bit of garden going – cabbage, sprouts, shallots, lettuce – and see what potatoes were native to that particular soil. 'I'll go to the pub,' he said, 'stands to reason, but I'll pace myself, no going back to skid row for Rafferty.' The bungalow was not in his own part of the country, but still it was home and he asked out loud if it was likely that he would once again hear the cry of the corncrake, that distinctive call which had never faded from his memory.

Birds in their truant giddiness were swooping and scudding about the gravestones, but a few pugnacious ones had converged on a plastic lunch box that had the remains of a salad, and were conducting bitter warfare by brandishing torn shreds of limp lettuce. Their beaks were a bright, hard orange.

When I am sitting on a rocking chair over there, on the borders of Leitrim and Roscommon (he continued), and they ask me how it was in the building work, I'll tell them it was great, great altogether, and I'll tell them about Paddy Pancake. Shrove Tuesday we were all on site, itching to get off early, because we'd sworn to give up drink for Lent. Paddy Pancake sprung a surprise on us. Never touched a drink himself, and wore his total abstinence badge for all to see. He was a night chef, somewhere in Ealing. From a black oilskin bag he took out flour, eggs, milk, caster sugar, salt, and a small bottle of dangerous-looking blue liqueur. He'd even brought a basin to make the batter. Then, looking around, he picked up a big shovel, washed it down a couple of times with a hose, and presto, he had his frying pan. Two lads were told to get a fire going, as plenty of wood from timbers and old doors was scattered on a nearby site. Paddy tossed the pancakes on the shovel like a master. He had an assistant to sprinkle on the caster sugar and a few drops of the liqueur, and lads grabbed and gobbled like wolves. To crown it all, a shy Galway boy stood up on a skip and belted out a rebel song, 'Roddy McCorley Goes to Die on the Bridge of Toome Today'. The words and his voice so beautiful, so heartfelt.

Tears welled in his eyes as he recalled that revel, a winter evening, the glow of the fire, the leaping flames of red and blue, dancing in that London wasteland, as if in some roman amphitheatre.

As he tucked the letters back in his wallet, a photo of himself fell out. It was a snap really, taken on some riverbank, where he and his friends had obviously been swimming. The sheer life in his expression was breathtaking. His hair was tousled. His eyes as youthful and moist as any young man's eyes could be. Not a single feature in that photograph resembled the man sitting beside me.

'Well, that's youth for you,' he said, suddenly bashful, as I had guessed, it was a fleeting farewell.

Less than two weeks later, when I called into the pub, for a moment I thought that I must be hallucinating. Sitting in his usual place, with a pint on the table in front of him, was a man the spitting image of Rafferty. Same wide-brimmed black hat, wrinkled jacket, and the pint. I looked away, but then Adrian gave me the nod, and I looked again. It was Rafferty. It was him. He was quiet and took his time before he acknowledged me, showing none of the warmth that he had on that day in the graveyard. 'It happens,' he said, then taking his leave, the unfinished pint on the table, he added that the rolling stone gathers no moss.

Adrian relayed to me what had happened. The bungalow was new and clean, too new and too clean. The old man, Denny, sat in his chair all day looking out at the low-lying fields, invariably shrouded in mist, checking his blood sugar every few hours, having an insulin injection, and taking four different sets of tablets. A Miss Moroney came to do the dinner, and drove them mad. The landing was like a shrine, with statues, Miss Moroney spouting homilies about the evils of drink and touching them for alms for unfortunate children in the third world. Even when he went to the pub, Rafferty didn't feel at home. It was noisy and brash, young people coming and going, no quiet corner to brood in, and no one had any interest in his stories. As for the garden that he had intended to plant, the grounds around the house had been landscaped with bushes and yellow flowering shrubs. Nothing was wrong, as he told Adrian, but nothing was right, either. The benefactor took the news of his sudden departure well, said he could come for a week in the summer if he wished, and that he had no hard feelings. The same young minicab driver who had collected him from the airport was the one to bring him back again, drove like a lunatic while also conducting a business transaction on a mobile phone, telling the would-be purchaser to get stuffed, that no way would he take two hundred. Seconds later he rang someone else to report on matters, saying that they would be mad to let it go for less and they would hold out for the jackpot. According to Adrian, Rafferty surmised that it was either a motorcycle or an old banger that was for sale. At the airport, the minicab driver mashed his hand in effusive farewell and said what a pity the holiday had been so short.

Roisin had persuaded the council to give him his little room back, and, as Adrian said, the brown suitcase with the missal, the crucifix, and the striped pyjamas was shoved back under the single bed.

'He doesn't belong in England and ditto Ireland,' Adrian said, and, tapping his temple to emphasise his meaning, added that exile is in the mind and there's no cure for that.

I was flabbergasted the day my analyst broke the news to me that he was leaving London and going to work in a hospital in Bristol. With solicitude he had procured a railway timetable and showed me how frequently the trains ran, saying I could come twice a month and have a double session.

I went back to the pub, to say goodbyes of a sort. Adrian treated me to an Irish coffee, and Rafferty came across and stood by us, as Adrian recounted his big night at the greyhound track in Wimbledon, picking four winners because of tips that he got from the barmaid, a Connemara girl, whom he hoped to be seeing again.

'Mind yourself.' Those were the last words Rafferty said to me. He did not shake hands, and, as on the first morning, he raised his calloused right hand in a valediction that bespoke courtesy and finality. He had cut me out, the way he had cut his mother out, and those few who were dear to him, not from a hardness of heart, but from a heart that was immeasurably broken.

Under the pavement were the lines of cable that linked the lights of the great streets and the lesser streets of London, as far distant as Kent. I thought of the Shovel Kings, and their names suddenly materialised before me, as in a litany – Haulie, Murph, Moleskin Muggavin, Turnip O'Mara, Whisky Tipp, Oranmore Joe, Teaboy Teddy, Paddy Pancake, Accordion Bill, Rafferty, and countless others, gone to dust.

Madame Cassandra

At last at last. I have been perambulating for the best part of an hour . . . luckily I had my brolly to keep off that glaring sunshine. It must be at least twenty-three Celsius . . . the poor earth is baked . . . even the old weeds are passing out and the foxglove expiring. I always love the way the bees snuggle into the foxglove . . . for the coolth and the nectar . . . make themselves at home – 'Where the harebell grows and the foxglove purple and white' . . . a favourite . . . from the anthologies.

My, my . . . what a pretty caravan . . . so gaily coloured and flowers, flowers. Steps painted in three different shades. 'Madame Cassandra' – how beautiful, how ancient. You know your mythology I am glad to see. It says 'No appointment necessary' but Madame your door is shut . . . your half door is shut and your heavy red curtain is drawn all along your picture window. I am a little weary . . . trudging here and so forth . . . not to mention the inconvenience of having to ask people directions, when I alighted from the bus. I shall rest a little on one of your steps, on one of your painted steps.

Eureka. I know what it is . . . you are expelling, if that is the word, the karma of the previous incumbent and a good thing too . . . I must say I would love a glass of water or a glass of angostura bitters . . . such a thirst – parched. I see you collect stones, large stones, small stones, rocks, and that fearsome boulder . . . I expect each has a significance for you, a hidden power. Those ponies are pretty and dappled, but wild . . . wild and quite unpredictable. It must be common ground . . . I noticed people – strays, youths, louts – and one or two caravans, much drabber than yours. To tell you the truth I am quite breathless . . . I have been over yonder for the last hour . . . I saw that you were occupied . . . I saw your sign – 'Do Not Disturb'. Made myself scarce. The previous client . . . I happen to know her. We are, neighbours. Her people's land abuts onto our avenue which of course is more exclusive what with our belt of trees, yews, and cypresses that have matured down the years. Good lady, I imagine that you are resting . . . it stands to reason . . . you are drained. When a young girl, may I say a buxom young convent girl such as your last client, comes for advice it is usually pertaining to matters of the heart . . . Comprendé. I hope you don't mind my sitting here and gabbling away . . . it lessens the fret. I shall try to admire the surroundings . . . though to be honest I would rather I were not observed. Matters of the heart must be strictly confidential. Comprendé. I am Mildred . . . wife of Gerhardt, Mr Gentleman . . . my maiden name was Butler . . . we are descended from the House of the Ormonds . . . our flower gardens and our fruit gardens were renowned – open on certain summer Sundays to the public whence teas were served in a little summerhouse. As a matter of fact Mr Gentleman wooed me in the kitchen garden, in and out between the raspberry canes and the loganberry canes and the tall delphiniums. Many girls, it seems, had set their caps on him, this young and eligible barrister, set their caps on him to no avail. My yearning was for the stage . . . how I loved the magic, the make-believe. Even at the age of six or seven when my mother took me to the Gaiety Theatre in Dublin for the pantomime and we sat in a box, I drank it all in – the orchestra, the miming, the intrigues, the dames, the villains, the skits and the ever-happy ending. My father would wait for us at his club in Stephen's Green, and we would have dinner in a very salubrious dining room. I played Desdemona in my boarding school . . . Othello, well she/he was somewhat uncouth . . . ah yes, one who loved not wisely but too well. So when I met Gerhardt I was full of Desdemona but not for long. You see my heart went on a ninety-mile . . . what is it called . . . revolve. I lost my head. I waited for the ring of our garden bell. Oh what a chirpy sound from that big fat copper bell . . . Mr G coming on any excuse, the flimsiest of excuses, in a suit or in old dungarees and always when least expected . . . how the heart registers these thunderbolts. I was much younger and younger still for my actual years . . . yes, in and out between the raspberry canes, and the loganberry canes and would you believe it our dog Hector got so jealous he would bark and chase Mr Gentleman, in venom, and one day he took a great scoop out of the side of Mr Gentleman's hand, kept his teeth there, and what did Gerhardt do . . . he did a strange thing, a rather cruel thing – he kicked Hector, beat him into submission, and Hector became his friend . . . Mr Gentleman could handle beast or man or woman or girl . . . In time he was welcomed indoors . . . a sherry and so forth . . . his pursuit of me was both adamant and subtle, which was why they thought him ideal. He always brought gifts – chocolate or cherry brandy truffles – he was one-eighth foreign, Normandy stock, which added to his mystique. He proposed in a country churchyard and it was dusk and there was not a soul about . . . just like the elegy – 'the lowing Herd winds slowly o'er the Lea' – and he made a ring of grasses . . . a magic ring, engagement and eternity so to speak. A couple of nights before our wedding he was in the library with my father . . . they had become bosom friends or should I say bosom buddies – they played backgammon, they reminisced, they drank port or Armagnac – in those days I did not drink . . . slept like a baby . . . whereas now the evening tipple is mandatory. I overheard them speak of women – how much they loved women, idealised women – dilated on their necks, their sloping shoulders, their hindquarters, their ankles . . . all very detached . . . almost clinical . . . my father did not mention my mother, Alannah, not once. Stressing how certain pieces of music reminded them of their trysts with certain women, either because the music was being played on a gramophone in some lady's drawing room or perhaps, some more . . . obtuse reason, my dear mother . . . so beholden. I could always tell when they had been intimate because next morning my father would be most imperious, quite snappy, munching his toast . . . crumpling his newspaper, and my mother a trifle foolish and obliging. Yes I stood in the doorway half expecting my husband-to-be or my father to say 'Ah Millie come in' but they didn't, either because they were so engrossed and did not see me or else they thought my presence was inappropriate. Madame I know you are resting . . . each séance, each session, call it what you will, must take a lot out of you, reaching into the soul of the person and drawing out the inmost secret, the kernel.

Perhaps you are praying – 'And death shall be no more, nor mourning, nor crying, nor sorrow shall be any more.' I regard myself lucky to have found you, to have tracked you down . . . now where was I . . . oh yes, oh yes our wedding . . . it was beautiful . . . it was written up in more than one daily newspaper . . . the smell from the lily of the valley drenched the little country church in County Waterford . . . our own lily of the valley at that – tiaras of it for the bridesmaids and bunches for the little maidens of honour – it was intoxicating . . . a choir . . . hymns . . . me poured into my ivory slipper-satin. My husband could not take his eyes off me that June morning . . . I should like for a moment to say something about my husband's eyes . . . they are in the normal course of things, as he broods over his papers and his briefs, they are not unlike an oyster, which is to say that they are grey with a milkyness . . . but when, as for instance our wedding morning, when the dart of Cupid has struck, they are opal, which is to say they have the merest hue of silver, limned with blue . . . I saw them then and many other times and . . . and I see them now and they are not on me and they are not for me and it is awful . . . and it is awful. Our honeymoon was . . . well it was sailing into the sunset . . . pure bliss . . . unadulterated bliss . . . there is no other word quite so appropriate . . . or so nuanced, devoid of affection and small talk.

But which does one want more, bliss or affection, and moreover I had brought a stack of books . . . the Aegean Sea a palette of blues . . . and all those guidebooks with tales of the ancients, the gods and the goddesses . . . what spitfires they were . . . with their intriguings . . . always plotting to get the upper hand of one another . . . if Hera liked you, Athena didn't, and Juno marrying her own brother Jupiter, who wooed her in the guise of a cuckoo . . . not to mention old Poseidon . . . who could stir up a storm in a flash . . . yes . . . essential to keep on the good side of Zeus, and as for poor Dido it was not a willow in her hand with which she bade her love to come again to Carthage, it was a sword on which she impaled herself . . . poor poor Dido. It was there that I read how the Egyptians were the first to master the art of clairvoyance . . . they could by knowing the date of a person's birth, tell the character, the life's eventualities, and the day of death – but it was not called astrology, not until Roman times was it connected to the stars . . . but good lady you know all about that – those gods and goddesses had their seers . . . people just like you . . . they in their shrines and you in your painted caravan and I cannot tell you what a relief it is to be here . . . to be able to let off a little steam. Yes, it was bliss . . . the ever-changing light of the sea and no dusk . . . just daylight and then darkness . . . amorous dark, and when we came home it went on being bliss but life does stretch on, does it not, like a great yarn . . . and married people have to get to know one another's peculiarities . . . one another's habits . . . moods. Gerhardt was in the city in his chambers all week and then Fridays he drove home and the welcome, or should I say the host of welcomes, the two dogs, my wolfhound and his red setter, our little daft helper Aoife, and myself all rushing onto the drive, waving – Odysseus did not have such a welcome at Ithaca, far from it. A delicious dinner, roast with potato gratin, and apple fritters or charlotte russe for afters. Later, in the gloaming, we sat in the conservatory and discussed our week . . . the little highlights and the little lowlights,

and he smoked a cigar and I would have a taste, yes a taste, more
than a puff, and Mr Gentleman . . . well he knew so much . . . so
much more than me and amazing how versatile even a cigar
can be. Grand Marnier soufflé Sundays before he took off for the
city . . . not a grass widow but a barrister's widow. For our holidays
we never went abroad . . . we sailed . . . we loved sailing and with
a windfall from a great aunt we bought a small houseboat and
named it after her – Violet Rose. We would set out from Athlone
and come all the way down along the Shannon, so beautiful,
the breezes, the reeds, the quiet . . . endless preparations beforehand . . . rubber cushions, rugs . . . the primus stove . . . methylated
spirits . . . a first aid kit . . . straw hats and rain hats . . . cream for
the creepy crawlies . . . scarcely speaking . . . just ambling along,
and the smile, the smiles . . . what a lovely thing a smile is . . . it
speaks multitudes. I lost two children very early on . . . he too was
cut up – 'there above the little grave, we kissed again with tears.'
Good lady, I confess, I am most afraid. Quite by chance I came on
it, a white shoebox, tucked into the folds of a wide cedar that
borders their fence and ours . . . slippers . . . Cinderella slippers
with rosebuds, concealed in tissue paper . . . they were not my
size . . . I have rather large feet . . . the following morning they
were gone . . . someone had removed them. On that rare occasion,
I did tackle him, but he would not engage . . . said he wanted to
hear no more outlandish stories or delusions. It was in the
bedroom, in the very early morning . . . I feared for my life. There
are some moments, or perhaps they are mere seconds, that stay in
the deep freeze of the mind forever. I might have dreamed it . . . I
convinced myself for a time that I did dream it . . . I said Millie,
put it behind you . . . you have been sleepwalking . . . you walked
down the avenue in your sleep. I got to be an ace fisherwoman on
our Shannon cruises . . . G couldn't believe it . . . he said it was
something to do with not just the lightness but the swivel of my
wrist. I was a tad unpopular with all the other fishing folk . . . a

witch they called me. Of course at first I did not know how to play a fish, I rushed it and lost several . . . but Gerhardt schooled me and before long I excelled, I surpassed him. In the month of May, in the dapping season, we stayed out all day . . . all those millions of mayflies . . . the air scudded with them . . . Gerhardt said their courtship and their demise happened in the course of a single day . . . poor mayflies . . . nature's trick . . . poor mayflies . . . poor Dido. 'Never give all the heart outright' – Who said that? I have read that men have cycles just like us women . . . we have cycles because of the presence of the uterus – hence we are subject from time to time to hysteria – whereas men's cycles do not answer to the womb or the moon but to their own dastardly whims . . . they simply go on and off the creatures they call women. Of course anyone could have left the shoebox . . . any yokel or passer-by. Of late he stays out in the greenhouse till all hours . . . just like my father and his dog – my dog, I should say, Hector the fourth – yes Gerhardt stays there tending his vines, his cucumbers and his marrows which cross-pollinate . . . don't ask me how . . . he just places them side by side next to each other and somehow they cohabit . . . they breed . . . the saffron pollen wends its way to the opposite sex and . . . they propagate . . . .

He rarely falls in love . . . three times to my once and a half. A scandal occurred in his chambers in the Four Courts . . . one morning a junior happened to come in with a mound of papers and the secretary, a Miss O'Hanlaoin, was where she should not be and engaged in some hanky panky . . . fortunately it was hushed up . . . he did not feature half naked in a tabloid with his braces down, and moreover the junior was quite discreet, quite sterling. The overweening secretary not so. I found her notes in his pockets – demanding a showdown with me. Oh la la la. It taught him a lesson. 'I will never leave you Millie . . . I will never leave you' was what he said. We went on a cruise for a reconciliation . . . some of the wives had at least twelve changes of attire . . .

and the jewellery, so ostentatious, so unnecessary . . . we sat at the captain's table. I did get tiddly once or twice . . . the high heels and the ship's swaying did not help matters. When we docked for two days in a strange port, my husband played with children on the beach . . . a ball game – he and they tossed and kicked an orange ball . . . strangers' children . . . dusk-coloured children . . . certainly not white children, and they loved him. You see he has this aura – it emanates from him – by which people fall in love with him. They were seen – the buxom girl, the hussy, who has just left your caravan – they were seen one evening of late out on the lake and were caught in a squall . . . had to take shelter . . . something I learned as one does through the offices of a best friend. It was when Dido and Aeneas took shelter that the fateful arrow of love struck. I do have one card up my sleeve, the most powerful card in the pack. One of our national poets, one of the triptych of Greats, has said that a young wife's, or for that matter, a young convent girl's trump card is the young cunt . . . but an older wife has a more powerful card . . . a darker card . . . one that we must not speak of. Are you with me, good lady . . . comprendé? I see you also do the tarot cards as well as the Crystal . . . I am familiar with some . . . the Hanged Man . . . La Tour . . . Temperance . . . The Scales of Justice. That hussy has no right to our gooseberries . . . none whatsoever . . . our apples . . . our crab apples . . . our pippins . . . our pears . . . our marrows . . . our redcurrants . . . our blackcurrants . . . our loganberries . . . our quinces . . . our greengages . . . our sugar plums . . . our medlars . . . our strawberries . . . our hops . . . our vines . . . our root vegetables . . . our harvests. Please, please. Open your door to me. I won't ask too much. I realise that it is a matter of some delicacy, of some discretion on your part . . . the Hippocratic oath or something akin to the priest in the confessional . . . you are bound to secrecy . . . all I ask is this. Being as you are a seer, what did you see? Have they gone in deep? By that I mean . . . you know what I mean. He's not old enough to be her father . . . he's old enough to be her grandfather . . . it is preposterous . . . it is absurd . . . it is, unthinkable . . . I think of Dido . . . I think of confit of duck in the fridge, since Sunday . . . I think of my husband's opal eyes and the card he wrote me last Christmas . . . 'twenty-two years and still my Queen' . . . I think I think I think. Good lady, open up . . . open your door . . . open your curtain . . . open it now . . . I cannot wait a second longer . . . do you understand . . . these louts are looking at me . . . they're laughing at me . . . the wild ponies are galloping . . . raising the dry dust in swarms. You are there. I know. I know it. I feel your presence in the non-rustle of the thick, dark-red lined curtain.

The journey hither takes three hours and thirty-five minutes, not allowing for mishaps. More than once, in our godforsaken part of the world, some wretch or beast has surrendered to the embraces of the rail track. Yes, the evening train winding and wending its way and all that fabled scenery and sky and skyline and torrents of rain.

Farewell dear callous lady.

Madame! There has been a strange development for which you are indirectly responsible. Had you seen me, it could not have occurred as I would have had to take the later train and not the six o'clock Express.

I had found an empty carriage and as the train gave its preliminary lurches, a door behind me, that I presumed led to the driver's cabin, was unlocked and a passenger ushered in. Even before I turned to look I knew, by the quickening of my pulse. It was not the footfall and not yet the voice, because no one had spoken; you could almost say my hunch was ethereal, yes, plucked from the ether. There was my husband, with his squashed briefcase, wedged under his elbow, and a stack of papers in his arms which he was holding awkwardly. He was flushed at having to race to catch the train.

'Millie,' he said, incredulous. As the train started his papers skived all about and he flopped onto the seat opposite and looked at me almost with wonder, as if he was seeing me in some way altered, his wife of twenty-two years leading a secret life, having a day up in Dublin, a rendezvous perhaps, and wearing a black cloche hat with a soft furry feather that tapered along the cheek.

'Where did we buy that hat?' he asked.

'We,' I said, lingering on the word, 'we bought it in Paris on the Rue du Dragon one Christmas Eve, as it began to snow.'

'So we did,' he said, and gazed into space as if he would have given anything to see falling snow.

The countryside, like our lives, is rolling by, stacks of chimney pots higgledy-piggledy, rooks and jackdaws whirling in the dusk of heaven, making that vast expanse their own.

In a while, he will lead me along to the dining car, a little agitation at the core of both our hearts, and we shall sit quietly, uncertain at what the future may hold.

Plunder

One morning we wakened to find that there was no border – we
had been annexed to the fatherland. Of course we did not hear of
it straightaway as we live in the wilds, but a workman who comes
to gather wood and fallen boughs told us that soldiers had
swarmed the town and occupied the one hotel. He said they drank
there, got paralytic, demanded lavish suppers, and terrorised the
maids. The townspeople hid, not knowing which to fear most, the
rampaging soldiers or their huge dogs that ran loose without
muzzles. He said they had a device for examining the underneath
of cars – a mirror on wheels to save themselves the inconvenience
of stooping. They were lazy bastards.

The morning we sighted one of them by the broken wall in the
back avenue we had reason to shudder. His camouflage was
perfect, green and khaki and brown, the very colours of this
mucky landscape. Why they should come to these parts baffled us
and we were sure that very soon they would scoot it. Our mother
herded us all into one bedroom, believing we would be safer that
way – there would be no danger of one of us straying and we
could keep turns at the watch. As luck had it, only the week before
we had gathered nuts and apples and stored them on wooden
trays for the winter. Our mother worried about our cow, said that
by not being milked her poor udder would be pierced with
pain, said the milk would drip all over the grass. We could have
used that cow's milk. Our father was not here, our father had
disappeared long before.

On the third morning they came and shouted our mother's
name – Rosanna. It sounded different, pronounced in their tongue,
and we wondered how they knew it. They were utter hooligans.

Two of them roughed her out, and the elder tugged on the long plait of her hair.

Our mother embraced each of us and said she would be back presently. She was not. We waited, and after a fearful interval we tiptoed downstairs but could not gain entry to the kitchen because the door between it and the hall was barricaded with stacked chairs. Eventually we forced our way through, and the sight was grisly. Her apron, her clothes, and her underclothes were strewn all over the floor, and so were hairpins and her two side combs. An old motorcar seat was raised onto a wooden trough in which long ago she used to put the feed for hens and chickens. We looked in vain through the window, thinking we might see her in the back avenue or better still coming up the path, shattered, but restored to us. There was one soldier down there, his rifle cocked. Where was she? What had they done to her? When would she be back? The strange thing is that none of us cried and none of us broke down. With a bit of effort we carried the stinking car seat out and threw it down the three steps that led from the back door. It was all we could do to defy our enemies. Then we went up to the room and waited. Our cow had stopped moaning, and we realised that she too had been taken and most likely slaughtered. The empty field was ghost-like, despite the crows and jackdaws making their usual commotion at evening time. We could guess the hours roughly by the changing light and changing sky. Later the placid moon looked in on us. We thought, if only the workman would come back and give us news. The sound of his chainsaw used to jar on us, but now we would have welcomed it as it meant a return to the old times, the safe times, before our mother and our cow were taken. Our brother's wooden flute lay in the fire grate, as he had not the heart to play a tune, even though we begged for it.

On the fifth morning we found some reason to jubilate. The sentry was gone from his post, and no one came to stand behind that bit of broken wall. We read this as deliverance. Our mother would come back. We spoke of things that we would do for her. We got her clean clothes out of the wardrobe and lay them neatly on the bed. Her lisle stockings hanging down, shimmered pink in a shaft of sunlight, and we could imagine her legs inside them. We told each other that the worst was over. We bit on apples and pelted each other with the butts for fun. Our teeth cracked with a vengeance on the hazelnuts and the walnuts, and picking out the tasty, fleshy particles, we shared them with one another like true friends, like true family. Our brother played a tune. It was about the sun setting on a place called 'Boulevouge'.

Our buoyancy was shortlived. By evening we heard gunshot again, and a soldier had returned to the broken bit of wall, a shadowy presence. Sleep was impossible and so we watched and we prayed. We did that for two whole days and nights, and what with not eating and not sleeping, our nerves got the better of us and, becoming hysterical, we had to slap each other's faces, slap them smartly, to bring common sense into that room.

The hooligans in their camouflage have returned. They have come by a back route, through the dense woods and not up the front avenue as we expected.

They are in the kitchen, laughing and shouting in their barbarous tongues. Fear starts to seep out of us, like blood seeping. If we are taken all together, we might muster some courage, but from the previous evidence it is likely that we will be taken separately. We stand, each in our corner, mute, petrified, like little effigies, our eyes fastened to the knob of the door, our ears straining beyond it, to gauge which step of stairs they are already stomping on.

How beautiful it would be if one of us could step forward and volunteer to become the warrior for the others. What a firmament of love ours would be.

A deathly emptiness to the whole world, to the fields and the sacked farmyards and the tumbledown shacks. Not a soul in sight.

Not an animal. Not a bird. Here and there mauled carcasses and bits of torn skins where animals must have fought each other in their last frenzied hungers. I almost got away. I was walking towards somewhere that I didn't know, somewhere safe. There had been no soldiers for weeks. They'd killed each other off. It was hard to know which side was which, because they swapped sides the way they swapped uniforms. My mother and later my brother and my two sisters had been taken. I was out foraging and when I came back our house was a hulk of smoke. Black ugly smoke. I only had the clothes I stood up in, a streelish green dress and a fur coat that was given to my mother once. It used to keep us warm in bed, and sometimes when it slipped onto the floor I would get out to pick it up. It felt luxurious, the hairs soft and tickling on bare feet. That was the old world, the other world, before the barbarians came. Why they came here at all is a mystery, as there was no booty, no gold mines, no silver mines – only the woods, the tangly woods, and in some parts tillage, small patches of oats or barley. Even to think of corn, first green and then a ripening yellow, or the rows of cabbage, or any growing thing, was pure heartbreak. Maybe my brother and sisters are across the border or maybe they are dead. I moved at dusk and early night, bunched inside the fur coat. I wanted to look old, to look a hag. They did not fancy the older women; they wanted young women and the younger the better, like wild strawberries. It was crossing a field that I heard the sound of a vehicle, and I ran, not knowing there was such swiftness in me. They were coming, nearer and nearer, the wheels slurping over the ridged earth that bordered the wood that I was heading into. The one who jumped out picked me up and tossed me to the Head Man. They spluttered with glee. He sat me on his lap, wedged my mouth open, wanting me to say swear words back to him. His eyes were hard as steel and the whites a yellowy gristle. Their faces were daubed with paint and they all had puce tattoos. The one that drove was called Gypsy.

That drive was frantic. Me screaming, screaming, and the Head Man slapping me like mad and opening me up as though I was a mess of potage. They stopped at a disused lime kiln. He was first. When he splayed me apart I thought I was dead, except that I wasn't. You don't die when you think you do. The subordinates used their hands as stirrups. When I was turned over I bit on the cold lime floor to clean my mouth of them. Their shouts, their weight, their tongues, their slobber, the way they bore through me, wanting to get up into my head, to the God particle. That's what an old woman in the village used to call it, that last cranny where you say prayers and confide in yourself the truth of what you feel about everything and everyone. They couldn't get to it. I had stopped screaming. The screams were stifled. Through the open roof I saw a buzzard glide in a universe of blue. It was waiting for another to be with it, and after a time that other came that was its comrade and they glided off into those crystalline nether-reaches. Putting on their trousers, they kept telling each other to hurry the fuck up. The Head Man stood above me, straddled, the fur coat over his shoulders, and he looked spiteful, angry. The blood was pouring out of me and the ground beneath was warm. I saw him through the slit in my nearly shut eyes. For a minute I thought he might kill me and then he turned away as if it wasn't worth the bother, the mess. The engine had already started when Gypsy ran back and placed a cigarette across my upper lip. I expect he was trying to tell me something. As children we were told that why we have a dent in our upper lip is because when we are born an angel comes and places a forefinger there for silence, for secrecy. By degrees I came back. Little things, the air sidling through that small clammy enclosure and the blood drying on me, like resin. Long ago, we had an aluminium alarm clock with the back fallen off, that worked on a single battery, but batteries were scarce. Our mother would take out the battery and we'd guess the time by the failing light, by the dusk, by the cockcrow and the one cow, the one faithful cow that stood, lowing, at the paling, waiting to be milked. One of us would go out with a bucket and the milking stool. When she put the battery back the silver needle would start up and then the two hands, like two soft black insects, crept over each other in their faithful circuit. The lime-green dress that I clung to, that I clutched, that I dug my fingernails into, is splotched with flowers, blood-red and prodigal, like poppies. Soon as I can walk I will set out. To find another, like me. We will recognise each other by the rosary of poppies and the speech of our eyes. We, the defiled ones, in our thousands, scattered, trudging over the land, the petrified land, in search of a safe haven, if such a place exists.

Many and terrible are the roads to home.

My Two Mothers

In the dream, there is a kidney-shaped enamel spittoon, milk-white and a gleaming metal razor such as old-fashioned barbers use. My mother's hand is on the razor and then her face comes into view, swimming as it were towards me, pale, pear shaped, about to mete out its punishment, to cut the tongue out of me. Then with a glidingness the dream is over and I waken shaking, having escaped death not for the first time. In dream my mother and I are enemies, whereas in life we were so attached we could almost be called lovers. Yes, lovers insofar as I believed that the universe resided in her being.

She was the hub of the house, the rooms took on a life when she was in them and a death when she was absent. She was real mother and archetypal mother. Her fingers and her nails smelt of food – meal for hens and chickens, gruel for the calves and bread for us – whereas her body smelt of myriad things, depending on whether she was happy or unhappy, and the most pleasant was a lingering smell of a perfume from the cotton wad that she sometimes tucked under her brassiere. At Christmas time it was a smell of fruitcake soaked with grog and the sugary smell of white icing, stiff as starch, which she applied with the rapture of an artist.

Anything that had wonder attached to it was inevitably transposed onto her. For instance, when in the classroom one learned that our vast choppy lakes had the remains of cities buried beneath them, it seemed that in her, too, there were buried worlds. At mass, when the priest turned the key of the gold crested tabernacle door, I had the profane thought that he was turning a key in her chest. As if reading my mind she would pass her prayer book to me, solemn words in Latin, a language that neither of us was very conversant in.

We lived for a time in such a symbiosis that there might never have been a husband or other children, except that there were. We all sat at the same fire, ate the same food, and when a gift of a box of chocolates arrived looked with longing at a picture on the back, choosing our favourites in our minds. That box might not be opened for a year. Life was frugal and unpredictable, the harvests and the ripening hay subject to the hazards of rain and ruin. Hovering over us there was always the spectre of debt. Yet in our house, there were touches of grandeur – silver cloches that resembled the helmets of medieval knights stationed along the bog-oak sideboard, and mirrors encrusted with cupids kissing and cuddling. In drawers upstairs were folds of silk from the time when she worked long before, in the silk department of a department store in Brooklyn, the name of which ranked second only to Heaven. On Sundays for mass, she would hurriedly don her good clothes that had been acquired in those times, or later, cast-offs sent by relatives, voile dresses cut on the bias that seemed to sway over a body, over hers. I would beg of her to re-don them in the evening so that we could go for a walk, and in summer at least enjoy the evening intoxication of stock in other people's gardens.

We had an orchard, ploughed fields and meadows. Somehow I thought that a garden would be a prelude to happiness. The only flowers I had occasion to study were those painted on china cups and plates, splotches of gentian in cavities of moss, and on the wallpaper tinted rosebuds so compact, so life-like, one felt that one could squeeze or crush them. Those walks bordered on enchantment, what with neighbours in some sudden comraderie, greeting us profusely, and always, irrationally, the added possibility that we might walk out of our old sad existence. She was beautiful. She had beautiful hair, brown with bronzed glimmers in it, and blue-blue eyes that held within them an infinite capacity for stricture. To chastise one she did not have to speak – her eyes did it with a piercing gaze. But when she approved of something, everything seemed to soften and the gaze, intensely blue, was like seeing a stained-glass window melt.

On those walks she invariably spoke of visitors that were bound to come in the summer and the dainty dishes she would prepare for them. There was a host of recipes she had not yet tried. Sometimes her shoes hurt and we had to sit on a wall while she rolled down her stockings and mashed and massaged her poor reddened toes. Once, a man that we scarcely knew came and sat down beside us. He wore a torn flannel shirt and spoke in a wild voice, kept asking us 'Any news ... any news'. She laughed over it afterwards and said he was a bostoon. I secretly thought she would have liked a city life, a life where she could wear those good clothes and her rareified Sunday court shoes with their stout buckles. Yet at heart she was a country woman, and as she got older the fields, the bog, her dogs, and her fowl became more important to her, were her companions once I had left. I had always promised not to leave. I promised it aloud to her and alone to myself as I looked at the silver knights on the sideboard and the about-to-burst rosebuds in the wallpaper.

Our house had quarrels in it, quarrels about money, about drinking, about recklessness, but not content with real fear she also had to summon up the unknown and the supernatural. A frog jumped into the fire one night and she believed it was the augury for the sudden and accidental death of a neighbour. Likewise a panel of coloured glass above a vestibule door broke again and again, and she insisted that it was not wind or storm but a message from beyond. One evening, sitting in the kitchen in some dread, she conceived the thought that a man, a stranger, had come and stood outside the window preparing to shoot us. We moved to the side of the window and sat on two kitchen chairs, barely breathing, waiting for our executioner. We sat there till morning, when her husband, who had been gone for days, appeared, unslept, still half drunk and vexed at having to return to us. She and I were mendicants together – cooking, making beds, folding sheets, doing all the normal things in the so-called normal times, and in opposite times cowering out of doors, under trees, our teeth chattering in mad musical shudder. We were inseparable.

I cannot remember when exactly the first moment of the breach came. There were tiffs over food that I refused to eat and disapproval about gaudy slides that I put in my hair. I began to write – jottings that had to be covert because she would see in them a sort of wanderlust. She insisted that literature was a precursor to sin and damnation, whereas I believed it was the only alchemy that there was. I would read and I would write and she, the adjudicator of what I was writing, had to be banished, just as in a fairy tale. One day she lost her temper completely when I read aloud to her a quotation of Voltaire's that I had copied – 'Illusion is the queen of the human heart'. She looked at me as if I had escaped from the lunatic asylum twenty miles away.

'Illusion, queen of the human heart,' she said, and went on with her task. She was pounding very yellow oatmeal with boiling water, and the vehemence with which she did it was so great she might have been pounding me. Those passions, those sentiments that were in Voltaire or in Tolstoy, the recklessness of a Natasha willing to elope with a cad through a window, those were the heights I now aspired to. She sensed the impulse in me the way a truffle hound sniffs the spoils buried beneath, and a current of mistrust sprang up between us.

She searched my eyes, she searched my clothing, she searched my suitcase when as a student I returned home from Dublin – the few books I had brought with me she deemed foul and degenerate. The battle was on, but we skirted around it. I wrote and she silently seethed. She would tell me what others – neighbours – thought of what I wrote, tears in her voice at my criminality. Flings, youthful love affairs were out of the question, yet I threw my lot in with a man I had only known for six weeks. Though hating him by merely seeing a photograph of him, she nevertheless insisted on my marrying to give the seal of respectability to things and there followed a bleak ceremony, which she did not attend. With uncanny clairvoyance she predicted the year, the day, even the hour of its demise. Ten years and two children later, when it happened, she wrote her ultimatum. It was sent postrestante and I read it in a street in London. She enjoined me to kneel down on the very spot as I was reading and make the vow to have nothing to do with any man in body or soul as long as I lived, adding that I owed it to God, to her, and to my children. She lamented the fact of my being young and therefore still in the way of temptation. She had reclaimed me.

Then came years and years of correspondence from her. She who professed disgust at the written word wrote daily, bulletins that ranged from the pleading to the poetic, the philosophic, and the commonplace. I never fully read them, being afraid of some greater accusation, and my replies were little niceties, squeezed in with bribes and money to stave off confrontation. Yet there was something that I wanted to ask her about. I sensed the secret inside her. An infant before me had been born prematurely and had died, and I believed it was caused by some drastic transaction between the two of them. Why else was its name never uttered, prayers for it never said, and never did we visit the grave where even the four letters of its name were not inscribed on the tombstone underneath that of distant forebears. She had not wanted another child, three children and waning finances were hardship enough, and by being born two years later I had in some way usurped her will.

For twenty-odd years I had postponed opening the bundle of letters that lay in my house, in a leather trunk, enjoinders that I had not read and had not the heart to destroy. Then one day, deluding myself into the belief that I needed for my work to revisit rooms and haunts that had passed into other hands, I lifted the little brass latch and took them out. It was like being plunged into the moiling seas of memory. Her letters were deeper, sadder than I had remembered, but what struck me most was their hunger and their thirst. Here was a woman desperately trying to explain herself and to be understood. There were hundreds of them, or maybe a thousand. They came two, three a week, always with apology for not having written in the intervening days. I read them and stowed them away. She would wonder whether I was at home or away, wonder how soon we would meet again, wonder what new clothes I had got, or any other extravagant item of furniture. She would swear to cross the sea to England, even if she had to walk it, and slyly I postponed these visits. She would send things from her linen press, and the letter which preceded the parcel read – 'I sent you yesterday eighteen large doyleys, eighteen small ones and four central ones . . . I didn't get to wash and starch them as it takes so long to iron them properly, when starched.' The next letter or the one following would be about toil. She had drawn one hundred buckets of water and sprayed the entire avenue with weedkiller to kill off the nettles. One Sunday she had gone for a walk, further than she had ever gone before. It was a scorching day, as she said, and she felt a strange kind of energy, an exhilaration as when she was young. Up there on the slopes of the mountain there were ripe blackberries, masses of them on the briars, and not wishing to have them rot she began to pick them to make blackberry jelly. Without basket or can, she had to remove her slip and put the blackberries inside it where they shed some of their purple juices. Her letter kept wishing that she could hand me a pot of clear jelly over a hedge and see me taste and swallow it.

I had no intention of going back to buy a house or a plot of land, but nevertheless she had her eye out for holdings that might suit me. One was called Gore House, named after an English landlord, long since dead. She said it was a pity I had not bought it instead of the German clothier, who not only never set foot in it but had bought it when he saw it from the air, travelling in his private jet. Continentals loved the place and therefore why not I?

The letters about her dogs were the most wrenching. She always had two dogs, sheep dogs, who sparred and growled at one another throughout the day, apart from when they were off hunting rabbits, but who at night slept more or less in each other's embrace, like big honey-coloured bears. They were named Laddie and Rover and always met with the same fate. They had a habit of following cars in the avenue and one, either one, got killed while the other grieved and mourned, refused food, even refused meat, as she said – kept listening to the sounds of dogs barking in the distance, and in a short time died and was buried with its comrade. She would swear never to get another pair of dogs, but yet in a matter of months she was writing off to a breeder several counties away and two little puppies in a cardboard box, couched in a nest of dank straw, would arrive by bus and presently be given the identical names of Laddie and Rover. She gloried in describing how mischievous they were, the things they ate, pranks they were up to. She looked out one May morning and thought it was snowing, but when she went outdoors she found that they had bitten the sheets off the clothes line, chewed small pieces and spat them out.

Her life got increasingly harder – there were floods and more floods, and heating-oil got costlier each year while the price of cattle went rock bottom. People were killing their own beef, but as she said for that one needed a deep freezer, which she did not have. A mare that my father loved and had despatched to a trainer was expected to come first in a big race but merely came third, and the difference in the booty was that of a few pounds as opposed to several hundred pounds, thereby crushing all hopes of riches. The mare could have come first but that she was temperamental – could be last in a race, then out of the blue pass them all out or purposely lag behind. Not having the means, she nevertheless lived for the day when she could afford to get me a chandelier and to have it so carefully wrapped that not a single crystal would get broken. I did not have that much of a wish for a chandelier.

As she got older she admitted to being tired and sometimes the letters were in different inks where she had stopped writing or maybe had fallen asleep. Death was now the big factor, the six-mark question that could not be answered. She was bewildered. She began to have doubts about her faith. One morning for several moments she went blind, and from that day onwards she hated night and hated dark and said she lay awake fearing that dawn would never come. Life, she maintained, was one big battle, because no matter who wins nobody does. I began to see her in a new light and resolved to clear up the differences between us, get rid of the old grudges and regain the tenderness we once had. I always pictured her at work, removing the clinkers from the ash pan in the morning and separating them from the half-burnt knobs of anthracite, which she mixed in with the good stuff as an economy. She loved that Aga cooker that was kept on all night, because formerly it was a hearth fire that would have to be quenched and had to be coaxed with balls of newspaper, sugar and paraffin oil. I realised that what I admired in her most was her unceasing labour, allowing for no hour of rest, no day of rest. She had set me an example by her resilience and a strange childish gratitude for things.

She began, as things grew darker, to implicitly forgive my transgressions, whatever they might have been. I was going to America and she asked me to track down a gentleman at an address in Brooklyn. He must have been a sweetheart. She believed that it had been opened and therefore read. It was like finding a hidden room in a house I thought I knew. I remembered something that as a child I had blushed at overhearing. We were in a hire car – my mother, a newly married woman called Lydia, and myself – waiting outside a hospital for a coffin to be brought out to the hearse. My father and the driver had gone inside. Lydia chain smoked, laughed a lot, and was vibrantly happy. My mother was delighted that we had given her a lift and began to get talkative. Normally guarded with neighbours, my mother began to tell this stranger of her glorious time in Brooklyn, the style she had, the dances she went to, the men she met. Pressed on that point, she said that yes there was one in particular, dark, handsome, and with a beautiful reserve. He had been such a gentleman, had given her little gifts, and on their Sunday outings had seen her back home to her digs and shook her hand on the doorstep. Yet one night, passing a house of ill repute with its red lights and its sumptuous velvet curtains, he had nudged her and said that maybe they should go in there and see what went on. She did not say if the friendship had been broken off abruptly but it was clear from a little shiver in her body in which desire and disgust overlapped, that she had probably loved him and wished that she could have gone through that forbidden door with him.

Even as I was resolving to go to that address in Brooklyn she was taken ill at home and driven to a hospital in the city, hundreds of miles away. Like many another in a time of reckoning, she decided that she wished to change her will with regard to her house, which had for her the magic of a doll's house. She wished to give it to me. Her son, hearing that he was about to be disinherited, came in high dudgeon and they quarrelled in the gaunt hospital hall. She got into some sort of fit there and was brought back to bed, her mind rambling. Late in the evening she began her last letter – 'my hand is shaking now as well as myself with what I have to tell you'.

It remains unfinished, which is why I wait for the dream that leads us beyond the ghastly white spittoon and the metal razor, to fields and meadows, up onto the mountain, that bluish realm, half earth, half sky, towards her dark man, to begin our journey all over again, to live our lives as they should have been lived, happy, trusting, and free of shame.

Manhattan Medley

Midsummer night or thereabouts. The heat belching up from the grids in the pavement, trumpet, or was it trombone, and the hands of the homeless, the fingers thin and suppliant, like twigs, outstretched for alms. We were relative strangers to each other and strangers in that lively, pulsing city.

To leave a party that was held in your honour, we risked the odium of the ever-wrathful Penelope, but yet we did. You gave me the signal, a knowing glance and a nod, even as a coven of women had swarmed around you in evident and gushing admiration. Your scarlet cummerbund was much remarked upon.

On the stairway we accidentally kicked some marbled boules balls that were there as ornament and that came skeetering down along with us. Nor was that our only miscreance. In the pocket of your dinner jacket was a coffee cup, severed from its fragile handle, which had somehow affixed itself to my little finger. In order to avert a crisis, you simply put both in your pocket and mum was the word. It was a turquoise coloured cup and white handle with gold edging, which with a nicety you placed courteously by the foot scraper at the top of the flight of steep steps.

Cities, in many ways, are the best repositories for a love affair. You are in a forest or a cornfield, you are walking by the seashore, footprint after footprint of trodden sand, and somehow the kiss or the spoken covenant gets lost in the vastness and indifference of nature. In a city there are places to remind us of what has been. There is the stone bench for instance, where we sat that night to quench our thirst, but really to call into existence a wall with two water nozzles cemented together, metal tubers bearing the trade name 'Siamese'. A bit of concrete wall against which you threw me cruciform-wise to press your ebullient suit.

'Is there a place for me in some part of your life?' was what you asked. Yes. Yes, was the answer. We walked uptown and down, not knowing what to do with ourselves, not knowing whether to part, or to prolong the vertigo and sweet suspense. I asked what you thought of the tall, brown building that seemed to tilt like a lake above us, a brown lake of offices, deserted at that hour and poised as if to come heaving down into the street. You admired it but said you would have varied the cladding. I found the word so quaint and teased you over it. By asking for a place in the margin of my life, you were by inference letting me know that you also were not free, that you were married, something I would have assumed anyhow.

Only fools think that men and women love differently. Fools and pedagogues. I tell you, the love of men for women is just as heartbreaking, just as muddled, just as bewildering, and in the end just as unfinished. Men have talked to me of their infidelities. A man I met at a conference described to me how he had been unfaithful for twenty-odd years, yet upon learning of his wife's first infidelity, went berserk, took a car ride, beat up his opponent, came home, broke down, and sat up with her all night thrashing out the million moments and non-moments of their marriage, the expectations, the small treacheries, the large ones, and the gifts that they gave or had failed to give. Then, weary and somewhat purged, they had made love at dawn and she had said to him – this unslept, no-longer-young, but marvellous wife – If you must have an affair, do, but try not to, and he swore that he would not, but feared that somewhere along the way he would succumb, yield to the smarms of the Sirens.

Of all the things that can be said about love, the strangest is when it strikes. For instance, I saw you once in a theatre lobby in London and you struck me as a rather conventional man. I thought, there is a man with a wife and undoubtedly two motor cars, a cottage in the country to which he repairs at weekends, one car stacked with commodities, wine, cheeses, virgin olive oil, things like that, a man not disposed to dalliances. Maybe like my friend you have sat up with a wife one entire night, atoning, and maybe it seemed as if everything was forgiven, but something always remains and festers.

Of course, I knew you by reputation and read complimentary articles about your buildings, those wings and temples and rotundas that have made you famous and bear the granite solemnity that is your trademark. Between that austerity and your wine-red cheek, where the blood flowed in a velvety excitement at the dinner party, I saw your two natures at odds, your caution and your appetite.

We walked and walked. The truffle hound and his Moll, chambering. Then we stood outside my hotel and looked at the display in a glass case of the larger bedrooms, which were decorated in gold and apricot shades, with bright chintz upholstery. You did not come up. But it was a near thing, holding each other, unable to let go, and melting.

Your gift arrived the next afternoon, after you had left to go home to England. It was an orchid that stood in a cake box, the pot filled with pebbles, grey-white pebbles that recall wintry seashores. The white-faced petals high on the thin slender stalk, suggested butterflies poised for flight. Flight. Have you fled from me? I imagine not. Unable to sleep at night, I look at it, and from the slice of light that enters where the curtains do not meet, it looks somehow spectral.

You had put me in such a flowing state of mind and body that I determined to befriend all those whom I met. A tall black wraith of a man with one missing eye put his hand out imploring and I gave, liberally. He launched into an irrational spiel of how he had fought in the Civil War, to defend the right of God and man, had been there alongside Ulysses S. Grant. The fawn flap over the missing eye was pitiful. He walked along with me, unwilling to cut short his lament.

Strange how suited we were. The right height, the right gravity, the right tongues and oh, idiocy of idiocies, the right wall. Does something of us remain there, some trace, like the frescoes in caves, scarcely visible? You asked if we might make love in all the capital cities throughout the world, if we might go to them in secrecy and return in secrecy, hoarding the sweet memories of them. We would not enter into a marriage that must by necessity become a little stale, a little routined. Yes, yes was the answer. Yet the friend Paul who saw us leave Penelope's gathering said that I looked back at him disconcerted, like Lot's wife before she was turned into a pillar of salt.

An affair. It is a loaded word. A state of flux, fluxion. So many dire things happen, plus so many transporting things. Letters get opened by the wrong source or the gift of a trinket gets sent to the wrong address by a novice in the jewellers. A woman I know secretly read the list that her husband's newest mistress had jotted down for her Christmas stocking – Krug champagne, lingerie, a bracelet, and last, but by no means least, a baby. Yes, in capitals – A BABY. The wife went into action. She took him to the Far East on a cruise, to various islands, all very rustic, remote, wooden boats with wooden chairs, huts to sleep in, dancing girls and garlands of gardenias put around the necks of this mistrustful pair. Before they left home, the wife had done something rather clever and rather vicious. She had sent the predatory young woman copies of other letters written by other women, enabling her to see the graspingness and the similarity of these missives, reminding her that unfortunately she was one of many. A touch of the Strindberg. Another woman told me that she first got a whiff of her husband's affair, not from rifling his pockets, but from the simple fact that when his mistress came to their house for cocktails, she brought her rival a bunch of dead flowers. Carnations. Later that evening, when they had all repaired to a restaurant, she saw husband and mistress in cahoots, then remembered the dead flowers, stood up and made her first ever, somewhat pathetic scene – 'I am going to the bathroom now and then I am going home', was what she had said. He did not follow immediately, but soon after he did and found her on a sofa eating the flowers as if they were coconut shreds, then spitting them out, and he simply said that he hated scenes, women's scenes, then went out onto the balcony and walked up and down, but stayed, as she said, stayed.

Clarissa calls me from the west coast most days. I met her after I had given a lecture out there and she sensed that we had something in common. A little thing happened to unite us. The contents of her bucket handbag fell out and I said, 'What's wrong Clarissa, what's wrong,' at which she turned and asked if I believed she was having a breakdown. She is seeing a trauma specialist. Her mother, whom she scarcely knew, has recently died and in the wake of this death, a mountain of troubles has assailed her. Her mother's death has opened a trap door into the unknown. Her mother, who was beautiful and also rich, never really discussed things, and this now is causing Clarissa to drop handbags, over-salt the food, and have a sherry in the morning, she who does not even like drink. She wants to ask her dead mother a key question about a naked man in her bedroom. She was a toddler who had ambled across a landing, whereupon the mother shouted at her to get out. The man must have been an old flame. At camp, to which she was sent aged twelve, she saw a photograph of a woman who resembled her mother and kissed it when others were out of sight. She kissed it, and at home she smelt a nightgown that was hanging forlornly in a wardrobe. It smelt of mother. She has something important to tell me but she does not know how to say it. She trusts me because of the debacle of the handbag.

Graffiti, graffiti, graffiti. They seem to be done by the same unseen hating hand. Parables of rage. On walls, on vans, even on the torn leatherette of the back seat of a taxi. The driver was angry. His photo staring out of a hanging tag showed a disappointed, no longer young man. Suddenly he was shouting to another driver who cut in on us. Then he railed against the jarvey cars, horses fouling the street, pissing artificial flowers clipped to the side of their carriages.

When they drank a toast to you at Penelope's dinner party, I could see that you were nervous, your face flushed from the blaze of candle flame. We were not at the same table, but in the same archipelago, as you said. You were talking to a woman, and I knew by your hesitance that you knew she desired you and that you could not return her ardour. She spilt red wine on her thigh and pleaded for sundry advice. Someone suggested white wine to neutralise the red; someone else suggested salt and handed you a dainty silver cruet, with which to minister to her. It was then you looked across at me; it was then you caught my eye through the spaces between the trellises of branching candelabra. You gazed, indifferent to the red and white wine that flowed in an estuary on the woman's thighs. In that milieu of high society, scorching flame, and brittleness, we fell. Later, when we had all stood up to repair to the salon for coffee, you saw me link a man, both to be friendly and marginally to nettle you. Quite testily you nudged me, 'Am I taking you home or have you better fish to fry?'

I wish you were only torso, only cock. No pensive eyes to welcome me in or send me packing. No mind to conjure up those qualms that clandestine lovers are prone to. No holdall of incumbents – mother, father, wife, child, children, all, all calling you back, calling you home. I wish I were only torso in order to meet you unencumbered. I recall an image on a postcard from the seventh century, that of a headless woman, a queen, leaning a fraction to one side, her robe torn, breasts like persimmons, one arm missing, yet pregnant with her own musks.

I have been to our wall, to pay my respects. You would think it was the Wailing Wall in Jerusalem, where I once was and stuck a petition written on a piece of paper, in between the cracks. People see me standing by our shrine but make nothing of it, for they are just loitering. It is a city of nomads. You see a man or a woman with carrier bags or without carrier bags, walk up to a corner, cogitate and walk back in the direction from which they came. Everyone eats on the street, discarded hollows of bread, stumps of pickled cucumber, noodles phosphorescent in the sunlight, fodder for the starving. People sit on steps or sit at empty outdoor tables and stare. The place is teeming with the lonely and the homeless, both. One such woman, who sits by a fountain for hours each day, was, or so I was told by another woman, a bridesmaid at Grace Kelly's wedding, but came down in the world and went cuckoo. Cuckoo is a word they use a lot. Why is the cuckoo always a she? Treachery perhaps. Woman's treachery, different to man's. A mutual woman friend said your name, said it several times in my hearing, to unnerve me. Her eyes glittered like paste jewellery, that pale unchanging glitter, which palls. The canker of jealousy, jealousies. 'I don't want to see you get hurt', your best buddy Paul said, having observed us slip away from the party. Waspishly, he then mentioned how slender your wife was.

A tall red-bearded figure, a 'Finn McCumhal' of the pavement, with green eyes, is enfolded in a tartan rug, which he wears toga-wise. He sells things – cheap abstract prints, black and white cubes, and the wounded orchids of Georgia O'Keefe that appear both spent and fertile. I give him a coffee in the mornings, since he is stationed outside the deli. I asked him if he ever felt down in the dumps. He looked surprised. Said never. He was a mountain man and a Green Beret man. 'Plus, I have God.' Yes, that was his reply – 'Plus, I have God.'

Hot food.

Home-made pizza.

Warm brisket.

I could scarcely eat. I had gone downtown to do some chanting, to chant the taste, the smell, the touch, the after-touch and the permeability of you out of my mind. I thought I knew the building from a previous excursion, but found myself in wrong hallways, talking to janitors, who were surprisingly friendly, the old homeland and so forth. I went back into the street to telephone information. The kiosk looked to have been someone's abode – a dirty baseball cap, punched cans, orange rinds and a cassette tape in such a tangle that it looked as if it might presently scream. On the wall there was a card with neat lettering – 'WordPerfect in ten hours: Lotus.' WordPerfect in what? Further up the street were two pugilistic women, denouncing pornography. They held up photographs of sliced breasts hanging off, their voices rasping above the roar of traffic and sirens.

In a café, a newly married woman at a table next to me gave a dissertation to her friend on marriage, 'Yes . . . it's good to be married . . . he's a great anchor, Frank . . . I wouldn't have said that six months ago, but I do now . . . not overnight do you trust a husband, but it comes . . . it comes.' Then she dilated on their getting a dog. Her husband wanted a large dog, a Labrador. She wanted no dog. Eventually they settled on a small pedigree poodle as being a compromise between no dog at all and a large dog. They have named her Gloria, after Gloria Swanson.

Clarissa called very early. There was something she needed to tell me. She has had female lovers as well as male. It is not that she is promiscuous, her needs change. I asked her what it was like. She said it was a hunger for a ghost, a hunger not altered by man or woman and not altered by marriage. Then she said something poignant. She said the reason that love is so painful is that it always amounts to two people wanting more than two people can give.

My room is a rose pink with gilded mirrors and a chaste white bureau, which looks like a theatre prop. The centre drawer does not open, the side ones do. On the white lining paper of one, I wrote 'Remember.' I wrote it with the expensive pen you gave me, as we were parting, asking me to send you a word, words. Even though you hadn't come up that first night, I knew you wanted to, and I stood in my bedroom doorway, watching as the lift door was opened each time and people were disgorged, some boisterous, one couple gallingly amorous, and others weary from the day's hassle.

One young creature yesterday, on her throne of rubbish, wept. It was in front of a very select jewellers. I asked why she was weeping so. A man had played a dirty trick on her. He had put a hundred dollar bill in her white plastic cup and then taken it back. There had been an altercation. In the window behind her, a ruby necklace blazed on a dainty velvet cushion and a note simply said, 'circa 1800', but no price. Yes, a man had played a dirty trick on her. The word dirty had set me thinking. Had there been a proposition of some kind? Further along, a man dangled his empty cap and urgently said the same thing, again and again – 'I'm broke I'm homeless I'm broke I'm homeless' – scratched his bald head, saying he had travelled hundreds of miles from Georgia. Across the street came a more vociferous voice, shouting, calling it a city of abuse, a shit-hole, a hell-hole and saying that everyone sucked. The cart, which he must have taken from a supermarket, was lined with magazine covers featuring the latest movie stars. On the wall above him, someone had written, 'You're dead'.

I have never felt so alive, so ravenously alive. I walk for miles and miles. Yesterday evening the sky darkened and thunder began to rumble as if marching in from the back woods, from Georgia itself, marching in on the city and on the elect in limousines, stately as hearses, impervious to the plight of wretchedness. I saw the fiend urinate on the roped muscles of the movie stars and laugh wildly. His cart was a swamp. Outside a restaurant a man was bent over a refuse bag. What struck me was his hair. A short bouclé crop of it, Titian-coloured. He had the stealth of a hunter. What he hauled out was a loin bone, with shreds of meat half cooked and dripping. Without ado he began to gnaw. His eyes were incomparably placid. I thought to approach him to give him some coins but did not dare. The pupils of his eyes were too proud and full of distance, that unfathomed distance of the deprived. Moreover, his orgy with the bone was utter.

Stella, a friend from long ago, invited me to a hen party at her sister's house. It was out of town. Down in the dark cavern of an underground I could not find a single human being who might direct me towards the right track. A mass of people in mindless urgency hurtling through the turnstiles and with no time to speak. I came up and hailed a taxi. Passing row after row of identical tall blocks of flats, and occasionally from a billboard sighting a glamorous face, male or female, peddling cosmetics or trainers or a television station, I had this impatience to get to Stella's house and leave presently, because I was convinced that you were returning to this city in search of me. I even imagined you sitting in an armchair in the undistinguished lobby, watching the swing doors for my return. Stella's sister's house was a white clapboard, identical houses all along the street, and mown lawns, and a sense of everything being neat and hunky dory. The women guests were of two kinds – those who were slightly shy, wore long skirts and sandals, and the go-getters in very short skirts and slashed hairdos, all blonde. 'What hat de clock,' one woman said, remarking on the fact that the root of the English language had originated in her part of Saxony. Her husband had but recently left her for a younger woman. Stella wore a stricken look. She stood in the dining room, her small child clinging to her, holding a handful of cutlery and trying by her expression to tell me that much had happened since we last met. 'In a moment, pet,' she kept saying to her second daughter, who had a silvered paper crown, which she needed to be clipped to her hair. Stella's sister Paula was an altogether more assertive type, and looking through the French windows into the garden, she complained about the table being unlaid.

'I ironed the cloth,' Stella said feebly. It was only half ironed. The creases on it were a mimicry of tiny waves upon water. It had begun to drizzle. The glasses in which the drinks were going to be served had incrustations of fruit. Pineapple and melon in ungainly wedges. Each woman arrived bearing a gift. It was a birthday for an elderly aunt, who was sitting in an armchair, dazed. As she was handed a bunch of white roses, her eyes filled up with tears and she held them to her chest as if she was holding an infant. The woman who brought the roses wanted Bourbon and inveighed against iced tea, which was being passed around. Another, who had that morning arrived from Europe, said she had found the perfect cure for jet lag. Wherever you are, or happen to be, you simply alter the time on your clock and get on with things. She was of the thin brigade, the hem of the red skirt level with her crotch. 'What hat de clock.' I ground a biscuit out of irritation. Stella got down on her knees to pick up the crumbs and by mistake overturned a glass. She asked if I remembered Mrs Dalloway, how much we both loved Mrs Dalloway, who threw a shilling in the Serpentine, bought flowers in Bond Street, and wished that she could live her life all over again, live it differently, as we assumed. The rain by now was coming down in buckets and loneliness seeping into me. I thought I wanted to think only of you and to think of you I would have to be alone. Paula, who was making a raspberry salad dressing, said I could not leave so abruptly, but I did. I was given a present on the way out, and in the street I opened the red crepe wrapping. It was a ladle onto which the rain fell in fat spatters, and standing there in that leafy suburban limbo, I thought of you with every pore of my being, drew you into me as if you were sun, moon, and rain, praying that nothing would cancel those journeys to cities around the world.

I went to Penelope's townhouse near the river, where we had met. So many quickening memories. It looked ghostly, black-veined creeper over the brick wall and no sign of life within and no coffee cup by the foot scraper. In the little walkway, by the railings, were the invalids and their nurses. Nurses in starched uniforms standing rigid, behind the wheelchairs. It was the invalids that unsettled me most. The spleen in their expressions was quite shocking and quite pitiless. It was like a sick room there, although we were out of doors. Somehow, the sight of them recalled those sad, studious, forgotten misfits in some of Rembrandt's haunted interiors. Their eyes frightened me most. Eyes onto which pennies would soon be pressed. Their lives, their youth, even their wealth, was already dead to them, and I thought, I am alive, you are alive, and remembered in detail the night of our simmer, your throwing me against the wall in an urgency, as if you intended to smash my bones.

Mercedes cleans the room. She is from Colombia. We have got into the habit of chatting. Frequently she cries, her tears are torrents. Some months ago her man failed to come home, he who had shared her bed for over a year. Only next day at work did she learn why. He had had a massive heart attack while holding the car door open for his boss and had died in an ambulance on the way to the hospital. Neither the boss nor any of the people in the apartment building knew of the man's relationship with her, because of their not being married. It was discovered by a note in his pocket, on which was written her name and address. His funeral, which she had to arrange, was a bleak affair – only a lawyer, herself, and one wreath. Chrysanthemums she thinks, fattened with eucalyptus leaves. His wife, from Jamaica, is strenuously making her claims. First it was his satin waistcoat, then his watch, then his engraved cufflinks, and then the one valuable watercolour that he possessed. She dreads that his wife will come and occupy the apartment. She has had to bring her brother from Colombia to stay indoors all day and keep guard. He plays the guitar and eats incessantly. Every day she says the same prayer, asks God to help her to bear it, and embraces me as if I had some influence in that quarter. She says he was the kindest man that ever lived, washed her feet, pared her corns, indulged her. She also says that if I can get a photograph of you or a sample of your handwriting, she can have a friend do a voodoo spell. It involves the blood of cockerels, but she assures me that it is not sinister.

Clarissa has guessed my predicament. I am invited to the coast. She has a cottage for me in the grounds. We make no secret of our muddles. She says to have a woman carnally opens up as many minefields as to have a man. She thinks a visit might help me. She is not sure about you. She has misgivings. She thinks you might be a philanderer. I tell her that is not so. I bought an English newspaper, to somehow reach you. Reading one of the supplements, I began to picture little hamlets, steep country roads, the faded coats of arms on manor gates, old people's homes, and flutes of white convolvulus attaching themselves to everything within reach. Then the picture slid into night, that hushed, de-peopled time of night, when the cottages that Shakespeare occasionally wrote of, are sunk in dew, poplars like ghosts along a hillside, fairy lights still twinkling outside the shut public houses, and I thought of you as being part and parcel of that landscape and prayed that you would admit me to it, to those cold mocking sensibilities, to those men and women sprung from the loins of admirals. I wonder why you chose me. A death perhaps. Often it is the death of a close one that sends us in search, so that we run here, there and everywhere, run like hares, knowing that we cannot replace that which is gone.

I detest these cosy hush-hush affairs, which your kind excels at. Women in their upstairs drawing rooms, made up to the nines, at lunch hour, standing by the folds of their ruched curtains, with glazed smiles. Sherry and gulls' eggs in wait. The marital chamber stripped of all traces of a spouse. Lamb cutlets and frozen peas and lots of darling, darling.

When one is smitten, what does one want imparted and what hidden? If for instance you say 'I am hell to live with', it has a certain bravura to it. Does it simply mean that you are lazy and sullen indoors, expect someone else, a wife or a servant, to pour the coffee or to put a log on the fire, but that you show yourself to best advantage when visitors are heard coming up the path, just as you are decanting the choicest wine? How I hate these games and subterfuges. Sunday lunches, Sunday dinners, Sunday teas, the gibberish that gets trotted out. A woman telling the assembled guests how clever her Dave is, while notching up grievances inside. It's ubiquitous. I was with a couple one Sunday when the wife pronounced on some book of poetry, whereupon her husband said 'Have you read it', and oh the look, the withering look that she gave back to him, saying have *you* read it, and in the icy aftermath, the hatred congealed.

The most telling moment was when you saw me in that crowded nightclub come up from the Ladies, utterly lost. It was bedlam. You were leaving the next morning. I had to make my way back to our long table and took a detour so that I would have to pass closer to you, but of course not touch you. Suddenly you stood up and said my name with great anxiety, as if we were about to be separated. Then you kissed me. They saw you kiss me and were surprised by your indiscretion. I don't remember how I got to my chair.

Again and again I pay my respects to our wall. Last evening, I went on a little foray before dark. The violet hour was quite beautiful, balmy and pregnant with the kind of promise that evening in this city heralds. Musicians had gathered and taken up their posts at several corners. Skeins of sound sweetening the air. At one corner an African boy held up his wares, ropes of pearls and scarves that fluttered like veiling. They looked quite magic. The whites of his eyes were orbs, full of the wonder of evening, the wonder of Africa, the sense of a day almost done. It mattered not to him that I didn't buy anything, that I ignored his entreaties to look. The violet hour. The homeless had already decamped for the night, in doorways, in recesses, on church steps, lying there in heaps, like sacks of potatoes. I saw one sleeping man pat his stomach and smile benignly. Perhaps he was dreaming of food, not the oily noodles left as refuse, but a banquet such as he had glimpsed through the window of some restaurant, a bounteous offering, the fruits of the earth. To think that he would waken hungry. Hungers of every denomination are on display.

Thunder shook the foundations of the hotel, but I was shaking anyhow. I had wakened from a dream of having telephoned your hotel in Paris, thereby showing my need. I was told that you were out. I telephoned again and again. At one minute to midnight I called again, but was told that you had not returned. Then five minutes later, when I called back, I was put through and you answered gruffly, having gone to sleep. I reckoned that you must have come in tired, or maybe a little drunk, and flopped down on your bed. In the dream, you recognised my voice immediately and asked how I knew that you were in such and such a hotel in Paris. I put the phone down because I sensed the naked terror of a man who believes he has just been trapped. It freaked me.

Without any deliberation, I decided what I must do. I rang the airline and found they had spare seats, probably because it was midweek. I decided to take up Clarissa's invitation, to spring a surprise on her. The guest bungalow has its own kitchen and a little patio that opens onto a garden. I imagine at this time of year there will be those sharp, needly red flowers that resemble the beaks of tropical birds, and the pale pink corollas of flowering cacti, in terracotta pots. Why I imagine this, is beyond me.

No doubt the atmosphere at supper will be tense and there will be plenty of wine and false gaiety to relieve the strain, because strain there must be, considering the undercurrents. Clarissa is unsure, recognising that she has a reliable husband in Todd, but keeps harking back to a favourite story by D. H. Lawrence, in which a woman rides into the desert, where she is stripped not only of her clothing and her worldly possessions, but stripped of her former self and her attachments.

Clarissa comes each morning, laden with boxes of tiles and grout and phosphorescent paints. She arranges the shells in panels and fonts, magical configurations for houses and grottoes, bringing the whoosh of the ocean and intimations of the disgorged creatures that once lived and throve inside them.

Your name comes up all the time and the very utterance of it sends shivers through me. I have shown her one or two of your postcards, the more elliptical ones, but not of course, your letters. She has her doubts. Even your handwriting she questions. She cites clandestine loves in life and literature strewn with concealment, jealousies and betrayals. But I tell her, it has already begun. Even if I lingered here, there or anywhere it would still run its course, in letters, in longings and the whet of absence.

Not to go to you is to precipitate the dark and yet I hesitate. It is not that I do not crave the light. Rather, it is the certainty of the eventual dark.

Inner Cowboy

Flat, watery land. Big lakes, little lakes, turloughs that filled up in the rain and rivers a reddish brown from the iron in the soil. Curly didn't pay much heed to scenery, he was used to it. But he did notice the mist through the window when he got up early, everything blurry, the pots and the wheelbarrows in the backyard, the magpies lined up on the chimney stacks, and the cat, pleased with herself after her fill of mice and bats in the night – black night people called it. That cat was run over and got renamed 'Lucky to be alive' and had a ridge in her tail, like a ponytail. Felim, Curly's boss, collected him every morning and brought him to the hardware shop, in the other town, eight miles away. Riding along, he'd see the mist lift and it was like seeing a grand lady lifting the veil of her hat, gradual, gradual, but he did not say so to his boss or he'd be jeered at.

He disliked his boss. *I dislike this man* he'd say, sitting as far apart from him as he possibly could. Curly often confabbed with himself in private.

He had a brown shop coat, even though he wasn't let serve customers. All day he was hauling things back and forth from the store room, across the yard, over the puddles, crates of paint and filler and wallpaper and lino and mats and carpeting and buckets and bundles of kindling. There was a big high counter of cherry wood and, behind it, loads of drawers for nuts and bolts and nails, which Curly had to keep tidy, because things got jumbled. Felim was pure ignorant towards him and once went so far as to call him a 'retard' in front of customers. He was vexed, but he swallowed his pride, because he needed the wages for the rent of his room. The council paid some and he had to pay the rest. When Felim got the hump or had a hangover he kicked all before him and one day he kicked Curly in the shins. He could sue him for that, but he was too afraid of the guards.

The singing in the choir was what kept him going. They learned the words from a big songbook that took three pairs of hands to hold. Miss Boyce played the piano and conducted the choir. She was a lady. She would make an apple cake and bring it in and give it round. Then she got an infection, was out for a month, and after she came back she slid off the piano stool and fell. She died in a week. They sang for her in the church, sang with all their might – 'Here I am Lord, Lord of the sea and sky.'

He kissed her in the coffin before they put the lid on it. The other person he kissed was a nun kneeling in the grotto, because she looked sad. They were the two people, apart from his granny, that he kissed. He didn't remember his mother because she died when he was young and his father scooted. *No, there is no romance in my life and that is something I miss*, he would say to himself, believing that it would come, that it was like a little mustard seed and would grow. His granny said he was the best person alive and that made him feel great and not a retard.

His granny loved the olden days, when shops were drapery and grocery and hardware all in one. At the town square on a fair day, every Christmas, she sold her turkeys and was still calling her turkeys back. After she lost her husband and was all alone she got a pattern book and crocheted a beautiful white bed shawl. That kept her alive. But she wasn't as clued up as she used to be and dozed a lot in the chair and came awake always saying the same thing, 'Oh Curly, you asked for a biscuit and Coca Cola and I gone and got you a biscuit and a glass of milk.'

Curly preferred the bog to the quarries. The quarries were big ugly places, cross places and noisy, flying dust everywhere, showers of it black and gritty, from all the crushing and the blasting. The bogs were more peaceful, stretching to the horizon, a dun brown, with cushions of moss and spagunam and the cut turf in little stooks, igloos, with the wind whistling through them, drying them out. The birds flew high up in the air, only came down at night to feed and to suck. At school, the master read from an encyclopedia that bogs were a place to bury butter, to take a shortcut, and to dispose of a murdered one. Curly helped in the bog in the summer, because even though turf was cut with machinery it still needed humans to lay it and foot it and bag it and bring it home.

One day his friend Roddy wanted to be alone with his girlfriend and he got Curly up on the tractor, put it in first gear, and said, 'Take your boot off the brake and 'twill go.' And he did. And he was driving all over the place, slurping and lurching, the wheels sunk in the mire and he rollicking about, like he did in the dodgem cars at the carnival. Ever after in his dreams he was behind the wheel, powerful. When he got on Roddy's red Honda, that was different, that was trouble. Big time. Only a few hundred yards down a country road and didn't a squad car drive up and he was stopped and questioned, asked for his driving licence and insurance. He had neither. After ten days he received the summonses, one for not having the said documents and the second for failing to produce them. That day in the local district court, he wore a white baseball cap and made sure to address the judge as Judge. The reason he gave for speeding was because of the carburettor – said it would blow out if he went any slower, that he had to open her up for a mile or so. The judge was furious, boomed that he did not tolerate balderdash and called Curly a *brazen ingrate*. On a document, he was listed as P.O.A., which meant some kind of offender.

A crowd went to the races at Cheltenham in England and, feeling left out, he said to himself, *Curly, why don't you do something really wild*. He had a twenty-pound note and at lunch break he went down to the bookies, looked up numbers, and just went for number thirty-seven. Just like that. He watched the race in the hardware shop, in between doing things, and saw that his horse didn't fall, but didn't see the finish. When he went back to the bookies, Tilda asked him was he going out that night and he said he was skint and then she told him to go down into the little reception area and help himself to hot chocolate from the machine. When she came a bit later, there was a couple there and she said, 'Give a guess what this young man has won,' and they couldn't and neither could he. Oh, she teased it out, saying what a lucky lad he was and he'd be going places. Then she whispered in his ear, his horse had come in at fifty to one. He was flabbergasted. She gave him the money in the back room. It was one thousand pounds in different notes. He had been invited to a twenty-first that night and treated himself to a new suit, a striped suit, and got a radiator for his granny, one with the dial high up so she didn't have to bend, and a pink feather boa for Tara, the birthday girl. He had his hair cut and then spiked with gel. The life and soul of the party, everybody congratulating him and saying they'd all go to a match in Dublin, make a weekend of it. He sang the song that he always sang – 'The Walking Man I Am.' With the rest of the money he bought a black mare that turned out to be very bold, but she'd have a foal and he could sell it. The mare was in one of Donie's fields. Donie lived in the next county and was a third cousin of the family.

Every third Saturday Curly worked for Mrs Mulkearns, who ran a bed and breakfast. He put horse manure around a belt of young trees – maples, pines, and birches that were planted up near the main road to muffle the sound of the passing cars and lorries. Conor was the gardener, always muttering to himself. He said rich bastards were ruining Ireland, poisoning it, the McSorley brothers and their ilk grabbing, buying up every perch of farm, bog, and quarry they could get their hands on. Hadn't they destroyed a sacred wood with its yew trees, bulldozed it, in order to make pasture to fatten livestock. With the mist vanishing,

Conor would point to the last wisps of dew on the palings and on the posts, like diamonds, zillions of diamonds. If only they could catch them, they'd be as rich as the McSorleys.

Mrs Mulkearns did something gorgeous. She invited him and his granny to come and stay for a night. It was like going abroad. They got there at dusk. Being autumn, the trees up along the avenue were all sorts of plum colours and there were still flowers in the flowerbeds and in the hallway a tall clock in a glass-fronted case and the polished pendulums, solid as truncheons. There was a big fire in the room, pictures on every inch of wall, and books and ornaments and a second clock on the mantelpiece ticking. Mrs Mulkearns carried in a tray with sandwiches, scones, a variety of jams, and a cake, and she sat with them and explained the different flavours in the jams and how she came upon the Austrian recipe for the cake, which was shaped like a log and had a soft white butter icing. It was called a Stollen, from an old Prussian name that meant 'awaken'. All of a sudden she decided to tell a story of her youth, her harum scarum youth. She was in a convent and, with two other girls, plotted to get over the stone wall to meet two boys and walk three miles out of the town, to look at a haunted house. It was creepy, them just pushing the door in and every stick of furniture still in the rooms, and in the music room, a piano, sheet music strewn all over, and a beeswax candle in a brass holder – the very same as if the dead owner was about to come in. When they heard footfalls they ran and ran, and she and the two girls were expelled from the convent. His granny began a story but lost the thread of it and then it was his turn and he told about going to the bookies and picking number thirty-seven, but he did not tell what had transpired between him and Donie.

Lying in the strange four-poster, he thought on the matter and said, *Awaken Curly, awaken*. There was things in the media every single day about the haul from the notorious bank robbery in the north – how some traceable notes were retrieved, more found in chimneys and broom cupboards, and there were warrants for people whom the state intended to call. He might be one of those people. One evening, at closing time, Donie called to the shop and brought him across to the chipper, where he had his favourite things, chips with prawn sauce and grated cheese and mince. Donie wanted a favour, he wanted something hidden. A bag. He said Curly was not to worry, as he would not do anything to harm him or his granny and that it was only temporary. It could go in the granny's shed. That shed beat all for clutter. There was stuff in it going back hundreds of years, an old sidecar with a trap wedged over it, milk churns, milk tankards, breast slanes and foot slanes from when turf was cut by hand, and fenders and picture frames and old chairs and a horsehair sofa with the leather slashed and the coarse hair spilling out. There was a hole in the floor under the sidecar, where his great-grandfather hid his pike in Fenian times and his grandfather hid the bottles of potcheen and where he would hide the bag. Donie said there would be a reward and he asked what and Donie said, 'Name your poison', and he did. He wanted a mobile phone and straight away, when they'd finished the tea, they went to the phone shop, where there were hundreds and hundreds of phones all standing up, like little soldiers, waiting to be claimed. He picked a pink one, light pink, the colour of cake icing, and next day people at work were gaping at it and touching it, mad jealous. He put three telephone numbers into the memory, his granny's, Donie's, and his boss. He put the boss's number in because he longed for the morning that he could ring up and say, *I'm not coming in today, Mutt, and I'm not coming in ever*. He longed for that day.

The money was in a black plastic bag inside a holdall, and feeling it in his bedroom that first night he wondered how many thousands were in it, because he knew it was money, it wasn't anything else. He placed it on the floor of the wardrobe, laid it into his jacket and tied the buttons so that it looked like a dead person, a dead person with the legs sawn off. Then he put the baseball cap on it. If anyone came into that room and opened the wardrobe, they'd get a fright, but no one would.

It is winter evening and the men in the quarry are already knocking off. But in Mr McSorley's office there is uproar, as Daragh McSorley himself thunders at Seamus the foreman, who stands mute, lank and unable to control the shaking.

'Tell me more Seamus . . . moremore . . . it's music to my ears, it's Beethoven and Boyzone and Glenstall Monks rolled into one,' and before Seamus can even attempt to answer, McSorley is yelling what he has already been told, what he has already ingested – Hanrahan, a fucking eejit, a fucking moron, on his mobile, not thinking, rams his digger straight into the tank of diesel and, presto, thousands of litres have spewed onto the rained-on yard, making those rainbow colours so beloved of youngsters – said diesel already flowing through the porous limestone down to the river and onwards to the estate of houses in the valley below. Forty fucking families who hate his guts are now alerted to a peculiar smell in their kitchen and weird patches of damp seeping up through their foundations. Forty families baying at the gates; the Gardai, the council, the fisheries board all on his back, his quarry shut down indefinitely, loaders, crushers, lying idle, men laid off, bank repayments to the tune of fifty grand a month. Marvellous, inspirational, a whammy, a catastrophic environmental and human fuckup. At that, he reaches for his calculator and with instantaneous lucidity begins to tot up the gargantuan sums about to be lost.

Seamus watches the savage snarling expression, not yet knowing how long it will take for the spree of rage to subside, but guessing the finale – McSorley tearing wads of newspaper to chew, then spit out, because his anger can no longer be contained in a violent welter of words.

'Hanrahan is very sorry . . . he was ringing the hospital to inquire about his mother and getting no answer,' Seamus said, only to be silenced, because McSorley does not give a tinker's curse if Walter Mitty and Walter Mitty's ailing mother are dead in a ditch. The tank has got to be removed and a cleanup operation commenced at once.

'It can't be done tonight,' Seamus says.

'Can't! Can't!' McSorley roars. Can't is a verb he does not tolerate. Can't does not close a deal. There are no prizes for can't. Can't is the breast that losers are suckled on. That tank goes and is replaced with an identical one, all surface evidence is erased, stones taken up, crushed, buried, and clean unsmelling stone put in their place.

Alone, he drops down into his chair, drenched in sweat, and spits out the last gob of wet newspaper, then reaches into his bottom drawer for the brandy and his pewter mug. The first slug he drinks direct from the bottle and studies his reflection in the mug, his mouth foaming, his features distended. He does not like what he sees, because he is a vain man, proud of his jutting jaw, his mineral-blue eyes, his ramrod posture, and the cropped tawny mustache that singles him out from the lubbers and jobbers all around. He asks himself, 'Who am I, what am I' and answers 'I am Daragh McSorley, from the big house on the hill' – lawns, topiary, sculptures the size of cannon, a fragrant wife, Kitty, panelled walls, priceless paintings, a library of first editions, a yacht named after his daughter bobbing in the wintry waters off the coast of Spain, and a family to assuage his every mood, his bursts of temper, a devoted family that is his pride and joy.

But no one really knows him as he is, no one knows the scope of his ambition, the passion, the relentless unrest. Only Dr Tubridy got a glimpse of it once – Tubridy, aping the English mores with his tweeds and his trilby hat, put it to him in the surgery, after the second by-pass – asked him what made him tick.

'Lust,' he answered.

'For the fair sex,' Tubridy said.

'For everything . . . Medbh the Connaught Queen, has nothing on me, with her avarice for dominions, herds, jewels and booty.'

'And thy fellow man?' Tubridy put it to him.

'A cheque book speaks louder than the act of perfect contrition,' he answered and laughed, and Tubridy laughed with him, but nervously.

He was famous for his loud laugh that had little mirth in it. It confused people, it kept them dangling. As for bad feeling, there was so much bad feeling vented on him that he could bottle it and sell it like holy water. His wife, Kitty, mortified that Sunday after mass, when a mad eejit of a woman who had done upholstery for a block of houses, came up to him cursing and screaming, 'You broke me, you broke me, Mr McSorley,' and he not losing the cool one bit, giving her the big smile and assuring her that it would be looked into. Soon she was timorous, almost apologetic, and he walked tall to the car, Kitty pinching him and asking, 'In the name of God Daragh, in the name of God, what did you do?' It wasn't long after that that the stone eagles were hacked off the piers of his front gates and dogs were set on Kitty when she was out for a walk.

Another thing, never in his cups did he luxuriate in that maudlin stuff about hunger and privation. He knew it in his marrow. Lesser men than him would go on about crubeens and a turnip for Christmas dinner, or a grandmother pulled off her bicycle when she was taking the salmon that her man had poached from the river, to sell to the fishmonger in the town, taken down off her bicycle and brought to the county jail.

'Be absolute in your aim' was what he told himself while he was still in short trousers. On the day when he hired his first lorry and trusted that guiding star that led him through mountain gorges to his Eldoraldo, a disused quarry. He got out, looked at a sheer wall of rock over two hundred feet high, and imagined the wealth that lay hidden within the belly of it.

It is Friday night, the night he and Kitty – along with Ambrose, his brother and partner, and Ambrose's wife, Isolde, the ex-beauty queen – will go up the country to a simple olde worlde pub for dinner. It's his way of letting it be known that he hasn't lost touch with his roots and, moreover, they have taken on a young chef who had just got his degree in Switzerland. Walking to his car after work, the jacket over his shoulder, he can see the men, the few trusted ones breaking the stones with their jackhammers. Lights gleamed in the valley down below, and from a hillside farmstead comes the sound of a cow in labour. He knew that sound. Sometimes the memory of it took him unawares, that low grieving sound of a cow in labour, but instantly he shut it out. Such things belonged to his former and unhardened self. He is no longer that man. He is a man frequently described in the newspapers as ruthless and with a criminal coldness.

Yes, it's their evening for up-the-country, and Isolde, with her range of accessories – because she's an accessory freak, in the black gloves with sequins – raving about too much dairy in her diet, too much frigging Krug in her diet, not like his little Kitty, one gin and tonic that she nurses faithfully, because she read somewhere that Winston Churchill always nursed his drink. Isolde falling not once, not twice, but thrice at their barbecue at the end of summer, whereas his little Kitty is up with the lark, morning Mass, a bit of baking, her prize herb garden and a brisk walk in the afternoon to keep her figure. Chalk and cheese, Kitty and Isolde, like Daragh and Ambrose, quiet and staid, brothers yoked together, in their crooked deeds and their crooked deals. Kitty knew how to keep her man, that lady journalist sashaying up to him at the function in Dublin, to ask how she could get in touch so as to raise his profile, stressing his works for charity and his role as a family man, and Kitty answering from the far end of the festive table, 'Through me, through me.'

Next day Curly was a hero. The words ran away with him, boasting how he had pulled a calf from its mother, up there on Pat-the-Bonham's bit of land, Pat having gone to Lourdes as a volunteer, when lo and behold, up there in the silence and the gloom there was this hullabaloo from down in the quarry below, security lights turned off and he reckoning that it was some gang stealing diesel or stealing stones. Then, as he told it, the cow got very agitated, running around in circles, and the noise was atrocious, a drilling sound, a zzzzzzzzzzz, like from the key-cutting machine in the shop, only louder, and then the claps of metal hitting other metal and echoing back, so that the cow bolted from the building and ran off. He followed, but each time she got away, over grass and thicket, he demented, in case she got caught in a crevice of the ravine, or that the calf would slip out and split its head on rock or bits of drainage pipe embedded in the earth. When he got to the moment when he knew he would have to deliver a calf, he asked them, his listeners, to just picture it – he with only a small torch and not a bit of rope or twine, seeing the forelegs jutting out, but not able to catch them because of their being so slimy, and doing the only thing he could think of, which was to take off his sweater, get a grip on them, and pull and pull, until the calf came out in a big plop on the damp ground and he, as he said, roared with joy and relief. Then nature took its course, the mother licked the sac, took her time over it, licked the crusted eyelids, chewed the cord, and the calf began its pathetic attempts to get up, the mother unable to do that for it, only the calf itself could do that, and eventually, staggering on its little legs and going straight to the udder.

'*Euphoria*' was the only word Curly could find to describe what he felt.

By nightfall, as he told it in the chipper, the pitch black was blacker, the noise from the quarry suspicious, but worst of all, the birth was complicated, as one of the calf's feet was folded back inside the mother and he who knew nothing about veterinary had to put his hand in, jiggle it around to get it forward and enable the calf to slide out, which it did.

The *euphoria* would be short lived.

Over the next days, the environmental agency was flooded with complaints, some in person and some by phone, families up there, irate at the fact that their water was contaminated, that smears of greasy film appeared in their sinks and on their baths, and the springs that fed the reservoir had lagoons of oil floating upon them. Men were called to monitor the damage, and when fish were found dead in the river an enquiry was set up as to what might have caused such spillage, though those up there already knew that it had only come from one place, the detested quarry.

It was the tapping on the window at night that Curly came to dread and he being called out. First it was Seamus the foreman, telling him that he would have to comply, otherwise the McSorleys would punish him. Then it was Ambrose, saying that they knew he had made a statement to the Guards, but that he would have to retract it. He could say that he saw nothing and that he heard nothing and that anyhow, he had bad sight. The proof that he had bad sight they had already ascertained, because of the many pairs of glasses Curly had been prescribed down the years. Finally, it was Daragh McSorley himself, just dropping by for a friendly chat, asked who was his favourite pop group, when last had he been to Galway, and how was his granny doing on her lonesome out there in the wilds. Then he said that Curly had nothing to worry about, all he had to do was stand up in the court and say he had made up a story to keep himself company out there on the lonely mountainside. Muldoon, a friendly solicitor, would help, coach him and put him through his paces. If he played ball and the case was quashed, Santa would come and Santa would come to his granny also and to tell her that. Curly looked at Mr McSorley's big tall frame silhouetted against the shiny chrome of his car, and then into the distance the church spire tapering up into the sky until it seemed like a long needle. His knees had turned to water.

I am afraid of that man, that man Mr McSorley, Curly was saying to himself on the stepladder, stacking floor tiles on a shelf, when in walks Muldoon the crooked solicitor and tells him that the case is called for first Thursday in Michaelmas and to come in next day at his lunch break, so that they can get their act together. In his mind he now stood in the witness box, the judge firing questions at him, tripping him up, a barrister warning him that the case for the prosecution rested on his evidence. He saw himself being asked to stick out his tongue for the signs of a lie and he began to shake uncontrollably and the ladder underneath shook with him. He could do a runner, he could just vanish to some destinationless place, but where and how. He knew that he was being watched.

After work he went straight to Widow Nell's, not to the bar, but to the back room, where he sat at a table, by himself, lads saluting and gassing and he talking back but not knowing a single thing he said. There was a newspaper open on the table and a big article about the price of cattle feed gone sky high and fears for the decline in agriculture. The money in his granny's shed, his fingerprints on it. He should have used rubber gloves, but he didn't. He should have refused Donie, but he didn't. *I am so far in that I can't get out* was what he kept saying, kept piecing the bits together – if he denied what he saw that would be perjury and he would go to jail, and if he didn't deny that he saw what he saw the McSorleys would get him. Either ways he was sunk. When Curly was a young man, there was a girl two doors down that got a toy at Christmas that could talk. It was clothed in red fur, the mouth wide open and the tongue hanging out. It had two plastic knobs for eyes and an orange fur nose, and every so often it said 'Elmo wants you to know that Elmo loves you'. He was Elmo, only it was him saying it to himself – *I am so far in that I can't get out*. It wouldn't stop. Shelagh, the barmaid, an older woman, could see that he was upset and kept bringing him saucers of chips that were free and asking if he was sure he wanted another drink and oughtn't he be heading home for bed.

After he'd downed three pints, two large whiskies, and a Bailey's liqueur, he felt better. All of a sudden he asked himself, 'Why should I stay here, why should I loiter?' and got up and went out, pulling up his hood.

He was not drunk but he was not sober as he got on his bicycle and pedalled and pedalled through the drizzly night. Up the high street, past the church, past the monument, and down the back road, where people jogged at all hours and were a menace. Up to the junction that forked to the main road with a sign that said 'Dublin', except that it was invisible, cars flying by at one hundred miles an hour. Then pedalling at breakneck speed to get to the far side, and three and a half miles along to the forestry gates. When he entered the forestry he felt safer, tarred avenue with trees on either side and the big lake still and black and glassy. Everything black, save for one little light in the turret window of the ruin of the Castle. He'd never noticed that light before, because he'd never set foot there at night. That little light belonged to his other life, before he fell into the clutches of the McSorleys and before he buried the cursed bag in his granny's shed.

When Curly didn't appear at the beep of the boss's hooter and when it was discovered that his bed wasn't slept in, it was expected that he would mooch into work at some point with a cock-and-bull story. But when he was not seen and not heard of for twenty-four hours and had not kept the appointment with Muldoon, the Gardai had to be alerted. A guard drove up to his granny's house and, being as she was an old woman, he didn't want to upset her too much, did not immediately get out his notebook and biro to take down any evidence. He was amazed at the amount of clobber she had accumulated, every single chair and armchair a throne of old newspapers and bags and flattened cardboard boxes. There were bits of crochet, dolls, dolls' prams, and a multitude of small china animals along the mantelpiece, above the unlit stove. Sensing that Curly was in some trouble, she got very flustered and jumped up and took her hat and coat off the hook on the hall stand saying 'What have I got to do now, sir,' and he had the greatest trouble in calming her down. He said to leave it to them, that Curly had not boarded bus or train, and that Gardai were following up every lead and had their ears close to the ground.

It was a German woman who found him, or rather traced the sound of a ringing telephone. Eerie it was, up there in that empty wilderness, her two big dogs chasing each other and sniffing the territory where they had never been before. She was new to the neighbourhood and had come to look at a portion of bog with a view to renting it, so that they could have a turf fire the year following. Various sections were pegged with names and numbers, but there were still allotments for rent.

The phone was almost buried in a thicket of golden-crown heather, the 'auroras of autumn', as she had read in the guidebook. The ringing stopped just as she got to it and, bending in the near dusk to pick the phone up, she was startled by the sight of a sneaker, a man's dirty white sneaker, at the side of a deep black trench. She backed away, not knowing which apparition would be more terrifying at that instant, that of one living or dead. The phone felt alive in her hand, like a viper, a pink viper, and she walked, or rather she ran, holding it and whistling sharply to call her dogs.

The guard who answered the intercom could not hear her very distinctly, but when he saw her walk into the station, he guessed by her expression that she had come with a story.

It was all over the town, how Curly was missing and how sad, how very sad. The divers were not expected until later, since they were dashing all over the country, but the superintendent was promised that they would come, even if it had to be at night. Rumours were rife and ominous. Those who had barely thrown a word to Curly were now picturing him, so harmless, going up the street in his old windcheater, his brown mop of wet hair over his wet rosy cheeks, recalling his little impertinences, going up to people in pubs and saying *Why can ye not talk to me* and crashing weddings because he loved, adored, the taste of champagne. Some said that it must have been a rotten footbridge that gave way under him and that most likely the bog hole he fell into was deep, or the woman would have seen him. One pundit said that he might not be found for hundreds of years like an Elkman. A more sinister theory was that he had been brought there in the black night by those who wished him gone and an extra twist to the various scenarios was that he had indeed been got rid of, but somewhere else, that the mobile phone and the shoe were a decoy and Curly was lost in the vast swells of the Atlantic Ocean.

Only Donie knew, or rather guessed, that Curly, having heard that he was to appear in court, lost the nerve and believed that the judge could read his mind and would trip him up, so that somehow he would have to own up to the stash in his granny's shed. That's why he went at night and salvaged the bag to bury it – it was for her. It was love of her. The minute the news broke, Donie drove to the grandmother's to give her some kind of comfort and felt a villain, an out and out villain. He saw how the carts in the shed had been overturned and the empty hole with dirty black slashed cobwebs. It was in the bog now, beyond the grasp of mankind. 'I wouldn't do any harm to you or to your granny,' he had told Curly and he meant it, but he did, he did do harm and he felt rotten. When Phonsie the car dealer asked him to hide the haul, he was promised a bonus and a scooter for Kathleen, so she could hop down to the shops or have her hair done, when she felt like it. He did it for graft.

Never before had there been a hearse parked on that isolated road that led to the bog. How grim and inhospitable the place was, not a single bird-note, a universe of black-brown, frozen over and luridly lit by the fitful flares of the torches. The divers brought the body up slowly and laid it on the bank for the sergeant to identify Curly. Then it was placed in the black zipper bag and carried ceremoniously on a stretcher of tarpaulin. It would be taken first to the morgue for forensic examination and then to the chapel where the mourners would foregather.

It was in an annexe between the bar and the kitchen, poorly lit, that Shelagh asked the sergeant if she could have a word with him. He had gone in very late for a pint, to try to wind down. He could feel the emotion in her, but he could not see her face very clearly. She wanted to know one thing. What did Curly look like when they brought him out. He thought before answering. He knew that she needed reassurance of some kind and he heard himself say, 'He was fairly close to perfect.' He saved her the other things, how Curly's clothes were all soggy, his face and hands ash white from being suspended in the freezing water, and that when they pulled him out, the diver had to wipe the frothy fluid around his mouth, the egg white stuff, before putting him in the body bag. He spared her that.

'And the cause of death?' she asked.

'Probably death by misadventure,' he said. Picking up the carving knife that was on a sideboard, she drew it in mock execution across her neck and said woefully, 'Poor Curly, a lamb to the slaughter.'

The tradition still held to lay down the sword for a funeral. Everyone came. Bouquets of flowers lined the entrance hall, Isolde's the most exquisite of all – blue and purple – not like any flowers that might grow in the ditches, but like flowers in a dream. Curly's granny had to be contained, kept from trying to open the sacristy door, believing Curly was in there, even though she had already seen him in the coffin and put one of her china mice in along with him. Donie stood at the back. He was over a barrel, hadn't slept. At moments he thought he was keeling over and had to grasp the baptismal font for balance. He saw the McSorley brothers in their long black coats of finest nap, pillars of neighborliness and loyalty, their wives weeping beneath their mantillas.

Father McDermott spoke fondly of Curly, his innocence, his always offering a helping hand, his love of shooting stars and his love of the small things in life, like being invited into a house for hospitality. He said how poignant that Curly should lose his young life in the very bog where, only the previous June, he had helped a neighbor to foot and stack turf and then, somewhat melo-dramatically, he said, 'Whom the Gods love die young.' Gazing out at his parishioners, he asked them not only to grieve for a sensitive youth of one score years, but to open their hearts and examine their consciences, and then he reddened and his voice grew vehement. Greed, he said, was ruining the country, people no longer showed the compassion that they once had, and while he was not pointing a finger at any single individual, he said someone must have known that Curly was in some sort of jinx to go riding off into a bog in the dead of night.

Then Curly's voice, sweet and boyish, filled the chapel as a tape of his party piece was played and the mourners wept openly –

> The walking man I am
> I've been down on the ground
> I swear to God

If ever I see the sun
For any length of time
I can hold it in my mind
I'll never again go underground

They were filing out now and Donie filed out with them. He would drive straight away to Phonsie's place. Phonsie was an affable man but a ruthless man and with a cock-up of this magnitude, anything could happen. He might be next, dispatched to the wild blue yonder. Being a third cousin, people shook his hand and offered their condolences, but he was miles away.

The strength in their hands was mighty.

Black Flower

'It's a dump,' Mona said.

' 'Tis grand,' Shane said, looking around.

For an hour or more they had driven, under the prow of a range of mountain, in search of a restaurant that would be quiet but also cheerful, and now they had landed themselves in this big, gaunt room that seemingly served as both ballroom and dining room. A microphone on a metal stand took pride of place, and a bit of orange curtain lay crumpled on the bandstand, as if someone had flung it down there in petulance. One end of a long refectory table was covered with a white lace cloth under which there had been put a strip of red crêpe paper, and it was there they would most likely be seated.

It was late spring and when from the roadway they had spotted the rusted iron gates and the long winding avenue, they thought how suitable, and how enchanting it seemed. Moreover, the hotel had a lovely name – Glasheen. They drove up the long avenue, trees on either side, oak, sycamore, ash, all meshed together, fighting amiably as it were for ascendancy, and birds in their evening sallies, busier than the pigeons who cooed softly in their roomy roosts.

A battered jalopy with a 'For Sale' sign stood in the car park that was separated from a nearby meadow by a rope of green cable. A sign on a post read 'Danger – High Voltage', and from a metal box there issued a burping, that every few seconds rose to a growl.

Close to the entrance was a butcher's van with the owner's name printed in tasteful brown lettering, and on the step a child's tractor filled with toy soldiers and wooden blocks. In the hallway, a nest of candles glimmered on a high whatnot and a luxurious flowering plant trailed and crept along the floor, amoeba-wise. The petals were a soft, velvety black, with tiny green eyes, pinpoints, and there was something both beautiful and sinister about it. She had never seen a black flower before. Since nobody answered, she went into an adjoining room, where a man had his face so close to the television screen he seemed to be conversing with it and took no notice of her. Two dogs dozed on a torn leather armchair. Presently, a girl came, a strapping young girl who could not say for certain if they did or did not do dinners, as the season was not yet in full swing. Nevertheless, she led the way to the gaunt, cheer-less dining room.

They had driven so many miles, first to a town with a lake and a round tower, where they had strolled, then sat on dampish rough-hewn picnic stools and noted to each other how strange that others who had driven there had simply sat in their motor cars and stared out at the lake. He liked being with her, she could feel that. She didn't know him very well. She had volunteered to give painting lessons in the prison in the Midlands, where he was serving a long sentence. Though many came for the first few classes, they eventually dropped away and by the end, Shane was the only one. Sitting with his back to her, finishing off a self-portrait, which was in viscous gold and mustard yellows, she had asked him if he had ever seen the paintings of Van Gogh, to which he said he hadn't. She was reminded of Van Gogh because of the upturned stump of a sneaker, on which the dry paint bristled.

Walking in the graveyard beside the round tower, she had asked very quietly, 'How do you find the world, Shane?', since he was only out of prison a few short weeks.

'Crowded,' he had said, and half smiled.

While in prison, his wife had been shot, bathing their child, shot in lieu of him and not long after, the child, who was being reared with relatives, had also died, of meningitis. On the evening that his wife had been shot, he had gone to sleep while it was still bright, and though the warders knocked and pounded on his cell door, to tell him of it, he did not hear them. He reckoned that in sleep he was postponing the news that he could not bear, but would have to learn to bear. How he managed never to crack up was a mystery to Mona.

A few days before Christmas, the governor of the prison had rung to tell her that there was a parcel left for her in his office. It was the portrait wrapped in assorted carrier bags, and on the greeting card he had written, 'For Mona . . . I'm sorry it's so crude.' Something about the message seemed unfinished, as if he had wanted to say more, and it was this hesitancy that emboldened her to ask if he would like to meet in Dublin, when he was let out. He was due out that spring, but it was kept a secret to avoid a media jamboree. She knew how reserved he was, he having mentioned that, though he ate in the refectory and played tennis three times a week, he kept to himself, and the best times were at night in the cell, listening to tapes of Irish music and songs. She imagined that on those nights he would mull on the past and on the future, too, possibly envisaging how the world had changed in the fifteen years since he was captured. It was a hair-raising capture that attracted the attention of the nation and confirmed him as a dangerous outlaw.

It so happened that he was released three days earlier than he had expected and she could scarcely believe it when he telephoned her in her studio in Dublin and said somewhat bashfully, 'It's me . . . I'm free.'

They had made an appointment to meet in a hotel, and standing on the steps on a crisp frosted morning, the winter boughs and branches in the park across the way jewelled in frost, she felt he was not coming, that something had prevented him. After almost an hour, a young boy in a braided outfit came and told her that she was wanted on the phone and brazenly repeated Shane's full name. He was in another hotel a mile away, and she told him, somewhat sternly, to wait there and not to budge.

Sitting with him in a booth of the second hotel, drinking tea, there was a tentativeness. It was strange to see him in a gaudy shirt and jeans, because in the prison Portakabin where she had visited him, everything was muted. Moreover, a policeman had always stood behind them, listening in, except for the odd time when he took a stroll, maybe to smoke a cigarette. They had not shook hands when they met on the steps of the hotel, but she knew by his way of looking at her that he was glad to see her and remarked on her hair being much nicer, loose like that. For the painting class it had always been tied back and made her look more severe.

'So you're free,' she said.

'I had only ten minutes' warning,' he said.

'How come?'

'The governor came down to the sewing room and said, "You have a car and a driver at your disposal for twenty-four hours, it'll take you anywhere you want."' As he said it, she remembered exactly having asked the governor if things would be all right for Shane when he got out.

As he spoke she recalled the shiver she had felt as the governor told her that there were many people who wished Shane dead.

'You mean the Brits?'

'Them and his own ... feuds ... feuds ... Put it this way, he'll always be a wanted man,' and he raised his arms to fend off questions.

'What were you sewing?' she asked, in surprise.

'Oh, bits and pieces for the lads ... zips, darns, patches ... there was a long queue.'

'Who taught you to sew?'

'We were ten children at home ... the mother had a lot of other things to do,' he said shyly.

'So the lads will miss you?'

'They might,' he said, but without any show of emotion, then looking straight ahead he began to roll a cigarette, thoughtfully. He seemed then to be the very incarnation of loneliness, of isolatedness.

Some friends had pooled together to get him a second-hand motor car, and a few weeks later he suggested that they drive out into the country of an evening. It was agreed that she would travel by train and meet him in the town about eight miles north of Dublin, where he had found lodgings with a black woman, who chattered all day long to her humming birds and as he said did not ask questions.

Now they were in the big dining room, famished and waiting for the owner to come and tell them what she could possibly give them to eat. When she met Shane as arranged at the railway station, he was sitting against the outside wall eating an ice cream, and she wondered why a wanted man with a host of enemies would sit there, visible to all, in his new jeans and jazzy shirt.

His car was a little two-seater with a fawn coupe top. They had tried various restaurants along the way, to no avail. In one, a sullen owner pulled the door barely ajar and said there was no hope of teas as he was laid up. Several times she got out of the car and went in, only to discover that the restaurant was too rackety or too dismal. She joked about these places when she got back, described the tables, the lighting, the dried flowers and so on, giving each place marks ranging from one to ten. Shane didn't talk much, but he liked letting her talk. The years inside had made him taciturn. Judging by the newspaper photographs that had been taken on the day he was captured, he had changed beyond recognition. He had gone in, young and cavalier, and had come out almost bald, with a thin rust moustache that somehow looked as if it were spliced to his upper lip. He said once to her and only once that she herself could be the judge of his actions. He had fought for what he believed in, which was for his country to be one, one land, one people and not have a shank of it cut off.

When they came to the gateway leading to Glasheen, she felt it was ideal, so sequestered and the building far below, smothered in a grove of trees. Holding open one half of the iron gate – she had put a stone to the other half – she saw to one side a public telephone kiosk that looked glaringly forlorn, the floor strewn with litter. The horse chestnut trees were in full bloom, pink and white tassels in a beautiful droop, and in the meadow lambs bleated ceaselessly. It was pandemonium, what with them bleating and racing around for fear of losing their mothers.

'It's like a maternity ward,' Shane said and she wondered if he had ever been in one, as he was already in prison when his wife had given birth. Only his wife truly knew him and she was dead.

Looking at the stranded microphone, she said it was lucky they hadn't come on a dance night, as she was not a dancer.

'Me neither,' Shane said.

'Oh you'd dance if you were made to,' the owner said as she hurried in, drying her hands on a tea cloth, and told them about the lovely hunt ball they had had in the winter, people from all around, gentry and farmers and cattle dealers and highwaymen and God knows what.

'Are we bothering you?' Shane said.

'Aren't ye what I have been hoping for,' she said, and led them across to the long table that stretched almost to the window. When he sat down he smiled. It was the way he smiled that drew people to him, and the owner, quick to recognise it, introduced herself as Wynne and said proudly that they were in luck because her good-for-nothing husband had caught a salmon and she would poach it, along with potatoes and cabbage. Meanwhile, she said, they should tuck into the drink and she would bring bread to mop it up. There was a slight hitch, as she was inexpert at opening the bottle of wine, which Mona had already ordered. The corkscrew buckled and bits of crumpled cork floated in the pale amber liquid.

'Just enjoy the view and the rolling countryside,' Wynne said, and sallied off muttering what a nice man Shane was and what nice manners and how manners maketh man.

'This is nice,' he said. He liked the wine, though he was not used to it. She could tell he was not used to it because his eyes became a little foggy, like steam on a kitchen window when pots are boiling over. They could hear Wynne talking to the dozy girl in the kitchen, as their arrival had created a little flurry.

'Your eyes are the colour of tobacco,' Mona said.

'Is that good or bad?' he asked.

'It's good,' she said.

Turning to Wynne, who had just come in with a loaf of bread, he asked what the room rates were for the night.

'We could negotiate that,' Wynne said, and winked as she toddled off.

'You're not thinking of staying in this dungeon,' Mona said.

'No one would find me here,' he said, gravely.

'Where will you live Shane?'

'Maybe in the west,' he said, but vaguely. She pictured him in some cold, isolated cottage, by himself, wrapped in an overcoat, on edge, day and night on the look-out.

'Do you worry about . . . about reprisals?' she asked.

'I'd be worried for others,' he said, and looked at her with such concern, such tenderness, across the reaches of the wide table, the flames from the stout candle guttering in the breeze from the open window, half his face in shadow.

'Do you think you'll go back to . . .'

'The fight isn't over . . . isn't done,' he said grimly.

She didn't ask anything further. There were always distances between them, a part of him cut off from her and from everyone, a remoteness. How different the two hims, the young invincible buccaneer and the man sitting opposite her, ageing and dredged, his deeds locked inside him.

'It's alright,' she said, not even sure of what she was saying.

'It is,' he answered, also unsure.

The poached salmon was a sturdy lump from which the head and tail had been cursorily lopped. The skin, hanging in a long shred, looked like fly paper, and though the outside was cooked nicely, the inside was rawish and around the bone the juices were a pale blood colour. Wynne hacked it jubilantly with an old carving knife and conveyed pieces onto Shane's plate with bravado. She then picked up the hot boiled potatoes with her bare hands and filled his plate in her desire to please him. Mona asked for a smaller portion as Shane apologised for the mound he had been given.

'There'll be jelly and custard, so leave a gap,' Wynne said and went off proudly, humming.

Very soon after, he listened as if he had heard something that was no longer the bleating lambs, because in the fading light they had gone quieter.

'What?' Mona asked.

'Car.'

The car drove in at hectic speed, lights fully on and then drove off again, with a vengeance.

'Ah, youngsters, hoping there was a disco,' Wynne said, having come back in with the white sauce for the salmon. But he was not listening to her, he was only listening now to his own thoughts and his appetite had gone. He drank a few more swigs of wine and jumped up.

'Toilet,' he said and reached out and touched her sleeve. She watched him go, something so wounded about him, his clothes clinging to his thin body, his sleeves rolled up as he tugged at the loose door knob. Then peculiarly, he ran back and took his jacket off the back of the chair.

Since he was away for quite a while, Wynne, who had been coming in and out, brought an old dented cloche to put over his dinner, as both of them watched through the open door into the dark passageway. The two dogs, so inert a short while previous, raised an ongoing terrible howl, as if catastrophe was about to befall the house. Wynne said it portended thunder, as they never yelped at visitors, not even at tradesmen, but the onset of thunder always sent them crazy. She predicted that presently there would be flashes of lightning, the grounds and the meadow intermittently lit up. They waited, but the summer lightning did not come.

'I wonder what's keeping him,' Wynne said.

'He's not used to drink,' Mona said quietly.

'Lovely man . . . lovely smile,' Wynne said, and again looked, expecting him to appear, in that quick, stealth-like way of his.

At length, Wynne said, 'Do you think I should get Jack to go and investigate?'

They had left the dining room and were in the hallway facing the door that said Gents, with the metal 'G' askew on a loose rusted nail. Mona thought how awful if he had passed out and how ashamed he would be. Jack was summoned from where he was stationed, close up to the television screen, and rising he muttered something, then went into the Gents and closed the door behind him. Soon Wynne pushed it in so that they could be of assistance.

'He's not here,' Jack called.

'Where is he then?' Wynne shouted.

'He went out . . . he got change for the pay phone,' Jack said and instantly she guessed that he had gone to phone one of his comrades to come for her, as he would have to disappear.

The dogs were already on the avenue, running back and forth in a froth, and ready to tear anyone to pieces.

Both women ran and Jack followed behind, calling after them.

People stood on the far side of the gate, muted and in shock. Shane lay half in and half out of the telephone kiosk, his eyes, his tobacco-coloured eyes, still open, staring up at the sky with its few isolated stars. He was gasping to say something, but the strength had almost left him. He could not say what he most wanted to say. The onlookers stood in a huddle, baffled, not knowing who they were looking at, or why he had been slain, while simply making a telephone call. The guards had already been called, and one woman, who had been first on the scene, said she had heard him repeatedly utter, 'Oh Jesus, oh Mary,' but her companion stoutly contradicted that. Mona wanted to kneel by him and shut his eyes, but she was too afraid to stir. If only someone would shut his eyes, but she dared not, for fear of them. He looked so desolate and so unbefriended, the breath just ebbing away and the instant it left him, she let out a terrible cry. He was dead. Dead for a cause that others did not believe in, and as if on cue a youth who had been going by, stopped, dismounted his black brutish motorcycle, threw down his helmet, and crossed with the officiousness of a pallbearer. Looking down at the corpse, he recognised Shane and repeated his name with evident outrage and disgust. He seemed almost ready to kick him. The group recoiled, stricken, not only with fear, but with revulsion. The brief spate of pity had turned ugly. Wynne shrieked at Mona – 'A murderer . . . you brought a murderer under my roof where my grandchildren slept,' and then lunged fiercely, as Jack caught her, repeating the same phrase over and over again, 'It's all right . . . it's all right . . . he's history now . . . he can't harm us anymore.'

The police cars had arrived and big burly men, in a lather of curiosity and vindication, hurried to look at the assassin, in whose bloodied death, they rejoiced.

'What goes around comes around,' one said with a smugness.

Those that had been first on the scene were told to drive to the police station in the town, while Jack, Wynne, and Mona were ordered back to the hotel for interrogation.

Jack and Wynne hurried on, as the dopey girl and a boy came to meet them, clinging to one another for protection. Mona lagged behind, dreading their questions and their abhorrence of her. It had begun to drizzle. A brooding quiet filled the entire landscape and the trees drank in the moisture. There would be another death to undo his and still another and another in the long grim chain of reprisals. Hard to think that in the valleys murder lurked, as from the meadow there came not even a murmur, the lambs in their foetal sleep, innocent of slaughter.

Send My Roots Rain

Men and women hurled themselves through the revolving door of the hotel with an urgency, and so quickly did they follow one upon the other that Miss Gilhooley imagined it was bound to end in a stampede. Discharged into the hotel lobby, they flung out their arms or tossed their scarves, triumphant at having arrived. Miss Gilhooley drew back, waiting, as she hoped, for a pause in the hectic proceedings. It was then that Pat-the-Porter noticed her, standing somewhat tentatively on the lower entrance step – not a young woman but a striking woman in a gray Cossack hat, such as he had seen on an actress in a Russian film many years before. He held the door and drew her in, as he put it, 'to the most distinguished address in Dublin'. He was an affable man, with sparkling blue eyes, proud of his girth inside that fine uniform and certain of the importance of his station. He had, as he soon told her, been working there for thirty-three-odd years, barring the two years when the establishment was closed for the massive revamp.

The hall was a veritable Mecca. Marble floors of shell pink, which an unthinking being could easily slide on, and countless chandeliers, blazed and gave out a beautiful light, that surpassed daylight and trembled within the many mirrors. A fire was blazing and on either side were dented leather buckets filled with consignments of logs and turf. The flower arrangements were particularly fetching – golden gladioli and lilies in high vases and then nests of littler vases, which had deep blue orchids that had been severed from their stems squeezed inside, their faces pressed close to the glass, chafing at their imprisonment.

Pat-the-Porter was regaling her with some of the hotel's history from the time when it had opened its doors in 1824 – the perilous days during the Rebellion of 1916, when gunfire whizzed in Stephen's Green across the road, and sure, wasn't the lounge famous for having been the very place where the Irish constitution was drafted. In between these snatches of history, he snarled at young boys, bellhops, with their grey pillbox hats set at jaunty angles, reminding them of their various charges and all smiles. The couple in the Horseshoe Bar, as Pat-the-Porter said, were still waiting for their oysters, and the front steps needed more salt; he didn't want people breaking their ankles or their hips or any part of their anatomy. He was able to change his manner at a wink, soft and confiding with her, severe with the underlings, and giving a knowing half nod to the various swanks and habitués who came skiving through the swing doors and headed for either of the two bars or the Saddle Room. He would give her a booklet later on in which she could read all about the hotel, from its inception to the present time as a hot-spot for movers and shakers, not to mention the English gentlemen who came for the stag parties.

Miss Gilhooley, he opined, would feel more at home in the sedate ambience of the Lord Mayor's Lounge, and so he escorted her to a table that was not too close to the entrance, in a recess, a little round table covered with a white linen cloth and on which there rested a folded menu. The elderly pianist, in an excess of energy, was bent over his piano, hitting the keys so fervently that a waltz sounded like a recruiting song. His bald pate glistened in the winter sun that poured through the bay window and onto his knitted grey-white eyebrows and his small purple dickie-bow.

It would be true to say that her heart fluttered somewhat. Strange to think that she was about to come face-to-face with a great poet whom she rated above all other poets and especially the young whippersnappers with their portfolios of clever words and hollow feelings. His poetry evoked the truth of the land, dock and turnips and nettles, men behind their ploughs, envying the great feats of Priam and Hector, tormented men in small fields battling their desires. Again and again she recommended his poems to borrowers in the library where she worked, and once, she organised a little entertainment, where there were readings of his poems and refreshments afterwards. The audience was restless, finding the poems too depressing, so that there was fidgeting and coughing throughout.

Each time a new poem of his appeared in a newspaper she cut it out, assembling a scrapbook of him. Finding one addressed to a woman, whose name he wrote, she thought, he is not made of stone after all. They had first communicated some years before when she asked if she could impose upon him to sign a copy of his collected poems, to be placed in a glass cabinet in the library hall. He sent a white, ruled, adhesive sheet, which carried his name and the date, February twenty-second. It was in deep black ink and the handwriting being so cramped and tiny she felt he had a reluctance in writing it or sending it at all. The photograph on the back cover showed a formidable man, his forehead high and domed, the eyes hidden behind thick horn-rimmed spectacles.

One autumn night, in an expansive mood, she sat down and wrote him a letter about the white mist. It appeared from time to time, wraith-like, twining the three adjacent counties: frail as lace and yet sturdy as it wandered, or rather seemed to float above the fields, above the numerous lakes and separating into skeins and then meshing again. He wrote back warning her not to get too carried away by the mist and concluded by saying, 'I reject miracle in every form and shape.'

Now, she was here, picturing him arriving, somewhat awkward, in a long overcoat, looking around and being looked at, because he was famous and rumoured to be fiercely abrupt with any who ventured near him. She had come for poetry and not love, as she kept reminding herself. Miss Gilhooley had had her quota of love, but had never managed to reach the mysterious certitudes of marriage. In her small town she was mockingly referred to as the Spinster.

She began imagining things they might talk about at first, the changes that had occurred in their country, changes that were not for the better, bulldozers everywhere and the craze for money. Money, money, money. The rich going to lunch in their helicopters, chopping the air and shredding the white mist, their wives outdoing each other with jewellery and finery, stirring their champagne with gold swizzle sticks, and Mrs Ambrose boasting about their drapes from the palazzo of a gentleman in Milan and a tea-set shipped from Virginia that had once belonged to a president of the United States. Pictures on their walls of bog and bogland, where they no longer set foot, priceless pictures of these lonesome and beautiful landscapes and pictures of bog lilies that lay like serrated stars on pools of purple-black bog water. It was not only the rich but those who aped them that were also money mad. That little hussy who sued the Church Fathers because the sleeve of her coat singed as she was lighting a candle, actually employed the family solicitor to press for compensation and he did, egging her on, encouraged her in this rotten ploy.

The invitation to meet had come some weeks after Christmas, but the stamps on the envelope had pictures of various snowed-on Santa Clauses, so it seemed that he had deliberately delayed posting it or else it had lain in his coat pocket.

Though frozen, when she arrived, one of her cheeks was now scalding from the blaze of the fire and the pile of ash under the grate that was a molten red. She moved her chair back a fraction, as she did not want to be flushed when he arrived. She reckoned on his being late, poets always were. Her bus journey had been long and cheerless, the fields along the way flecked with snow, and in places small mounds of snow lay like hedgehogs crouching inside their own igloos. She had walked briskly from the bus station through the busy streets, strains of music, melodeon and guitar, fraught young mothers wielding their pushchairs, and beggars of various nationalities. She stopped by one older woman because of the little begging bucket, a blue bucket such as a child would take to the seaside with his spade to make a sand castle, and soon regretted her mistake in trying to have a conversation, as the woman had a cleft palate and could scarcely pronounce her own name, which was Mary. A frost, sheer and unblemished, coated the bonnets of the cars that were like sentinels around the grand garden square, and the railings, clad with icy snow, felt damp through the palm of her glove. She stopped a second time to admire a statue of Wolfe Tone, flanked by tall columns of stone, the valorous figure sprung, as it were, from earth, the green-bronze of his boots, his jacket and his torso, curdled and glinting in the wintry sun.

Though feeling hot she felt too constrained to remove her coat, merely opened the top buttons and let it fall capewise over her shoulders as she gradually eased her arms out of the sleeves. Under no circumstances would she mention the fact that she had written snippets of her own locality, little nothings for which she had received a flurry of rejection slips, polite and useless. There was one literary editor who had befriended her and who believed that one day she might become a Poet and in his tutoring of her became a little smitten. He would take her for a drive each week, to discuss this or that piece of writing and always on the dashboard there was a packet of toffees or glacier mints for her to take home. Eventually, they drove a distance away to the seaside, whence they would get out of the car and look or listen as the Atlantic waves vented their fury and now and then surprise them with a rogue wave that sent them toppling. One evening at dusk, when she could not see his face, he said that he was happy with the woman to whom he had been married for many years, but that those drives, the two of them witness to the hungers of the sea and the cry of the seagulls, were dear to him. Though young, she sensed for the first time how inexplicable love was.

She had been in love more than once, gloriously, breathlessly in love, but it was the last attachment that had been the deepest, that was as she believed, ordained. Such happiness. The long walks at weekends, scaling mountains which she would never have done alone, but she felt safe and confident next to him, and indeed if she missed her footing, as she often did, he was there to catch her and plant a kiss. Once they were loaned a grand house in County Galway and in the evening went to the pub in the hotel and talked with the beaters and the gillies and it was there she learned the yodel used to raise woodcock – 'Waayupwaayupwaayup'. It became their favorite password. By the open fire she read poetry to him, read from a book of foreign poets with the English translation on the opposite page and they swore that they would learn languages, that she would learn French and he Spanish and would converse in their adopted tongue. In one letter she was rash enough to tell him that she would walk water to reach him and he replied in kind. It was reciprocal.

His letter breaking it off was wedged half in and half out of her letterbox. She thought that he was merely postponing a date they had made to meet in Dublin at the end of the month, but she was wrong. He praised her qualities in English and in Irish and she cursed him for not having had the gumption to tell her in person. She hid it so as to return it to him in due course, but put it somewhere so safely that she could not remember where that safe place was.

'They'll find it, when I'm dead,' she said spitefully.

After the initial shock she felt the magnitude of the loss, and her whole will was directed towards getting him back. She so convinced herself of this that she bought wooden tubs to plant bulbs in the garden and new towels that were stacked in the bathroom, on a stool, waiting for him. They were a beautiful oatmeal color. She lost friends, having no time for them and they, for their part, were aghast at how she was letting herself go, hair wild and uncombed, her clothes streelish, she who had once been so proud of her appearance. Her boss in the library – a sombrous man – asked if she had had a bereavement, to which she could only reply, yes, yes. After work she went straight home and locked her door and before sleep she would wait for his footsteps, thought she heard a friendly tapping on the windowpane. How often did she switch on the light, stare into the empty room and curse her daft imaginings. She turned to poets as she would to God. Gerard Manley Hopkins was her favourite poet at that time and the line she repeated again and again and which incurred much disparagement, was 'O thou Lord of life, send my roots rain.'

Hearing of a psychic in another country, who lived on a caravan site, she drove there one Saturday and begged, yes begged, for a reading. How her spirits lifted when the woman described in detail things that had actually happened, a hand-painted scarf which her lover had given her and which he placed shyly on her head in the shop, and the time that they had met by surprise in a hotel, their astonishment as they withdrew to an alcove and without exchanging a word, his placing his hand on her chest to calm the violent heartbeats. The psychic then foresaw them setting up house together. It was a cottage by the sea, which they would do up and extend. She drew a picture of their future life together, one or other, whoever got back first of an evening, kneeling to light a fire and praying that the chimney would not smoke, though at first it would, but in time that would clear, once the flue had its generous lining of soot. So real did this become for Miss Gilhooley that she began to furnish the imaginary house, choose wallpapers for various bedrooms, bathroom tiles with specks of gold, such as she had seen in a catalogue and she also added a balcony to the main bedroom where they would stand at night and hear the roaring waves and in the sunny mornings watch the several waterbirds wade gracefully on the soft muddy shore.

Her only sensible action during that wretched time was not to take the pills the doctor insisted she must take. One evening at dusk she drove to the lake, unscrewed the can and dropped the contents into the dark water that was scummed with debris. Many secrets lay hidden in the depths of that lake, condoms, unwanted pups, unwanted kittens sewn into sacks, and incriminating letters. In time, she would bring her own batch of letters, written on sleepless nights, some proud, some craven, all foolish, and assign them to this watery pyre.

She became more and more isolated, but the one person she did not shrink from was Ronan. He was a young man who lived in a caravan on the back avenue of the manor house where Mr and Mrs Jamieson lived. In return for being able to park there, he did odd jobs, cleared the woods, sawed timber, walked the greyhounds and lit the fires if the family was home of an evening. Now and then Mrs Jamieson gave her one of her husband's castoffs but warned him not to let Sir know, as he was very sentimental about his belongings. Ronan and she made a pilgrimage together, for their special intentions, climbing up a steep mountain in Mayo, on a hot June day, with a busload of people who had been driven from the south. How relieved they both were that there was no one from their own vicinity, no one to spy on them. Often she wondered which of the locals had set upon the idea of torturing her with anonymous calls. They would come at all hours and always concerned Emmet, because Emmet was her lover's name, in honour of the hero Robert Emmet. Emmet, she would be told, had just got engaged to be married, Emmet was dating a dentist, Emmet was seen with a famous actress in Dublin, Emmet was seen in a shower with a brunette in a new spa in Westport. She knew they were lies, and yet to hear his name uttered and in such vile connotations, she longed to speak to him and warn him of these terrible calumnies.

It began to lessen. In her small gardens, one Sunday, she saw the stirrings of spring, the leaves of the camellia bush green and glossy, white buds, tight and tiny as birds' eggs, poised to open. She skimmed the sodden leaves from the rain barrel and standing there, looking, seeing, feeling the world around her, she realised that it was the commencement of her convalescence. A blackbird had found a luscious morsel of pink worm and was gobbling it, yet glancing left and right in case a fellow creature would snatch it away. Then, at the car boot sale, to which she went to pass the time, not one, but three different men smiled at her and she smiled back.

On the night when she gave herself to the minister, she believed, indeed knew, she had turned a corner. In their teens and while he was still a student, the minister and herself had met at a dance hall, had clicked and later sat in his motorcar, fondling and reciting poetry. She knew from the annual Christmas card down the years that he still remembered her and that he hankered in some way. When they found themselves at the same Summer school their joy at being reunited was immense. He was opening the event and she was giving a paper on the occult in Yeats's work. During the formal dinner, to which he had her invited, they exchanged glances, the odd word across the table, and eventually, not without a little detour, they found themselves in the same elevator and thence in his suite, which was so vast they had to grope their way to find a table lamp. Their lovemaking was at least twenty years too late, and they were too shy, lying in that enormous four poster bed, to laugh about it. At breakfast they were already on their separate ways, he to his house outside Dublin, and she further north, to the seat of the white mist.

She re-established friendships, went back to playing whist on Friday evenings and made a rhubarb jam flavoured with ginger, which she distributed among those who had been spiteful to her. Only Ronan knew. Ronan with his sideburns, dreaming of Elvis, of doing gigs in small towns, then graduating to big venues and finally to Dublin and afar. One night they watched a video of Elvis that she had hired, sitting in her front room by a warm fire and drinking red wine from the good cut glasses. There was Elvis, like a midnight God, in a midnight blue leather jacket and sideburns, wooing the world, Elvis asking a female member of the audience for the loan of her handkerchief to dab his brow, Elvis shivering as he half sang, half spoke, 'Are you lonesome tonight?' Ronan later strummed a song that he had written on his guitar, which he hoped would be a sensation at one of these imaginary gigs –

> Oh hollow heart you were so real
> I put my hand there
> I could feel
> Your hollow heart . . .

He looked at her, blinking – Ronan blinked out of nerves – and waited. She had to admit that it was not catchy enough and was somewhat bleak. Young people went to gigs to get high, to forget heartbreak and tedium.

'I can't do that . . . I can't forget,' Ronan said.

'Then don't,' Miss Gilhooley replied. But beyond that they did not dare go.

She came across her lover at a function a few years later, as she was wending her way through a room full of people, to table twenty-four. There was a priest with him and a young girl, perhaps his fiancée, though she could not tell. She stopped to say hello, not recalling a word of what was said, but she did and would remember how his arm, with a stealth, coming around the back of her waist and resting there for an instant, saying, without the words, what now would never be said. She drank somewhat immoderately at table twenty-four and kept repeating a line of Yeats's – 'A sweetheart from another life floats there' – much to the bafflement of the people around her.

At home she would mostly quell her desires, but when she went abroad in the summer, they ran amok. In that town on the Mediterranean, in stifling heat, everything quivered, even the knotted guaze scarves that swung from one of the stalls. The chrome of cars and motorcycles seemed to rasp in the head and in the jeweller's windows gold chains and gold wedding rings were at melting point. It was a crowded market, with a glut of goods – meats, fish, shellfish, fruits, vegetables, clothing, cutlery, handbags, seersucker skirts the colour of cotton candy, the locals knowing exactly what they had come for, steering their way with a certain pique through the loitering swell of visitors. The sun through the slits in the canvas awnings beat down relentlessly. A man wearing a faded blue shirt appeared as from nowhere and slid between the milling crowd with a curious, knowing smile. He was dark-skinned, his left jaw showing a strawberry mark, fiercely vivid, as if just slashed. He stood right before her as if she had willed him there, the encounter so thrilling and so unnerving, his eyes, which were a soft brown, moist and lusting, asking her to say yes. On one arm he carried a willow basket filled with gardenias, the smell so intoxicating, adding to her fluster and on the other arm there lay a snake, coiled and inert, its scales iridescent in that hot light. She drew back startled and he made some barely audible sound in order to reassure her. And yes, she would have said yes, gone down one of the narrow alleys, followed him to wherever he silently bade her, to lie with him. All that stopped her was that her friend Amanda was nearby, trying on different straw hats and beckoning her across. He took the measure of the situation and sauntered off with the ease of a panther.

The poet was late. The tall manageress blamed this lateness on the hopelessness of the train service. She herself had been five hours getting home to her parents the weekend previous.

'Where is home?' Miss Gilhooley asked.

'North east Galway,' she was told and tried to imagine the little townlands on the big map in the library hall, their names squeezed together in a cluster. After chatting to Miss Gilhooley, the manageress insisted on bringing one order of afternoon tea, saying that she would bring a second pot of tea when he arrived. She somehow guessed that it was a man. Presently a banquet was set before Miss Gilhooley – dainty sandwiches on white and brown bread, warm scones with helpings of clotted cream and raspberry jam, slices of rich fruitcake dense with raisins, currants, candied peel, cherries, and green strips of angelica and on the very top tier, as a final arpeggio, small gateaux of a sweet lemon flan, that trembled as the cake plate was put down. Except that she was not hungry.

She consulted her watch, regularly putting it to her ear to listen for the almost imperceptible ticking. A bellicose man at a centre table kept calling every other minute, to voice his complaints, addressing each of the passing waitresses as 'Serving person, Serving person.'

'An oddball . . . comes every day . . . lives alone somewhere in Ranelagh,' the manageress said, and hastened to his table, removing the cup and the saucer that was slopped with tea and speaking to him pleasantly.

People were munching and chatting, some consciously over-reserved, and from one table loud guffaws and peals of laughter at the richness of their jokes. She debated whether she should look, in the two bars and the Saddle room, but the truth was that she did not feel confident enough to wend her way past all those people. The heat in the room was now quite oppressive and a mobile phone rang repeatedly from the depths of someone's handbag. The pianist, sensible to the fact that he was being ignored, ran his hands along the keyboard with a flourish, then stood holding those self-same hands out, as for a requiem.

All of a sudden, she pictured her own hallway, with the storage heater about to come on and the radio playing full blast in the kitchen, a deliberate ploy, as there had been several break-ins in the town of late. The bellicose man was reading a newspaper, when suddenly he bashed his hand through the centre pages, shouting as obviously he had read something which infuriated him. His face was moist with rage and his ears, which were a blazing red, stuck out from his head as he looked around for an opponent to argue with. It was not at that precise moment that she admitted to herself that the poet was not coming. It was fifteen minutes later.

A little girl wearing a tam o'shanter came across and asked if she would care to buy a raffle ticket for an extension to be built at their school. As she wrote her address on the counterfoil, lest she came first, second, or third, the little girl rattled off the prizes, which were all of a culinary nature. As she walked off, her parents waved their gratitude and at that precise moment Miss Gilhooley put her arms back into the sleeves of her tweed coat, rising with as much composure as she could muster.

She paid at the cash register near the arched entrance and asked for the tip to be left on her table, as she dreaded the embarrassment of encountering the manageress, who was bound to be sympathetic.

Pat-the-Porter met her beaming. He had the booklet, the very last one, staff always swiping them, but he had it for her to take home as a souvenir. She mentioned the poet's name.

'Our Laureate,' he said, misquoting a line about a sod of earth rolling over on its back from the thrust of the plough.

'We had a . . . rendezvous,' she said, smarting at the pretentiousness of the word, and for a moment he was lost in perplexity, then drew her aside and in a low confidential voice began to mutter – 'Look . . . it's like this . . . I know the man . . . I can vouch for his honour . . . he comes here all the time with them bowsies . . . the barstool poets as I call them . . . and he sits like a man in a trance . . . he'd have every intention of meeting you . . . he'd want it . . . I can just see it . . . him shaving . . . putting on a clean shirt and tie, getting the good overcoat and setting out . . . coming as far as the corner by Wolfe Tone and all of a sudden . . . balking it.'

'But why . . . why would he balk it?'

'Shy, shyness . . . the shyest man I ever came across . . . I'll bet you he's walking the street now or maybe on a bench by the canal, reproaching himself for his blasted boorishness . . . his defection.'

It was left like that.

He steered her through the revolving doors and watched her go down the street. She held herself well, but there was a hurt look to her back.

The air in the bus was freezing, passengers not nearly so buoyant or talkative as they had been on the way down in the morning. She was glad that no one had sat next to her. In the various towns through which they passed, Paud, the young driver, drove with caution, because he had been stopped several times by the sergeant, but once onto the country roads he was reckless, the bus trundled, raising slush out of the ruts, grazing the hedges and twice coming to a skidding halt when a vehicle met them from the opposite side. Passengers were flung forward and afterwards there were irate calls to him 'For feck's sake, cool it, cool it.'

The dark seemed to get deeper and darker and the land itself swallowed within a primeval loneliness.

She had been dozing on and off, when suddenly, she came awake with a start. What an awful dream and where had it come from. She had been drinking the hot blood that spurted from the throat of a wounded animal, a wolf she reckoned. It was in a strange forest, the trunks of the trees massive and covered with white fleshy toadstools, a forest that was already receding from her mind, but the taste of blood lingered in her mouth. The horror. The horror. Was this the true her, a she-wolf drinking blood. Looking around, she sought in vain for deliverance, then wiped the window and saw that they were passing the low white building that had once been a creamery and was about twenty miles from home.

Home, the small town that so cried out for novelty that a few fairy lights, since Christmas time, still dangled from the lower branches of the big chestnut tree in the market square, home to the loamy land and the brown-black lakes fed from bog water, home to the rooks convening and prattling at evening time in the church-yard grounds and home to the intangible white mist. Pressed to the window she said aloud the name of the man she had so loved, a name that had not passed her lips in almost twenty years, and all of a sudden she was crying, soft, warm, melting tears and she thought of the poet, that lonely clumsy man, walking streets in Dublin or, as Pat-the-Porter said, sitting on a bench staring into greenish canal water. She knew then, and with a cold conviction, the love, the desolation that goes in to the making of a poem.

'Welcome to Mullaghair . . . and all in one piece,' the grinning Paud said with Olympian pride.

People were slow to get down as the steps were slippery and so was the pavement, the goodnights were cursory and everyone, including her, drew up the collars of their coats, to guard against the biting wind.

Old Wounds

In our front garden, there were a few clumps of devil's pokers – spears of smouldering crimson when in bloom, and milky yellow when not. But my mother's sister and her family, who lived closer to the mountain, had a ravishing garden: tall festoons of pinkish-white roses, a long low border of glorious golden tulips, and red dahlias that, even in hot sun, exuded the coolness of velvet. When the wind blew in a certain direction, the perfume of the roses vanquished the smell of dung from the yard, where the sow and her young pigs spent their days foraging and snortling. My aunt was so fond of the piglets that she gave each litter pet names, sometimes the same pet names, which she appropriated from the romance novels she borrowed from the library and read by the light of a paraffin lamp, well into the night.

Our families had a falling out. For several years there was no communication between us at all, and, when the elders met at funerals, they did not acknowledge one another and studiously looked the other way. Yet we were still intimately bound up with each other and any news of one family was of interest to the other, even if that news was disconcerting.

When the older and possibly more begrudging people had died off, and my cousin Edward and I were both past middle age – as he kept reminding me, he was twelve years older than I was and had been fitted with a pacemaker – we met again and set aside the lingering hostilities. About a year later, we paid a visit to the family graveyard, which was on an island in the broad stretch of the Shannon River. It was a balmy day in autumn, the graveyard spacious, uncluttered, the weathered tombs far more imposing than those in the graveyard close to the town. They were limestone tombs, blotched with white lichen, great splashes of it, which lent an improvised gaiety to the scene. Swallows were swooping and scudding in and out of the several sacred churches, once the abode of monks but long since uninhabited, the roofs gone but the walls and ornamental doorways still standing, grey and sturdy, with their own mosaics of lichen. The swallows did not so much sing as caw and gabble, their circuits a marvel of speed and ingenuity.

Now I was seeing the graveyard in daylight with my cousin, but once, a few years before, I had gone there surreptitiously. The youngster who rowed me across worked for a German man who bred pheasants on one of the other islands and was able to procure a boat. We set out just before dark. The boy couldn't stop talking or singing. And he smoked like a chimney.

'Didn't yer families fight?' he asked, when I trained a torch on the names of my ancestors carved on a tall headstone. Undaunted by my silence, the boy kept prying and then, with a certain insouciance, informed me that the family fight had come about because of what Edward had done to his widowed mother, flinging her out once she had signed the place over to him.

'That's all in the past,' I said curtly, and recited the names, including those of a great-grandmother and a great-grandfather, a Bridget and a Thomas, of whom I knew nothing. Others I had random remembrances of. In our house, preserved in a china cabinet, on frayed purple braid, were the medals of an uncle who had been a soldier of the Irish Free State and had met with a violent death, aged twenty-eight. I remembered my grandfather falling into a puddle in the yard, when he came home drunk from a fair, and laughing jovially. My grandmother was stern and made me drink hot milk with pepper before sending me up to bed early. She was forever dinning into me the stories of our forebears and how they had suffered, our people driven from their holdings and their cabins down the years. She said that the knowledge of eviction and the fear of the poorhouse ran in our blood. I must have

been seven or eight at the time. For Sunday Mass, she wore a
bonnet made of black satin, with little felt bobbins that hopped
against her cheek in the judder, as my grandfather drove helter-
skelter so as not to be late. The traps and the sidecars were tethered outside the chapel gates, and the horses seemed to know one
another and to nod lazily. As a treat, my grandmother let me smell
a ball of nutmeg, which was kept in a round tin that had once held
cough pastilles. The feather bed, which I shared with her, sagged
almost to the floor and the pillow slips smelt of flour, because they
were made from flour bags that she had bleached and sewn. My
grandfather, who snored, slept in a settle bed down in the kitchen,
near the fire.

About two years after my clandestine visit to the graveyard,
Edward and I met by chance at a garden centre. I was home on
holiday and had gone to buy broom shrubs for my nephew. As we
approached each other on a pathway between a line of funereal
yew trees, my cousin saw me, then pretended not to and feigned
interest in a huge tropical plant, behind which, he slid. Deciding
to brave it, I said his name, and, turning, he asked with a puzzled
look, 'Who do I have here?', although he well knew. And so the
ice was broken. Yes, his eyes were bad, as he later told me, but he
had indeed recognised me and felt awkward. As we got to be
friends, I learned of the journeys to the eye doctor in Dublin, of
the treatments required before the doctor could operate, and when
I sent him flowers at the hospital the nurse, bearing them to his
bedside, said, 'Well, someone loves you,' and he was proud to tell
her that it was me.

We corresponded. His letters were so immediate. They brought
that mountain terrain to life, along with the unvarying routine of
his days: out to the fields straight after breakfast, herding, mending
fences, fixing gates, clearing drains, and often, as he said, sitting
on a wall for a smoke, to drink in his surroundings. He loved the

place. He said that people who did not know the country – did not know nature and did not stay close to it – could never understand the loss that they were feeling. I felt that, in an oblique way, he was referring to me. He wrote these letters at night by the fire, after his wife had gone up to bed. Her health was poor, her sleep fitful, so she went to bed early to get as many hours as she could. He sometimes, while writing, took a sup of whiskey, but he said he was careful not to get too fond of it.

He knew the lake almost as well as he knew the mountain, and, through his binoculars, from his front porch he watched the arrival of the dappers in the month of May, a whole fleet of boats from all over the country and even from foreign parts. They arrived as the hatched mayflies came out of the nearby bushes and floated above the water, in bacchanalian swarms, so that the fishermen were easily able to catch them and fix them to the hooks of their long rods. He himself had fished there every Sunday of his life, trolling from his boat with wet or dry bait, and so canny was he that the neighbours were quite spiteful, saying that he knew exactly where the fish lay hiding, and, hence, there was not a pike or a perch or a trout left for anyone else.

He was a frugal man. In Dublin, he would walk miles from the railway station to the eye hospital, often having to ask the way and frequently going astray because of his ailing sight. His wife and son would scold him for not taking a taxi, to which he always said, 'I could if I wanted to.' Yet I recalled that time when, young, he had brought my sister and me a gift, the same gift, a red glassy bracelet on an elasticated band. The raised red beads were so beautiful that I licked them as I would jellies. My sister was older than me, and it was for her that he had a particular fondness. They flirted, though I did not know then that it was called that. They teased each other, and then ran around the four walls of our sandstone house, and eventually fell into an embrace, breathless from their hectic exertions. I was wild with jealousy and snapped on the band of my new bracelet. They aped dancing, as if in a ballroom, she swooning, her upper back reclining on the curve of his forearm as he sang, 'You'll be lonely, little sweetheart, in the spring,' and she gazed up at him, daring him to kiss her. He was handsome then, not countrified, like most of the farmers or their grown sons, and he wore a long white belted motor coat. He had a mop of silky brown hair, and his skin was sallow.

I met Moira, the woman to whom he got engaged some two or three years later, on the way home from school one day. She stopped me and asked if I was his cousin, though she knew well who I was and pointedly ignored the two girls who were with me. She asked me jokingly if she was making the right choice, as someone had warned her that my cousin was 'bad news'. She repeated the words 'bad news' with a particular relish. She was wearing a wraparound red dress and red high-heeled toeless sandals, which looked incongruous but utterly beautiful on that dusty godforsaken road. She was like flame, a flame in love with my cousin, and her eyes danced with mischief. It was not long after they got married that he called his mother out into the hay shed and informed her that his wife felt unwanted in the house and that, for the sake of his marriage, he had to ask her to leave. Thus the coolness from our side of the family. There was general outrage in the parish that an only son had pitched his mother out, and pity for the mother, who had to walk down that road, carrying her few belongings and her one heirloom, a brass lamp with a china shade, woebegone, like a woman in a ballad. She stayed with us for a time, and did obliging things for my mother, being, as she was, in her own eyes, a mendicant, and once, when she let fall a tray of good china cups and saucers, she knelt down and said, 'I'll replace these,' even though we knew she couldn't. In the evenings, she often withdrew from the kitchen fire to sit alone in our cold vacant room, with a knitted shawl over her shoulders, brooding. Eventually, she rented a room in the town, and my mother gave her cane chairs, cushions, and a pale-green candle-wick bedspread, to give the room a semblance of cheer.

But, with so many dead, there was no need for estrangement anymore.

Edward sent me a photograph of a double rainbow, arcing from the sky above his house across a patchwork of small green fields and over the lake toward the hill that contained the graves of the Leinster men. On the back of the photograph he had written the hour of evening at which the rainbow had appeared and lasted for about ten minutes, before eking its watery way back into the sky. I put it on the mantelpiece for luck. The rainbow, with its seven bands of glorious colour, always presaged happiness. In his next letter and in answer to my question, he said that the Leinster men were ancient chieftains who had come for a banquet in Munster, where they were insulted and subsequently murdered, but in a remaindered gesture of honour someone had thought to bury them facing their own province.

Each summer, when I went back to Ireland, we had outings, outings that he had been planning all year. One year, mysteriously, I found that we were driving far from his farm, up an isolated road, with nothing in sight except clumps of wretched rushes and the abandoned ruins from famine times. Then, almost at the peak, he parked the jeep and took two shotguns out of the boot. He had dreamed all year of teaching me to shoot and he set about it with a zest. He loved shooting. As a youngster, unbeknownst to his mother, he had cycled to Limerick two nights a week to learn marksmanship in a gallery. With different gundogs, he shot pheasants, grouse, ducks and snipe, but his particular favourites were the woodcock, which came all the way from Siberia or Chernobyl. He described them to me, silhouetted against an evening sky – they disliked light – their beaks like crochet hooks, then furtively landing in a swamp or on a cowpat to catch insects or partake of the succulence of the water. Yet he could not forgo the thrill of shooting them, then picking them up, feeling the scant flesh on the bone, and snapping off a side feather to post to an ornithologist in England. September 1st, he said, was the opening of duck shooting on the lake, a hundred guns or more out there, *bang-bang*ing in all directions. Later, adjourning to the pub, the sportsmen swapped stories of the day's adventure, comparing what they'd shot and how they'd shot and what they'd missed – a conviviality such as he was not used to.

For a target, he affixed a saucepan lid to a wooden post. Then, taking the lighter of the two guns, he loaded it with brass bullets, handed it to me, and taught me to steady it, to put my finger on the trigger and look down through the nozzle of the long blue-black barrel.

'Now shoot,' he said in a belligerent voice, and I shot so fearfully and, at the same time, so rapidly that I believed I was levitating. The whole thing felt unreal, bullets bursting and zapping through the air, some occasionally clattering off the side of the tin lid and my aim so awry that even to him it began to be funny. He had started to lay out a picnic on a tartan rug – milky tea in a bottle, hard-boiled eggs, slices of brown bread already buttered – when out of thin air a huge black dog appeared, like a phantom or an animal from the underworld, its snarls strange and spiteful. Its splayed paws were enormous and mud-splattered, its eyes bloodshot, the sockets bruised, as if it were fresh from battle.

'He'll smell your fear,' my cousin said.

'I can't help it,' I said and lowered the gun, thinking that this might, in some way, appease the animal. There wasn't a stone or a stick to throw at it. There was nothing up there, only the fearsome dog and us and the saucepan lid rattling like billio.

Edward knew every dog for miles around, and every breed of dog, and said that this freak was a 'blow-in'. Eventually, he sacrificed every bit of food in order to get the animal to run, throwing each piece further and further as matador-like he followed, bearing the stake on which the lid was nailed, shouting in a voice that I could not believe was his, so barbaric and inhuman did it sound. The dog, wearying of the futility of this, decided to gallop off over the edge of the mountain and disappear from sight.

'Jesus,' my cousin said.

We sat in the jeep because, as he said, we were in no hurry to get home. We didn't talk about family things, his wife or my ex-husband, my mother or his mother, possibly fearing that it would open up old wounds. There had been so many differences between the two families – over greyhounds, over horses, over some rotten bag of seed potatoes – and always with money at the root of it. My father, in his wild tempers, would claim that my mother's father had not paid her dowry and would go to his house in the dead of night, shouting up at a window to demand it.

Instead we talked of dogs.

Having been a huntsman all his life, Edward had several dogs, good dogs, faithful dogs, retrievers, pointers, setters and springers. His favourite was an Irish red setter, which he called Maire Ruadh, for a red-haired noblewoman who had her husbands pitched into the Atlantic once she tired of them. He had driven all the way to Kildare, in answer to an advertisement, to vet this pedigree dog, and his wife had decided to come along. Straightaway they had liked the look of her; they had studied the pedigree papers, paid out a hefty sum, and there and then given her her imperious name. On the way back, they'd had high tea at a hotel in Roscrea, and, what with the price he'd paid for Maire Ruadh and the tea and the cost of the petrol, it had proved to be an expensive day.

I told him the story of an early morning in a café in Paris, a straggle of people – two men, each with a bottle of pale-amber beer, and a youngish woman, writing in a ruled copybook, her dog at her feet, quiet, suppliant. When she finished her essay, or whatever it was that she had been writing, she groped in her purse and all of a sudden the obedient dog reared to get away. She pulled on the lead, dragging it back beside her, the dog resistant and down on its haunches. Grasping the animal by the crown of its head, she opened its mouth very wide and with her other hand dispatched some powdered medicine from a sachet onto its tongue. Pinned as it was, the dog could vent its fury only by kicking, which got it nowhere. Once the dog had downed the powder, she patted it lovingly and it answered in kind, with soft whimpers.

'Man's best friend,' my cousin said, a touch dolefully.

We came back by a different route because he wanted me to see the ruin of a cottage where a workman of ours had lived. As a child, I had been dotingly in love with the man and had intended to elope with him, when I came of age. The house itself was gone and all that remained was a tumbledown porch with some overgrown stalks of geranium, their scarlet blooms prodigal in that godforsaken place. We didn't even get out of the car. Yet nearby we came upon a scene of such gaiety that it might have been a wedding party. Twenty or so people sitting out of doors at a long table strewn with lanterns, eating, drinking, and calling for toasts in different tongues. Behind the din of voices we could hear the strains of music from a melodeon. It was the hippies who had come to the district, the 'blow-ins', as Edward called them, giving them the same scathing name as the fearsome dog. They had made Ireland their chosen destination when the British government, in order to avoid paying them social benefits, gave them a lump sum to scoot it. They crossed the Irish Sea and found ideal havens by streams and small rivers, building houses, growing their own vegetables and their own marijuana, and, he had been told on good authority, taking up wife-swapping. He had the native's mistrust of the outsider. We had to come to a stop because some of their ducks were waddling across the road. We couldn't see them in the dusk but heard their quacking, and then some children with their faces painted puce came to the open window of the jeep, holding lighted sods of turf, serenading us.

'Hi, guv,' one of the men at the table called out, but my cousin did not answer.

It was in his back yard, still sitting in the jeep, that he began to cry. As we drove in, he could see by the light in the upstairs room that his wife had gone to bed early, so I declined his invitation to have a cup of tea. He cried for a long time. The stars were of the same brightness and fervour as the stars I had seen in childhood and, though distant, seemed to have been put there for us, as if someone in the great house called Heaven had gone from room to room, turning on this constellation of lamps. He was crying, he said, because the families had been divided for so long. He had even tried to find me in England, had written to some priest who served in a parish in Kilburn, because, according to legend, Kilburn was where Irish people flocked and had fights on Saturday nights outside pubs and pool halls. The priest couldn't trace me but suggested a parish in Wimbledon, where I had indeed lived for a time, before fleeing from bondage. What hurt my cousin most was the fact that his wife's cousins, as she frequently reminded him, had kept in touch, had sent Christmas cards and visited in the summer, each of them rewarded with a gift of a pair of fresh trout. In his wife's estimation, his cousins, meaning my family, were heartless. It took him a while to calm down. The tissues that he took from his pockets were damp shreds. Eventually, somewhat abashed, he said, 'Normally, I am not an emotional man,' then, backing the car toward the open gate, he drove down the mountain road to the small town where my nephew lived.

One evening soon after that, when I telephoned him from London, he said that he had known it would be me; he had come in from the fields ten minutes before the Angelus tolled, because of this hunch he had that I would be ringing. We talked of recent things: the cornea transplant he had undergone, a robbery in a house further up the mountain, where an old man was tied with rope, the weather as ever wet and squally. He told me that it was unlikely he would make silage anymore and therefore intended to sell the cattle that he had fattened all summer. He might, he said, buy yearlings the following May, if his health held up. He did not say how happy the call had made him, but I could feel the pitch of excitement in his voice as he told me again that he had come in early from the fields because he knew that I would ring.

We took to talking on the phone about once a month. When his wife went to Spain with their son, from whom he was estranged, he wrote to tell me that he would phone me on a particular evening at seven o'clock. I knew then that these conversations buoyed him up.

It was the third summer of our reunion, and he had the boat both tarred and painted a Prussian blue. We were bound for the grave-yard. The day could not have been more perfect: sunshine, a soft breeze, Edward slipping the boat out with one oar through a thicket of lush bamboo and reeds, a scene that could easily have taken place somewhere in the tropics. He took a loop away from the direction of the island, in order to get the breeze at our backs, then turned on the engine and, despite his worsening sight, steered with unfailing instinct, because he had, he said, a map of the entire lake inside his head. The water was a lacquered silver, waves barely nudging the boat. We couldn't hear each other because of the noise of the engine but sat quiet, content, the hills all around sloping toward us, enfolding us in their friendliness. It was only when we reached the pier that I realised how poor his sight was – by the difficulty he had tying the rope to its ballast and his having to ask me to read the handwritten sign on a piece of cardboard, nailed to a tree-trunk, that said 'Bull on island'.

'We'll have to brave it,' he said. Our headway was cautious, what with the steep climb, the fear of the bull, and, presently, a herd of bullocks fixing us with their stupid glare, and a few of them making abortive attempts to charge at us. Once through the lych-gate that led to the graveyard, we sat and availed ourselves of the port wine that I had brought in a hip flask. Sitting on the low wall opposite the resting place of our ancestors, he said what a pity it was that my mother had chosen not to be buried there. Her explanation was that she wished to be near a roadside so that passers-by might bless themselves for the repose of her soul, but I had always felt that there was another reason, a hesitation in her heart.

'I came here twice since I last saw you . . . to think,' he said.

'To think?'

'I was feeling rotten . . . I came here and talked to them.' He did not elaborate, but I imagined that he might have been brooding over unfinished business with his mother, or maybe his marriage, which had grown bleaker amid the desolations of age. It was not money he was worried about, because, as he told me, he had been offered princely sums for fields of his that bordered the lake; people were pestering him, developers and engaged couples, to sell them sites, and he had refused resolutely.

'My wants are few,' he said and rolled a cigarette, regaining his good humour and rejoicing at the fact that we had picked such a great day for our visit. He surprised me by telling a story of how, after my mother died, my father had gone to the house of Moira's older sister, Oonagh, recently returned from Australia and had proposed to her. Without any pretence at courtship, he had simply asked her to marry him. He had needed a wife. He had even pressed her to think it over, then narked at her refusal, he had gone on the batter for several weeks. I could not imagine anyone other than my mother in our kitchen, in our upstairs or downstairs rooms; she was the presiding spirit of the place.

He then said that Moira had also expressed a wish to be buried in a grave near the town and he could not understand why anyone would want to be in a place where the remains were squeezed in like sardines.

Birds whirled in and out, such a freedom to their movements, such an airiness, as if the whole place belonged to them and we were the intruders. He spoke of souls buried there in pagan times, then Christian times, the monks in the monasteries fasting, praying, and most likely having to fend off invaders. It was a place of pilgrimage, where all-night Masses were celebrated; he pointed to boulders with little cavities, where the pilgrims had dipped their hands and their feet in the blessed water.

'Hallowed ground,' I said. The grassy mound that covered our family grave was a rich warm green strewn with speckled wildflowers.

'You have as much right to be there as I have,' he said suddenly, and my heart leaped with a childish joy.

'Do I really?'

'I'm telling you . . . you'll be right beside me,' he said, and he stood up and took my hand, and we walked over the mound, measuring it, as it were, hands held in solidarity. It meant everything to me. I would be the only one from our branch of the family to lie with relatives whom I had always admired as being more stoic than us and closer to the land.

When his wife got sick the next winter, his letters became infrequent. He rarely went out to the fields, having to tend her, and the only help was a twice-weekly visit from a jubilee nurse, who came to change her dressings. They could not tell whether it was the cancer causing all the wounds down her spine or whether she was allergic to the medicines that she had been prescribed. Sometimes, he wrote, she roared with pain, said that the pain was hammering against her chest, and begged to be dead. I was abroad when she died and he telephoned to let me know. A message was passed on to me and I was able to send roses by Interflora. To my surprise, I learned that she had been buried on the island after all, and on the phone, when I later spoke to him, he described the crossing of the funeral procession, the first boat for the flowers, as was the custom, then himself and his son in the next boat, and the mourners following behind.

'A grand crowd . . . good people,' he said, and I realised that he was vexed with me for not having been there. I asked whether she had died suddenly, and he answered that he would rather not describe the manner of her passing. Nor did he say why she had changed her mind about being buried in the family plot.

I could not tell what had caused it, but a chasm had sprung up between us. The friendliness had gone from his voice when I rang, and his letters were formal now. I wondered if he felt that his friendship with me had somehow compromised his love for his wife, or if he was in the grip of that spleen which comes, or so I feared, with advancing years. A home help, a very young girl, visited him three days a week, put groceries in the fridge, cooked his dinner, and occasionally went upstairs to hoover and change the sheets.

'Maybe you should give her a bonus,' I said, suggesting that she would then come every day.

'The state pays her plenty,' he said, disgruntled by my remark.

I got out of the habit of phoning him, but one Christmas morning, in a burst of sentiment, I rang, hoping that things might be smoothed over. Over-politely, he answered a few questions about the weather, his health, a large magnifying machine that he had got for reading, and then quite suddenly he blurted it out. He had been looking into the cost of a tombstone for his wife and himself and had found that it was going to be very expensive.

'Have you thought of what you intend to do?' he asked.

'I haven't,' I said flatly.

'Maybe you would like to purchase yours now,' he said.

'I don't understand the question,' I said, although I understood it all too clearly and a river of outrage ran through me. I felt that he had violated kinship and decency. The idea of being interred in the graveyard beside him seemed suddenly odious to me. Yet, perversely, I was determined not to surrender my place under the grassy slope.

There were a few seconds of wordless confrontation and then the line went dead. He had hung up. I rang back, but the telephone was off the hook, and that night, when I called again, there was no answer; he probably guessed that it was me.

It was August and pouring rain when I travelled to the local hospital to see him. A nurse, with her name tag, 'M. Gleeson', met me in the hallway. She was a stout woman with short bobbed hair and extremely affable. She eyed me up and down, guessed correctly whom I had come to see, and said that her mother had known me well, but, of course, I wouldn't remember, being a toff. If my cousin had come in at Easter, things might have been different now, she said, but, as it was, the news was not promising.

'How's the humour?' I asked tentatively.

'Cantankerous,' she said, adding that most patients knew their onions, knew how to play up to her, realising that she would be the one to wash them, feed them, and bring them cups of tea at all hours, but not cousin Edward.

'I should have brought flowers,' I said.

'Ah, aren't you flower enough!' she said and herded me toward the open door of his little room, announcing me bluffly.

He was in an armchair with a fawn dressing gown over his pyjamas, as thin as a rake, his whole body drooping, and when he looked up and saw me, or perhaps only barely saw me, but heard my name, his eyes narrowed with hatred. I saw that I should not have come.

'I couldn't find anywhere to buy you a flower,' I said.

'A flower?' he said with disdain.

'They don't sell them in the garden centre anymore – only trees and plants,' I explained, and the words hung in the air. The rain sloshed down the narrow windowpane as if it couldn't reach the sill quickly enough, then overflowed onto a patch of ground that was smothered with nettle and dock.

'How are you?' I asked after some time.

He pondered the question and then replied, coldly, 'That's what I keep asking myself – how am I?'

I wanted to put things right. I wanted to say, 'Let's talk about the tombstone and then forget about it forever,' but I couldn't. The way he glared at me was beginning to make me angry. I felt the urge to shake him. On the bedside table there was a peeled mandarin orange that had been halved but left untouched. There will be another time, I kept telling myself. Except that I knew he was dying. He had that aghastness which shows itself, months, often a year, before the actual death. We were getting nowhere. The tension was unbearable, rain splashing down, and he with his head lowered, having a colloquy with himself. I reminded myself how hardworking, how frugal, he had been all his life, never admitting to the loneliness that he must have felt, and I thought, why don't I throw my arms around him and say something? But I couldn't. I simply couldn't. It wouldn't have been true. It would have been false. I knew that he despised me for the falsity of my coming and the falsity of my not bringing the matter up, and that he despised himself equally for having done something irreparable.

'Have you been to the grave?' he asked sharply.

'No, but I'm going this afternoon. I've booked the boatman,' I said.

'You'll find Moira's name and mine on my grandfather's tomb . . . chiselled,' he said.

'Chiselled.' The word seemed to cut through the shafts of suffocating air between us.

I knew that he wanted me to leave.

As it turned out, the trip across the lake was cancelled because the weather was so foul. The boatman deemed it too rough and too dangerous. It was the day of a big horse race and he and his wife were in their front room with the fire lit, the television on, and an open bottle of Tia Maria on a little brass table.

Strange to say, neither Edward's name nor Moira's was on the tombstone when I went to his funeral, on a drizzling wet day that November. The grave had already been dug. 'Ten fellas,' as Jacksie the boatman said, had turned up to do the job. Buckets of water had been bailed out of it, but the clay itself was still wet, with a dark boggy seepage. His coffin would rest on his wife's, hers still new-looking, its varnish undimmed, and, in an exchange of maudlin condolences, women remarked that most likely Moira was in there still, waiting to welcome him.

Underneath his wife's remains were those of his mother, the woman she had quarrelled with and driven out of her home, and down in succession were others – husbands, wives, children, all with their differences silenced. When my turn came, I would rest on Edward's coffin, with runners underneath to cushion the weight. These thoughts were passing through my mind as the priest shook holy water over the grave and three young girls threw in red roses. I did not recognise them. Neighbours' children, I assumed. They threw the roses with a certain theatricality, and one of them blushed fiercely. They might as easily have been at a beauty contest.

When the priest started the Rosary, there were nudges and blatant sighs, as it became clear that he was going to recite the full five decades, and not just one decade, as some priests did. He was in a wheelchair and had to have a boat all to himself. Men had had to support him up the gravel path to the graveyard. Despite his condition, his voice boomed out onto the lake, where the water birds shivered in the rushes, and over it to the main road, where crows had perched in a neat sepulchral line on the telephone wires as the coffin was being removed from the hearse. The mourners answered the Our Fathers and the Hail Marys with a routine drone, and the gravediggers stood by their shovels, expressionless, witnessing a scene such as they witnessed every other day.

At the end of the prayers, a purple cloth was laid over Edward's coffin, the undertaker tucking it in as if it were a living person that he was putting down to bed. I felt no sorrow, or, to be more precise, I felt nothing, only numbness. I watched a single flake of snow drift through the cold air, discoloured and lonesome-looking.

Most of the people ambled down toward the pier, but a few stayed behind to watch as the men closed the grave. The wreaths and artificial flowers in their glass domes were lifted off the strip of green plastic carpet, which had been temporarily placed over the open grave to lessen the sense of grimness. The gravediggers shovelled hurriedly, gravel and small stones hopping off the coffin and the purple sheath, and finally they unrolled the piece of turf and laid it back where it belonged. Wildflowers of a darkish purple bloomed on graves nearby, but on the strip that had been dug up they had expired. The undertaker, who was full of cheer, said that they would grow again, as the birds scattered seeds all over and flowers of every description sprouted up.

On the way down the steep path, Nurse Gleeson tugged at my arm as if we were old friends. First it was a slew of compliments about the tweed suit I was wearing, singling out the heather flecks in it, and she said what a pity it was that she was size 18, otherwise I could pass it on to her when I grew tired of it. Then it was my head scarf, an emerald green with other vivid colours, quite inappropriate for a funeral, except that it was the only one I had thrown into my suitcase. She remembered my flying visit to the hospital, had, in fact, gone to get a tray of tea and biscuits, when, holy cripes, on returning to the room, she saw that I had vanished.

'Did he say anything?' I asked.

'Oh, he sang dumb,' she said, then, gripping my arm even tighter, she indicated that there was something important that she needed to impart to me.

A few days before the end, my cousin had asked her for a sheet of notepaper in order to write me a letter. There was a cranberry bowl in the kitchen at home, which he wished me to have, he had said. As it happened, she had found the sheet of paper in the top pocket of his pyjamas after he died, but with nothing written on it.

'The strength gave out,' she said and asked if I knew which bowl it was. I could see it quite clearly, as I had seen it one day, while waiting in his kitchen for a sun shower to pass, rays of sun alighting on it, divesting it of its sheath of brown dust, the red ripples flowing through it, so that it seemed to liquefy, as if it were being newly blown. It had been full of things – screwdrivers, a tiny torch, receipts, and pills for pain. When I admired it, he turned the contents out onto the table and held it in the palm of his hand, proudly, like a chalice of warm wine.

I hoped that the unwritten letter had been an attempt at reconciliation.

Sitting in the boat with a group of friendly people, I could still see the island, shrouded in a veil of thin grey rain. Why, I asked myself, did I want to be buried there? Why, given the different and gnawing perplexities? It was not love and it was not hate but something for which there is no name, because to name it would be to deprive it of its truth.

Acknowledgements

'The Love Object', 'Irish Revel', 'The Rug', 'Paradise' and 'The Mouth of the Cave' from *The Love Object* (Volume) © Edna O'Brien, 1968. First published in Great Britain in 1968 by Jonathan Cape. 'The Love Object' and 'Irish Revel' first appeared in somewhat different form in *The New Yorker*.

'A Scandalous Woman' and 'The Creature' from *A Scandalous Woman* (Volume) © Edna O'Brien, 1974. First published in Great Britain in 1974 by Weidenfeld & Nicolson.

'A Rose in the Heart of New York', 'Number Ten' and 'Mrs. Reinhardt' from *Mrs. Reinhardt* (Volume) © Edna O'Brien, 1978. First published in Great Britain in 1978 by Weidenfeld & Nicolson. 'Number Ten' and 'A Rose in the Heart of New York' first appeared in somewhat different form in *The New Yorker*.

'The Connor Girls', 'Tough Men', 'The Doll' and 'Sister Imelda' from *Returning* (Volume) © Edna O'Brien, 1982. First published in Great Britain in 1982 by Weidenfeld & Nicolson.

'Oft in the Stilly Night', 'What a Sky', 'Brother', 'The Widow', 'Storm', 'Long Distance' and 'Lantern Slides' from *Lantern Slides* (Volume) © Edna O'Brien, 1990. First published in Great Britain in 1990 by Weidenfeld & Nicolson. Some of the stories first appeared in somewhat different form in *The New Yorker*, *Paris Review* and *Antaeus*.

'Shovel Kings', 'Madame Cassandra', 'Plunder', 'My Two Mothers', 'Manhattan Medley', 'Inner Cowboy', 'Black Flower', 'Send My Roots Rain', 'Green Georgette' and 'Old Wounds' from *Saints and Sinners* (Volume) © Edna O'Brien, 2011. First published in Great Britain in 2011 by Faber and Faber Limited. Some of the stories first appeared in somewhat different form in *The New Yorker*, *Zoetrope*, *Atlantic Monthly* and *The Sunday Times*.

Country Girl

Edna O'Brien's debut novel *The Country Girls*, published in 1960, caused great outrage and was banned on publication. Undeterred, O'Brien continued to write and has since created a hugely acclaimed body of work. *Country Girl* is a rich and heady account of the events, people, emotions, and landscape that imprinted upon and enlivened O'Brien's lifetime. From a deteriorating house in Ireland in the 1930s, her story moves through convent school, elopement, divorce and single-motherhood, to a new life in sixties London. During this wild and exciting time, O'Brien encountered Hollywood giants, pop stars, and literary titans, such as Marlon Brando, Paul McCartney, Norman Mailer and R. D. Laing. In prose that sparkles, Edna O'Brien has recast her life in a book of unfathomable depth and honesty.

'Get ready to applaud, ladies and gentlemen, because there is no one like her.' Anne Enright, *Guardian*

'In *Country Girl* there is great honesty and struggle, and joy and sorrow leaping together – pure life!' Alice Monro

ff

Saints and Sinners

Winner of the Frank O'Connor
International Short Story Award

Full of powerful evocations of place and an often heart-breaking grasp of people and their desires and contradictions, this beautiful collection is full of passion, pain and beauty.

'Edna O'Brien writes the most beautiful, aching stories of any writer, anywhere.' Alice Munro

'O'Brien has . . . an unflinching, uncompromising gaze that lays bare love, longing and families; and an acute insight into the tragedy of human existence.' *Irish Independent*

'Subversion is what catapulted Edna O'Brien to literary stardom an incredible half century ago and, at the top of her game, she can still cut the ground from under your feet.' *The Times*